KNITORIOUS MURDER MYSTERIES BOOKS 1 - 3

A Knitorious Murder Mysteries Collection

REAGAN DAVIS

Carpe Filum

www.CarpeFilumPress.com

ISBN: 978-1-7772359-1-8 (ebook)

ISBN: 978-1-990228-10-0 (print)

❀ Created with Vellum

A Knitorious Murder Mystery Book 1

Knit One, Murder Two

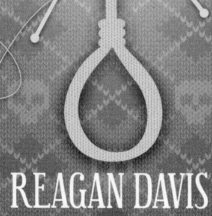

REAGAN DAVIS

COPYRIGHT

ISBN: 978-1-9990435-3-7 (ebook)

ISBN: 978-1-9990435-2-0 (print)

CHAPTER 1

TUESDAY SEPTEMBER 10TH

In theory, making half a bed should take half the time as an entire bed. It doesn't. At least not for me. I take just as long to make half the bed as the entire bed. My bed-making skills are an example of Parkinson's Law: "Work expands to fill the time available for its completion."

See also: the junk in my junk drawer expands to fill the entire drawer, my yarn stash expands to fill all the storage in my house, and my wardrobe expands to fill the entire closet when my husband and his wardrobe move out of our bedroom and into the guest bedroom across the hall.

I pull on my favourite jeans and my plum-coloured top, then open the washroom window to clear the steam still lingering from my shower. A generous application of tinted moisturizer, with SPF 30 of course, a touch of mascara around my hazel eyes, and a smear of lip balm complete my makeup routine. With a sigh, I contemplate my damp brown hair. Because curls are unpredictable, it's too soon to tell if today is a good-curl day or a bad-curl day. I slip a hair elastic on my wrist, just in case. Phone in hand, I leave my bedroom with coffee on my mind.

Walking past Adam's room, his unmade bed catches my eye. I close the door so I don't have to see it.

"Just a few more weeks, Megan," I mutter to myself. "Just hang in there a little longer."

With Hannah away at university, Adam can focus on finding an apartment. With any luck, he'll find a place for the first of the month.

Like a woman on a mission, I walk straight to the coffee maker, pop a pod of caramel coffee in the machine and place my *I'd rather be knitting* mug under the spout.

While I wait for it to brew, I open my planner to today's date. I have a 10 a.m. fundraising committee meeting at the Animal Centre, and work from 1 p.m. to 5 p.m. I've been working part time at Knitorious, Harmony Lake's only knitting store and my second home, for just over five years.

I glance at the clock on the microwave. 8:30 a.m. I have an hour to savour my coffee and some knitting before it's time to leave.

I settle in my favourite corner of the family-room sofa, legs crossed and feet tucked under my butt like a kid in kindergarten who's waiting for story time. I place my phone on the armrest.

"Oscar, play my playlist," I announce to the empty room.

"OK," Oscar replies.

A few seconds later, thanks to the miracle of modern technology, Gwen Stefani's voice fills the quiet space.

Oscar is a digital voice assistant. Hannah and Adam gave him to me for Mother's Day. They love technology, so most holidays I can look forward to getting their new favourite gadget. They make me look more tech-savvy than I am.

Like most technology, Oscar is useful. He can play music, keep my grocery list, provide weather updates, read news headlines, remind me to flip the laundry, and a myriad of other internet-based tasks I haven't tried yet. He is the size of a hockey puck and sits on the end table next to my yarn bowl, where he waits in silence for his next instruction. It's like having a useful pet that never needs food or water.

I savour my much-awaited first sip of coffee and follow the warmth as it travels down my throat and spreads through the rest of my body. I return the mug to the end table and take my knitting out of the yarn bowl.

Ding!

The vibration of my phone makes the sofa shake. It's a text message from a number I don't recognize.

Mystery texter: Hi Mrs. Martel. My name is Fred Murphy. My wife, Stephanie, works with Adam and they've been having an affair.

I didn't see this coming. How did he get my number?

He sends a second message. A screenshot of an intimate text conversation, allegedly between Adam and Stephanie. I know it's easy to fake a text conversation, but I trust the queasiness in my gut. This screenshot is the real deal.

Our marriage has been over for months and Adam is hardly home, even by workaholic lawyer standards. Since Hannah left for university, some nights I'm not sure he comes home at all.

A third text:

Fred: Can we meet to discuss? I have more proof, but I'd like to discuss it with you in person. I can come to Harmony Lake. Let me know when and where.

I immediately text my best friend, April.

Me: Adam's having an affair!

I send a follow-up text, the screenshot of the steamy text exchange.

Me: Her husband wants to meet me. Says he has more to tell me.

April: Wow! Do you want to meet him?

That's a good question. I'm not sure. Fred's texts have piqued my curiosity, that's for sure, and there must be a reason he's reaching out to me. Every instinct I have screams at me to do it.

April: Somewhere public. Meet him at the bakery so T and I can keep an eye on him.

T is what we call April's wife, Tamara. April and Tamara own Artsy Tartsy, the bakery up the street from Knitorious. Tamara is a talented pastry chef, and I stop by to taste her creations every chance I get.

Resolved to find out what Fred wants, I reply to his request for a meeting.

Me: Noon at Artsy Tartsy?

Fred: See you then.

I return my phone to the armrest and pick up my knitting. I'm working on a sock in plain stockinette stitch, a perfect project for knitting in front of the TV or trying to process your feelings about your soon-to-be-ex-husband having a girl-friend. A married girlfriend.

I find my rhythm and work one stitch after another by instinct while my mind replays the text conversation with Fred Murphy.

What is the appropriate reaction to finding out your soon-to-be-ex-husband is seeing someone? I'm not angry. I don't feel betrayed. I'm shocked. It hadn't occurred to me that Adam might have a girlfriend, much less one who's married.

Ding! Dong!

Twenty rounds of knitting and contemplation later, the doorbell brings me back to the here and now. It's April. I know it's her before I put down my knitting. I know because I would do the same thing; I'd rush to her side and make sure she's OK.

April and I have been friends for sixteen years. We met at a mummy-and-me group when Adam, Hannah, and I first moved to Harmony Lake. Our daughters are the same age and best friends. The girls just started university together in Toronto. It comforts us knowing the girls have each other so far from home, and April and I have each other as we adjust to their absence.

When I open the door, April and I have a tight hug. When we pull apart, she hands me a small white confectionery box.

"It's a maple carrot cupcake with pecans, topped with maple cream cheese frosting. T is thinking of adding them to the fall menu and she wants your opinion."

"Halfsies?" I ask over my shoulder, already halfway to the kitchen.

"No, thank you! I ate at least a dozen of them while she tweaked the recipe. I've eaten so many, I dreamed I was being chased by maple carrot cupcake-people, and they were pelting me with pecans."

"More for me!" I sit down at the kitchen table and open the box. "She's outdone herself, April. It's almost too pretty to eat. Almost."

I peel the paper liner away from the cupcake, and April sits in the chair across from me.

"How are you doing?" she asks. "Have you heard anything else from Fred?"

My mouth is full, so I shake my head while I chew.

After I swallow, I say, "I knew it would happen, eventually. It's not like I expect him to spend the rest of his life alone because our marriage didn't work out. I'm just shocked he didn't wait until he moved out, you know? And that she's married."

April nods and stares at me, searching for signs of an emotional breakdown. She's a good friend.

April and I are alike in so many ways. We share the same sense of humour, values, and taste in music. But we are physical opposites. I'm short with an hourglass figure. She's tall and lean. I'm a curly-haired brunette with hazel eyes, while she is a straight-haired blonde with blue eyes. I have fair skin, and she has a perpetual, year-round, sun-kissed glow.

"He could've waited until we announced the separation,"

I complain. "Other than Hannah, the only people who know are you and Connie."

Connie is my boss at Knitorious, but she's more like family than my boss.

April nods, her mouth pressed into a tight smile.

I finish my cupcake and ask April to please tell T to add it to the menu. It's fabulous and needs to be shared with the entire town as soon as possible.

I shrug. "I'm not in love with Adam anymore." It's cathartic to say it out loud, and a wave of honest relief washes over me. "I love him because he's Hannah's dad, and the three of us will always be a family, you know? But our marriage is definitely over."

My lack of intense feelings about Fred's texts confirm this for me once and for all.

Mindlessly, I twirl my wedding ring with my right hand. I'm a fidgeter, and if I'm not knitting, my hands find something else to keep busy. April reaches across the table and takes my hand, stopping me mid fidget.

"OK, Megastar, but can I ask you one question?" April likes to make up punny nicknames that are puns of my actual name. "If you're at peace with your marriage ending, why do you still wear your wedding ring?" She picks up my left hand and shows it to me as proof.

The ring is a thick band of white gold with a row of square and marquis-cut amethysts—my birthstone—in the centre and a row of diamonds above and below it.

"We agreed to wear them until we announce the separation," I explain. "It was part of our plan not to ruin Hannah's senior year of high school." I shrug. "Also, I love this ring. I designed it myself. When we got married, we were too young and poor to couldn't afford an engagement ring. We had simple, white-gold wedding bands. Adam always wanted to upgrade my ring, so for our tenth anniversary he told me to pick a ring. I designed this one."

I slip the ring from my left hand to my right. A perfect fit, like it was made for that finger.

"Better?" I ask, holding my right hand in front of April's face.

"As long as you're happy." She smiles and stands up. "Are you ready to head to the bakery and meet Fred?"

CHAPTER 2

IT'S A BEAUTIFUL, sunny day, so we walk to Artsy Tartsy. Soon, the weather will change, and I'll miss walking to Water Street without bundling myself into layers of winter outerwear.

Water Street is to Harmony Lake what Main Street is to other small towns. It's our downtown, and where many of the town's businesses and stores are located. Most of the businesses are on the north side. On the south, a park runs parallel to the lakefront.

Weather permitting, I prefer to walk to work because it's only about a ten-minute walk from my house. Harmony Lake is small geographically and in population. Almost anywhere you need to go is within walking distance. The town is nestled snugly between the lake on the south, and the Harmony Hills mountain range on the north. Nature left no room for expansion, but provided a perfect foundation for a tourism-based economy.

The Harmony Hills mountain range's two popular ski resorts are booked all winter with skiers and snowboarders, and booked again in the summer with city-escapees who flock to the lakefront. Except for a few weeks in the fall and summer, the town is full of tourists.

Autumn is my favourite time of year. The town is so pretty with the leaves turning shades of red and yellow; the storefronts have their fall window displays set up, and arrangements of pumpkins and fall flowers punctuate town. Our summer tourist season is over, and the winter tourist season hasn't begun, so for a few precious weeks, we locals have the town to ourselves.

We cross Water Street so we can walk through the park. A few boats dot the lake, and the park is full of townsfolk enjoying the postcard-perfect day.

My phone vibrates in my pocket. It's Adam. I don't have the mental bandwidth to deal with him right now. I clear the notification and return the phone to my pocket.

Across the street, I spot Paul Sinclair walking along the sidewalk in front of The Pharmer's Market, our local pharmacy.

"Shoot!" I duck behind April, then leap to her left side, hoping her height will shield me from view.

"What is it?" She asks, confused by my sudden ducking and weaving around her.

"It's Paul Sinclair," I reply. "There was a fundraising meeting this morning, and with all the kerfuffle, I forgot. I didn't call and let them know I couldn't make it. You know how he is."

I crane my neck to sneak a peek across the street behind April's back, hoping Paul hasn't spotted me. I'd rather deal with him after I deal with Fred.

It's too late. Paul is crossing the street. He saw me, and now he's catching up with me, probably to scold me for my thoughtlessness and lack of respect for the other committee members who *bothered* to attend the meeting. Paul derives an inordinate amount of satisfaction from chastising his fellow townspeople.

Besides being a member of the Town Council, Paul Sinclair is also the president of the Water Street Business

Association (known by the locals as the WSBA), the town council representative on the WSBA board, the WSBA representative on the Town Council, and a member of every committee, organization, and community group in town. To say he's involved in the town is an understatement.

Paul is also Harmony Lake's self-appointed, unofficial bylaw officer. He has a remarkable ability to recite any town bylaw by heart and takes it upon himself to enforce personally every one of them. No matter how minor or justified the infraction.

Paul Sinclair is the town bully.

He doesn't seem threatening at first, but if you violate a bylaw, miss a committee meeting, or otherwise displease him, he'll make sure you know it.

Paul is tall with perfect posture and a year-round tan. His unnaturally white teeth are almost always on display thanks to his carefully molded smile. His smile reminds me of the smile fairy tale wolves have before they eat you or blow down your house.

He even maintains his smile when he's in bully mode, which is confusing when you're his target. I've only ever seen him in a suit, and his dark hair is always perfectly coiffed, because his wife, Kelly, is also his hairdresser. She owns Hairway To Heaven, our local hair salon.

"Megan!" He's almost caught up to us now. April and I stop and turn toward his voice.

My phone vibrates again. Adam. Again. I reject the call and drop the phone in my tote bag.

"Hi Paul." I sigh. "Listen, I'm sorry I missed the fundraising meeting at the Animal Centre this morning. There's been a..."

I've drawn a blank. What do you call an unexpected text message from your husband's potential girlfriend's husband?

"...family emergency...and it took over my day. The meeting completely slipped my mind."

You could call it a family emergency.

"Oh no! Is Hannah OK? Is anyone hurt or anything damaged?" He asks, somehow sounding compassionate and concerned while making me feel like an irresponsible git.

His smile stays constant. His carefully cultivated veneer never cracks.

"Yes," I reply, knowing full well this is a set-up. "Everyone is fine. It's not that kind of emergency."

I attempt my own toothy grin and tilt my head as I look up at him.

"Well, that's a relief! If someone was hurt, I could understand you failing to keep your commitment, but surely you could've called to let us know you would be absent. I mean, imagine if we all just stopped being accountable, and just did whatever we want. It would be chaos, and I'm sure you don't want to contribute to chaos, do you, Megan?"

Still smiling. Him, not me.

I shift my weight from one foot to the other and try to muster the mental fortitude to defend myself. I'm laser focused on this meeting with Fred.

"This is the first meeting I've missed, Paul. Ever. I always follow through with my commitments, except for this morning, which was unavoidable. I'm sure you and the other committee members had a productive meeting, despite my absence. Please forward the meeting minutes to me, and I'll look them over before the next meeting." I'm not in the mood for his bullying right now.

"Will you have time to read the minutes with this emergency? Maybe if you told me what the emergency is, I could help."

He's not trying to be helpful; he's being nosy and condescending.

"Actually, Megan, I was hoping to speak with you alone after the meeting about a different matter. Do you have a few minutes now? Or we could meet later, as long as it's today. We can talk about the meeting and discuss the other thing."

"Today isn't good for me, Paul. You can email the minutes to me along with whatever else you want to discuss."

I sneak a peek at Paul's watch. Almost noon. We need to get to Artsy Tartsy.

"Just fifteen minutes later today?" he implores.

He's not letting this go.

"Paul, we're in a hurry." April holds up her right hand between Paul and me with her palm facing Paul in a stop gesture. "Megan told you why she missed the meeting, and she apologized. Let it go. Email the meeting notes to her and if she has questions, she'll call you."

As April finishes speaking, she grabs my hand and starts walking fast toward the bakery, dragging me along like a fed-up mother pulling a determined toddler away from the toy aisle in a store. Her long legs take longer strides than me, so I do an awkward shuffle-walk-jog to catch up with her.

"Thank you," I say, giving April's hand a squeeze.

She reciprocates my squeeze, looks down at me, and winks.

"The only way to deal with bullies is to confront them," she insists. In a softer voice she adds, "You're going to be OK, you know. You and Hannah always have T and I, and whatever happens today with this Fred person, we've got your back."

We're more than friends; we're family.

CHAPTER 3

As soon as we walk into Artsy Tartsy, the intoxicating aroma of fresh-baked pastries and bread envelop me like a hug. I inhale deeply and the comforting smell fills me with warmth.

I smile and wave to Tamara, who is serving a customer behind the long, glass counter. Tamara smiles and waves back. Without turning her head, she raises her eyebrows and moves her eyeballs to the left toward a man sitting alone at one of the bistro tables, staring at his phone.

April wishes me luck under her breath and hovers a few steps behind me as I approach his table.

"Fred?"

I extend my right hand for him to shake. He looks up at me from his phone.

"Megan?"

We shake hands.

"The owners have offered us the use of the office so we can speak in private," I say.

I gesture toward the back of the bakery. Fred stands up and follows me to the office with April in tow.

The office is a small, windowless room with a simple

white desk, two chairs, and a low profile, white filing cabinet. The walls, floor, and ceiling are also white, which makes the room feel less small and dark. There are accents of teal on the upholstery and teal office supplies. Family photos in teal frames of April, Tamara, and their two kids dot the walls.

I claim the chair closest to the door. Safety first. Fred has no choice and sits in the other chair.

He's tall and thin, with a wiry physique, light brown hair, a receding hairline, and glasses. I'd guess early thirties. His vibe is casual; jeans, a leather belt with an oversize, metal buckle, running shoes, and a button-down plaid shirt. He wears a plain gold wedding band.

From the doorway, April offers refreshments. Fred declines, and I ask for a glass of water. In part because I'm thirsty, and in part so she'll have a reason to come back. She closes the door behind her when she leaves.

Fred unlocks his phone and reveals more screenshots of alleged text conversations between his wife, Stephanie, and Adam. I'm about to ask him how I can verify the screenshots are real when he swipes again, showing me an intimate and revealing photo of Adam.

His face isn't in the photo, but there's no doubt it's Adam. A photo like this is harder to fake than a text conversation.

Fred scrolls through more intimate photos of Adam, then offers to text me the proof. Rendered momentarily speechless from shock, I nod. He explains how he discovered the affair two days ago when, by accident, Stephanie sent him a photo of Adam instead of a photo of their cat in a cardboard box.

Fred says when he confronted Stephanie, she confessed and told him everything. She even gave him access to her phone.

How could Adam be so stupid! I can't count how many times we lectured Hannah about the dangers of sending photos to people on the internet. You never know when those photos will come back to haunt you, or who else will see them. Yet here he is, sending compromising photos of himself to some random woman, who shared them with her husband, who then shared them with me. How many other people have seen these? Or, heaven forbid, have copies. Unbelievable.

A gentle knock at the door distracts me from my inner rant. April has a tray with water and a small plate of pastries to sample. She stands behind Fred so he can't see her.

"Are you OK?" she mouths, exaggerating her words so I can read her lips.

I smile and nod. She asks if we need anything else, then reminds us she's just outside if we do. She leaves and closes the door behind her.

I cross my legs and lean toward Fred.

"What do you want, Fred?" I ask. "We didn't need to meet face-to-face for you to send me your proof. You must want something."

"We want Adam to leave the firm," he replies.

Fred said *we*. His wife knows he's here. They're working together. He waits for me to speak. I stay silent, worry my lips between my teeth, and maintain constant eye contact. Don't show any signs of weakness, Megan.

"Stephanie and I are working it out, but it can't happen if she works with Adam every day," he explains. "Stephanie is a junior associate, and Adam is a senior partner. It would be easier for him to find another job than her."

He takes a deep breath and adds, "Their relationship violates the firm's fraternization policy. Also, as a senior partner, Adam is in a position of authority over Stephanie, and it could appear to the other partners that his influence as her superior coerced her into having an affair with him."

Anger bubbles up from somewhere deep inside me. My mouth is dry and hot, and my face is flushing with heat. I sip my water and try to compose myself.

I'm well aware of the firm's fraternization policy, and so is

Adam since he wrote it. It states employees cannot date or engage in intimate, personal relationships with other employees.

Did Adam use his position as partner to coerce her into having an affair? For years he has passionately represented victims of workplace harassment. I've seen how disgusted he is with the perpetrators; the Adam I know would never do this. But I guess that's what the wife always says when stories like this become public.

I pull myself up to my full seated height. "Are you implying my husband *forced* your wife to have an intimate relationship with him?"

I try hard to remain calm and composed, but the hostile, defensive tone in my voice betrays me.

Fred shifts in his chair and averts his eyes to his hands, which he's wringing in his lap.

"No." He shakes his head, still staring at his hands. "Stephanie says she made the first move, and I believe her."

He sits up, composes himself, and adds, "But that doesn't change the fact that the firm has a strict policy prohibiting employees from dating each other. Adam is technically her superior, and the firm has a history of representing victims of workplace harassment. The optics of this relationship wouldn't be good for the firm's reputation, or your husband's."

There it is. Fred and Stephanie Murphy are using the photos and screenshots to blackmail Adam into leaving the firm. Fred is right about one thing. A scandal like this would damage Adam's career, and maybe even end it.

It could ruin us financially when we have university expenses, and a separation that's about to add the costs of a second household to our family budget.

How will we explain this to Hannah?

"You said, 'we want Adam to leave the firm.' Do you

mean *we* as in you and Stephanie? She knows you're here today? Are you speaking on behalf of both of you?"

"Yes." He nods. "She knows I'm here. She told me to speak to you in person to avoid a technological trail of evidence."

I clear my throat to stop myself from laughing out loud at the irony. The Murphys don't want any technological evidence, yet they're using a technological smoking gun to blackmail my family. She's a lawyer for crying out loud, an officer of the court, and she's taking part in blackmail.

Fred's expression is dead serious. I don't think the Murphys are bluffing, I believe they'll follow through with their threat if Adam doesn't leave the firm.

"What EXACTLY are you asking ME to do?" My volume increases in proportion to my decreasing patience.

No more proof or explanations. Just tell me what I need to know. I need to get away from Fred Murphy before I throw up.

"We expect today to be Adam's last day at the firm. Steph called in sick yesterday and today, but she's going back to work tomorrow. If Adam is still there, she'll go straight to the partners. I met with Adam earlier, and he knows what we expect. I thought you should know. You're a victim, like me. You and I are collateral damage, victims of this mess. But encourage him to do the right thing, so you and your daughter won't have to deal with the fallout if he doesn't."

"Does Adam know you contacted me?" I ask, wondering if this is why Adam has been blowing up my phone with calls and texts all morning.

"No, he doesn't," Fred shakes his head. "I'll leave that up to you."

"I see." I stand up and squeeze the doorknob, my knuckles white from channelling my pent-up emotions into my grip. "I'd say it was nice to meet you, Fred, but it wasn't." I flash him an insincere smile. "Enjoy the rest of your day."

Fred stands up, and I step into the bakery so he can walk past me and leave. I pick up the water and a plate of pastries, follow him to the door, and watch him leave. Good riddance.

The bakery is empty. Tamara comes out from behind the counter and locks the door behind Fred. She turns the OPEN sign to CLOSED and wraps her arms around me. Feeling safe now that Fred is gone, I cry.

I tell April and Tamara about my conversation with Fred. Then, compose myself, dry my tears, and thank them for letting me use the office and always having my back.

It's almost time for my shift at Knitorious, and I need to tell Connie everything that's happened.

Tamara accompanies me to the door, and as she unlocks it, she makes a joke about flipping the CLOSED sign to OPEN before Paul Sinclair hears Artsy Tartsy is closed and comes rushing over to recite and enforce the many bylaws that are probably violated when a Water Street business closes in the middle of a business day. We chuckle and I step into the warmth of the midday sun.

It's not even 1 p.m., and today already feels like the longest day of my life.

On the walk to Knitorious, I reach into my bag and retrieve my phone. Adam phoned and texted again when I was with Fred.

I'm trying to work out what to say to Adam, when I notice Paul Sinclair and Fred Murphy. Together. Sitting in a car in front of a parking meter. Both men are animated and have angry expressions on their faces. They're so engrossed in their discussion, they don't notice me.

As I pass the parked car, I slow my pace to hear them. I can't hear a word, but they're speaking at the same time, and their facial expressions and exaggerated hand gestures make me think they're arguing. The two people who tried to bully me are shouting at each other. I think this is what April would call karma.

What could they be arguing about? Maybe Paul is reprimanding Fred for parking wrong. Or not putting enough money in the meter. Or violating some other bylaw.

I'm so distracted thinking about their heated discussion that I almost walk right past Knitorious.

CHAPTER 4

THE JINGLE of the bell over the door comforts me. Stepping into Knitorious always relaxes and inspires me. It's my second home.

The store is spacious with dark wood floors and yarn-filled, white shelving along the walls. The counter is in the centre. Behind it there is a long wooden harvest-style table with ten chairs where we teach classes and sit at knit night. The cozy sitting area is in front of the counter, off to the side. Knitorious is classic yet contemporary, just like its owner, Connie.

Connie stands at the winding station with her back to me. The winding station is a small wooden table with a yarn swift and ball winder attached to it. A yarn swift is a wooden contraption that holds a skein of yarn while it's being wound into a ball. We wrap the skein of yarn around the yarn swift, then attach one end of the yarn to the ball winder. We crank the ball winder so the swift spins and pulls the yarn from the skein to the ball that's being wound. Aside from knitting itself, winding yarn is the most meditative knitting activity there is.

I walk toward Connie, but stop at the harvest table when

Harlow, Connie's cat, flops onto the tabletop and exposes his belly. Unable to resist his soft under fluff, I'm compelled to rub him. He knows I can't resist his fluffiness. His body rumbles with purrs as soon as I touch his soft, warm tummy.

"It's been a heck of a day so far!" I declare.

I'm eager to fill in Connie on the events of this morning, but she turns, raises her left index finger to her closed lips in a shushing gesture, then bends her finger to her right. My gaze follows her finger, landing on Kelly Sinclair, who's browsing in the bulky yarn section. I nod to Connie, acknowledging her message.

I stash my tote bag under the counter and admire the skeins of ice-blue, bulky yarn on the counter.

"This is beautiful," I say, petting and squishing the yarn. "Is it new?"

The yarn tag says it's a bulky weight, merino-cashmere blend, and the colour name is *Breathless.*

"These skeins are going to be a new wrap for my sister." Kelly turns from the shelf of yarn where she's browsing and walks toward me. "She's always complaining her office is freezing. This colour is perfect for her!" She joins me with her perfectly manicured hands in petting and squishing the skeins of yarn. "Isn't it gorgeous?!

Kelly owns Hairway to Heaven. She and Paul live in the apartment above the salon. Kelly is nothing like her husband. She's pleasant, genuine, and kind. The opposite of her pushy bully of a husband.

Kelly is one of the most glamorous women in Harmony Lake. Her long, blonde hair is always blown out, so it's smooth and bouncy, her make-up is applied with professional precision, and her nails are meticulously manicured. She wears classic, elegant clothes, and her smile lights up a room. She's a walking testimonial to the services her salon provides. Sometimes, I wonder what she and Paul have in common. They're living proof that opposites attract.

"Connie offered to wind a skein for me," Kelly explains, "so I can cast on between clients. I doubt I'll get the chance, though, I'm booked for the rest of the day." Kelly checks the time on her phone, then retrieves her wallet from her purse. "And... oh... look at the time! I have to get back. Mrs. Willows is coming in for roots and highlights at 2 p.m., and the plumber said he'd come by to clear the drain after 1:30 p.m. I should go before I'm distracted by more yarn!" She giggles.

"Is it Archie or Ryan who's coming to unclog the drain?" I ask.

Archie and Ryan Wright are Harmony Lake's local father-son handyperson service. Most of the businesses on Water Street, and pretty much everyone else in town, rely on them for handy work and repair jobs. Their white van with the words "The Wright Men For The Job," painted on the side in red letters, is a common sight around Harmony Lake.

"We don't hire Archie and Ryan anymore." Kelly's smile disappears, and a more serious expression appears in its place. "Paul says Ryan isn't trustworthy. He said Ryan isn't welcome in the salon or the apartment ever again."

"Oh. Did Paul say why?"

I've heard no one complain about either Archie or Ryan. Ever.

Kelly shakes her head. "No, Paul just said he doesn't trust him and doesn't want me to hire him." She shrugs and pulls her credit card from her wallet.

Connie stops winding and grabs a pair of large knitting needles from the needle display. The fifteen-millimetre wooden needles look more like drum sticks than knitting needles. Bulky yarn requires big needles.

"If you don't get gauge with these, Kelly, just bring them back, and we'll exchange them for a different size." Connie smiles.

Connie hands me the needles, and I ring them up. Kelly pays, I put her yarn and needles in a paper bag with handles, and she rushes out the door to beat Mrs. Willows and the plumber to Hairway to Heaven.

"What do you think that's about? Paul not trusting Ryan?" I ask Connie now that we're alone.

Connie waves her hand in front of her face like she's waving away an unpleasant smell. "Who knows? Paul is always picking on someone, and if he's not picking on them today, he's looking for a reason to pick on them tomorrow. You know how he is, I'm sure it's something from nothing."

I reach under the counter and retrieve my knitting bag from my tote bag. I've carried around this purple yarn for a week, waiting for the chance to cast on a new hat and cowl for Hannah.

I take my knitting to a sofa and settle in. While I knit, I tell Connie about the texts from Fred, the encounter April and I had with Paul Sinclair, my meeting with Fred, the blackmail scheme, and the weird argument I saw between Fred and Paul on my way here. I'm trying to knit while I talk, but Harlow decides he'd rather nap on my lap than on the table, so I put my knitting aside to stroke the purring, sleepy cat.

Connie is a superb listener and a source of sage advice. I know she worries about Hannah and me, especially with Adam and I separating. I don't want her to worry more than she already does, but not telling her would feel like lying. I tell her and April almost everything. She even introduces me to people as her daughter-friend, and I call her my mother-friend.

At sixty-eight years young, Connie is the smartest, most sophisticated woman I know. She's wise in the ways of the world, yet the concept of sexting seems to elude her. She keeps asking how I can be certain it's Adam in the photos if his face isn't in any of them.

Without being explicit, I assure Connie it's definitely him in the photos. She's worried the photos are fake, and we're being conned. She asks to see them for herself. Obviously, that can't happen, so to stop this awkward conversation from becoming even more awkward, I tell her Adam's tattoo is in the photos. Adam has Hannah's birth date tattooed in roman numerals over his heart.

Thankfully, she accepts this and stops asking to see them. I change the subject, and we discuss ideas for the fall window display.

I'm pretty sure this isn't a lie because I recall seeing his tattoo in at least one photo, but I'm not certain. I haven't looked at them since Fred sent them to me. I'd like very much never to see them again.

When Connie gets up to answer the landline, I check my phone and find more calls and texts from Adam.

How do I tell him I know about the affair? At a loss for words, I send him a screenshot of the text conversation between him and Stephanie, careful to send him the least intimate one. As soon as I hit send, three dots on the screen indicating Adam is typing a reply.

Adam: I'm sorry. I will take care of this today. You spoke to Paul?

What does *taken care of* mean? Does that mean he's leaving the firm, or does it mean something else? He knows Paul was looking for me? I miss one meeting in sixteen years and Paul calls my husband? Seems like a bit of an overreaction on Paul's part, but OK.

Me: Yes, he found me on my way into town.

I want to tell him about my meeting with Fred, but I'm a bit paranoid about putting it in a text since I've got a phone full of incriminating photos and screenshots of text conversations that are being used against my family. I hit send and no dots appear. Instead, my phone rings with Adam's name appearing on the screen.

"Hi," I whisper, aware Connie is on the phone in the kitchenette behind the store.

I stretch to look through the doorway. Her back is to me,

her sleek, shoulder-length silver hair bobbing as she talks on the phone.

Connie is an animated talker. She uses her hands and facial expressions to add emphasis when she speaks. If people were books, most of us would be novels, but Connie would have full colour illustrations. She uses gestures to add context to what she's saying.

"Meg, I'm so sorry. I didn't know this would happen."

"Which part didn't you know, Adam?" I hiss. "That your girlfriend is married? That dating an employee is against the company policy *you* wrote? That you're technically her boss? That they could use those photos against us? That sleeping with an employee might hurt your career? That I might see a bunch of photos I wish I didn't know exist? You'll need to be more specific, Adam."

There's a long, angry silence. Well, angry on my end; for Adam, it might be an awkward silence.

"I know I messed up, Meg, and I'm fixing it. I've been in meetings with the other partners all day, and I'll be here late tonight tying up loose ends. If you're still awake when I get home, I'd like to talk, and explain things to you. If it's too late tonight, maybe we can talk tomorrow."

He says he'll be late like it's a rare occurrence, like he hasn't been working late and bringing work home with him on weekends for the better part of fifteen years. We need to talk about this, though, he's right.

"Fine," I agree, sighing. "Let's talk tonight or tomorrow."

I'm about to ask him what "taking care of it" means, but I'm interrupted by the jingle of the bell over the door. A local yarn dyer is struggling to hold the door open while carrying a tub of yarn that Connie must have ordered. I tell Adam I have to go. We end the call, and I rush to hold the door for the dyer.

In between serving customers, helping a knitter recover a stitch she dropped about three hundred rows ago, and petting

Harlow on demand, I unpack the tub of yarn, add the skeins to the store inventory, take photos of them for the shopping section of the store website, and rearrange some shelves to make room for the new, fall-coloured skeins.

Harlow and I look at each other when we hear dishes clinking. Harlow's pupils dilate, his tail twitches, and his ears are at attention. He's on full alert. The *ffffffffpp* of a lid peeling off a can of cat food confirms his suspicion that it's dinner time. He runs to the back of the store and into the kitchenette. He meows loudly when the spoon *tinks* against his dish as Connie doles out the gross-smelling loaf of cat food.

How is it dinner time already? According to the clock on the cash register, it's 6:20 p.m. We should have closed twenty minutes ago. I get up to lock the door and turn the sign to CLOSED. When I get there, it's already locked, and the sign turned.

"I closed up twenty minutes ago, my dear." Connie is out of the kitchenette and sitting at the harvest table. "You were so focused that you didn't notice."

"I was focused on keeping busy. To keep my mind off Murphygate." It didn't work.

Credit goes to April for coming up with, Murphygate. She used it a couple of hours ago when she texted me for an update.

"Have you heard anything from Adam or the Murphygate people, my dear?"

Connie's reference to the *Murphygate people* makes me smile.

"I would tell you if I did. I'm hoping no news is good news, and I'll never hear from them again."

"You should stay for supper tonight. We'll make tacos and drink wine. We can watch that British murder mystery show we like and have a sleepover! We haven't had a girls' night in ages." Connie claps her hands in front of her, like she just thought up the best idea ever.

Connie dotes on me. She's choosing tonight for a girls' night to help keep my mind off Murphygate, and to stay close in case there's another dramatic development.

"I'd love a girls' night, but can we do it another time? Today was exhausting and I think I'd fall asleep in my tacos and wine."

I'm moving around the store, picking up mislaid skeins of yarn, and returning them to their proper shelves when the half-wound skein of "Breathless" yarn at the winding station catches my eye.

"Kelly was in a rush and left without it," I say, nodding toward the winding station.

"Oh mothballs! I completely forgot to finish winding it." Connie turns around in her chair and starts cranking the ball winder.

I finish tidying the store while Connie finishes winding the skein of yarn.

"I'll drop it off on my way home," I offer. "I have to walk past the salon, anyway."

I place the yarn in a small bag and drop it in my tote. Connie follows me to the door so she can lock it behind me.

"I'll see you in the morning." I open my arms for a hug.

Connie squeezes me and rubs my back.

"Call me tonight if you need anything." She pulls away and points at my nose. "I mean it. I don't care how late it is."

"I will, I promise! Goodnight."

The lock clicks behind me as I walk down the street.

CHAPTER 5

It's after hours, but the lights are on inside the salon, so I check the salon door before heading around to the back door that leads to the upstairs apartment.

I grip the handle and read the business hours posted on the door. The salon closes at 6 p.m. on Tuesdays. It's almost 7 p.m. now. I pull, but the door is locked. I try pushing it anyway, because I've made that mistake before, and determine it's definitely locked.

Bringing my right hand to my forehead to reduce the glare of the setting sun reflecting off the salon window, I squint.

Kelly is standing at a sink tending to a client. Her back is to me. I pull the yarn from my tote bag and knock on the window. When Kelly turns around, I wave, smile, and hold up the bag. She smiles in acknowledgement, turns to her client, then turns back to me and walks toward the door, wiping her hands on a black towel with a pink, embroidered salon logo. Kelly opens the door and I step inside.

"One of your lovely skeins of yarn was left on the winder," I tell her.

The chemical smell inside the salon burns my nose and

throat. I wonder if the fumes bother Kelly, or if she's used to it. I hand her the bag, and she peeks inside.

"Thank you for dropping it off. I've been too busy to notice it's missing. I never work this late, but Mrs. Pearson and her husband are leaving for a cruise tomorrow for their forty-fifth wedding anniversary, and this was the only time I could fit her in before she leaves."

Kelly looks toward Mrs. Pearson, who is reclined with her head in the sink. "We want to make sure your hair looks sun-kissed in your vacation photos, don't we, Mrs. Pearson?" Kelly asks in a raised voice so Mrs. Pearson can hear her from inside the sink.

Mrs. Pearson raises a freshly manicured thumb in acknowledgement.

Still looking toward Mrs. Pearson and holding the yarn bag up high enough for Mrs. Pearson to see, Kelly says raising her voice, "I'll be right back to finish taking out your foils, Mrs. Pearson, I just need to run this upstairs to the apartment."

Mrs. Pearson again gives a thumbs-up acknowledgement. Kelly turns to me and wrinkles her nose.

"I don't want to leave it in the salon, it'll absorb the chemical odours," she explains, her voice back to its normal volume.

"I can take it upstairs for you," I offer. "You finish getting Mrs. Pearson's hair cruise-ready, and I'll take the yarn up to your apartment." I smile and take the bag from Kelly's hand.

"Thanks, hun, you're a star. I think Paul is at a meeting somewhere. But, if he's up there, just give him the bag. If not, there's a table on the right, just inside the door. The door should be unlocked." By the time Kelly finishes speaking, she's already back at the sink, her fingers crinkling the foil strips as she removes them from Mrs. Pearson's hair.

I flip the light switch in the small back room. Towels, bottles of shampoo, conditioner and other salon products are organized on floor-to-ceiling shelves along two walls. The back door that leads to the parking lot is in front of me and propped slightly ajar with a unique, heart-shaped grey rock. I assume Kelly opens it so the fresh air can combat the chemical smell in the salon. The stairs are on my left.

At the top of the stairs, muffled voices come from the apartment. I assume Paul is home and either watching TV or listening to the radio. I sigh, not looking forward to ending my day with another conversation with him.

I knock on the door, hoping he doesn't greet me with a reprimand, lecture, or any other lengthy conversation. My belly is rumbling, and I'm thinking about the leftover lasagna waiting for me in the fridge. I can get home and have it in the microwave within ten minutes of leaving here.

He doesn't answer. I knock again, louder. Still nothing. I put my ear to the door. A TV or radio, but nothing else. Maybe he left the TV on and went out. Or maybe he's asleep.

Tentatively, I turn the doorknob to confirm the door is unlocked. It is. I open the door enough to poke my head inside the apartment.

"Hello?" I call. "Paul? It's Megan. I'm just dropping off some yarn for Kelly."

No response. A sense of chilly apprehension makes a shiver run down my spine. I dismiss my unease, brace myself, and go over my plan. Open the door, step inside, put the yarn on the table. Leave, and tell Kelly on the way out that Paul didn't answer, and the yarn is on the table.

Deep breath.

I open the door slowly and step inside the apartment. There's a table on the right; just like Kelly said. The table has a bowl of keys, two pairs of sunglasses, a wallet, and the bag I handed to Kelly at Knitorious this afternoon. I place the small bag of yarn next to the larger bag, feeling relieved to avoid another unpleasant confrontation with Paul.

I turn to leave and Paul is sitting at the kitchen. His back is to me. He's slumped forward. I can't see his head; it must be on the kitchen table. What an odd place to fall asleep.

"Hi Paul." I watch to see if he wakes up, or twitches, or something. He doesn't.

With hesitation, I take a step toward the kitchen table.

"Paul?"

No response, no movement.

I attribute the growing knot of anxiety in my stomach to the eerie atmosphere of the apartment and creep toward the kitchen table. I stop and swallow hard when the knot of anxiety rises to my throat. This knot in my stomach is familiar; I feel it whenever something isn't right. It's one way my intuition communicates with me. The knot hasn't been wrong in almost forty years.

I inch closer to Paul. There something around his neck. Something blue. I squint in case my eyes are playing tricks on me. A skein of yarn? Why would he drape a skein of yarn around his neck? I recognize the yarn; it's a skein of *Breathless*, the same yarn I admired at work today, and the same yarn Kelly bought four skeins of.

The skein is untwisted and draped around Paul's neck like a back-drop necklace, tight in the front with the excess yarn draping down the back of his white undershirt.

I bend to look at his face, except it's immersed in a large bowl. I check for signs of life. He's too still, and his body isn't rising and falling like a body should when it inhales and exhales.

"Paul, I'm going to check your pulse," I tell him.

It's been more than a dozen years since I've had CPR training, but I remember the instructor saying it's important to talk to the person and tell them what you're doing each step of the way.

His hands are on the table, on either side of the large bowl. His cell phone is next to his left hand.

I check his wrist for a pulse. No pulse. He's warmer than room temperature, but not as warm as he should be.

Maybe this just happened. Maybe there's still time to help him.

"Paul, can you hear me? I'm going to lift your head out of the bowl."

Please hear me, Paul. No reaction.

Please be a bizarre household accident or medical episode. Please be all right.

I put one hand on either side of Paul's head, just above his ears, and lift his head from the bowl. It's heavier than I expect. Milk drips from his face into the bowl and onto the table. There are pieces of soggy cereal stuck to his nose and cheek.

He won't be all right.

Paul Sinclair is dead.

CHAPTER 6

THE KNOT in my stomach explodes, shooting panic throughout the rest of my body. My heart thumps double time, banging in my chest like it's trying to escape. With my heartbeat pounding in my ears, and my face flushing with heat, I try to catch my breath and swallow. I have to get help. I have to get out of here.

Should I put his face back in the cereal bowl? Do I move the cereal bowl and lay his head on the table? The CPR course didn't cover this.

How can he be dead? I just saw him this morning, and he was alive. Controlling and bossy, but alive.

Did he drown in a giant bowl of cereal? Was he strangled by the skein of yarn?

I turn his head to the left, and gently rest it on the bowl, making sure not to submerge it again. I walk backwards toward the door, watching him in case I'm wrong, and he moves.

Please move, Paul! Please wake up!

Groping behind me, I find the door, and back out of the apartment.

Running down the stairs to the salon, I hear myself scream.

"Kelly! Kelly! Call 9-1-1! It's Paul! Something's wrong with Paul!"

Confusion clouds Kelly's face, and she looks like she's in slow motion.

My phone is in my shaky hand, and I call for help.

While I answer the dispatcher's questions, Kelly looks from me to the stairs, then back to me again. I sense she's about to run up to the apartment. Should I spare her from seeing her husband like this? What if it's a crime scene? I position myself between Kelly and the stairs while answering the dispatcher's questions. Kelly wipes her hands on a towel, then sprints to the back room, pushing past me and racing upstairs.

"Paul!" She screams.

I run up the stairs after her. She's kneeling at his side, checking for a pulse. She checks the same wrist I checked moments before. I hope she has a different outcome.

The dispatcher instructs me to unlock the door. I run downstairs and pass the back door, telling her it's propped open with a rock. I unlock the front door and crack it open to confirm it's unlocked.

Aluminum foil crinkles behind me, and I turn to see Mrs. Pearson on her feet, removing the last of the foils from her hair. She bends forward into the sink and gives her short hair a quick rinse, then while rubbing her wet hair with a towel, walks over to me and tells me that she'll take over door duty. I nod in response.

I stand guard at the back door in case the ambulance pulls up behind the salon. She's still on the line, but the dispatcher stops asking questions. We're silent except for her saying, "Are you still with me, Megan?" at regular intervals, and me responding with, "Yes, I'm here." After which, she says,

"Help is almost there." Then, after a brief silence, we do it again.

An ambulance pulls up in front of the Hairway To Heaven, and the lights create a red and blue strobe effect on the walls inside the salon. The dispatcher and I end our call.

In what feels like seconds, the salon is full of first responders. Paramedics, police officers, and firefighters rush around me.

The salon is smaller with all the commotion. To stay out of the way, I find a nearby wall and lean against it, trying to take up as little space as possible.

A police officer leads Kelly down the stairs, and I get her a glass of water from the kitchenette. At least I'm doing something. Anything. I just need to do something useful.

The officer leads Kelly to a chair in front of a sink and helps her sit. I hand her the water and place a box of tissues from the kitchenette on her lap.

A second police officer guides me to a stylist's chair across the room.

I notice a third police officer with Mrs. Pearson at the reception desk.

They're keeping us apart on purpose.

Many years of binge-watching murder mysteries with enthusiasm while I knit has taught me that police keep witnesses at a crime scene apart, so they can interview them separately, and they won't influence each other's statements. People are highly suggestible, particularly when in shock. We can influence each other's recollection of events. For example, if I think something at the crime scene is blue, but I hear another witness describe it as green, I might question my recollection, and convince myself the blue thing was green.

My police officer opens her notepad and starts asking me questions. I fiddle with my wedding ring, now on my right hand, and provide her with my name and contact information. I reach for my wallet to show her my identification.

37

Adam's voice is inside my head, telling me not to answer any more questions without a lawyer. But I have done nothing wrong, and I have nothing to hide. I decide to cooperate and help any way I can.

She asks me why I'm at the salon and why I went upstairs. She also wants to know how I found Paul, where I touched him, and what else I touched while I was up there. I tell her everything, starting from when Connie and I noticed the skein of yarn Kelly left behind at Knitorious earlier today.

The firefighters leave and more people arrive to take their place. A tall, official-looking man in a suit among them.

My police officer and I both notice the suit, and she excuses herself to speak with him. My experience as an avid viewer of murder mysteries tells me the suit is a police detective.

In the background of my mind, I've been telling myself that Paul had a medical episode, or an accident, and it wasn't murder. I don't want to believe one of my neighbours could be a murder victim. Murders don't happen in my cozy, sweet town. However, a detective's presence makes it difficult to convince myself that either theory explains Paul's death.

If Paul's death is a murder, I was at a murder scene moments after the killer fled. This realization increases my anxiety and leaves a sick taste in my mouth.

Suddenly, I'm hot, my breathing is shallow, I've developed a tremble, and my mouth is too dry. I take deep breaths to bring the trembling under control, but the chemical smell in the salon works against me, so now, on top of everything else, I'm also nauseous. I close my eyes and put my head between my knees.

"Are you all right?" asks an unfamiliar man's voice. "Do you need medical attention?"

I raise my head and try to focus on the suit standing in front of me.

"Would it be possible to step outside for some fresh air?" I gulp, hoping to swallow the wave of nausea rising inside me.

"Of course," he replies, "follow me."

He extends a large, warm hand and helps me up. He leads me to the front door and onto the sidewalk where I inhale as much of the crisp, evening air as my lungs can handle.

"Heavy shoulders, long arms," I mutter to myself.

Heavy shoulders, long arms is a relaxation technique to help release tension from the neck and shoulders. I learned it in a yoga class in my twenties and still use it all these years later.

"Pardon?" the suit asks, looking down at me, and stooping to so he can hear me. "Did you say something?"

I shake my head and lean against the cool brick wall of the salon. I put my hands on my knees and take a few more deep breaths.

Feeling a little less nauseous and shaky, I stand upright. Friends and neighbours line the sidewalk across the street. Police officers and barriers prevent them from coming closer.

A uniformed officer appears and positions himself in front of me, holding up a large white sheet. Is he trying to shield me from seeing the people across the street, or is he trying to shield them from seeing me? Either way, it's too late.

"Someone is getting you a glass of water," the suit informs me.

"Thank you." I look up at him and nod. "I'm feeling better. We can go back inside."

I return to the same chair I was in before, and Mrs. Pearson, followed accompanied by her police escort, hands me a glass of water and rubs my back reassuringly.

This woman is good in a crisis.

Just when I'm feeling like this day will never end, my police officer appears at my side and asks me if there's anyone I can call to pick me up.

My first thought is to call either April or Connie, but it seems silly to ask them to escort me home when I can walk there myself in ten minutes. Also, they'll fuss over me and ask a ton of questions I'm not ready to answer. I'm not prepared to relive this again tonight. I'm tired and hungry. I want to go home and put on my jammies.

I could call Adam. Not for emotional support, but because he's a lawyer. If ever there was a situation where a lawyer might come in handy, this would be it.

I decide not to call anyone. The police officer offers to drive me home, and I accept.

WALKING through my front door reinvigorates me. Five minutes ago, I was exhausted and overwhelmed, and now I'm wide awake and wired. This must be what shock feels like. Tonight I learned that shock is a process with a wide spectrum of reactions ranging from panic, fear, sadness, and nausea, to energetic, hyper, alert, and overwhelmed.

I try to recall something I read once about adrenaline and stressful situations, but can't remember the details.

Adam isn't home yet, and I'm relieved I don't have to answer questions about what happened or sit through reminders about not answering police questions without a lawyer.

I put a piece of lasagna in the microwave. While it warms up, I retrieve my phone from my bag and unlock the screen to see dozens of texts from friends and neighbours wanting to know what's happening, and if everyone is OK.

I reply to April and Connie first, letting them know Kelly, Mrs. Pearson, and I are OK, but Paul isn't. I also tell them I need a few hours to process everything, and I'll talk to them tomorrow. They offer to come over and promise not to ask questions. I appreciate it, but thank them and decline. Right now, I want to be alone and end this long, awful day.

Scrolling through my missed messages, Adam texted to

say I shouldn't wait up, and he'll be around in the morning to talk.

I text him back and tell him Paul is dead, and the town is in shock. He'll find out anyway, so it may as well be from me. I don't tell him I was the one who found him or it looks like murder. I'm not ready to deal with questions yet.

He doesn't respond.

It's much later than I normally eat dinner, but I haven't eaten since this morning, and I'm famished and nauseous at the same time. As a result, I eat my lasagna faster than I should, and hope I won't be up all night with indigestion.

I put my dishes in the dishwasher and make a mug of chamomile tea while I finish scrolling through the missed text messages.

In bed, I toss and turn. My body is exhausted, but my brain refuses to yield to its demand for sleep. When I close my eyes and try to be still, I relive it. Paul hunched over the table. Kelly sprinting for the stairs. The chemical odour in the salon. Milk dripping off Paul's nose and the pieces of cereal stuck to his face. His not-quite-warm-enough skin. It plays over and over in my head, a movie I can't pause.

To distract myself, I turn on the TV and find a channel that only airs 1990s sitcoms. I leave it on until I either fall asleep, or it's time to get up.

With the theme song from Friends filling my bedroom, I close my eyes and take deep breaths.

CHAPTER 7

WEDNESDAY, September 11th

I wake up to Paul and Jamie Buchman arguing about a pretty nurse on Mad About You. Sleep was elusive and occupied by a dream that had me running around the edge of a huge fountain of cereal, trying not to fall in while a giant skein of blue yarn chased me.

I turn off the TV, hurry through my morning routine, and rush out the door.

Adam's car isn't in the driveway. His briefcase, shoes, and coat aren't where he leaves them, so I assume he didn't come home last night.

I walk into town in case Water Street is still closed in front of Hairway to Heaven. Also, I'm too tired to drive.

When I round the corner onto Water Street, yellow crime scene tape glistens in the light of the dawning sun and wafts in the breeze. I cross the street because the police officer stationed in front of Hairway To Heaven is blocking the sidewalk.

There are fewer bystanders this morning, but still a good-sized crowd. As I thread my way through clusters of curious onlookers, someone calls my name. I stretch my neck and scan the crowd, my gaze landing on April who's waving me over to her and Connie.

They envelop me in a group hug.

"How did you sleep, my dear?" Connie squeezes my shoulder with one arm and hands me a coffee with the other.

"Thank you!" I say, accepting the coffee and holding it under my nose before I take a sip. It's hazelnut-French vanilla medium roast, and right now, it's my favourite coffee in the world.

April leans in and whispers in my ear, "Phillip was here early to receive a delivery, and he saw Kelly. She got in the back of a police car and they drove her away."

Phillip Wilde owns Wilde Flowers, the florist shop next to Knitorious. He also lives next door to me; we're neighbours at work and at home.

"Poor Kelly," I say.

I thought my night was bad. I can't imagine what she's going through.

People notice me, and word of my presence makes its way through the crowd. Soon, people are approaching me to ask how I'm doing. Some people are sincere, some are trying to find out what I know, and the rest fall into both categories.

In light of the attention, Connie suggests we make our way to Knitorious, and we walk away from the crowd.

I'm not trying to avoid answering my friends' and neighbours' questions, I'm just not sure what I should and shouldn't say. I want to respect Kelly's privacy and the police investigation, but Harmony Lake is a small, tight-knit community, and a tragedy like this affects all of us.

After we've put some distance between us and the crowd, April asks if anyone official declared Paul's death a murder.

"I don't know," I reply. "I answered a lot of questions last night, but I didn't ask any. It didn't look like he passed away peacefully in his sleep, but it also didn't look like a gruesome murder scene."

This is the most I've said to anyone other than the police.

"Not all murders are gruesome, my dear," Connie reminds me. "Look at those murder mystery shows set in quaint British villages, they're never messy."

Connie shares my enthusiasm for murder mysteries. We're both experienced armchair investigators.

INSIDE THE STORE, I lock the door behind us. We don't open for two hours, and I'm not ready to deal with people.

Connie excuses herself and goes up to her apartment for a shower, while April and I sit in the cozy sitting area sipping our coffees. Harlow runs into the store, jumps onto the sofa, and nestles into April's hip, settling in for his early morning nap.

"I know Paul was a bully and rubbed many people the wrong way, but someone would have to hate him a lot to kill him," April speculates as she absentmindedly strokes Harlow. "Especially with his wife in the same building. I mean, they risked being caught by Kelly unless they entered the apartment from the roof."

"If they were already in the apartment when Paul got home, they only risked being seen when they left," I point out.

I fiddle with my ring, still getting used to wearing it on my right hand.

"Either the killer knew Kelly was working late in the salon and Paul was alone in the apartment, or they intended to kill both of them, but Kelly wasn't there, so they settled for only killing Paul," she theorizes.

"I wonder if Mr. and Mrs. Pearson left for their cruise?" I wonder out loud.

"You mentioned her last night in your text, but we didn't see her there. I don't think anyone saw her, and other than you, no one else has mentioned her," April says.

"She was the client Kelly stayed late for. No one else knows that?"

"No. We only knew you were there because you came outside for air. The police held up sheets to block the view when anything, or I guess anyone, left the salon."

April leaves for Artsy Tartsy, where she'll work behind the counter while Tamara works her magic in the kitchen.

Alone with my thoughts, my mind replays last night's events on a constant loop, and I worry I missed something important, or compromised the crime scene when I found Paul and tried to help him. Maybe I shouldn't have lifted his head and put it in a different position.

Harlow wakes up and meows loudly at me.

"I know what you want, handsome. You only ever want one thing." I pick him up, carry him to the kitchenette and put him on the floor. He weaves in and out of my ankles while I spoon his breakfast into a dish and place it on the floor in front of him.

When I walk back into the store, Adam is outside waving at me through the window. I let him in.

"I knocked, but I guess you didn't hear it in the back."

He's wearing a suit. Either he's on his way to the office, or on his way home. We sit on the sofa, and he tells me he didn't get my text about Paul's death until this morning. I fill him in.

"You were dropping off yarn?" Adam asks, stunned. "I assumed you went there because Paul was blackmailing me. He's the person who told you about Stephanie Murphy and gave you the screenshots, right?"

"No!" I reply, confused. "Fred Murphy gave me the photos, not Paul," I clarify. "Paul knew about you and Stephanie? How? And how did he get the photos?" I take a breath and let sink in that Paul had the photos. "Paul was blackmailing us?" I ask. "In *addition* to Fred and Stephanie Murphy? Or did they all work together?" I shake my head as though it will help the pieces fall into place and everything will suddenly make sense. "Was there one blackmail scheme or two? I'm so confused."

Seriously, what's going on? I might need a chart or something.

Adam brings his hands together in front of his chest.

"You spoke with Fred?" he asks, then points to me. I nod. "Fred told you about Stephanie and me, and gave you the photos?" He points again and I nod again. "OK, Fred and Stephanie Murphy blackmailed me to leave the firm. Then, Paul contacted me yesterday morning and told me to transfer a certain amount of money into his account by noon. He said if I didn't do it, he would send the photos to you," Adam explains. "There's no way I would give in to Paul's demand. I didn't send him any money. I tried calling and texting you, but you didn't answer. Then you texted me the photo, so I assumed when I didn't pay him, Paul followed through with his threat and told you about Stephanie."

This explains why Paul wanted to talk to me yesterday.

"How did Paul get the photos you sent to Stephanie?"

"I have no idea," Adam replies with a one-shoulder shrug.

"I saw Paul and Fred together yesterday," I tell him. "They were arguing in a car outside Artsy Tartsy. I assumed Fred parked wrong, or didn't use his blinker, or some such thing. But maybe they knew each other and were discussing blackmail."

Adam leans toward me and rests his elbows on his knees.

"Meg, the texts and the photos on Paul's phone, and his text conversation with me, give us motive to kill him. The police will want to question us. Soon."

"Where were you last night?" I probe. "The police will want to know."

He didn't come home, and I assume he wasn't with his blackmailer-girlfriend, Stephanie Murphy.

"A hotel near the office," Adam explains. "The firm keeps a courtesy suite." He sighs. "I resigned yesterday. Effective today. I stayed late tying up loose ends. It was late when I left, and I was too tired to drive home, so I stayed at the hotel."

Wow. He left the firm! This is the end of an era. Under normal circumstances, this would be a monumental event, but considering everything that's happened since yesterday, it seems almost insignificant.

I want to ask him if this affair with a married woman that cost him his job, and got us blackmailed twice over, was worth it. But I bite my tongue. We need calm, level heads, not heated arguments and accusations.

The floorboards creak when Connie descends the stairs. Adam stands up, smooths his tie, smiles, and walks toward her to greet her as she enters the store.

Adam is a dangerous combination of handsome and charming, packaged in a well-tailored, expensive suit. He looks at you like you're the only person in his world.

Even Connie isn't immune to his charm. As he takes her hands and kisses her cheek, his charisma draws her in like a moth to a flame. He compliments her perfume and still holding her hands, tells her how beautiful she looks in blue because it brings out her blue eyes. She blushes like a school-girl. He can't help it. He doesn't know he's doing it. It's not predatory, he's sincere and means everything he says. It's just how he is. He's oblivious to the effect he has on people, particularly women, and his naivete is part of his charm.

They're talking about Paul and how his death shocked the community. Adam doesn't mention Paul was blackmailing us.

He throws a few more compliments at Connie, then goes home to shower and change, leaving Connie and I alone in the quiet store. Except for Harlow purring and the gentle clickity-clack of our needles, we knit in silence until it's time to open the store.

"It's showtime." Connie smiles at me, puts her knitting on the table and gets up to unlock the door and flip the CLOSED sign to OPEN.

CHAPTER 8

WATER STREET IS busy for a typical Wednesday. But today isn't a typical Wednesday; it's the day after our neighbour was killed in his home.

People stroll along Water Street, meandering in and out of stores. They're trying to make sense of what happened. They find comfort in reassuring each other and not being alone today.

As shocked people wander in and out of Knitorious, Harlow makes himself available to provide comfort, accept rubs, and takes on the role of self-appointed emotional support animal.

Almost everyone asks me what I saw yesterday. The few who don't ask me themselves hover nearby so they can hear what I say. I tell them I can't talk about it until the police tell me otherwise. Word must have spread that I'm not talking because, by lunchtime, fewer people ask me about it.

Connie and I take turns having lunch. When it's my turn, I go upstairs to her apartment and have a sandwich she made for me. I rarely take a full lunch break. Usually, I'm content to eat in the kitchenette then go back to work. Today I take my time and use the full hour.

I return from lunch to find Connie dangling a shimmery pom-pom on a string in front of Harlow.

"Will you be all right if I leave for my appointment, my dear?"

I forgot about Connie's appointment today. She mentioned it yesterday before I went to Hairway To Heaven.

"Of course!" I say, "You go. I'll be fine. Besides, Stitch-Fix is this afternoon, so I'll be busy and the afternoon will fly by."

Stitch-Fix is a knitting clinic we host one afternoon each week where knitters bring in their knitting problems and mistakes, and Connie and I help fix them. I love the challenge.

"Only if you're sure. I don't mind rescheduling. I meant to reschedule this morning, but in all the excitement I forgot." She shrugs, chuckling at her forgetfulness.

"I'll be fine," I tell her, again.

She leaves through the back door, and for the first time today, the store is empty. I tidy the shelves and return mislaid skeins of yarn where they belong.

In the bulky yarn section, I stare at the remaining skeins of Breathless. A now-familiar wave of nausea washes over me and in my mind's eye I see this yarn wrapped around Paul's neck with him hunched over the kitchen table. The yarn dangling down the back of his white undershirt. I decide I'll remove Breathless from the shelf. Out of sight, out of mind, and all that.

While contemplating which yarn to put in its place, the bell over the door jingles. A tall, fortyish-year-old man in a suit looks around. He's familiar, but I can't place him. He's not our usual demographic. If he was a return customer, I'd remember him for sure.

We make eye contact and walk toward each other, meeting at the harvest table.

"Hi," I say, smiling.

"Hello, again," he responds, also smiling.

He extends a hand and offers me a business card:

Detective Sergeant Eric Sloane
Ontario Provincial Police

He's the suit from the salon last night.

"Of course!" I exclaim. "You're the detective from Hairway to Heaven!"

I extend my hand, we shake, and I gesture for him to have a seat at the harvest table.

"Why the OPP?" I ask. "Isn't the Harmony Lake Police Department investigating?"

The OPP is what the locals call the Ontario Provincial Police.

"Harmony Lake PD doesn't have a major crimes division, so they asked us to assist," he explains. "Apparently, there isn't enough crime in Harmony Lake to warrant a major crimes division."

"Not until yesterday," I confirm.

It's true. Compared to bigger towns and cities, Harmony Lake has a low crime rate. We have our share of parking tickets, jaywalkers, and the occasional drunk-in-public tourist. A few years back, there was a spate of wallet robberies, but we've never had a murder. Until now.

Eric Sloane smells good. Like a forest after it rains. I didn't notice yesterday with everything else going on. And not to be shallow, but he's hot. If you're into tall men with dark hair, brown eyes with flecks of gold, and friendly smiles.

Don't stare, Megan.

"How are you?" he asks. "I know yesterday was a shock. You weren't feeling well at the salon last night. Are you feeling better?"

"It was a shock, for sure, but I feel better today," I reply. "Thank you for asking. I've been thinking about Kelly. How is she doing?"

"She has family with her, and we're making sure she has access to all available resources to help her."

It's amazing how well he answered my question without actually answering my question.

"Well, please tell her everyone is thinking of her and sending her lots of love and support."

I doubt he'll say those exact words, but hopefully he'll relay the sentiment.

"How can I help you, Detective Sergeant?"

"Please, call me Eric."

"Only if you call me Megan."

Eric pulls a small notebook and pen from his breast pocket, and I notice his nice hands. You know, if you're into large, powerful hands with clean, well-groomed nails.

Don't stare at his hands, Megan. Breathe. Act normal.

"Can you tell me about the yarn that Ms. Sinclair purchased yesterday?"

He finds a blank page in his notebook, and pen in hand, is poised to write.

"Sure."

I walk over to the shelf and pick up a skein of Breathless. I return to my seat and place the skein between us.

He asks me how many skeins she purchased, if they were the same, and if she purchased anything else. I print a copy of her receipt and give it to him so he can see the transaction details.

"Other than the yarn, did Ms. Sinclair leave anything else behind yesterday?"

"Nope," I reply, shaking my head. "Just the yarn I dropped off."

"Are you sure she left the store with everything else, including the knitting needles?"

"Yes. I put them in the bag myself. She definitely had the needles when she left."

"Did she have both needles? Could she have left one knitting needle behind?"

I retrieve a pair of needles identical to the ones Kelly

purchased, return to my seat, and place the needles on the table between us, beside the skein of yarn.

"They're packaged together," I explain. "To lose one, the packaging would have to rip or tear in two spots. Connie handed me the needles, I rang them up, and put them in the bag. One of us would have noticed if the packaging was torn to that extent. Connie wouldn't have them on the rack if they were torn, never mind sell them."

He nods and makes a note. I try to read it, but his penmanship is messy. It's also small, and from my vantage point, upside down. I can only decipher the date at the top of the page.

"Can you tell me about the altercation you and Ms. Shaw had with Paul Sinclair yesterday at the park?"

He stares at me, gauging my reaction.

"Hmmm... I wouldn't call it an altercation." I shake my head. "It was a typical interaction with Paul. If it was an altercation, every interaction Paul ever had was an altercation. I missed a committee meeting yesterday morning at the Animal Centre, and Paul chased me through the park to reprimand me. He wouldn't let it go, so April—er, Ms. Shaw —told him to back off." I shrug. "Then we left."

He scrawls another note, then looks at me again.

"Why did you miss the meeting at the Animal Centre?"

I take a deep breath and let it out.

"My husband's girlfriend's husband texted me and asked to meet." *Good luck connecting those dots, Eric!* "This is a new situation," I explain. "It distracted me, and derailed my morning," I explain.

He nods and writes in his book.

Harlow jumps onto the table, nudges Eric's pen, and steps onto the page Eric is writing on. Eric stops writing; Harlow doesn't give him much choice. He scratches Harlow between the ears, and Harlow flops onto the notebook, purring contentedly.

"I need to ask you some more questions, Megan. Can we meet again so I can take a full statement?"

My heart thumps double-time in my chest, and I swallow hard.

"Am I a suspect?"

CHAPTER 9

My heart and stomach switch places while I wait for Eric's response.

"Everyone is a suspect until they're eliminated, Megan, and your statement will help to eliminate you."

Again, he answers my question without actually answering my question. This must be a skill cops learn at the police academy.

"I didn't do it," I insist, panicking. "I'd never hurt anybody, never mind kill them. Besides, I don't think I'm strong enough to strangle someone, even with a skein of yarn."

"Hold on." Eric raises his right hand in a stop gesture. "Why did you say that, about the yarn? Why do you think that's how Mr. Sinclair died?"

"I found him, remember?" I remind him. "I saw the yarn around his neck. Also, if he died of natural causes, or an accident, I doubt you'd be here. Based on what I saw, he either drowned in a giant bowl of cereal or was strangled with a skein of yarn and fell forward into the cereal. It would be weird to eat cereal while wearing a yarn-necklace. And if he *was* wearing a yarn necklace, it wouldn't have been pulled tight against the front of his throat. Therefore, I assume the killer strangled Paul from behind, then left his face in the bowl."

I stop incriminating myself long enough to take a breath. To Eric, it must sound like I just confessed to killing Paul by strangling him with yarn and letting his face fall into a huge bowl of cereal.

Now I understand why Adam is so keen on people having a lawyer present when they talk to the police.

The bell above the door jingles. Harlow jumps down to greet the new arrival.

Eric closes his notebook, clicks his pen, and returns them to his breast pocket. He pushes the skein of yarn and needles aside and places his hands palms down on the table between us.

"Megan, can you do me a favour please? Don't tell anyone else what you just told me. Can you please keep it to yourself?"

Terrified, I nod. If I wasn't a suspect before, I am now. Why didn't I stop myself from talking myself all the way to the top of Eric's suspect list? What was I thinking?

"I think someone's here for Stitch-Fix." I stand up and push my chair in.

At the front of the store, a scowling knitter holds a partially completed blanket with a large hole in it. I greet her, smile knowingly at her blanket, and tell her I'll be right back to help her with her knitting problem.

I walk Eric to the door. We agree to meet tomorrow, so I can give him a statement and answer more questions. He says he'll be in touch in the morning to arrange a time.

After he leaves, I shudder. Paul was murdered. There's a murderer in our midst. If it were tourist season, we could blame an outsider for what happened, but the summer tourist season is over and the winter tourist season hasn't begun, which means a local murdered Paul. One of my neighbours is a killer.

I WISH the last Stitch-Fix knitter a good day after helping her close a hole in a sweater sleeve made when she accidentally created a stitch about sixty rows ago. My tummy rumbles and I head to the kitchenette for a snack. I'm opening the fridge when the door jingles. I poke my head into the store and see April carrying one of my favourite things, a white confectionery box with the Artsy Tartsy logo on the lid. I grab two glasses of water and join her on the sofa.

She opens the box and reveals still-warm pumpkin oatmeal cookies for her and I, and a small container of whipped cream for Harlow.

While we enjoy our treats, I tell April about Eric Sloane's visit and my theory about the killer being local, and possibly someone we know and see all the time.

"In books and on TV, the killer is almost always the spouse," April comments. "I mean, Kelly had access to him, and it was her yarn that killed him."

What did she just say? She knows about the yarn?

"You know how Paul died?"

"It was in the WSBA group chat." April shrugs and picks up another cookie. "Mort mentioned it to someone. He said the coroner had to be careful when he removed Paul to not disturb the yarn around his neck. Whoever he told mentioned it to someone in the group chat and now the entire WSBA knows."

Which means the entire town knows. The Water Street Business Association (WSBA) group chat is for members only. I'm not a member, but Connie and April are members because they own businesses on Water Street. They use the chat for things like announcing sales, reminders about meetings, and gossip.

Mort Ackerman is our local funeral director. He owns Mourning Glory Funeral Home in Harmony Hills.

I make a mental note to text Eric and tell him the thing he wants me to keep to myself is common knowledge, and make it clear I didn't let the yarn out of the bag, so to speak.

"Kelly had to leave Mrs. Pearson long enough to go upstairs, kill Paul, compose herself, and come back downstairs. When I got there, she was her usual, friendly, laid-back self. There was no hint she just killed her husband," I reason.

"She would be composed if she's a psychopath," April deduces. "Psychopaths don't lose their composure after they kill. And they can act normal, that's how they trick the rest of us into believing they aren't psychopaths."

The thought of a psychopathic killer roaming the streets of our community weirds us out.

I take the last cookie and offer it to April, but she waves it away. I break it in half, offer her half, but she waves it off, too, so it's all mine!

"I saw Paul and Fred in a car together when I left the bakery yesterday. They were arguing. I'm not sure if they already knew each other, or if Paul caught him breaking a bylaw and confronted him."

"That's interesting…" She nods, her gaze wandering to the left.

"Paul had an issue with Ryan too…" I say with my mouth full. These cookies are so good, I forget my manners. I raise my right index finger until I swallow the cookie. "Something must have happened between."

"Paul had issues with lots of people, and lots of people had issues with him. If having an issue with Paul gets your name added to the suspect list, almost everyone in town is on the list."

She makes a good point.

"Speaking of issues with Paul," I say, "I'm pretty sure Adam and I are at the top of the suspect list."

I take a deep breath and tell April about Paul having the photos and using them to try to blackmail Adam.

Before she can react, we're interrupted by the jingle of the front door, and Connie swoops in and joins us. We fill her in until it's time to lock the door and flip the sign to CLOSED.

CHAPTER 10

As soon as I walk in the house, I text Hannah and ask her to FaceTime.

Adam isn't home, and I know he'd want to be here when I tell her about Paul, but April and I agreed we need to tell our daughters tonight about Paul's murder. We agreed to Face-Time our respective daughters as soon as we get home. This way they'll hear it from us instead of from each other, a friend in Harmony Lake, or a social media post.

I hit Send on my text to Hannah, then pull out Eric's business card and fire off a text explaining the information he asked me to keep to myself is all over town because of someone else. I don't tell him it was Mort because, first; I don't know for sure it *was* Mort, I only know what April told me she read in the WSBA group chat, and second, Eric is a detective. He can use his detective skills to figure it out.

Hannah calls me on FaceTime, and I tell her about Paul. A few minutes into our conversation, the doorbell rings. I look through the living room window. Eric Sloane is standing on the porch. Two visits in one day. Lucky me. I open the door and gesture for him to come in as I say goodbye and I love you to Hannah and end our chat.

"I sent you a text," I say, leading Eric into the living room.

We sit, I offer him a beverage, and he declines.

"I was driving, but I read it when I pulled into your driveway. It's difficult to keep things under wraps in a town this small. The yarn was a hold-back, but it's all right."

"What's a hold-back?" I ask.

Eric explains that a hold-back is evidence or information from the crime scene that only the killer would know about. The hold-back is useful when interrogating a suspect. If they mention the hold-back, it's a good sign they were there. A hold-back can also eliminate someone who confesses to a crime they didn't commit, because according to Eric, people actually do that. If they don't mention the hold-back, it's less likely they were at the crime scene when the crime occurred.

"I'm hoping to see Mr. Martel," he says.

Relief washes over me, followed by guilt about feeling relieved because he wants to question Adam instead of me.

"He's not here," I tell Eric. "I can text him, let him know you're here and ask when he'll be back?"

Eric nods, "Thanks, that would be great."

I text Adam and wait for a reply.

"Do you have any idea where he might be?" Eric asks.

This is a loaded question. I'm pretty sure Eric figured out Adam and I aren't an example of matrimonial bliss. Telling him I met with my husband's girlfriend's husband was a big clue, and so are the photos and texts between Adam and Stephanie that Eric would have found on Paul's phone. I sense he's looking for me to clarify our marital status and give him some back story without coming out and asking me.

"We still live under the same roof, but Adam and I separated months ago. I don't know where he is, and we don't monitor each other's comings and goings." That's the short version.

"Was the separation triggered by the photos on Mr. Sinclair's phone?"

He asks carefully, trying to be sensitive to the situation which I appreciate.

"No." I shake my head. "As far as I know, Adam's affair with Stephanie is recent. I found out about it yesterday from Fred. He and Stephanie threatened to make the photos public if Adam didn't leave the firm. I found out Paul had the photos this morning when Adam told me. I swear I didn't know Paul was blackmailing Adam when I went to the salon yesterday." My phone dings. "It's Adam. He says he's only a few minutes away."

"That's great. Thank you," Eric responds. "Is it possible Mr. Martel's desire to keep the affair secret made him do something drastic?"

"No!" I answer quickly and emphatically, hoping to convince Eric that Adam didn't kill Paul. "Adam wouldn't hurt a soul. He takes spiders outside instead of killing them, and in the winter, he puts them in the garage instead of outside, so they won't freeze," I explain.

"But spiders weren't blackmailing him, Megan."

"Adam is a smart man and an excellent lawyer," I reason. "He knows eliminating Paul wouldn't eliminate the evidence that Paul blackmailed him. At the very least, he would have taken Paul's phone with him and disposed of it or deleted the evidence to slow down the investigation. But Paul's phone was on the table with the yarn, I saw it. I doubt the contents of his phone were the only motive for Paul's murder."

"You're very observant," Eric comments, looking impressed. "Have Mr. Martel and Ms. Sinclair ever had an intimate relationship?"

Excuse me? Did he just suggest Adam and Kelly are having an affair? Why would he ask me this? Adam and Kelly? Do they even know each other? Adam gets his hair cut by a barber in the city. He's always at work and hardly ever in town. How many women has Adam been seeing? Does he send these intimate photos to all of them?

Speechless, I hope the look on my face convinces Eric this is news to me.

"Are they?" I ask in a barely audible whisper. "Having an affair, I mean?"

"We found communication between them, and evidence they've met face-to-face. What do you know about that?"

Searching for words, I shake my head. Did Eric blindside me on purpose? It makes me feel like I can't trust him.

We both turn toward the door when it opens. Adam walks in with a laptop box under his arm. He slips his shoes off and walks past us and into the dining room where he places the box on the dining room table.

Adam greets us, then he and Eric introduce themselves and shake hands.

Would Adam like to go to the police station? Or would he like to talk here and I can go out? They look to me for an answer, but I'm still speechless and processing the bombshell about Adam and Kelly. All I can do is shake my head and shrug.

Adam opts for the police station and puts on his shoes. Eric joins Adam at the door with one hand on the doorknob.

"Thank you, Megan." Eric smiles.

I nod in response. His smile offends me; it's like he's pleased with himself for playing head games with me.

"Lock the door behind me and don't wait up," Adam says.

He smiles and closes the door behind him. I lock it, even though we never lock the door when one of us is home. Everything has changed so much in 24 hours.

Adam and Kelly having an affair? It doesn't feel right. Yesterday, my instincts told me Fred was telling the truth about our spouses. Today, my instincts tell me the opposite; if there is a relationship between Adam and Kelly, it's not an intimate one. Too bad instincts aren't evidence.

If Adam and Kelly were having an affair, it gives Kelly a motive to kill Paul. Maybe Paul found out and was planning to leave her. Or maybe she wanted to leave him for Adam, but Paul made it difficult. Maybe murder is less expensive and faster than divorce. Maybe Paul blackmailed her too.

Kelly is always so sweet and kind to me. Could she be sleeping with my husband and still act totally normal around me?

April would say, yes, she could, if she's a psychopath.

An affair with Kelly would give Adam another motive too. Maybe Paul threatened to tell Kelly about Stephanie, his other mistress. Or maybe Paul wouldn't go quietly and let Adam and Kelly to be together.

All this what-iffing makes my head hurt. In the kitchen, I pour myself a small glass of wine. My phone dings.

Connie: According to the WSBA group chat, Kelly left the police station. She's staying with her sister in the city. She can't go home because the apartment and salon are still crime scenes.

Why would she want to? Paul has been dead for twenty-four hours. If I were Kelly, the murder scene is the last place I'd want to go.

Ding! This time it's April. It's a group text to Connie and me.

April: Did you guys hear Kelly is staying with her sister?
Connie: Yes, that poor girl! At least she has her sister!
Me: Eric and Adam just went to the police station. Eric hinted that Adam and Kelly are having or have had an affair.
April: ?!?!?!
Connie: Oh my!
April: Maybe he's speculating?
Connie: I was about to say that!

Connie's exclamation points are the text-equivalent of speaking with her hands, and it makes me smile. We text for a while longer, until I decide to get ready for bed.

CHAPTER 11

THURSDAY, September 12th

On my walk to work through the drizzle and fog, I stop at Latte Da and pick up two café mochas with whipped cream.

At Knitorious, I stop to turn on the computer then hang up my jacket. I leave Connie's coffee on the counter in the kitchenette for her to find when she comes downstairs.

I only work a half-day today. I want to pack the online orders and drop them off at the post office when I leave at lunchtime.

Tending to the technology-related tasks at Knitorious is my job because Connie claims she doesn't like technology. Despite her insistence that she hates it, she's a proficient texter and user of social media. But given the choice, she'd prefer ledger books and checklists to keep track of the accounts and manage inventory. Administrative tasks are one of my happy places; I majored in economics and minored in accounting. I like being in charge of the behind-the-scenes organization.

I print the online orders and walk from shelf to shelf, collecting the yarn and notions to fill them. Then, I pull out tissue paper, envelopes, and bubble mailers from under the counter. The crinkling of the tissue paper lures Harlow like a beacon to the harvest table where I'm working. He loves tissue paper, so I ball-up a couple of sheets for him to play with, and toss them onto the floor, at the opposite end of the store. He chases and attacks them a safe distance from the sheets I'm using to pack the yarn; I'm sure customers would prefer their yarn to arrive free of cat fur.

While I wrap, pack, and label, my phone dings. Eric wants to know what time we can meet. I'll text him later; I want to finish up and put everything away before Harlow loses interest in his tissue paper balls and helps me.

Also, I'm not eager to talk to Eric. I'm still bitter about how he dropped the Adam-and-Kelly bombshell with no regard for my feelings and seemed to take pride in shocking me.

Connie is puttering around in the kitchenette. It's Thursday, so I assume she's cleaning out the fridge and checking our supplies of coffee, tea, snacks, cat food, and such.

"What the...? Oh, my."

"Is everything all right, Connie?" I shout without losing my rhythm, packing and addressing bubble mailers.

Connie comes into the store holding a thingamajig in her hand.

"I opened the dishwasher to empty it and this,"—she holds the offending thingamajig in front of her nose—"was sitting in the bottom and is probably the reason the dishes are still dirty."

"I'm sure The Wright Men can fix it. Ryan's van was on Water Street when I was walking to work. If he's still around, maybe he can fix it today, and maybe I can ask him some questions while he's here."

"Ask him a few questions about what, my dear?"

"About Paul not trusting Ryan and not wanting him in the salon or the store. Right now, Adam and I are pretty high on the suspect list, and if I can find the real killer, I can clear our names."

"Are you suggesting that Ryan Wright killed Paul?"

Connie sounds incredulous, and I get it. Ryan is one of the last people I'd ever suspect of murder. But on TV, the killer is always the last person everyone suspects.

"No," I reply, "but maybe whatever happened between them will shed some light on what happened to Paul."

Connie picks up the landline and calls Ryan. He's servicing the walk-in cooler next door at Wilde Flowers and says he can look at the dishwasher in about an hour. I finish packing orders while Connie returns to the kitchenette and hand-washes the dishes.

AN HOUR LATER, on the nose, Ryan knocks at the back door. I open the door and Ryan and his toolbox get straight to work assessing the dishwasher situation. I hand him the thinga-majig we think is causing the problem, and Harlow and I hover around him while Connie serves the handful of customers milling around the store.

Harlow rubs against Ryan's ankles while he and I talk about Paul's murder and how shocked we were. I ask him if he's heard any rumours. He visits so many homes and businesses each day, he must hear things.

He says he's heard nothing other than sympathy for Kelly. The consensus is that it was a targeted murder by someone Paul disagreed with, not a random attack or serial killer.

"Are you one of the people Paul disagreed with?" I ask, trying to be delicate.

He doesn't seem fazed by my question and continues tightening, or loosening, I can't tell the difference, the thing he's either tightening or loosening, without losing his rhythm.

"Now, why would you ask me that, Megan?"

"The day Paul died, Kelly mentioned Paul wouldn't let her hire The Wright Men For The Job anymore. He told her he didn't trust you."

Ryan stops working and pops his head out from inside the dishwasher.

"If anyone isn't trustworthy, it's Paul." He places the tool he was using back in the toolbox and pulls out a different tool. "Six weeks ago, Paul offered to pay me to burglarize Hairway To Heaven."

Ryan pauses while I take in what he said. I'm taken aback and need a few seconds to catch up.

"Why would he want to steal from his wife's business? What did he want you to steal? Shampoo and conditioner?" I ask, spinning my ring.

"Kelly's invested in new equipment this year. New computers, new styling tools, and other stuff that Paul said wasn't cheap. He said he'd keep Kelly away from the salon overnight and give me a list. I'd steal the items on the list and deliver them to a buyer he lined up. I'd collect the cash from the buyer, give half to Paul, and keep the other half for my trouble. He insisted it wasn't stealing because they insure everything, so Kelly could file an insurance claim and replace it."

Theft *and* insurance fraud. That's a big job to ask your local handyperson to do.

"What did you tell him?" I ask.

Ryan chuckles. "I told him no way. But Paul didn't like my answer. He said if I didn't do it, he'd tell everyone I'm a felon."

I close the door to the kitchenette. In Harmony Lake, all walls have ears.

"Are you a felon, Ryan?" I ask in a whisper.

"Technically, yes," he replies matter-of-factly. "Remember about five years ago when I moved to Ottawa to work for my Uncle's construction company?"

I nod.

"Well, I wasn't in a good place then. I made some poor decisions. I discovered some guys on the site were stealing copper wire, and other things, and reselling it. They offered to cut me in if I didn't rat them out. I accepted. For the next few months, they stole from worksites, and I pretended not to notice. Once a week a guy would bring me a coffee from the coffee truck, but it was an empty cup filled with cash. I didn't know one of them was an undercover cop who infiltrated the group to bring down the theft ring. When they busted us, they charged me along with everyone else. I copped a plea and spent three months in jail."

"Wow, Ryan. I had no idea. How did Paul know? Did you tell him?"

"After my release, I was on probation. For three years, I drove into the city to visit my probation officer. Paul saw me go into the probation office and snooped around." Ryan shakes his head. "He was probably in the city visiting the casino," he mumbles.

Ryan ducks his head into the dishwasher and continues working.

It seems Paul had a habit of blackmailing people. First Adam, and now Ryan. Maybe that's why he and Fred argued in the car. Maybe Paul blackmailed the Murphys too. But how did he know Adam was seeing Stephanie Murphy? Did he see them together, like he saw Ryan in the city?

"How did you avoid being blackmailed? I mean, Paul didn't tell anyone, right?"

Ryan's head pops out of the dishwasher again.

"Paul likes to gamble. It used to be a big problem for him, but he learned to control it after Kelly threatened to leave him if he didn't. Lately, his gambling problem hasn't been under control. He borrowed money to hide his gambling debt from Kelly. I told Paul I know about his gambling habit and debt and threatened to tell Kelly about it, tell her about his plan to rob the salon." Ryan shrugs. "He stopped talking to me. It sounds like he lied to Kelly to make sure she wouldn't talk to me either."

"How do you know about Paul's gambling debt?"

"I do a lot of work for Jay Singh. He's a money lender who lives in Harmony Hills. We're friends. He's super smart, so when Paul tried to blackmail me, I asked Jay for advice. Jay told me he loaned Paul money to pay off his gambling debt, and Paul was behind making the repayments. He told me to use the information to get away from Paul. He said he also hoped it would pressure Paul into getting his payments up to date. And before you ask, I was with Jay when Paul died. He hired me to assemble a backyard play set for his twins."

Ryan's head and shoulders disappear into the dishwasher. I open the door and return to the store.

Ryan replaces the thingamajig and puts the dishwasher back together. Then he gives Connie an invoice, which she pays out of the till, and leaves.

When Connie and I are alone, I disclose to her what Ryan told me. I know she'll keep Ryan's past to herself. She isn't as shocked as I expected about Ryan's criminal past, but she shares my shock about Paul's scheme to burgle the salon.

This means people without the last name Martel had a motive to kill Paul.

If Hairway To Heaven was robbed, the entire town would've heard about it, so I assume Paul didn't pull it off. Maybe he tried to hire someone else to rob the salon, it didn't work out, and they killed him. Or maybe the buyer he lined up for the equipment killed him when Paul failed to deliver.

If Paul owes money to Jay Singh, maybe Jay killed him. That would be bad for Jay's business though, since dead people don't make debt repayments. But sometimes on TV, the loan shark kills the debtor as a warning to other debtors.

Maybe Kelly found out about the burglary plot, her husband's gambling habit, secret debt, or all of the above, and it pushed her over the edge, and she killed him.

Maybe Paul used the photos of Adam and Stephanie to blackmail the Murphys, and they killed him.

Or maybe Ryan is lying. If he is, it's an elaborate lie. There's one way to find out.

"Since I'm not scheduled to work this afternoon, I'm going to visit Jay Singh."

"That doesn't sound very safe, my dear. What if he is the killer?"

"I promise I'll only go if April comes with me." I make an X over my heart to assure Connie I mean it. "We won't go anywhere alone with him. At the very least, he might verify Ryan's alibi and eliminate him as a suspect."

Connie says nothing. She purses her lips and squints. The look on her face makes it clear that while she doesn't like my plan, she won't try to stop me.

"I have a book club meeting tonight, and Archie is a member, so I'll ask him if he remembers where Ryan was when Paul was murdered."

"Thank you," I say, smiling.

I pull out my phone and text April, asking if she's up for a road trip this afternoon. She is! We agree to meet after lunch and drive to Harmony Hills.

Eric texts me again, asking when we can meet. I holdback my reply until after April and I visit Jay. With any luck, I'll be able to give Eric a lead on a suspect that isn't Adam or me.

CHAPTER 12

I DROP off the online orders at the post office on my way home for a quick lunch before April and I visit Jay Singh. It's still cloudy and humid, but the drizzle has stopped for now. My curly hair expands in the damp air and, while I walk, I use the hair elastic on my wrist to secure it in a high ponytail.

Walking up to the house, it's weird to see Adam's car in the driveway on a weekday. Walking into the house, it's even weirder to see him sitting at the kitchen table on a weekday. He's focused on his new laptop, and I don't want to disturb him, so I walk into the kitchen unannounced.

"Hey!" He says without looking up.

"Hey. How's the new laptop?"

"I like it. I had to leave my old laptop with the firm when I resigned. It was company property. Anyway, I'll need a laptop to start a law practice in Harmony Lake."

He looks at me and smiles.

"Oh, you aren't joining another firm?"

I assumed he would pursue a partnership elsewhere.

"No, it's time for a change," he replies. "I can't work anywhere for thirty days because of the thirty day non-compete clause I have with the firm, but on the thirty-first day, I intend to hang out my shingle and open for business. There aren't any lawyers in Harmony Lake, it's an underserved market. The closest lawyer is at least half an hour away in Harmony Hills, and I think he limits his practice to real estate law, if he's still there. He might've retired. I should look into that."

He picks up a pen and makes a note in the planner beside his laptop.

"How was your visit to the police station last night?" I ask. "I didn't hear you come in. Eric must've kept you pretty late."

He makes a sweeping gesture with his hand, "It was fine. I answered Eric's questions honestly and thoroughly. He kept my cell phone, so I went out this morning and bought this."

Adam holds up a shiny new cell phone and waves his empty hand with a flourish that would make Vanna White proud.

"It's two models newer than the old one. It's really advanced, and it can interact with Oscar!"

New technology is Adam's happy place.

"I already texted Hannah and gave her my new number."

"How did you explain it to her?" I ask, trying to mask my panic.

She knows Paul's death was murder, but I'm trying to avoid her finding out her parents are suspects.

"Relax," Adam says, "I told her I left the firm to open a practice in Harmony Lake. I explained that the laptop and phone belonged to the firm, and I had to leave them. She's fine with it."

He taps the screen of his new phone, then puts it down on the table. My phone dings; a text from a number I don't recognize.

"I assume this is you?" I ask.

"Yup." He nods. "Now you have my new number too."

I save his number to my phone and delete his old office and cell phone numbers.

"Adam."

"Mm hmm." He's staring at his laptop screen again.

"Adam. Look at me." I need to look in his eyes when I ask him what I'm about to ask him. We make eye contact. "Are you having an affair with Kelly Sinclair?"

His eyes open as wide as they can, and he raises his eyebrows so high, they almost disappear into his hairline.

"Of course not!" He insists. "Meg, why would you ask me that?"

"Then why are you communicating with her and meeting her?"

"Did Kelly mention this to you?" The shocked expression morphs into one of confusion.

"No," I reply. "Eric did. He asked me if I knew you and Kelly were communicating and if I knew about any meetings between you. I told him I know nothing, because I don't."

Adam hesitates. He's choosing his words carefully.

"It would be inappropriate for me to comment on any communication between myself and Kelly Sinclair."

His lawyer voice. This isn't Adam, my soon-to-be-ex-husband speaking, it's Adam the lawyer. I know this routine well.

"Is your relationship with Kelly protected by attorney-client privilege?" I ask.

He puts his right hand in front of him, palm toward the floor, and rotates his wrist. "It's complicated."

"Complicated because you have a personal relationship with her?" *C'mon, Adam, give me a clue.*

"No! Absolutely not!" he laments. "Stephanie is the only personal relationship I've had, and it was a huge mistake, Meg. I've regretted it every day since it started–this summer, by the way. Long after you and I called it quits."

Not that long, but whatever.

"So Kelly isn't a client, and you don't have a personal relationship, but you can't give me a straight answer?" I clarify. "Is that what you're saying?"

"Kelly's not a client. She hasn't paid me for legal services, and I haven't represented her. Technically, we spoke as friends. I didn't even let her pay for my coffee, so I'm not violating attorney-client privilege if I tell you."

I sit across from him at the kitchen table, and he closes his laptop.

"Kelly texted me a couple of months ago and asked me to meet her for coffee. She asked me not to tell anyone, not even you. She insisted we meet away from Harmony Lake, and away from my office. We met at a coffee shop in the city. She told me Paul used to have a gambling problem and racked up significant debt. She said the gambling and the financial strain almost ended their marriage, but he got help for his addiction. They stayed together, and over time they paid off the debt. Now that they're back on their financial feet and the salon is doing well, Kelly worried what could happen if Paul gambled again. About her potential liability for gambling debts he might incur. She wanted advice on Paul-proofing her business and the building. We discussed various hypothetical options and scenarios for about an hour. After that, Kelly never contacted me again, but Paul did. A few days after Kelly and I met, Paul began texting me, demanding to know why I met with Kelly. He accused me of having an affair with her or trying to."

"What did you tell him? And did you tell Kelly that Paul contacted you?"

"I responded to one of Paul's texts and denied his accusation." Adam shrugs. "I told him I had no idea what he was talking about. He continued sending texts, and I ignored them. He left a couple of voicemail messages, and I ignored those too. I saved the messages, though, they're on the phone Eric kept. In one message, he said he knew Kelly and I were talking because he saw the text messages when he went through her phone, and he knew we met because he saw the entry in the calendar on her phone. I never told Kelly about it. She wasn't my client, and I didn't want to deal with Paul."

"Wow. Paul's control issues went beyond his role as town councilor to his role as husband." I get a glass of water and process what Adam just told me.

"Meg, I didn't kill Paul."

"I know."

"Have you given the police a statement yet?"

I'm not sure if Adam the lawyer is asking or Adam the soon-to-be-ex-husband.

"Kind of, I guess," I reply. "I answered questions that night, again yesterday morning at the store, and yesterday evening when Eric came to see you. And, he's been texting me today to meet again. He must be running out of things to ask me."

"You should have a lawyer present when he questions you. Let me give you a number…" He opens his laptop and starts tapping on the keyboard.

"I don't need a lawyer, Adam, it's fine. I haven't done anything wrong, and I have nothing to hide. I'd rather tell him everything I know and do whatever I can to help find the killer. I don't want to suspect everyone I know of murder. I want to eliminate us as suspects and get on with my life."

Did Paul make a habit of spying on Kelly? Why didn't he trust her? If she knew he was violating her privacy and checking up on her, would that make her angry enough to kill him?

Based on the conversation she had with Adam, it sounds like she knew, or at least suspected, Paul was gambling again.

CHAPTER 13

THANKS TO LIVING in the age of technology, a quick web search helped me find Jay Singh's address in Harmony Hills, and the GPS in April's car is helping us get there. It's raining, and we're on the highway almost halfway between Harmony Lake and Harmony Hills. Harmony Lake is on the south side of the Harmony Hills Mountains, nestled snugly between the mountains and the lake. Harmony Hills is on the north side of the Harmony Hills Mountains and is a suburb of the city located farther north. Harmony Hills is larger than Harmony Lake and doesn't have the same geographic restrictions, so it has a larger population and more amenities. Most residents of Harmony Lake make regular trips to Harmony Hills to visit the hospital, big box stores, various professionals, movie theatres, and everything else Harmony Hills has that our tiny town doesn't. The quickest route to get from Harmony Lake to Harmony Hills is a twenty to thirty-minute drive along the highway that runs through the mountains.

April and I agree it feels pushy showing up at a stranger's home unannounced, but I'm hoping the element of surprise will work to our advantage; Jay might not speak to us if he has time to think about it. And his reactions will be more candid than if he had time to prepare for our visit.

THE SINGH HOME IS A TWO-STOREY, two-car garage, red-brick house. It's in a newer subdivision with several speed bumps and no shortage of DRIVE SLOWLY: CHILDREN AT PLAY signs posted above the many NEIGHBOURHOOD WATCH signs. The front lawn and garden are meticulous, and the top of the driveway is littered with two tiny, training-wheeled bikes, hula hoops, a small basketball net, and remnants of chalk drawings washed away by the rain.

We pull up outside the house. It's not raining right now, but everything is wet. A thirty-ish year-old man wearing cargo shorts, a t-shirt and rain boots is jumping in puddles on the sidewalk with two small children. The kids wear identical bright green raincoats with frog eyes on the hoods and yellow rubber boots with toes painted like duck bills and eyes on the tops of the feet. They're freaking adorable!

"Ryan said Jay has twins. That's probably him," I say to April, whose eyes are also fixed on the two identical, adorable puddle jumpers.

"Awww, look at them!" she says. "Let's talk to him before our ovaries explode from the cuteness, or the neighbourhood watch wonders why we're sitting here."

We unbuckle our seat belts and April unplugs her phone from the car's console. We get out of the car and April locks it. The *beep* of the horn confirming it's locked gets the boys' attention. I smile and wave at them; they ignore me and jump in a puddle.

I introduce myself to Jay as a friend of Ryan's, and April introduces herself as a friend of mine. We shake hands and April and I gush over the cuteness of his sons. I tell Jay he has two of the cutest frog-duck puddle jumpers I've ever seen. He smiles at them with pride.

"If you're looking for a loan, there are online forms to fill out on the website, and I'll get back to you within twenty-four hours."

Jay Singh must be a modern, twenty-first century money lender.

"No. I'm not here for a loan, but since you brought it up, I am super curious about your business. Is it a legitimate business? You have a website and everything?"

"Of course. Everything is above board. The service I provide is more common than you think."

He tells us he's a stay-at-home dad, and his sons just turned four. He and his wife, Jenna, were both nurses at Harmony Hills hospital, but after the twins arrived, finding an affordable daycare situation to accommodate their erratic shift schedules was impossible, so they decided Jay would stay home.

They had some money from an inheritance, and to replace Jay's income they were going to purchase one of the luxury condos in the new Harbourview Condominium development at the end of Water Street and rent it to tourists. But the development was a year from construction, and they couldn't wait. Jay did some research and realized that the return on investment would be higher and the risk more diversified if they made several high-interest, short-term loans.

I relate to their daycare struggle. I found out I was expecting Hannah within a few months of getting married, and about five years sooner than we'd planned. I had to leave school three semesters short of my degree when she was born. When Hannah started school full time, I was eager to finish my last three semesters and graduate, but I couldn't find a daycare solution that worked for all three of us. I was about to give up and accept that I'd have to wait to finish school, when

Connie insisted that she and Colin, her husband, would love to help look after Hannah. They were like grandparents to her and spoiled her rotten. Colin passed away about five years ago, but Connie and Hannah still have a special bond.

"What I do is legal, though some people think it's unethical. Most of my clients are in Harmony Hills and Harmony Lake, and my job makes me privy to many secrets about many people."

Jay winks after that last sentence, and I get the sense he'd love to tell some of those secrets, but I already feel like, since Paul's death, I'm learning more about some of my neighbours than I care to know, so I interrupt him.

"That's why I'm here. I'd like to ask you some questions about a mutual acquaintance. Ryan tells me you know Paul Sinclair?"

"What about him? Does he owe you money?" Jay smirks.

Hearing him talk about Paul in the present tense makes me think he doesn't know about Paul's death, so I tell him someone murdered Paul on Tuesday.

"That's unfortunate. I guess I should expect a visit from the police soon," He says bluntly, sounding neither surprised by Paul's death, nor worried about a visit from the police.

"Ryan said when Paul tried to blackmail him, you helped him by giving him information to use against Paul. When Paul died, he was blackmailing my family, and I'm looking for information that might point the finger of suspicion away from us."

"He borrowed money from me," Jay offers. "I think he said it was to pay off some bad bets. He had trouble paying me back and fell behind with his scheduled repayments. He stopped returning my calls and emails, so my lawyer wrote a letter to Mr. and Mrs. Sinclair advising them I started the process of executing a writ of seizure on the building on Water Street."

I know about writs of seizure from Adam mentioning

them. A writ of seizure gives Jay the right to force the Sinclairs to sell the building to repay the debt.

"But the business belongs to Kelly, not Paul," April interrupts. "Did they borrow the money together?"

"No, Paul borrowed the money alone. One reason people borrow from me, instead of a bank, and pay higher interest costs, is because they don't want their partner to know about the loan. His wife might own the business in her name alone, but they both own the building, so they're both notified. The letter and the threat are often enough to scare the debtor into finding my money."

"Was it enough to scare Paul?" I ask.

"Sure was. I heard from him the day he got the letter. It was sent by registered mail, and he's the one who signed for it, so I doubt his wife ever saw it. A few days later he asked to meet and paid the loan in full. With cash."

"Where did he get the cash so fast?" I think out loud, looking at April, not expecting a response.

"He said his brother-in-law lent it to him," Jay responds. "I don't know if it's true, and I don't care. People who need my services often have secrets they lie to protect. I take what they say with a grain of salt."

One twin asks if they can go in the backyard to dig for worms. Both boys are carrying a small bucket and shovel. So cute!

We follow the boys to the side of the house. April hangs back close to the sidewalk. She's being safe, so if something happens, she can get help. Jay opens the gate, and the boys run into the backyard. There's a large wooden play set with a slide, two swings, and a playhouse with a rock-climbing wall.

"That must be the play set Ryan assembled on Tuesday?" I ask, pointing to the large wooden structure.

"He assembled it, but, like, two weeks ago, not on Tuesday," Jay replies.

As soon as the words finish coming out of his mouth, his

expression changes, and it's obvious Jay realizes that he just contradicted Ryan's alibi. "Actually, I can't remember for sure. Maybe Ryan was here on Tuesday night?" He furrows his brow, purses his lips, and directs his gaze down and to the right, trying hard to look like he's working out the correct date. Nice try, Jay. "Look, Ryan's a good guy," he asserts. "He's made a few mistakes and bad choices, but I consider him a friend. He must consider you a friend, too, if he told you about me and sent you here. There's no way Ryan killed Paul."

One twin offers his share of tonight's dessert if the other twin eats a worm. But only if he eats the whole worm.

Jay runs over to stop anyone from eating any portion of any worm. I yell after him, thanking him for his time, wishing him good luck with the worms, and telling him April and I will see ourselves out.

He waves to me in acknowledgement.

CHAPTER 14

"That was worth the drive!" I say as April navigates out of Jay's subdivision.

"I know, right! He said he has clients in Harmony Lake and is *privy to lots of secrets.* I wonder who else in Harmony Lake borrows money from him?"

"I'm not sure I want to know," I answer. "Life was easier forty-eight hours ago when the only secrets I knew were my own."

"And mine," April adds. "You know all my secrets."

"How can we find Paul's brother-in-law to ask him if he loaned Paul the money? If Ryan wasn't at Jay's house on Tuesday evening, where was he, and why would he lie?"

"I don't know the answers to those questions," April responds as she turns onto the main road that leads to the highway, "but I know that solving a murder in real life is harder than it looks on TV."

She's not wrong.

My phone dings: another attempt by Eric to arrange a meeting. I don't fancy being questioned at the police station, and I assume Adam will be home tonight. As luck would have it, Connie has a book club meeting this evening and Knitorious will be empty.

I reply to his text suggesting we meet at Knitorious after it closes. He confirms.

April puts on "No Scrubs" by TLC and turns it up loud. We sing at the top of our lungs as we merge onto the highway.

I GET to Knitorious twenty minutes before closing time and park behind the store.

Harlow is happy because my arrival coincides with his dinnertime. He corners me in the kitchenette and charms me until I feed him.

Connie is relieved I'm still alive, and the moneylender didn't kill April and me.

I fill her in about our visit with Jay Singh and remind her to please ask Archie about Ryan's whereabouts on Tuesday evening since Jay didn't confirm his alibi.

"He told you himself that he's not ethical, my dear. Maybe Ryan *was* there, and the money lender is mistaken or lying. But, of course, I'll ask. If the opportunity presents itself."

"He told me that some people believe his business is unethical, not that *he's* unethical," I correct her. "Also, you didn't see his reaction when he realized what he'd said."

I offer to close up so she can leave early, and tell her Eric is coming to the store to question me, but we'll leave before she gets home.

I haven't had dinner, and by the time Eric is due to arrive, I'm starving. Scrolling through the menu on the Ho Lee Chow website, I add items to the online cart until Eric knocks on the door.

I don't recognize him at first; he's not wearing a suit. He's wearing khaki, slim-fit trousers, a dark green, collared golf shirt, and brown leather slip-on shoes. The dark green shirt brings out the honey-coloured flecks in his eyes, and the short sleeves show off a pair of well-defined, muscular biceps and forearms. He's hot. I remind myself not to stare.

"Hi! Thanks for meeting me again," he says, standing aside, so I can lock the door after him.

He smells good, like a forest after it rains, and the sun comes out.

"No problem. You must be out of questions by now. Or will I be answering the same questions I've already answered?"

I wonder if he's met with everyone else three times in two days, or just the top contenders on his suspect list.

"A bit of both." He smiles and puts a hand on his flat, probably-has-a-six-pack stomach.

Don't stare, Megan.

"Have you eaten? I'm starving and I thought I might order something to be delivered if that's OK."

"Great minds think alike, Eric."

I spin the laptop to show him the Ho Lee Chow menu I've been picking items from.

He adds a few items to the cart, and I submit our order. While we wait for dinner to arrive, I get dishes from the kitchenette. Harlow forces Eric to notice him by jumping onto the harvest table and pacing back and forth in front of him with his tail in the air while Eric strokes him and asks me about yarn.

What's the difference between a hank, a skein, a ball, and a cake? I explain that a hank is a loop of yarn that's loosely twisted, similar to the yarn that Kelly bought. A skein is yarn that's wound into an oblong ball. A ball is yarn that's wound into a round ball, and a cake is yarn that's wound into a cylindrical shape. To confuse him further, I explain that most people use *hank* and *skein* interchangeably. I gather yarn from the shelves as I explain to show him examples of each.

What does *ply* mean? Yarn consists of multiple strands twisted together: single ply is one strand of yarn, two-ply is two strands twisted together, three-ply is three strands twisted together, and so on. The yarn Kelly purchased was twelve-ply.

He also has questions about knitting needles: straight vs. circular, metal vs. wood, how to decide which size needle to use with which size yarn. At first, I assume his curiosity is because of Paul's murder, then I wonder if his interest is genuine. I'm sure it's related to the case, but I offer to teach him to knit, anyway. He declines, saying his job keeps him too busy for hobbies like knitting.

When he finishes testing my yarn and needle knowledge, we sit in the cozy sitting area and I pick up the hat I'm working on. I start the crown decreases while he asks me questions about my routine on Tuesday, and pets Harlow, who is curled up contentedly on his lap.

Our food arrives, and while we eat, he asks me about yesterday. I tell him, again, about Adam's visit to Knitorious to tell me Paul had copies of the photos and used them to blackmail us. Then I tell Eric he caught me off guard last night when he suggested Adam and Kelly were having an affair.

"I'm sorry how that played out, and I'm sorry I upset you," he says. "I didn't think there was anything between them, but I needed to be sure, and your reaction helped confirm my hunch."

I appreciate his apology, but don't respond because I still think it was a cruel way to confirm his hunch.

"Adam's affair with Mrs. Murphy must have upset you though..."

Eric likes to use unfinished sentences to ask questions. He starts a statement and lets his voice trail off at the end while he looks at you to finish the thought for him.

"Adam and I were married for almost 20 years. We met in university when I was 18, and by the time I was 20, we were married. I became pregnant soon after. We had a great marriage for a long time, but somewhere along the way, we grew apart. Our lives stopped revolving around each other and neither of us noticed. He focused on his career, I focused on being a Mum and being involved in the community. Next thing we knew, Hannah was the only thing we had in common."

I stop to drink some water.

"If you both decided it was over months ago, why are you still living under the same roof and keeping your separation a secret? Most divorced couples can't wait to get away from each other."

I want to ask him if he's speaking from experience, but I don't.

"This year was a big one for Hannah. She finished high school and went away to university. We were determined that our separation wouldn't overshadow her last year of high school, so we decided Adam wouldn't move out until she left for university. The last thing she needed was everyone in town talking about our failed marriage and her broken home. Reputation is everything in a small town—especially in Harmony Lake. We're handling this transition like civilized, reasonable people. I've always put Hannah's interests above all else, and this divorce is no exception. We may not be a couple anymore, but we're Hannah's parents and we'll always be family. We're intent on coming out of this divorce as friends. Or at least friendly to each other. We'll see."

"No one in Harmony Lake knows you're separated?" Eric asks.

"The only people who know, other than Hannah, are April and Connie. Unless Adam confided in someone. I'm not angry or betrayed by his relationship with Stephanie Murphy. I haven't been in love with Adam for a long time. I want him to be happy and live a good life, I just wish he'd waited until he moved out, didn't send his girlfriend compromising photos, and maybe picked someone who wasn't already in a relationship."

Saying this out loud, to someone other than Connie or April, is cathartic. It's not easy pretending your marriage isn't broken. Living a lie is exhausting.

I wonder if Eric is married and is a dad. Has he ever disentangled his life from someone else's while causing as little damage as possible to his kids?

It's like playing catch with a hand grenade, except every time you throw it, you take one step backwards until you and the person you're playing catch with can't communicate anymore. So, you both just try to be slow, gentle, and intentional with each toss, grateful when the other person catches it, and it doesn't hit the ground, destroying your home, your lives, and your child.

We each choose a fortune cookie. Eric's says, "You are cleverly disguised as a responsible adult," and mine says, "Three people can keep a secret only if you get rid of two," which sounds ominous and creeps me out. I jokingly offer to trade fortunes with him, but he declines, saying he likes his non-creepy fortune better.

While clearing the dishes and throwing away the food packaging, I contemplate whether to tell Eric about my conversation with Ryan and the road trip April and I took to visit Jay. I want this case solved as fast as possible. The more information he has, the faster Eric can find the killer and clear the Martel name. I decide it's best to tell him.

If I'm lucky, maybe he'll tell me something in return that I don't already know about the case.

"I had an interesting conversation with Ryan Wright this morning."

I tell Eric about my conversation with Ryan, while watching him intently for a hint of a reaction. Nothing. Either this isn't new information, or Eric has an impressive poker face.

I double down and tell him about my conversation with Jay. Still no reaction.

When I finish talking, Eric gazes into the distance like he's thinking about something. Then he looks at me.

"I'm not from Harmony Lake," he states. "This is a small community, and the residents are... protective... of each other and information. They don't trust outsiders, and I'm an outsider. They're hesitant to open up to me."

He's choosing his words with intention. I live in this small, protective community, and he doesn't want to offend me. This is a pleasant change from last night. He's right, though. It takes a while for us to warm up to new people. We cater to tourists who visit Harmony Lake for a few days or weeks of the year. Some of them want the local experience, and we've learned to make them feel welcome and included while still protecting the heart of our community and keeping it just for us.

"I appreciate you sharing what you've found out with me," Eric continues, "but it's not a good idea for you to investigate and question witnesses. Asking the wrong questions to the wrong people puts your safety at risk. But if people seek you out and share information with you, I'd appreciate you passing that information along to me."

I'm choosing to interpret this as a verbal disclaimer, like an ENTER AT YOUR OWN RISK sign at a construction site. It doesn't mean you *can't* enter the site; it just means if you do, you might get hurt, and it'll be your own fault because you ignored the sign. He didn't say no, he said it's not a good idea, and that isn't the same as no.

It would be easier for both of us, and less work for me, if he would say what he means, but I'm learning that Eric speaks in subtext. He answers questions without actually answering them, and now, it seems, he gives permission without actually giving permission. It must be a cop thing.

It's getting late, and I'm tired. I try to fight it, but a yawn escapes me, and I ask Eric if we're done with questions for the night. I turn off the lights and we say goodnight to Harlow. The cat follows us to the back door, then slinks upstairs to Connie's apartment. When we leave through the back door, Eric and I wish each other a good weekend, which makes me hopeful he won't question me again until at least Monday.

CHAPTER 15

Friday, September 13th

Connie has yet another mystery appointment this morning. She doesn't tell me where she's going, which is unusual for her. I hope everything is OK and have to trust that she'll tell me if it isn't.

Friday and Saturday are our busiest days, so business is steady today. Harlow, planting his cuteness in a warm ray of sun in the front window for his morning nap, attracts a few passersby who come in to see him, making us appear busier.

Paul's murder is still the number one conversation topic around town. People want to know when the police will remove the crime scene tape. And when Kelly will come home.

I take advantage of the brief intervals between serving customers to update the inventory on the website and finish Hannah's hat; I bind it off just before noon.

When Connie returns from her appointment, she brings me a sandwich from Deliclassy. It must be tuna because Harlow appears on the counter like a flash, showing serious interest in the bag.

"How was book club? It was pretty late when I left, but you still weren't back."

"It was fun! There was some confusion about what our September book is, so half of us showed up having read one book and half of us read another book. We solved it by breaking into two smaller groups, one for each book, and next month we'll switch!"

"I'm glad it worked out. Did you ask Archie about Ryan's alibi?"

"Yes, I did. Archie insists Ryan was with him. They watched the baseball game on TV and barbecued steaks. He says Ryan was with him from late afternoon until the next morning."

"I guess Ryan mixed up his Tuesdays, then. He must have been in Harmony Hills the previous Tuesday," I shrug.

"I've known Archie a long time, my dear. He wouldn't lie. I believe him."

"So do I," I say.

At least I think I do. I want to. Would Archie lie to give his son an alibi? I think a lot of parents might tell a fib to protect their children.

Harlow and I eat our sandwich in the kitchenette, and the rest of the afternoon passes quickly.

We close the store and tidy up to prepare for tomorrow. Then I go home to have an awkward dinner with Adam. I can't remember the last time we had a meal alone. We struggle to find something to talk about aside from Paul's murder or Hannah.

As much as I enjoy a good small town murder mystery or true crime documentary, both feel a bit too close to home right now, so after dinner, I watch a stand-up comedy special, cast on the matching cowl for Hannah's hat, and knit until my eyelids feel heavy and I'm ready for bed.

SATURDAY, September 14th

Saturday is our busiest day. Today is no exception. We're getting into the busy season. Knitters are embracing fall and planning their holiday knitting. As soon as the snow falls, we'll also be busy with tourists staying at the ski resorts. Saturdays will only get busier until after ski season.

After lunch, Connie's phone chimes. She reads the message, then hands me her phone. Customers are milling around the store, and she doesn't want to read it out loud.

It's a message in the WSBA group chat:

Libby: Paul's body was released to his family. His funeral is on Wednesday. A private service for family followed by a public celebration of life at the Irish Embassy. Details soon.

Libby is the owner of Latte Da, and the Irish Embassy is our local pub. The Embassy, as it's called by the locals, is owned by the O'Brien family. Sheamus manages the pub, and his parents, who are mostly retired, divide their time between Harmony Lake and Dublin, Ireland.

I hand Connie's phone back to her, and literally seconds later, a symphony of cell phone notifications chime throughout the store. Customers talk amongst themselves about Paul's arrangements. The speed at which news travels through Harmony Lake is astounding.

Tonight is trivia night at The Embassy. The knitting group that meets at the store each week has a team called Knitty By Nature. The winning team gets a free meal (lunch only) at the pub. Tamara meets us after the store closes, and we head over to The Embassy to win the free lunch! Tamara is a trivia buff and an occasional knitter, so we recruited her for our team. She's alone tonight because April took their fifteen-year-old son, Zach, to hockey practice. We don't win the free lunch, but thanks to Tamara, we're a close second.

Everyone in the pub speculates about Paul's murder, and harasses Sheamus for details about Paul's celebration of life, but Sheamus doesn't confirm or deny anything, and says he'll tell us more when he can.

SUNDAY, September 15th

This is the third Sunday since Hannah's left home, and so far, Sundays are when I miss her the most. It's the day we would do something fun together. On Sunday evenings we would have dinner as a family when Adam came home.

Since we can't be together as a family in person, we do the next best thing. Adam and I FaceTime Hannah together and have a virtual visit with her. She tells us about her classes, her new friends, and the fun, touristy things she's doing in Toronto.

We're careful not to mention Paul's murder, blackmail schemes, or police interrogations. When Hannah asks how Kelly is doing, I tell her that Kelly is staying with her sister. Adam quickly changes the subject.

Several times each day, I get the urge to text Kelly, ask how she's doing, and let her know everyone is thinking about her. But I don't want to impose. She has so much to deal with. As far as I know, she hasn't been back to Harmony Lake since Paul died. If she's not ready to deal with us, I won't force us on her.

I spend the rest of Sunday missing Hannah, cleaning the house around Adam while he works on his laptop, and giving the lawn and garden some much-needed attention.

CHAPTER 16

MONDAY, September 16th

Knitorious is closed on Mondays, so it's my day to drive to Harmony Hills to grocery shop and run errands I can't do in Harmony Lake.

I pull into the Shop'n'Save parking lot, turn the car off, and text April.

Me: I'm in HH today, do you need anything?

Whenever one of us comes to Harmony Hills, we text the other to see if they need anything. It's become a habit.

I push the button that opens the trunk and get out of the car to retrieve my reusable shopping bags. As I close the trunk, my phone vibrates in my pocket.

April: So am I! I was about to text you. Just about to go into Shop'n'Save.

Me: I'm in the parking lot, where are you?

April: Meet me at the door by the pharmacy.

I shove my phone in my pocket and head toward the pharmacy entrance where I find my friend.

"Why are you here on a Monday?" I ask mid hug. "You know I shop on Mondays. I would've picked up whatever you need."

"I know, but we have this... situation... called Zach. He's fifteen and eats *constantly*. We shop three times a week just to keep him fed. Also, they're having a ridiculous sale on butter this week, and T wants me to buy as many as I can carry. She's afraid they'll run out before the sale ends."

"If there's a limit on how many you can buy, I'll buy up to the limit, too, so T won't have butter anxiety," I offer.

We each get a cart and decide to start in the dairy section.

April puts the maximum amount of butter they allow each shopper to purchase at the sale price into her cart, and I do the same.

With our carts stacked with literally enough butter to supply a bakery, we meander up and down the aisles, picking up items and checking them off our lists as we go. We talk about our weekends, update each other on Hannah and Rachel, and strategize to get Tamara on Jeopardy, so she can win all the money, and she and April can retire.

We turn into the freezer aisle, and as April says she doubts Tamara would retire if she won on Jeopardy because she loves working at the bakery so much, Kelly Sinclair walks past the end of the aisle. She's with a woman I don't recognize. She's pushing a cart.

I tighten my grip on the handle of my butter-heavy cart and speed walk to the end of the aisle, trying to catch up to her. April speed walks after me.

"Where are we going? I need to get frozen pizza in this aisle."

"Kelly just walked by," I say.

I make a sharp left, speed walk past a display of peanut butter, then toilet paper, and look up the next aisle. No Kelly. I continue toward the next aisle, past a display of tomato sauce, then baby food. April breaks into a jog, and in a few strides, she and her butter-filled cart are beside me.

"Kelly Sinclair?" she asks.

"Yes. With a woman. They have a cart."

I look up the next aisle, no Kelly. April uses her impossibly long legs to outpace me and beats me to the next aisle. She looks up the aisle, then looks back at me and smiles.

"Found them!"

She turns her cart into the household cleaning aisle. My cart and I follow her, and I think about how this would never happen in Harmony Lake; stores are too small for a foot chase. There are obvious benefits to small stores with short aisles.

Kelly is at the end of the aisle. Her hair is in a messy top knot, and she's wearing grey sweatpants, a matching grey hoodie, and white running shoes. She looks so different from the polished, glamourous Kelly I'm used to seeing in Harmony Lake that I'm surprised I recognize her. She's facing a shelf, comparing two items with one in each hand.

Her friend and I make eye contact. I don't recognize her. She's not from Harmony Lake. She says something to Kelly, then turns and walks away, disappearing as she turns at the end of the aisle.

When we're about halfway up the aisle, April calls her name.

Kelly turns to us, and her face lights up with recognition. April pulls her cart over to the side of the aisle, walks over to Kelly and gives her a hug. She says something in Kelly's ear and Kelly's red, swollen eyes become redder and fill with moisture.

I reach into my tote bag and grab my portable tissue holder. When April lets go of Kelly and steps back, it's my turn, and I give Kelly a long, tight squeeze. When we pull apart, I hold out the portable tissue holder for her to take, but she reaches into her purse on the top-level of her cart and pulls out her own portable tissue holder.

"I came prepared!" She attempts a laugh and dabs at her puffy, tired-looking eyes.

"Megan, I'm sorry I haven't been in touch. I meant to call

and thank you for helping me the other night. Everything's been so busy since... I just haven't had time to call anyone."

"Please don't worry about it, Kelly," I assure her. "You're going through so much. No one expects you to do anything except take care of yourself. Nothing else matters."

"Everyone in Harmony Lake is thinking of you and hopes you're doing OK," April adds. "Do you need anything? You only have to ask," April chokes up at the end of her sentence.

Now we're all crying. It was only a matter of time.

"I'm fine. My sister,"—Kelly gestures to her left, where her friend, who I now assume is actually her sister, was standing before she walked away — "and brother-in-law are amazing. They fuss over me, and they've both missed work to help me out. My sister is here, she popped over to the pharmacy to fill a prescription. This week is so hard..." Kelly's voice hitches on the last word.

April and I each rub one of her arms while we fight to keep our own tears from streaming.

This would be a strange scene for someone wandering up the aisle in search of dish soap; two emotional women with a bizarre amount of butter comforting a third, crying woman whose cart is... full to the brim with cleaning supplies? I try to hide my shock at the contents of Kelly's cart.

"What's with all the cleaning supplies, Kelly?" I ask quietly, trying not to sound critical or judgmental.

If purchasing excessive cleaning supplies is what Kelly needs to do to cope and get through this tragedy, we will support her.

"The police released the salon and the apartment," Kelly explains, "so I'm going over there when we're finished here. I plan to spend the rest of today and tomorrow deep cleaning."

She reaches for a box of rubber gloves on the shelf beside her and places them in her cart next to the box of rubber gloves already there.

"There's dust everywhere from fingerprinting and footprints from boots. Everything needs a thorough scrubbing."

"Do you need help?" I offer. "I'm a pretty thorough cleaner when I put my mind to it, and Knitorious is closed on Mondays, so I'm free."

"And after I deliver all this butter to the bakery, I can scrub too. The three of us could make quick work of it," April suggests.

"No, thank you, ladies. I want to do this on my own. I'm hoping it'll be cathartic. I plan to go home on Wednesday after Paul's service and open the salon as usual on Thursday."

"Well, you have my number if you change your mind."

I hope I don't sound relieved. I'm not prepared to go back there today. I'm not ready. The last place I want to go is where I found Paul's body. But I imagine it will be much worse for Kelly. She needs all the support she can get, so I'll suck it up if I have to.

Kelly invites April and I to attend Paul's celebration of life on Wednesday. We ask if we can bring anything or do anything to help, but she insists they've taken care of everything, and she wants people to focus on remembering Paul.

"He was such an amazing man. Everyone loved my Paul. My voicemail is full of people telling me how much they'll miss him and how generous and kind he was." She tears up and takes a moment to collect herself.

"Harmony Lake won't be the same without him," I say.

It's not a lie. Out of the corner of my eye, April glares at me.

"He was one of a kind," April adds.

It's my turn to glare at April.

"I should find my sister." Kelly puts both hands on the handle of her cart and prepares to move.

"Before you go…" I place a gentle hand on her cart. "If the police released the building, does that mean they know who did it? Are they going to arrest someone?"

"They haven't said, but they don't tell me anything. This

Sloane guy likes to ask questions, but he doesn't like to answer them."

"I've noticed," I sympathize.

Kelly's expression changes from sad to tense.

"I told Eric Sloane who did it," she exclaims. "I told him to arrest Ryan Wright, but he's still walking around Harmony Lake, a free man." She shrugs with both hands in front of her.

"How do you know it was Ryan?" April asks.

I'm glad April asked, because I want to know, but hesitated for fear of further upsetting Kelly.

Kelly looks at me. "Remember when I told you Paul didn't trust Ryan and didn't want him in the salon or apartment?"

I nod.

"Well, Ryan tried to talk my Paul into an insurance scam involving the business." She opens her eyes wide and pauses for a reaction. I open my eyes wide in response and make my best surprised face. "Ryan said he knows a guy who will pay big money for my new salon equipment. He told Paul it would look like a robbery. He said I could make an insurance claim to get the stolen equipment replaced. Ryan told Paul he would give us half of the proceeds."

"Wow!" I say out loud, despite intending to say it in my head.

"I know, right?" Kelly says. "I couldn't believe it. I thought Paul misunderstood him, but then he told me Ryan has done this kind of thing before. Apparently, he went to jail a few years ago for stealing from his employer and re-selling the stolen goods."

"What did Paul say when Ryan suggested this scheme?" April asks, shocked.

"He told Ryan we wanted nothing to do with it. He warned Ryan that if any of my equipment went missing, we'd go straight to the police and tell them it was Ryan who did it."

Paul has a pattern of lying and blackmail, and Ryan's

history includes time in jail for a similar robbery scheme. Which one of them is lying, and which one is telling the truth?

Kelly and her cart of cleaning supplies make their way toward the pharmacy to find her sister, and April and I resume shopping and checking items off our lists.

"They don't look alike, do they?" April observes, gesturing to Kelly and her sister who are leaving the store with their purchases. "Kelly is blonde and lean, and her sister is brunette and curvy. Like you and me."

"She seems convinced Ryan killed Paul," I point out.

"She also seems convinced everyone loved Paul and thought he was a great guy," April counters. "It was like she was describing a different person. Grief must have a way of changing our perspective and making us remember only the best parts of the person we lost."

"Is her judgment clouded by grief, or is she blaming Ryan to keep the investigation focused on him and not on her?" I ponder aloud. We cash out and I follow April to her car to transfer the butter from my cart to her trunk. "Who has a stronger motive, Kelly or Ryan?" I ask.

"I think it's relative," April replies. "What isn't a big deal to one person might be enough for another person to commit murder."

"And they both gain from Paul's death," I add. "Kelly's business would be protected from Paul's gambling, and Ryan's criminal history would stay a secret."

"But did they both have opportunity?" April asks as she closes her trunk. "If Archie is telling the truth, Ryan couldn't have done it. Kelly had the opportunity. She was in the salon while Paul was upstairs. She just had to distract Mrs. Pearson and go up there and kill him."

After we say goodbye, I load my groceries into the trunk, and head home to take something for the headache I feel coming on.

CHAPTER 17

<small>WEDNESDAY</small>, September 18th

I'm walking along Water Street en route to Knitorious to meet Connie. We're going to the Irish Embassy together for Paul's celebration of life.

The warm, sunny day is a stark contrast to the sombre, serious mood of the town. It's not everyday Harmony Lake buries one of its own. Never mind someone as young as Paul or a murder victim.

The WSBA and the town council decided Water Street businesses could close early today so everyone can attend Paul's celebration of life. The irony of Water Street closing early isn't lost on me. Paul devoted his life to enforcing compliance with every town and WSBA bylaw and ordinance. I doubt he would approve of closing early on a business day for anyone's funeral, even his own. But maybe the point is to honour Paul in a way that would mean something to him by changing the rules to accommodate him. Or maybe it's a passive-aggressive way to violate a bunch of bylaws at once, since there's nothing Paul can do about it.

What to wear was a tough decision. The weather is too fall-like for a summer dress, but too warm for a winter dress. I settled on a knee-length, black jersey-knit dress with three-quarter length sleeves, and black calf-high leather boots. I pulled my hair into a French twist and chose not to fight with the few rebellious curls around my face that refused to cooperate. To add a bit of colour to my all-black ensemble, I switched out my black tote bag for my pumpkin-coloured tote bag. I always carry a tote bag large enough to accommodate my usual purse items, along with a knitting project or two. Over the years, I've acquired an impressive bag collection.

Adam texted to say he'll be late due to an appointment. I overheard him on the phone yesterday, and it sounded like he was planning to view an apartment. I hope he likes it, wants to live there, and will move out any day now.

We agreed to tell friends and neighbours about our separation. After today, so we don't upstage Paul's day. Today, we'll attend Paul's celebration of life together to keep up appearances. We're quite good at faking it, we've had lots of practice. Arriving separately won't raise any eyebrows because the entire town knows Adam is a workaholic, and everyone is used to me arriving at events on my own.

I'm about to reach into my bag for my keys, but I decide to turn the handle and see if the door is already unlocked. It is. I open the door to Knitorious and listen for the jingle. The familiarity makes me feel warm and comfortable. Connie is in the cozy area with Archie Wright and two ladies from the book club.

"Hello, my dear!" Connie waves me over. "We're just having a quick cup of tea before we head over. We thought we'd arrive as a group, apparently several community groups are sending a delegation, so we decided we would too!"

Harlow is curled in a ball and sleeping on her lap.

I greet Connie's friends and make polite small talk while I help clear the teacups from the large square coffee table.

Our envoy leaves Knitorious, and we walk up Water

Street to the crosswalk in front of The Irish Embassy. There are a few people dressed in dark, conservative attire loitering outside the pub entrance. They're chatting and soaking up the pleasant weather.

Archie opens the pub door and holds it while the rest of us file past him. The pub is packed. One step inside and we hit a wall of darkly clad people crammed too close together. Personal space does not exist here, we're literally rubbing shoulders with each other. Being on the shorter side, I rub just below the shoulder of most people.

I'm used to standing room only during tourist season, but it's never been as busy as this wake.

The Irish Embassy is a good-sized pub. It's the equivalent of two stores. The main floor has a long, double-sided bar in the centre with stools lining both sides of the bar. The bar is surrounded by various seating, booths along the walls, tables and chairs in the centre, and a couple of cozy sitting areas with sofas and club chairs around a fireplace.

There's a centre hall staircase behind the bar that leads upstairs where two large function rooms and Sheamus' office are located. There's a large open foyer overlooking the main floor with an intricate wood railing to lean on. Upstairs is closed to the public and available only for private functions. Behind the staircase there's more seating and the patio doors.

"Wow!" I say as I turn to look at Connie.

"He was young and involved in every committee and group in town." She shrugs. "I expected a full house, but I never imagined this!"

We suck in our shoulders and try to make ourselves as small as possible as we move through the crowd.

Lucky for me, April is tall and easy to spot. Her blonde head is about ten feet ahead.

"Excuse me! Pardon me! Sorry! Can I just squeeze past? Thank you!" I repeat as I navigate through the packed space. I regret my tote bag because of the extra space it takes up, and

I'm envious of April who never carries a purse, just a wristlet that acts as both a wallet and phone case.

"I made it!" I declare triumphantly, then give April and Tamara a hug. "But I lost Connie along the way."

I scan the surrounding area, but there's no sign of Connie. The crowd absorbed her.

We discuss how warm it is with so many people so close together when Tamara points out the top of Adam's head, weaving its way through the crowd in our direction. I squeeze closer to April to make room for him.

Adam greets April and Tamara with a hug and cheek kiss. Watching them chat, I can't help but notice how flattering Adam's tailored suit is. He's always been handsome, but age and maturity have increased his attractiveness.

My mother said a well-tailored suit is to women what lingerie is to men. She was right. I catch myself giving him an appreciative head-to-toe-glance and feel a twinge of sadness remembering how once upon a time, seeing Adam dressed up and watching him charm a room would elicit a stronger physical response from me than just an admiring glance. I can't remember the last time my heart skipped a beat, or I felt the flutter of butterflies in my belly with Adam.

I'm trying to figure out the moment everything changed, and we stopped being in love, when the person standing behind me bumps me. We turn and apologize at the same time.

"Hi Phillip. Sorry to bump into you. Sometimes the force of the crowd just kind of moves me, you know?"

Phillip Wilde is my neighbour at home and at work. I smile and place a hand on his shoulder, steadying myself against the movement of the crowd. He leans in and we exchange a double cheek kiss.

"I know what you mean," he whispers in my ear because that's how close he is. "It took us twenty minutes to make our way over to Kelly to give our condolences. I don't think I'll last much longer in this suit. It's too warm in here."

He fans his hand in front of his glistening face.

"I hear ya!" I sympathize with him about the crowd. Being on the shorter side, crowds overwhelm me. I feel invisible when I'm surrounded by many people, like I'm being swallowed up. Suddenly, the atmosphere changes and the crowd loosens up. We can spread out a bit, move our elbows, and breathe deeper. I stand on my tippy toes to look around the pub. "Where is Kelly?" I ask.

Phillip points over his left shoulder, raises his eyebrows and says, "About twenty minutes that way. She's with her sister- and brother-in-law near the fireplace. You might get there in ten minutes since the crowd has eased up. And if you don't run into too many people."

"In this town?" I joke. "Where everyone knows everyone else?"

We laugh and I turn back to Adam, April, and Tamara.

"Sheamus opened the patio door and upstairs," Adam says, looking up and pointing toward the ceiling.

Grateful for the extra space, I silently thank Sheamus for relieving the pressure and letting in fresh air. I look where Adam is pointing and watch people spill into the open area at the top of the stairs. My gaze follows the wooden railing until it lands on Eric. He's leaning against the railing, drink in hand, scanning the crowd below. When our eyes meet, I smile and wave. He smiles back and lifts his drink.

Interesting. I guess it makes sense he would be here, watching and listening. Does this mean he thinks the killer is here? Blending in with everyone else, pretending to be a grieving friend and neighbour? I shudder and pull myself back to the here and now.

"We should find Kelly," I suggest. "Phillip said she's with her sister and brother-in-law near the fireplace." I jerk my head in the direction Phillip pointed to earlier.

We move single file through the less crowded room, stopping every few feet to say hello to a neighbour, or hug a friend.

When we get to Kelly, there's a line of people ahead of us waiting to offer their condolences. Even grieving and traumatized, she's beautiful and elegant. Her blonde hair is styled in a low chignon, and she's wearing a thin, black, long sleeve turtleneck, a pair of high-waisted, black, wide-leg trousers, and simple black pumps. Her wedding ring and gold stud earrings are her only jewelry. She's not wearing any makeup and her swollen eyes are red from crying, and probably from lack of sleep. She looks exhausted. Poor Kelly. She's having the worst week of her life, but she still puts on a smile and deals with a town's worth of people vying for a few minutes with her.

My heart breaks for her, and I feel like a huge jerk. She's devastated by her husband's death, and here I am wondering if she could be his killer.

Kelly handles everything around her with grace and poise. As I admire her strength under such stress, a man's hand comes into view. It disappears behind Kelly's upper back, and his arm moves up and down in a rubbing motion. I follow the arm to see the rest of the man attached to it.

It's Fred!

Why is Fred Murphy is rubbing Kelly's back?

CHAPTER 18

I LOOK AWAY from Fred just long enough to grab April's arm.

"Are you seeing this?!" My attempt to whisper sounds more like an angry hiss.

April's eyes widen when she sees Fred.

"Is that?" April asks, incredulous.

"Yup! Fred the blackmailer," I seethe before she finishes her sentence. "Why is he standing with Kelly?"

I should stop trying to whisper. Subtlety doesn't seem to be an option for me right now.

"If that's Fred"—April points to Fred—"is the woman on the other side of Kelly his wife, Stephanie?" She points to the woman. "Are Stephanie Murphy and Kelly sisters?" she asks with a puzzled expression.

April faces Fred, but looks at me when she speaks, "I'm sure she's the same woman who was with Kelly at the Shop'n'Save. Remember?"

Whoa! This realization blows my mind.

I scan the room for Adam. He's near the bar chatting with Sheamus. Narrowing my eyes on my target, I suck in my breath and march over there.

"Hi Sheamus." I smile at him and clench Adam's forearm,

"You have your hands full today. It's a full house. Do you mind if I borrow Adam?"

Without waiting for a response, I lead Adam to a less-populated corner of the pub. I look him in the eye.

"Is that your girlfriend standing next to Kelly Sinclair? Look behind me, eleven o'clock."

Adam looks. He blinks and does a double take. His reaction is response enough; the woman beside Kelly is Stephanie Murphy. Stephanie and Kelly are sisters. Fred Murphy was Paul's brother-in-law.

Overwhelmed as I connect the mental dots, I find the nearest table and sit down. It's already occupied, but there's an empty chair. I smile at the people already sitting there.

"Do you mind if I just sit for a moment and catch my breath?"

"Of course," they respond out of sync, smiling politely. One of them asks me if I need anything. "Just to rest for a moment, thank you," I force a smile.

I fiddle with my ring and observe Stephanie from the safety of the full table. Stephanie and Kelly aren't at all alike, and I don't just mean their appearance.

Where Kelly is blonde, slender, and graceful, Stephanie is brunette, curvy, and seems uncomfortable greeting people and making small talk. The word *mousy* comes to mind. Kelly has beautiful taste and a classic sense of style, Stephanie's grey pant suit is a size larger than her body, and her cream-coloured blouse and sensible cream flats are, without a doubt, function over fashion.

I bear a closer resemblance to Stephanie than Kelly does. We're the same height, both have curly brown hair, fair skin, and a similar body type—a good helping of boobs and hips with a small waist. The similarities are a bit creepy. Maybe Adam has a type. It would make more sense to me if he chose someone who bore no resemblance to me.

"I swear, I had no idea they were sisters." Adam appears

next to me. I get up, thank the other table occupants, and walk away. Adam follows me, continuing to speak. "Honestly, Meg, I didn't know Stephanie was married until Fred blackmailed me, never mind knowing anything about her extended family."

He sounds sincere. Gob smacked, I say nothing in response and purse my mouth into a thin line.

"She doesn't wear a ring," Adam continues. "She never talked about her family, and she didn't have any photos or personal items in her office. I knew about her cat. She talked about the cat and showed me photos of him on her phone. She never mentioned a husband. But now it makes sense why Kelly didn't want to meet for coffee near my office."

I glance at Stephanie's ring finger. He's telling the truth; she isn't wearing a ring. In fact, she isn't wearing any jewelry at all.

Maybe Stephanie didn't have any family photos in her office, but Adam did. Lots of them. The most recent addition to his collection was a photo of the three of us at Hannah's graduation ceremony.

When Stephanie and I made eye contact at Shop'n'Save on Monday, she must have recognized me from the photos in his office. That would explain why she disappeared to the pharmacy.

"She knew she was married, and you both knew you were married, even if it is in name only," I remind him. "You also knew that you were a senior partner, and she was a junior associate. The relationship was against company policy. Not to mention unethical. It put your livelihood and our family at risk," I admonish.

Maybe next time, he'll ask a few questions before he gets in bed with someone and sends them compromising photos.

We stand in silence. While I compose myself, he recovers from the shock of his wife and girlfriend being in the same room at the same time.

"We should say hello to Kelly and give our condolences," I finally say as I turn and walk toward the condolence line.

April and Tamara go first. I watch as April introduces herself to Fred as though they've never met before and shakes his hand. Well played, April.

Watching them shake hands reminds me I need to pick up more of those portable hand sanitizer bottles for my purse and car; it's almost cold and flu season. I'm about to reach into my bag and rummage around for a bottle, so I can use it before and after I shake Fred and Stephanie's hands, but Tamara moves on to talk to Kelly, and it's my turn to greet Fred.

Following April's lead, I shake his hand, fake-introduce myself as Kelly's friend, and tell him I'm sorry for his family's loss. He fake-introduces himself as Fred, Paul and Kelly's brother-in-law, and thanks me for coming. I tell him Kelly mentioned how supportive he and his wife have been, while silently hoping he feels as awkward as I do with all this pretending.

Tamara moves along to Stephanie, and I move along to Kelly. I wipe the hand that touched Fred on my dress to banish the disgust I feel after touching the blackmailer.

While Kelly and I hug, I tell her to call, text, or show up anytime day or night if she needs anything. I tell her the town already feels different without Paul. It's not a lie.

I move along to Stephanie and extend my hand. Her handshake is limp. When she tries to end the handshake, I tighten my grip just enough to prevent her from pulling her hand away. Then I place my other hand over our conjoined hands.

"I've heard *so much* about you." I let Stephanie pull her hand away from mine. She looks uncomfortable. Good. Though I get the sense she's generally uncomfortable. Blackmailing witch. "Kelly says you've been amazing this week.

She's so lucky to have you. She says you and Fred took time away from work to support her. What do you do again?"

I maintain eye contact, and when she averts her eyes, I move my head to compel her to look me in the eye again, engaging her in some kind of weird, passive-aggressive staring contest. I'm determined to win. I don't even blink.

"I'm an attorney," she replies, her voice squeaky and mouselike.

"Right! I remember now," I say, still maintaining eye contact. I force a fake smile and summon my most chipper voice. "I believe you know my husband, Adam Martel." I turn to Adam as he finishes his conversation with Kelly. "Adam, you know Stephanie, right? You work together, I think?" I look back at Stephanie. "I'm sorry, I meant to say *worked*. Adam resigned last week, but I'm sure you know all about that." I watch her squirm, then continue. "Such a small world! Stephanie, we're so sorry for your family's loss," I say, tilting my head and mustering a consoling tone of voice so sarcastic it sounds sincere.

I walk away, watching Adam and Stephanie's interaction. I don't see any sparks or chemistry between them. If there's still any attraction, it's not palpable. In fact, they look down-right awkward, but that might be because of the scene I made. They shake hands, and he walks away. I hope their exchange was as uncomfortable as it looked.

"What was that, Meg?" Adam asks.

"I'm sorry," I respond. "I've never met my husband's girl-friend before. I don't know what etiquette is in this situation. *Please forgive me.*" My words drip with disdain.

I look away from him because I'm fighting the urge to yell and say things I'll regret. I gravitate to April and Tamara.

"Stop calling her my girlfriend. She's not my girlfriend," Adam asserts, rolling his eyes, which only makes me more frustrated.

"Mistress? Concubine? Significant other? What label do

you two prefer?" I ask. "Is it awkward having your wife and *girlfriend* in the same room?"

"I'm going to the bar to get a drink and give you some space. I'll get you a drink too. You need one," he says calmly.

He turns to April and Tamara, "Ladies, can I get you anything from the bar?"

While avoiding looking at Adam, I notice an elderly couple approach Kelly with a plate of food and motion for her to sit by the fireplace.

The woman puts the plate down in front of Kelly and cuts the food into bite-size pieces. Recognizing a fellow mum when I see one, I deduce that the elderly couple is Kelly's parents.

The family settles in the sitting area by the fireplace. Then Fred leans over to Stephanie, says something in her ear, and she nods. Fred gets up, slips away from his in-laws, and strides toward the door. I'm right behind him.

CHAPTER 19

ADAM and I make eye contact as I follow Fred past the bar. I mouth, "Stay here," exaggerating each word so Adam can read my lips.

I follow Fred onto the sidewalk in front of the pub. He turns the corner and disappears in the alley beside the building. So that's what I do too.

Fred's upper body and left foot rest against the brick wall. His head lowered, his left hand cupping a lighter he's flicking in his right hand. There's a cigarette between his lips.

"Filthy habit," I say to announce my presence.

He looks at me, pulls a pack of cigarettes from his shirt pocket and extends his arm toward me, offering me one. I raise my hand in a stop gesture and shake my head no. I take a step closer, but make sure I'm visible from the sidewalk, so if I scream someone can find me.

"So, you're Paul's brother-in-law. I didn't see that coming."

Fred exhales a cloud of smoke.

"I assumed you knew," he says, "Doesn't everyone in this town know everything about everyone?"

I used to think so, but the past seven days have taught me

there are a lot of secrets in Harmony Lake, and I'm happier not knowing most of them.

"Well, you don't live in this town. I'd never seen you before you showed up to blackmail us. I saw you arguing with Paul the day he died, and I mentioned it to the police. Why did you give Paul the photos? So, he could blackmail us too?"

"I didn't blackmail you. I blackmailed Adam," Fred clarifies.

He takes a long drag from his cigarette.

"Same thing," I point out.

"I didn't give Paul the pictures. We didn't know how he got them until after he died. Steph texted Kelly and told her about the affair the day before Paul died and sent the pictures to her. Kelly told the police she thinks Paul found the pictures when he was nosing around her phone. He stole them. Steph didn't tell Kelly who she was having an affair with. She only said it was a guy from work," He chuckles. "You should've seen her face when she found out he was your husband."

Fred chuckles again and slaps his knee, then looks at me without turning his head towards me.

How did Paul know Adam was Stephanie's affair partner? He could have recognized Adam's tattoo, but I'm not sure Paul ever saw it. More likely, he knew Adam and Stephanie worked together and took a stab in the dark that it was Adam. Then, Adam unknowingly confirmed Paul's suspicion by not denying it when Paul blackmailed us.

"I would never give the pictures to Paul. He's sneaky, and he'd use them for his benefit." Fred flicks ash from the tip of his cigarette. "I don't want the world to know my wife slept with your husband. If Paul knew, that's what would have happened. The entire world would know. At least now that he's dead, I don't have to deal with him or his problems anymore."

He takes another long drag from what's left of the cigarette.

"What did you and Paul argue about in the car?" I ask.

I have nothing to lose by asking. This could be my only chance to question Fred, so I'm asking all my questions now, while he's talkative.

"Paul owes me money. He told me he would pay me back by blackmailing Adam with the pictures. I was angry that he had the pictures. I wanted him to delete them and pretend he never saw them. But Paul's greedy, and there's no way he'd delete them if he could use them to squeeze money out of someone."

Fred says all of this matter-of-factly, like he has nothing to hide. He flicks the cigarette butt into the distance, and we watch it disappear.

Paul told Jay his brother-in-law loaned him the money to repay his debt; Fred just confirmed that Paul owed him money.

"If Paul owed you money, why kill him? He can't pay you back if he's dead."

I take a big step backwards in case Fred freaks out about being accused of murder, and I need to run.

"I didn't kill Paul. But he tempted me more than once, trust me," he answers, shaking his head. "I was asleep when Kelly called from the police station to tell us what happened. I was so tired from the previous two days. After learning about Steph's affair, talking with her to save our marriage, dealing with you and Adam, and arguing with Paul, I was so exhausted, I passed out after dinner and slept like I was in a coma. Steph had a hard time waking me up to go to the police station. She had to drive because I kept nodding off and couldn't stay awake."

He uses his left foot to push himself away from the wall and stands with both feet on the ground, facing me.

"Look, I don't like Paul and I don't trust Paul, but Kelly

loves him, and I love her like a sister. I love my wife, and it hurts her when Kelly suffers, so I would never do that to them. Anyway, I never expected Paul to pay me back. Before he died, he was spiralling financially." He twirls his index finger down in a circular motion. "Even dead, he's still costing me money."

Fred chuckles and coughs a phlegmy smoker's cough.

"How is your dead brother-in-law costing you money?" I ask.

"Who do you think paid for all this?" he answers my question with a question and gestures vaguely around us. "Kelly can't afford this spread. She also can't cover the cost of the funeral or cremation. Steph and I are footing the bill. When I heard he died, I thought at least his life insurance would cover his final expenses, but we found out yesterday he let the premiums lapse almost a year ago. Aside from the business, Kelly has nothing."

With that, Fred walks past me, rounds the corner, and returns to the pub.

I follow him around the corner and lean against the wall near the pub door, taking a moment to process my conversation with Fred.

Instead of eliminating suspects, I'm uncovering more reasons to keep them on the list. First, Ryan, with his robbery scheme, criminal history, and revolving door of alibis. Next, Kelly, who wants to protect her home and business from her husband's financially destructive behaviour and stop him from snooping through her phone. Then there's Fred, who admits he hated Paul, admits he was angry when Paul threatened to expose Stephanie and Adam's affair, and was tired of giving Paul money.

As much as I hate to admit it and find it impossible to believe, I have to admit that Adam belongs on the suspect list too. Paul blackmailed him, and Adam didn't come home the night Paul was killed. He'd already lost his job because of the affair and maybe being blackmailed on top of everything else was too much to bear and pushed Adam over the edge.

Adam is just inside the pub door on the left, and Eric is on the right. I don't acknowledge Eric because I'm angry at him; he knew Kelly and Stephanie were sisters and didn't tell me. He stood back and let me get blindsided. Again. It's like watching me squirm is his hobby, or something.

I accept the glass of Pinot Adam offers me and take a long sip.

"Are you OK?" Adam asks. "I worried when he came back in and you didn't. I was about to look for you."

"I'm more confused than before I spoke to him, but other than that I'm fine," I mumble.

I take a deep breath and repeat, *heavy shoulders, long arms,* a few times in my head to help release the tension in my neck and shoulders.

Out of the corner of my eye, flailing arms get my attention. It's April. With the crowd thinning out, she, Tamara, and Connie found a booth.

Adam and I join them. I sit down, put my tote on the floor under the booth and fill them in on my conversation with Fred.

April and I are both in awe of Kelly's lying skills. At the grocery store, she didn't let on that she knew about Stephanie and Adam. Also, neither of us recall her referring to her sister by name, just as "my sister," and now I wonder if that was intentional. But Kelly invited me to Paul's celebration of life today, so she knew I'd find out her sister and Stephanie Murphy are the same person. Maybe I'm over thinking it. Kelly is so deeply mired in her own grief that lying to me or covering for her sister's poor decisions isn't on her radar right now.

"Well, either she's grieving and doesn't care, or she's an academy award worthy actor," Connie observes.

"Paul spied on Kelly's phone? Maybe she found out and

got angry. Or maybe she found out he blackmailed Adam and threatened to expose her sister, and it made her snap," Tamara surmises.

It seems like there were trust issues in Paul and Kelly's marriage, at least on Paul's side. Paul's reaction when he found out Kelly texted and met with Adam in the summer is proof of that. I'm careful not to share this bit of information because Adam told me in confidence. Aside from me, the only person he told is Eric Sloane. If only Adam was as discreet with his personal relationships as he is with his professional ones, we wouldn't be caught up in this tangled yarn of a murder investigation.

"Until today, I thought Fred was the least likely suspect because Paul owed him money, and it's hard to collect a debt from a dead man. But Fred said he didn't expect Paul to pay him back. Also, the family thought Paul had insurance, but yesterday they found out he stopped paying the premiums almost a year ago. So, maybe Fred killed Paul for the insurance and it backfired," I suggest.

"I think Fred is the strongest contender for the title of Killer," April says. "If we were betting, I'd put my money on him."

"I don't know," I say.

I bite the inside of my lip while I wrestle with the gut feeling that Fred didn't do it.

"He kept referring to Paul in the present tense, you know? Like he said, 'I *don't* like Paul. Paul *owes* me money. He *is* sneaky.' Wouldn't the killer use past tense? And he didn't hesitate to talk to me. He acts like he has nothing to hide."

Maybe he's fed up with being a murder suspect and wants to wrap this up already. If that's the case, I relate because I feel the same way.

"We know he's capable of blackmail, and lying, so how big of a leap is murder?" Connie theorizes.

Everyone shrugs and nods their heads. I'm conflicted.

Logically, I know Fred is a strong suspect, but my instincts don't agree.

"Are you ready to head out?" Adam asks me.

"I think I'll stay and have another glass of wine. Then I'll walk Connie home. I'll see you at home," I reply, smiling.

"Meg, there's a murderer in our midst, and you're asking questions and trying to figure out who it is. You could be in danger. I'll feel better if I walk you and Connie home."

He's lays out his argument using his lawyer voice, and I hate it when he uses his lawyer voice with me.

"I'll be fine, Adam," I insist brusquely. "You can leave. I'll text you when I leave. You don't have to worry."

"Archie and some members of the book club are coming to Knitorious for tea after this, so I won't be alone anyway, but thank you, Adam." Connie reaches over and squeezes his hand.

"I'll keep Megan safe," Eric offers, suddenly standing beside our booth. Where did he come from? He looks at me. "Megan, I'd like to speak with you before you leave. Then I'll see you home safely. If that's all right with you, of course."

"It's fine," I say. I look at Adam. "I'll see you at home."

Adam says goodbye to the table, thanks Eric, and leaves.

"I'll be sitting by the bar whenever you're ready," Eric says before he walks away.

"Megan? Why are you *Megan* and T and I are *Ms. Shaw* and *Ms. Shaw*?"

"Dunno." I shrug. "He told me to call him Eric, so I told him to call me Megan."

"I need to figure out who killed Paul so I can get on with my life," I say.

Connie places her hand on top of mine and gives it a gentle squeeze.

"I'm going to get us another round of drinks. Or two!" April announces.

CHAPTER 20

WITH A SLIGHT BUZZ from three glasses of wine on an empty stomach, I wander over to the bar. I find Eric perched on a bar stool with a plate of wings and a drink in front of him. I assume the drink is non-alcoholic because on TV police officers never drink while on duty.

"Is that from the local microbrewery?" I point to his pint glass.

"Only if the local microbrewery brews ginger ale," he replies, smiling. "Wing?"

He nudges a plate of wings toward me. Shaking my head, I raise my hand to say no thank you and climb onto the stool next to him at the almost-empty bar.

"I can't believe how busy it was in here earlier. I've never seen so many people crammed into The Embassy," I say, making small talk.

"It was crazy," he agrees. "It was difficult to observe everyone. But I observed you racing out of here after Fred. How did that go?"

He gets right to the point. All business, this guy.

"I'm sure he didn't tell me anything that you don't already

know. Like how you knew Stephanie and Kelly are sisters, and I didn't."

It's a relief to get this off my chest. One thing I've learned this week is to speak up when I'm upset and not shove my feelings aside. It's not my job to spare other people from having uncomfortable feelings at the expense of my own. I deserve to be heard too. Everybody does. As of today, I promise myself I will say how I feel and not ignore my feelings for the sake of not rocking the boat. And I will keep this promise at least until this wine buzz wears off.

"Until I saw the look on your face, I didn't know you weren't aware of the relationships. Harmony Lake is a small town, everyone seems to know everyone else, so I assumed you knew. I'm sorry that was awkward for you, it wasn't my intention."

Maybe he didn't blindside me on purpose.

"Thank you," I reply. "Why were you watching me?"

Was a cop assigned to watch every suspect?

"I wasn't watching *you*," he clarifies. "I was watching the condolence line. It was busy in here, and I had to narrow my focus, so I monitored the condolence line from upstairs while a few non-uniforms wandered the crowd with their eyes and ears open."

While Eric finishes his wings and ginger ale, I fill him in on my conversation with Fred and share the conclusions that Connie, April, Tamara, and I came to earlier.

"I appreciate the information, it's more helpful than you realize, but Adam is right to be concerned about your safety. There's a murderer in this town, and they might know you're asking questions and talking to me. If they think you're getting too close, you could be in danger. You need to stop investigating and get on with your life."

His concern seems sincere, and not an excuse to convince me to get my nose out of his case, though I'm sure that's part of it.

"I need you to solve this murder because Adam and I are suspects. We have a daughter. I don't want her to think her father had an affair with a married woman, someone blackmailed us because of it, and one of us killed the blackmailer. Part of it being true is bad enough. It will be easier to explain to her when someone else is behind bars for Paul's murder," I explain. "Adam is a lawyer. Being a suspect in a murder investigation could destroy his career. I mean, would you hire a lawyer who may have killed the person who was blackmailing him? The affair already cost him his partnership at the firm."

I choke up, and my cheeks flush with angry heat. Talking about how this could affect Hannah makes it too real. I take a deep breath, dab my eyes with a napkin from the bar and compose myself.

"If I tell you something, do you promise not to tell anyone?" Eric asks just above a whisper.

He makes a fist and extends his pinky finger for a pinky swear. I hook my pinky finger around his.

"Promise." I use my other hand to make an X over my heart, so he knows I mean it. "I pinky swear, *and* I cross my heart and hope to die, so spill."

"We've eliminated Adam as a suspect. Security video footage and his keycard for the office building verify that he arrived at work early in the morning and didn't leave his office until late Tuesday evening. Then, he went to a burrito place up the street. We have video of him ordering food, leaving with his order, and entering a nearby hotel a few minutes later. They issued him a keycard for the company suite. There's footage of him and his burrito entering the elevator, then exiting on the floor where the suite is located. We have video of him unlocking the door with the keycard. The door to the suite didn't open again until Wednesday morning. He couldn't have done it."

I tear up, overwhelmed by relief.

"Well…" I sigh. "At least if I go to prison for Paul's murder, Hannah will still have one parent on the outside."

When I hear the words come out of my mouth, I realize they sound glib, but I'm serious. I'm worried because the police haven't eliminated me as a suspect yet, but they've eliminated other people. The suspect list is getting smaller, and my odds of being charged are getting higher.

"As for you,"—Eric hands me another napkin to dab my tears—"you were with Connie until less than ten minutes before you found the body. You are, at best, an unlikely suspect."

I nod. An unlikely suspect, but still a suspect.

"I was planning to tell Adam tomorrow, but we can tell him when I take you home."

I nod. "That would be great, thank you, Eric."

"So, there's no need for you to keep asking questions and putting yourself at risk, right?" he nods at me, looking for agreement.

"Right," I say, nodding back.

Ready to leave, we say goodnight to Sheamus, and head toward the door.

"Thank you for offering to take me home, but you don't have to," I say. "I'll be fine."

"I know," he says, "but it's a good idea for everyone to be extra cautious right now. You know, safety in numbers and all that. Besides, I promised your hus—Adam, and this gives me a chance to tell him he's no longer a suspect."

At the door, I reach for my tote bag to get my lip balm. Where's my tote bag?

"Shoot! My bag. It's under the booth!"

I spot my pumpkin-coloured bag under the table where I left it. I grab it, stride back to Eric, through the door he's holding open, and onto the sidewalk, forgetting about my dry lips and wanting to apply lip balm.

Eric doesn't have a car. He rode with two colleagues who

took the car with them when they left. It's a nice evening, so instead of waiting, we decide to walk to my house. He'll text the station and ask for a patrol car to pick him up there.

On the walk to chez Martel, we talk about hockey, we're both Toronto Maple Leafs Fans. We talk about school. I went to U of T, and he went to Western. We talk about TV, we both hate reality shows, I prefer streaming services, he prefers cable. He even answers a few personal questions; he was divorced two years ago. They were married for ten years and she was a chiropractor. His job caused stress in their marriage, and he has no children. He doesn't have a girlfriend because he's married to his job, and when he tries to have a relationship and a career, one suffers, so he gave up trying to have both.

The porch light is on, and the door is locked. Adam isn't kidding around about our security; we never lock the door when one of us is home. I don't like feeling that I have to lock my door to feel safe in my home.

Instead of ringing the bell and disturbing Adam, I reach into my bag and grope around for my keys. I grab hold of something that feels… odd.

What is this? It's smooth and cylindrical, and Eric and I both watch as I slowly pull a twelve-inch-long, fifteen-millimetre diameter, bamboo knitting needle from my bag and hold it up between us.

"What the f—what is this? This isn't mine. It wasn't in here when I switched bags this morning."

I'm dumbfounded trying to figure out where this knitting needle came from and how it got into my bag.

"Are you sure it's not yours? Maybe it was already in your bag from the last time you used it, and you forgot it was there?"

Eric positions his hands cautiously around the needle, being careful not to touch it, like he's prepared to catch it if it falls.

"I'm sure. We sell these at the shop. In fact, this one is identical to the needles Kelly bought the day Paul died."

I look at his face for a reaction, but he's hyper-focused on the needle I'm dangling between us.

"I don't own needles this big," I explain. "I knit with fingering weight or worsted weight yarn, so my needle collection ranges from about two millimetres to five millimetres. Nothing this big, and I only use circular needles, even when I'm knitting flat. This needle isn't mine."

He looks at me blankly for a second, then returns his focus to the needle.

"I don't know what that means," he says, pressing the doorbell with one hand and guarding the needle with the other. "But this needle might be evidence. I need you to return it carefully to your bag without touching it any more than you already have."

Adam opens the door, looks at me, looks at Eric, then looks at the needle.

"Hey, guys!" he says with a big smile.

CHAPTER 21

HOLDING my bag at arm's length, I hurry from the front door to the dining room and, like it's a grenade instead of a bamboo knitting needle, place the bag on the dining room table. I step away backwards, keeping a watchful eye on it the entire time.

I switch on the dining room light. Eric is behind me on his phone. He requests a car and an evidence kit.

Adam watches the scene with obvious confusion. I tell him about the mysterious knitting needle I found in my bag. He doesn't look any less confused. Adam is used to finding random knitting needles in unexpected places—he's lived with a knitter for almost twenty years—and doesn't think a rogue needle in my tote bag is unusual. I explain this specific needle isn't mine, and Eric thinks it might be evidence. His confused expression morphs into one of concern.

"We have to take the entire bag and its contents for processing," Eric explains when he finishes his call.

"Oh. Can I keep my cell phone? That's the number Hannah uses to reach me."

"Not if it's in your bag, I'm afraid," he responds, shaking his head.

"They'll probably keep it for a while," Adam adds. "They've had my cell phone for almost a week." He snickers. "It might take them a week just to unpack your luggage."

I roll my eyes. Adam always teases me about my love of large tote bags. *Luggage* is one of his many terms of endearment for them. I know he's trying to lighten the mood and ease my anxiety, but I'm not amused.

"It's still early," Adam says, looking at his watch. "I'll go to the store and get you a new phone. You can text Hannah with your new number tonight, and if she needs anything in the meantime, she'll text me or call the landline. We'll tell her the phone got wet or something. It'll be fine."

I nod, sad about lying to my daughter. How would I tell her the police confiscated my cell phone because murder evidence—from a murder I'm suspected of committing—appeared in my bag?

Adam asks Eric if it's OK for him to leave.

"Go ahead," Eric replies, "but I need to ask you some questions when you get back."

"I'll be as quick as I can."

Adam is already at the door putting on his shoes.

"Can I get you a drink? Coffee or tea or anything?" I go into the kitchen to get myself a glass of water.

Eric stays in the dining room with the tote bag.

"No thanks," he replies. "When was the last time you reached into your bag? Before we got here and you went looking for your keys, I mean."

Retracing my day, I think back. I realized I didn't have my bag when I wanted to put lip balm on as we left the pub. It was under the booth where I put it when I first sat down. I remember wanting my hand sanitizer in the condolence line but forgetting about it because it was my turn to fake-introduce myself to Fred. I didn't need to reach into it for my keys at Knitorious because Connie already unlocked the door.

"When I left the house this afternoon," I shout from the

kitchen. "I locked the door and dropped my keys in my bag. I haven't reached into it since. It was on the floor under the booth most of the afternoon. When it wasn't under the booth, it was on my shoulder. I switched bags this morning, and I'm telling you, there were no knitting needles in my bag. Except for the ones that belong in my bag. I have a sock project in there that I work on in line-ups, waiting rooms, you know, when I'm waiting. But it's a sock and has tiny needles."

I remove my boots and put them in the closet. Then I sit on the living room sofa with my feet tucked under my butt. I'm able to position myself with an unobstructed view of the bag.

"Did anyone hold your bag for you?" Eric asks.

"No." I shake my head. "It was on my shoulder or under the booth. Lots of people bumped into it because the pub was so crowded. Are you going to explain why the knitting needle might be evidence?"

"They're here," Eric says, ignoring my question, walking to the front door, and letting in two police officers.

The three law enforcement officers proceed to the dining room, one of them places a black case on the dining room floor. She opens the case, pulls out a pair of latex gloves and puts them on. Then she grabs a large plastic evidence bag, which unfolds into an even larger evidence bag. She reaches into the case again and pulls out smaller evidence bags and lays them in front of her. The other officer reaches into the case and puts latex gloves on. They photograph, bag, and tag the contents of my tote bag. I'm glad Adam isn't here to crack a joke about the size of the evidence bag they need to fit the tote bag inside.

While his colleagues collect the evidence, Eric suggests we wait in another room. I lead him into the family room and resume my tucked-up position on the sofa there. Eric sits at the other end of the sofa.

"Well," I say, "why is this knitting needle potential evidence?"

By instinct, I pick up the sock-in-progress from the ceramic yarn bowl on the table next to me, and start knitting.

"That's a nice bowl. Did you make that?"

I swear this man will do anything to avoid directly answering my questions.

"Thank you. Yes, I took a pottery class a few years ago."

Eric slides closer, so he's in the middle of the sofa instead of the end. He smells good.

"Remember when I explained what a hold-back is?" he asks in a whisper.

"Yes," I whisper, leaning in so I can hear him. "It's evidence only the killer would know about. You keep it secret until you find the killer, then use it to verify their story."

"Pretty much," Eric whispers back. "One of the knitting needles Kelly bought at Knitorious was missing from the crime scene. We can't find it anywhere. We turned the apartment, salon, their cars, everything upside down looking for it. One needle was there, but we never located the other one."

"So, you think the killer took it?" I ask. "Like a sick souvenir or something?"

I cringe at the thought of someone disturbed enough to want a murder memento.

"Possibly," Eric replies with a nod. He pauses, like he's not sure he should say anything else. "The murderer might have used the needle as a garrote. Do you know what a garrote is?"

I look at him and nod. My stomach sinks, and I swallow hard.

A garrote is a weapon used to help strangle someone. The police suspect the killer might have used the knitting needle as a tool to tighten the yarn around Paul's neck. Its sudden appearance in my bag probably means Eric upgraded my status as unlikely suspect to most likely suspect.

"Will you be able to keep the knitting needle a secret,

Megan? It would help the investigation if we can keep it under wraps. I know you're close with April and Connie. Will you be able to keep this from them? The killer likely wanted you to find it and touch it, and I'd rather not give this creep what they want." Eric winks.

I give a small smile to his attempt at reassuring me.

I'm not reassured, I'm terrified. My fingerprints are on that needle, I touched it to pull it out of my bag. The killer probably took it with them after they killed Paul, wiped it clean of their own fingerprints, then planted it so I would leave my fingerprints on it. This needle is a direct link between me and Paul's murder.

"Of course, I'll keep it a secret." I tell him firmly.

In silence and with trembling hands, I knit while Eric paces between me and the officers in the dining room.

Adam comes home with my new phone and hands me the box. I take it into the kitchen and plug it in while Eric questions Adam in the family room. The two officers finish collecting the evidence and pack up their things.

I text Hannah with my new number. My mind wanders to the knitting needle while I wait for her to text back an acknowledgement. I touched a weapon that murdered someone. It was in my bag, and I didn't even realize it was there. The murderer got close enough to put it there without raising my suspicion.

A knitting needle, of all things. I love knitting; knitting has brought me comfort during the hardest times of my life, like when my mother passed away. Knitting helped me make friends when we moved to Harmony Lake, and now knitting might frame me for a murder I didn't commit.

I feel gross and dirty and can't wait for the police to leave, so I can lock myself in my room and have a shower.

I STAND under the stream of hot water for I-don't-know-how-long. The tips of my fingers are wrinkled and pruney.

Does Eric believe I'm innocent? Does everyone else believe I'm innocent? Why would the killer want me to find the murder weapon? Why not someone else? Was the murderer at Paul's celebration of life, walking around, acting normal, and doing it so well they didn't stand out?

The water runs cold and I shiver. I turn off the shower and step into the steam-filled washroom to dry off.

I put on my favourite flannel pyjamas with cats and yarn balls on them, a pair of thick, hand-knit, wool socks, and go to the kitchen to make a mug of chamomile tea.

Adam is at the kitchen table with his laptop open.

"Did you text your new number to Hannah?" he asks without looking up from the screen.

"Yes, it's all good," I reply. "Thank you for replacing my phone."

Choking up, I swallow the lump in my throat.

"Do you think I killed Paul?" I blurt out.

My eyes fill with tears, and I can't stop them from streaming down my face.

Adam gets up from the table, picks up a tissue box, and pulls out a couple of tissues. He hands them to me and places the box on the counter next to me.

"I know you didn't kill anybody, Meg," he says. "No one who has ever met you could think you're capable of murder. The killer must feel cornered and desperate to redirect the investigation," he theorizes, rubbing circles into my back. "Eric seems like a thorough investigator who's good at his job. I'm sure he's seen this before. He knows you didn't do it, and he'll find the monster who did."

Adam puts his arms around me, and I let him. I cry there for a while. At least if I'm charged with Paul's murder, I'll have one of the best lawyers around.

KNIT ONE MURDER TWO

After I pull myself together, I make my tea and say goodnight to Adam.

"Eric spoke to you about keeping the knitting needle secret, right?" Adam asks. "It's important, Meg. If we tell anyone, it could jeopardize the investigation." His voice is slow and gentle, like he's trying to reason with a disappointed child.

"I understand," I assure him. "I won't say anything. And I can keep a secret, you know. I've kept our separation a secret for months." As soon as I say it, I realize I sound bitter, which isn't my intention. "Eric told me he eliminated you as a suspect. He said he was going to tell you tonight," I tell Adam in case Eric forgot to mention it amidst all the commotion.

"He told me," Adam responds. "And I know you can keep a secret, Meg. I also know you confide in your friends. You can't confide in them about this. Tell them the same story about your phone you told Hannah. It'll be easier to keep track of the lies if we keep them consistent," he says, smiling at me. "Goodnight."

He sits down at the kitchen table and resumes working on his laptop.

I've become a person who has so many lies, she has to keep track of them. I need to solve this murder, so I don't have to lie anymore.

This isn't who I am.

CHAPTER 22

THURSDAY, September 19th

I didn't sleep well. I dreamed I was in prison with the cast of "Orange Is the New Black."

After tossing and turning most of the night, I'm wide awake. I may as well get dressed and go to Knitorious. There are online orders to ship, and I can finish the fall window display.

Realizing the police confiscated my keys with my bag last night, I retrieve the spare set from the hook on the laundry room wall and drive to the store.

Making as little noise as possible, I let myself in the back door. I don't use the front door because the bell might wake up Connie, and no one should be up this early.

Harlow runs downstairs and purrs while he wraps himself around my ankles. I pick him up, scratch under his chin, tell him how charming he is, and carry him into the store. I sit on a sofa, and he jumps onto my lap. He purrs while I stroke him, and we enjoy some quiet time together until he purrs himself to sleep.

I pick up the cowl I'm working on and knit for a while before I print the online orders. The clicking of the needles and Harlow's purring are the only sounds in the otherwise silent store. For the first time since Paul's murder, anxiety loosens its grip on me. I'm thankful for the reprieve, even if only for a few minutes.

Harlow wakes up, licks himself, and leaps off my lap. He meows and looks back and forth between me and the kitchenette.

"Are you hungry, handsome?" I ask the tuxedo cat.

I stand up, and he runs to the kitchenette. While I dole out Harlow's pungent food, footsteps thud on the steps behind me that lead to Connie's apartment.

"Good morning, sleepy head!" I greet Connie without turning around.

I place the cat dish on the floor and turn toward the stairs.

"Oh!" I gasp, "Where's Connie?"

"Good morning, Megan!" Archie replies. "Connie will be down in a minute. We didn't think you were coming in this morning,"

This is awkward. For both of us. I had no idea Connie and Archie were more than friends. Does her relationship with Archie have anything to do with Connie's mystery appointments?

Archie and I act like it's the most normal thing in the world for me to catch him doing a walk of shame from Connie's apartment on a Thursday morning.

"How are you doing, Archie? How's the sore hip been treating you?" I hold up a coffee mug to offer him a cup of coffee.

"It's stiff, but as long as I keep using it, it's OK." He shakes his head and waves away my silent coffee offer. "It seizes up when I stop using it, so I try to keep it moving." After an awkward silence he adds, "Listen, Megan, I was talking with Connie, and Ryan might have misinformed you about where he was the night Paul died."

"I wondered about that," I admit, turning on the coffeemaker.

"Well, we watched the game together. That part is true," Archie confesses. "But before that, he wasn't with his friend Jay, he was with me. You caught him off guard, and he didn't know what to say. He was protecting me as much as he was protecting himself."

"Just tell her, Archie!" Connie is coming downstairs, and this morning-after scene is getting more awkward.

"Good morning, my dear." Connie and I hug, and she kisses my cheek. "Stop beating around the bush, Archie, and tell her where you were," she says, taking his hand.

Archie takes a deep breath.

"Ryan and I were at an AA meeting at a church in Harmony Hills. He got his three-year chip that night."

"Archie, I had no idea!" I say. "Good for him. Tell Ryan I'm proud of him. Sobriety isn't easy. And please tell him his secret is safe with me. I won't tell a soul," I reassure him.

"Us," Archie corrects me. "We were both at the meeting, Megan. I've been sober for 23 years." He smiles at me and then at Connie. "Like father, like son," Archie continues, "I'm afraid my rugged good looks and seductive charm aren't the only things I passed down to my son."

Connie laughs and puts her spare hand on his shoulder.

"Ryan was taken aback when you asked him where he was," Archie explains. "He didn't want to out my sobriety. That's why he lied to you. He feels awful for lying. But he was with me the entire night, I swear."

"I'm proud of both of you." I hug him. "And I couldn't be happier for you and Connie. I feel better knowing you're staying here while there's a killer roaming around Harmony Lake."

I finish making my coffee, say goodbye to Archie and go into the shop to print the online orders. Connie and Archie say goodbye at the back door, then she joins me.

Connie looks happy. She has a glow about her and a spring in her step I haven't seen since her husband passed away five years ago. Archie obviously makes her happy, and that's enough to make me happy for them.

"I mean it, you know," I say. "I'm happy for you and Archie. But why the secrecy?"

"It's not a secret," Connie replies. "We just didn't announce it. We decided to live our life and let people figure it out for themselves. Making a big deal out of it at our age is exhausting, to be honest, and as soon as the right people figure it out, it'll be common knowledge, anyway." She shrugs.

Still smiling, Connie tidies the yarn on the shelves behind the sofa.

I process the online orders and think about what Connie said about her relationship with Archie becoming common knowledge. Until last week, I thought nothing could stay secret in Harmony Lake, but now I realize no matter how small and tight knit our cozy little community is, secrets lurk everywhere, everyone has one. Even our family has a secret, and if we can keep a separation secret for months, anyone can do it. It makes me feel like I don't know my friends and neighbours as well as I thought.

THE FAMILIAR JINGLE makes Connie and I look up at the same time. April strides in with a deep frown.

"There you are!" she shouts, narrowing her eyes on me, and crossing her arms in front of her chest. "I've been texting you all day. I worried, so I texted Adam to make sure you were OK. He said you have a new phone number, and I'd probably find you here. What happened to your phone, and why are you working on your day off?"

"What's this about a new number, my dear?" Connie adds, the skin around her eyes creased with concern.

"I'm sorry! I meant to text you my new number, but I don't *know* your phone numbers. I depend on technology and don't have anyone's contact information memorized or written anywhere." April and Connie continue staring at me, waiting for more of an explanation. "The phone is no big deal, I dropped it in water last night, and it didn't recover. I worried Hannah wouldn't be able to reach me, so Adam replaced it." I make a mental note to get one of those old-timey phone books and write down important numbers, in case the police ever confiscate my phone again.

I smile and look back and forth from April to Connie, hoping they believe me and hating that I just lied to them. Not telling them something is hard enough, but this is an outright lie.

"And?" April prods. "Why are you here? It's your day off."

"There are online orders to process, we need to finish the fall window display, and honestly, home is awkward right now with my soon-to-be-ex-husband there."

The last part isn't a lie, it is awkward having Adam at home so much. We're always in each other's space.

Connie walks over to the counter with her right hand extended, palm-up, and wiggles her fingers. "Give me your phone. I'll text myself, so we have each other's numbers." I hand her my unlocked phone. "I agree with April," Connie adds, "I would've panicked if I tried to reach you and couldn't. We still have a killer roaming around, remember?"

Despite claiming she understands nothing technological, Connie finds the text app, texts herself, and hands the phone back to me, with no help or tech support. I hold the phone out to April, who takes it and adds her and Tamara's numbers.

"Why were the police at your house?" April asks. "Phillip said two patrol cars were there for quite a while."

Uh-oh. Adam and I didn't come up with a lie to explain why the police were there. I wonder if Phillip saw the police leave with evidence bags?

"Eric walked me home after the wake, and his colleagues came to pick him up."

It's not an outright lie. I know I'm lying by omission, but it feels less awful than saying something completely untrue.

"Phillip said there were two cars," April says, holding up two fingers, "Eric needs two cars to drive him around?" She raises her eyebrows and tilts her head.

She's not buying it. April knows me too well. Connie stands next to her in some kind of show of solidarity, crossing her arms in front of her chest.

"Ok, Eric needed a ride back to the station, that's true. He also told Adam that they eliminated him as a suspect. And... he called his colleagues to pick up.... some.... evidence...that appeared suddenly last night."

"Keep talking, my dear," Connie says, moving her hand in a rolling motion in front of her.

"I want to tell you, but I can't," I blurt out. "Eric said it would compromise the investigation. Please stop asking because I want to tell you, but I can't. And please don't mention it to anyone." I bring my palms together in a pleading motion in front of my face.

"Of course, we won't say anything! We know you'd tell us if you could. Let's just hope whatever it is, it breaks the case wide open and gets this murderer off our streets."

"Your secrets are always safe with us, my dear." Connie says as she wraps her arms around both of us and gives us a tight squeeze.

"Now that we've sorted that out," April says, "Latte Da's fall menu starts today and I'm craving a spiced caramel apple latte. Come with me to see the other fall yummies they added to their menu this year." April rubs her tummy in a circular motion.

As much as I love coffee, April loves it more. Her commitment to caffeine is admirable. Coffee is kind of her hobby.

"Give me five minutes to pack this order, so I can drop these off at the post office on our way." I gesture to the pile of packaged orders on the counter.

I place the packaged orders into a large reusable laundry bag with a pink and brown tartan pattern.

"That laundry bag is almost as big as your purse!" April says, pointing at the large bag, laughing, and looking at Connie who's covering her mouth with her hand to hide her laughter.

"Ha! Ha!" I say, "Everyone likes to make fun of my bag until they need me to carry something for them, don't they, April?"

I shoot April a sideways glance without lifting my head. April only carries a wristlet which acts as her phone case and wallet, so whenever we go anywhere together, she puts whatever doesn't fit in her wristlet—which is basically everything —in my tote. At any given time, half the contents in my bag belong to her.

My cell phone dings.

Adam: Can you meet me at 845 Mountain Road at 1pm? I want to show you something.

Me: Yes! C u there!

I'm so excited, I almost add a smiley emoji to the end of my text reply.

"I don't want to jinx it, but I think Adam found an apartment," I say. "I overheard him on the phone the other day. It sounded like he was arranging a viewing. He just texted me to meet him at 845 Mountain Road at 1 p.m."

I'm grinning so wide my cheeks hurt, and I do a little happy dance behind the counter.

"Mountain Road...those are older houses, right? Some converted to duplexes and triplexes, I think? And a few renovated as offices? A bit off the beaten path, but nice and close to the highway." April nods.

"That reminds me." Connie snaps her fingers and interjects, "I have an appointment tomorrow, late morning. Will you be OK by yourself for a couple of hours?"

"Of course," I tell her. "Is everything OK, Connie? You've had several appointments over the last few weeks, should we worry?"

Scared the answer might be yes, I brace myself. Connie is like a mother to me, and I can't imagine anything happening to her. Sure, she's slowing down a bit, but she's still the healthiest, most active senior I know.

"Nothing to worry about, my dear." She waves her hand dismissively. "At my age a few extra appointments are to be expected," she adds with a reassuring wink.

"Promise you'd tell us if something was wrong?" April extends her pinky finger to Connie for a pinky swear, and Connie, hooking her own pinky finger around April's, says, "pinky swear, my dear."

CHAPTER 23

April and I move our sunglasses from the tops of our heads to our eyes in unison as we step onto the sunny sidewalk. We walk toward Latte Da, enjoying the sun on our faces while I tell her Ryan is off their suspect list. I'm careful not to disclose where Ryan and Archie were when Paul was murdered. I worry she might press for details about Ryan's alibi, but lucky for me, she forgets all about Ryan when I tell her I caught Archie leaving Connie's apartment this morning.

"Just wow!" April's mouth hangs open in disbelief. "I mean, good for them. They deserve to be happy. It's shocking how we live in such a small town, and are so close with Connie, yet we never knew."

"I know," I agree with her. "I've been thinking the same thing lately. We assume because Harmony Lake is so tiny and everybody knows one another, that it's hard to keep a secret, but since Paul died, all we've done is find out people's secrets. It makes me wonder how well we really know anyone."

"Well, you know me!" April pulls the door and motions for me to go ahead of her. "I have no secrets. What you see is what you get."

She lets the door close behind her and joins me in line. Latte Da is busy today. Everyone is checking out the fall menu and ordering their favourite fall drinks they haven't had since last fall.

We order our coffees and sit at the only available table. I put my mocha chip iced coffee on the table, settle into my seat and pull out my knitting. I want to finish Hannah's cowl and hat before she comes home for Thanksgiving in a few weeks. Hopefully Eric will solve Paul's murder by then, and Hannah won't come home to a mother who is a murder suspect. Thinking about Hannah and what could happen if the police don't find Paul's killer makes me tearful. I swallow hard, fighting the urge to cry.

"Hey…" April touches my knee. "Are you OK? You aren't listening to my review of this Spiced Caramel Apple Latte, or is it so boring it's bringing you to tears?"

"I'm sorry," I drop my knitting in my lap. "Hannah will be home for Thanksgiving in three weeks, and I'm still a murder suspect. We haven't even told her about the investigation. She has no idea I'm a suspect, or that Adam was a suspect. I just want it solved so badly."

A familiar voice gets my attention, and I look toward the cash register where Kelly is paying for her order. Hairway to Heaven is next door, so I'm not surprised to run into her here. Kelly looks over and our eyes meet. She waves.

"Hey ladies!" she calls. "Save me a seat. I'll join you when Gingerbread Spiced Coffee is ready."

We wave back and nod.

"I still have feelings about her knowing about Adam and Stephanie and not saying anything," I whisper to April.

"I get it," April whispers, "but Stephanie is her sister. You're like my sister, and I wouldn't rat you out if you had an affair. Even if she told you, would it have changed anything? You and Adam were splitting up, anyway. The affair was still a threat to Adam's career. And you both would have wanted the text messages and photos kept private. It wouldn't have changed anything."

"You're right," I agree, "but it sucks to feel like I can't trust her. And she's such a good liar."

I sit up and move my large, cinnamon-coloured tote from the chair between April and me to the chair on my other side. As Kelly walks over, I pat the empty chair, motioning for her to sit down.

Kelly sits, puts her drink on the table, her purse on the floor, and sighs. I smile at her. Convincing liar or not, if she didn't kill Paul, Kelly needs all the support she can get right now.

She looks tired and wears less makeup than usual. Her hair is in a low ponytail instead of the full blow out she usually dons when she's working. Her only jewelry is her wedding band and a pair of delicate, gold love-knot earrings.

"Those earrings are lovely," April says, as if reading my mind.

April excels at small talk, a quality I admire and am grateful for because her gift for gab has saved me from an awkward silence more than once.

"Thank you. They were a gift from my grandparents when I was a teenager. They gave us each an identical pair,"—Kelly gestures toward the counter where Stephanie is paying for a drink—"but she has a metal allergy and can't wear any jewelry. None. No gold, no silver, nothing. She breaks out in a horrible rash that lasts for days if she even touches the stuff."

Trying not to react to Stephanie's presence, I move my tote bag from the chair beside me to the floor to make room for her.

"Listen, ladies, thanks for coming to Paul's celebration of life yesterday," Kelly says, putting one hand on my lap and her other hand on April's lap. "I wish I could've spent more time with you, but it was busy, and overwhelming. I'm not sure I even talked to everyone once."

April puts her hand on Kelly's hand, which is on her knee. "How was your first night at home?"

"Not good." Kelly shakes her head. "Much harder than I expected." She perks up. "Stephanie! Over here!" she waves until Stephanie notices her and waves back.

I give April a look that says, *Really? We're going to have coffee with Stephanie and pretend we're all friends?*

In return, April shoots me a look I interpret as, *I know, just grin and bear it for Kelly.*

"I thought it would be comforting to go home," Kelly explains, "with all our stuff and happy memories. But I was an emotional mess. I ended up calling Stephanie. She came and stayed with me."

"That's understandable," I say. "It's only been a week, you're still in shock, and maybe until the police arrest the mur —person, it's safer to not be alone, anyway."

"Look, Megan, before Stephanie comes over..." The three of us glance toward the counter. Stephanie is still waiting for her coffee. "I'm sorry I didn't tell you about her and Adam. I didn't know until after Paul died. The day before he died, she told me she was seeing someone, but she didn't tell me who it was. I found out during the investigation."

"I understand," I say, nodding. "You were in an awful position."

Kelly's version of events matches what Fred told me outside the pub yesterday.

"But, even if I knew,"—Kelly shrugs—"she's my sister. I don't think I would have told you. I hated knowing, and I hope this doesn't hurt our friendship."

Kelly places her hand on my knee again. Her big, sorrowful eyes are full of sincerity.

"Did you know Fred and Stephanie used the photos to blackmail Adam into leaving the firm? So, Stephanie could stay there without Fred having to worry about her and Adam working together?" I ask.

There isn't time to gauge Kelly's reaction because Stephanie is on her way to the table. We all plaster smiles to our faces.

"Hi ladies," Stephanie mutters, looking down at her drink.

"Hi," April and I say weakly in unison.

To distract myself from Stephanie's presence, and obsessing over what the heck Adam saw in her, I pick up my cowl and resume knitting.

"Is the salon open again?" April asks, fussing with her bangs.

"Yes," Kelly replies. "My stylists need to work. They worried their clients might go elsewhere if we didn't open again. And it's good for me to keep busy."

"Kelly will work at the salon during the day," Stephanie adds, "and at night she'll stay with us." Stephanie smiles at her sister. "She knows there's always a room for her at our house."

"It's amazing how well I sleep at Stephanie and Fred's house," Kelly says wistfully. "Every night, within an hour of eating supper, I'm so relaxed and drowsy that I take myself off to bed, and the next thing I know, it's morning. Stephanie and our mom think it's all the crying and emotions. Grief is exhausting."

"You're lucky to have each other," I say. "So how's Fred doing?"

I couldn't care less about Fred; I'm trying to do my part in this awkward, painful conversation. I take a sip of my iced coffee.

"He's been so great!" Kelly says. "He's upstairs right now, packing an overnight bag. I couldn't cope with going into the apartment today. Fred and Stephanie are making sure I don't have to."

"I think he's packing the car." Stephanie looks behind her, "He said he'll pop in to let us know when everything's packed, and we can head out."

April fusses with her bangs again. "No pressure, Kelly, but when you have time, I'd love to see you for a bang trim, and maybe you could clean up my ends? There's no rush, I won't go anywhere else. Whenever you're ready."

"I think I can squeeze you in tomorrow, hun! Let's pop next door so I can look at my schedule." Kelly stands up, grabs her drink, and gestures for April to follow her.

Next thing I know, they're both gone and I'm alone with Stephanie, pretending this isn't the most uncomfortable situation of my life.

"Well, this is awkward," Stephanie states the obvious.

"What? Having coffee with my husband's girlfriend?" I shrug. "Just another Thursday, Stephanie."

My words drip with sarcasm, and I don't care. I sip my iced coffee and resume knitting while sending telepathic messages to April telling her to hurry up.

Stephanie clears her throat. "I'm not his g—," she starts with a meek, wimpy voice.

"Girlfriend?" I finish her sentence for her. "You and Adam agree on that. Neither of you want you referred to as *Adam's girlfriend*."

I smile and look around for another free table, hoping I can move, alone. Nothing. Latte Da's new fall menu is a big event in Harmony Lake, and all the tables are full of people enjoying their beverages and the company of friends and neighbours. Except our table. There's no enjoyment at our table. *Please come back, April.*

"Megan, I'm sorry. I never intended to interfere in your marriage. I regret the affair. I wish it never happened."

I don't buy Stephanie's attempt at a heartfelt apology. Her forced sincerity is fake and patronizing.

"So, the affair wasn't part of your blackmail scheme from the beginning?" I ask.

It's crossed my mind more than once that blackmailing Adam was Stephanie's goal all along. Adam's departure from the firm creates an opportunity for everyone below him to move up a rung on the career ladder, including Stephanie.

"No," Stephanie says with her feeble voice, shaking her head. "There was no scheme. It was a mistake. Adam is charming and handsome, and I was weak."

Sneaky, sneaky Stephanie. I see what you're doing. You're subtly branding Adam as the pursuer and minimizing your own role in this mess. I'm thinking Stephanie is a skilled manipulator who hides behind her meek, shy persona act.

"I didn't want to blackmail anyone. That was all Fred," She looks down at her drink. "But I didn't stop him."

I'm not a lawyer, but I know Stephanie just admitted to aiding and abetting a crime. Blackmail is a crime, and Stephanie, aware that it was happening, didn't stop it or report it. She's a lawyer, for goodness' sake, an officer of the court. We both know I won't say anything. It would be her word against mine; nothing will come from her admission.

"Adam is a senior partner. He has a well-established career and reputation. It's much easier for him to find a new position than for me. I'm a newer lawyer and junior associate. I love Fred and want our marriage to work, but Fred can't move past the affair if Adam and I work together. I truly am sorry for everything, and I hope your marriage survives this as well."

Stephanie gives me a meek smile and looks down at her cup. I put my knitting on my lap and lean toward her.

"I'm telling you this for one reason," I hiss, trying to whisper and control my anger. "You and your blackmailing husband have no influence over my life. None." Squinting, I focus my gaze into her eyes. "Adam and I separated months before you and he swapped dirty text messages and photos. You did not destroy our marriage. Because *you aren't significant enough*. Your six-week affair didn't end our twenty-year marriage, years of apathy and disinterest did. You aren't even a blip on the radar of my life. You came along after our marriage ended. And knowing Adam as well as I do, you were just a distraction." I sneer, shaking my head.

I snatch my tote bag from the floor and drop my knitting into it. Then I stand up, throw my bag over my shoulder, grab my coffee, and stride to the door without looking back.

CHAPTER 24

SQUINTING INTO THE HARSH DAYLIGHT, I slide my sunglasses from the top of my head to my eyes and get my bearings as I swallow the last of my mocha chip iced coffee.

I dump my empty coffee cup in a nearby recycling receptacle and keep walking. I'm about to text April to explain why I bolted from Latte Da when my left shoulder bumps into someone walking toward me. When I look up to apologize, Fred Murphy is looking down at me.

It feels like the Murphys are everywhere I go today. I acknowledge Fred with a curt nod and continue on my way. Determined to as far away as possible from the Murphys, I pick up the pace as I go.

I'm in the alley beside Knitorious, almost at my car, when my phone dings from inside my bag.

Inside the car, I lock the door because, on top of everything else that happened this week, I've become someone who locks her car and house to feel safe, even when she's in them.

I plug my phone into the console and check my texts. Adam. We were just talking about him. I bet his ears are burning, as my mother used to say when someone she was thinking or talking about would call or show up.

Adam: Where are you? Everything OK?

I start the car and look at the time on the dashboard: 1:05 p.m. I'm late.

Me: On my way. Be there in 10.

On the short drive to Mountain Road, I contemplate how the Stephanie I met at Paul's wake and the Stephanie today at Latte Da are like different people. Which version of Stephanie Murphy is real and which one is fake?

Since learning about Adam and Stephanie's affair, I've wondered who made the first move. Fred said Stephanie made the first move, but after meeting meek and mousey yesterday-Stephanie, I couldn't imagine her making a first move to get anything, and figured Adam was more likely the pursuer. But after talking to today-Stephanie, I'm considering a third possibility: she chased him until he caught her. Stephanie let Adam believe the relationship was his idea, but she was in charge the entire time. Passive aggressive and manipulative.

I'm also not convinced Stephanie sent Adam's photo to her husband by accident. Maybe it was a calculated move to expose the affair and eliminate Adam as an obstacle on her career path.

845 Mountain Road is a large, Victorian-era house. I park on the road and sit in the car, assessing my surroundings. Mountain Road is in one of the oldest areas of Harmony Lake. The lots are large, with stately houses set far back from the road. Mature, leafy trees and tall, imposing coniferous trees punctuate the large front yards.

Several houses have signs indicating they're now duplexes, triplexes, or professional buildings. The neighbourhood predates sidewalks, and old-fashioned lamp posts connected by electrical wires line the east side of the road. During tourist season, Mountain Road is busy with tourists coming and going from the two vacation resorts in the mountains; skiers in the winter, and city-escapees in the summer.

I text Adam and let him know I'm outside. I exit the car and lock the door, listening for the chirp.

As I approach the wraparound porch, the large front door opens with Adam on the other side, waving. With a wide grin, he bounces on his heels and beckons me inside. He's downright giddy. Adam hasn't been this excited since he made senior partner at the firm.

One step inside and I can tell right away this house wasn't converted to residential apartments. It was renovated into office suites. I try to hide my disappointment and not ruin Adam's obvious joy. Hopefully, he's wrapped up in his own excitement and doesn't notice my initial shock that this isn't his new home.

What was originally a grand foyer is now a reception area. The sitting area has a leather sofa, two leather chairs, a coffee table, and two end tables with magazines and brochures fanned out.

To my left is an ornate, wooden reception desk and coat rack that look like they were custom made to match the restored ornate woodwork of the railings, banisters, and moldings throughout the house.

Behind the desk, a young woman smiles and waves while answering the phone. Her black hair almost camouflages her hands-free headset. When she ends her call, Adam introduces us. Her name is Lin Chow. She's friendly and has kind eyes.

Lin offers me a refreshment, which I decline. Then, Adam takes me on a tour of the main floor; meeting rooms, a kitchen, two washrooms, and a supply room with printers, a fax machine, boxes of paper, shredders, and office supplies. Exactly what you'd expect to find in a professional building.

We climb the wooden staircase, and at the end of the hall, on the right, we enter Adam's future office. It's already furnished in the same ornate-wood theme that was prevalent on the main floor. I look around and decide it's professional and lawyerly. A very Adam-like office.

Adam tells me his professional neighbours are an accountant, an insurance broker, a financial planner, and a psychologist who specializes in relationship and family counseling.

Despite my disappointment that he won't be living at 845 Mountain Road, I do my best to join in Adam's excitement, and decide against telling him about my interaction with Stephanie Murphy. He's happier and more hopeful than he has been in ages, and I don't want to ruin it.

We FaceTime Hannah and give her a tour too. When we end our video call, I notice it's almost 2:30 p.m.

"Shoot! I have to get going," I say. "I need to get to the bank and hardware store before they close."

I need to replace my bank card and get another set of keys cut. Since I have no idea if or when the police will return the contents of my bag, I need to replace my stuff.

"I'll walk you out," Adam says as we leave his new office. I say goodbye to Lin and tell her it was nice to meet her. "Congratulations on your new office, it's great," I say to Adam on the porch.

"Thanks. I'll see you at home after your errands."

With an air of vigilance, Adam stands guard on the porch while I walk to my car, lock myself inside, and drive off.

Seeing how concerned he is about our safety is making me paranoid that I'm not concerned enough. Was the knitting needle a warning that I would be next? I shudder at the thought. When I arrive at the bank, I park in a metered spot on the visible, well populated street in front of the bank, instead of parking for free in the secluded parking lot behind it. Changing my routine because of this situation makes me sad, but maybe right now, safety is more important than my feelings.

CHAPTER 25

RYAN WRIGHT IS KNEELING on the front porch, changing the lock on the front door. Why is he here?

"Hey, Ryan!" I smile. "Whatcha doin'?"

"Hey, Megan." He pauses his work to talk to me. "Adam asked me to come over and re-key the house. So, here I am." He smiles and shrugs.

"Oh, he didn't mention it."

I try to control the tone of my voice, so it won't give away how annoyed I am. *Thanks for talking to me about the new locks, Adam!*

"Listen, Ryan, I'm sorry I questioned your alibi, and I'm sorry if I made you feel like a murder suspect. I spoke with your Dad, and he cleared things up," I say, and gently touch his arm. "Also, congratulations on your three-year chip. I'm proud of you, and I promise your secret is safe with me. I'd never disclose it to anybody."

"I know you won't say anything, Megan." Ryan smiles. "I'm not ashamed of being a recovering alcoholic, but my livelihood depends on people being comfortable enough to let me into their homes and businesses. Near their families.

Some people would think twice if they knew about my past... issues."

"You'll always have work at chez Martel! We're useless at fixing anything. If not for you and Archie, we'd have to sit on boxes of flat-packed, unassembled furniture, surrounded by drippy faucets and broken appliances," I joke. Sort of.

I walk past Ryan and into the house. Adam is speaking to someone. I assume he's on the phone and try to make as little noise as possible. Entering the kitchen, I see that he isn't on the phone; he's at the kitchen table on his computer, talking to the empty room.

"Oscar, stop!" Adam says when he sees me.

"OK, transcription stopped," Oscar responds.

"It's a transcription app," Adam explains. "Instead of typing a letter, or email, or whatever, I dictate to the app, and it emails a transcript to me. Then I can forward the transcript to my legal secretary who can clean it up and format it."

"That's cool," I reply, "It sounds like a real time-saver."

I'm still annoyed about Adam having the locks changed without discussing it with me first.

"Why is Ryan changing the locks?" I ask, trying to sound non-confrontational.

"Because yesterday a killer accessed to your purse and every-thing in it, including the keys to our home," Adam justifies.

That means they also had access to the keys to Knitorious. I should've made this connection sooner. I make a mental note to ask Ryan to re-key Knitorious.

"You should have discussed it with me first, since I live here too. In fact, I'm supposed to be the only one who lives here. We had a plan, Adam. You said you'd find somewhere to live this month, not find office space. Have you even looked for an apartment?"

"I'm not moving out until the police arrest Paul's murder-er," he replies matter-of-factly.

"What if the police never arrest Paul's killer?" I ask. "What if this turns into one of those cold cases?" Frustration seeps into my voice despite my best efforts to stop it.

"Meg, I'm not budging on this," Adam insists. "We might not be together anymore, but you're still my wife. You'll always be Hannah's mother, and we'll always be family. I have to protect my family. I'm not moving out while a killer roams around town, rummaging around in your purse whenever they feel like it. If you want to deny the seriousness of the situation, that's fine. But you and your denial should get used to having me as a roommate. At least until the police solve this murder and the killer is behind bars."

Seething with anger, I clench my jaw muscles so hard they hurt. Adam decided all of this without talking to me. And on top of everything else, he's using his condescending lawyer voice. I hate when he uses his lawyer voice to argue with me.

"Again, *Adam*." I emphasize his name in the most condescending tone of voice I can summon, my version of his lawyer voice. "I'm an adult with the right to make my own decisions. Including whether we change the locks and whether we continue to live under the same roof. Maybe *I* should move out and *you* should stay here."

It's an empty threat. I'd never leave my home. It's more my home than Adam's, and he knows it. I chose every piece of furniture, tchotchke, and paint colour. I clean it, maintain it inside and out, and have spent countless nights and weekends alone inside it, raising Hannah, while Adam was elsewhere, focusing on his career.

"Don't be so dramatic, Meg!"

He did *not* just call me dramatic!

"This house is big enough for both of us," Adam argues. "We can co-exist a while longer without getting in each other's way."

"You're dismissing my feelings, Adam!" I growl out of frustration. "Stop doing that!" I shout.

"OK, transcription stopped," Oscar says, interrupting my tirade.

We look at the small device on the end table. Oscar's light changes colour from yellow to blue, and Adam and I look at each other.

"He recorded our argument?" I ask, pointing at Oscar, "and emailed it to you?" I ask, pointing at Adam's laptop.

"Maybe," Adam says, swiping his fingers across the track pad on his laptop to wake it up. Staring at the screen, he types on the keyboard. "Sure did!" he confirms. "I just got an email of our conversation starting when I said, *I'm not moving out the police arrest Paul's murderer.* Before that, one of us must've said something that triggered the dictation app."

I try to recall what we said that could have triggered Oscar, but it's a jumble of raised voices and hurt feelings. Oscar probably said something like, "Dictation started," but we didn't hear it over our shouting.

As if I need another reason to solve this murder. Adam's determination to live here until the killer is behind bars just rocketed to the top of the list.

"That's creepy. Have you received emails of our conversations before?" I ask.

"No," he replies without looking away from his laptop screen, "but I only installed the app a few days ago. Maybe I should delete it."

We're interrupted by a knock at the door.

"Ryan," we say in stereo.

"I totally forgot he was here," I comment on my way to answer it.

"Sorry to interrupt." Ryan cranes his neck, moving his head from side-to-side. He's trying to look past me into the house, probably to see what all the shouting is about. "Here are your keys."

He dangles two keys and two business cards between his thumb and forefinger.

I open my hand and Ryan drops the keys and cards into it. The business cards have a seven-digit code on the back. Seeing my confusion, Ryan explains that Adam upgraded to smart locks. *Of course, he did!* And he didn't discuss it with me first, either. We can lock and unlock the house with a key, a phone app, or by talking to Oscar.

"Do you want me to demonstrate?" Ryan offers.

I'm not interested in downloading another app, so I decline Ryan's offer and silently resolve to continue locking and unlocking the doors the old-school way, with a key.

Before he leaves, I ask Ryan if he can change the locks at Knitorious, too, since the store keys were also on my missing key ring. He tells me he's leaving today for an out-of-town job until Monday night. In the meantime, his dad will install an extra lock on the inside of both doors. Ryan says he'll meet me at the store first thing Tuesday morning and re-key both locks.

I give one of the business cards with the code on it to Adam, but don't give him a key. He won't be living here much longer anyway, I reason, so he can use the app.

I retrieve the spare key we keep hidden under the mat on the back deck and replace it with a new key Ryan gave me. When I come back in the house, Adam is staring at me.

"You won't use it anyway," I say. "You love technology. You'll only use the app."

He flips the business card over and uses his cell phone to scan the code, so he can download the app and set it up on his phone.

"Did you know the app works anywhere in the world?" Adam asks, super excited about his new tech toy. "If we leave the country, we can still lock and unlock the house. And we can set it so the door locks automatically thirty seconds after it closes."

I text Hannah and tell her I misplaced my keys and send her the code and app info.

CHAPTER 26

FRIDAY, September 20th

When I arrive at Knitorious, I'm relieved to find that—just like Ryan said—Archie installed a brand-new, shiny barrel-lock on both doors.

Connie invites me for a sleepover after work, and I accept. We haven't had a sleepover in ages, and I'm looking forward to the break from Adam.

After a yummy spaghetti Bolognese dinner, we apply face masks that, according to the packaging, will make us look ten years younger. Then we eat too many chocolate-covered almonds and drink wine while we binge-watch a new-to-us show. It's about three suburban homemakers who hold up a grocery store to solve their financial problems and end up working with in international money laundering ring. Hijinks and hilarity ensue.

Lying in the silence and darkness of Connie's spare room with Harlow purring next to my head, I'm more relaxed than I have been in days and welcome a good night's sleep.

SATURDAY, September 21st

The store is busy, which helps the day pass quickly. Life is returning to normal in Harmony Lake. There's no more crime scene tape, the salon is open for business as usual, and Paul's murder is consuming less of the town's collective consciousness. Paul's murder is still the hottest discussion topic in town. But between concocting theories about Paul's murder, people are talking about other things again. By the way, the latest theory is Paul's murder was a professional hit because he confronted a mob boss for littering.

After work, Connie packs an overnight bag, and she and Harlow leave to spend the rest of the weekend at Archie's place until Ryan can change the locks on Tuesday. I head home to wash, dry, and fold laundry while I watch the second season of the show Connie and I watched last night.

SUNDAY, September 22nd

Adam and I have our weekly FaceTime call with Hannah, and she tells us all about university and life in the big city. We're relieved and happy to see how well she's adjusting to living away from home. She's coping better than us, but she's not embroiled in a police investigation.

I spend some time outside, giving the gardens some much-needed maintenance, then have a shower and go to April and Tamara's house for lunch.

April's cheddar pancetta quiche with thyme is delicious, and Tamara spoils us with homemade chocolate eclairs. They have a knack for making elegant food look easy to prepare, and for making easy to prepare food look elegant. I tell April about my girls' night with Connie and recommend the show we watched. While we're talking, April and Tamara's phones chime.

"It's the WSBA group chat," Tamara says.

"Fred Murphy, Kelly Sinclair's brother-in-law, is missing," April reads. "The police would like anyone with information to contact them. Then it has Eric's number."

"Interesting," I say.

"I bet he did a runner," April surmises. "He killed Paul, and he knows the police are about to arrest him, so he took off." She shrugs her right shoulder.

April believes Fred did it. He's been her number one suspect since we found out he is Paul and Kelly's brother-in-law.

"If he did it, and now he's on the run, let's hope he's far away from here," Tamara adds. "Someone that desperate might do anything to avoid being caught. And if he already killed once, he has nothing to lose. I hope none of us run into him."

"Me too," I say.

"I wonder how long he's been missing. The last time I saw him was Thursday, after my dramatic exit from Latte Da. He was on the sidewalk."

"I didn't see him on Thursday, but I remember Kelly and Stephanie telling us he was loading the car with Kelly's stuff. They were waiting for him to finish up so they could leave, remember?" April asks, nudging me, and I nod.

"Well, I haven't seen him since I shook his hand at the pub on Wednesday in the condolence line," Tamara adds.

"What if he's not on the run?" I ask. "What if he discovered who killed Paul, and they killed him?"

Since the knitting needle from the murder scene turned up in my bag, I've wondered if the killer was trying to send me a message: stop snooping and stop asking questions.

April and Tamara give me leftovers for Adam, and I somehow manage not to eat his eclair on the drive home.

"April and T sent leftovers for you," I announce, holding up the glass containers with the quiche and eclair inside.

Adam is lounging on the sofa, watching golf. "Do you want them now? Or should I put them in the fridge?"

Adam pauses the TV and comes into the kitchen. He opens the cutlery drawer, grabs a fork, closes the drawer with his hip, takes the rubber lid off the glass container with the quiche. He leans against the counter and eats.

"This is fantastic," Adam says, using his fork to point at the quiche in the container.

"I know, right?" I answer. "Did you hear that Fred Murphy is missing?" I throw it out there without warning.

"No." He shakes without looking up and stabs the quiche with his fork. "Where did you hear that?"

"The WSBA texted the girls about it during lunch."

Adam swallows the last forkful of quiche and puts the container and his fork in the sink. I bite the inside of my lip to stop myself from pointing out that the dishwasher is literally right beside him, next to the sink. Infuriating. Then he reaches for the container with the eclair in it.

"The last time I saw Fred was on Thursday, outside Latte Da, right before I met you at your office. When did you last see him?" I ask.

He turns his back to me and eats the flaky eclair over the sink.

"Wednesday. At the pub. With you," he mumbles with his mouth full and still facing away from me.

We stand in silence for a moment. Adam finishes his éclair and wipes his hands.

"That was good. I'll text the girls and thank them." Then he returns to the family room, resumes the TV, and picks up his phone.

CHAPTER 27

Tuesday, September 24th

Ryan arrives and gets to work changing the locks as soon as I flip the sign from CLOSED to OPEN and unlock the door. I unpack a yarn order at the counter, trying not to let the random jingle of the bell as Ryan works trick me into looking up.

"Thanks for getting here so fast, Ryan. I'm sure you have a waiting list after leaving town for four days. I appreciate it."

"Anything for family!" he replies.

I look at him confused.

"We're practically family now," he explains. "Archie's my dad and Connie may as well be your mom, so that kind of makes us...step siblings? I think?"

It's his turn to look confused, but he's right.

"So, when does Adam open for business at his new office on Mountain Road?" Ryan asks.

His question takes me by surprise; I didn't realize Adam told anyone about his practice yet. I mentioned it to April and Connie, so maybe Connie told Archie, and Archie told Ryan?

"Sometime next month," I respond. "I didn't realize he mentioned it to you."

"He didn't," Ryan clarifies. "Lin told me. I think he'll enjoy working there. The building is well-maintained. Dad and I do most of the maintenance, so it's quality work." He smiles.

"Did Lin mention it when you were there doing a job?" I ask.

"No, she told me last night." He looks up at me. "Lin and I are dating. We had dinner last night when I got home."

Another secret I've learned this week to add to my ever-growing list.

"Lin and I just started dating. Not very many people know yet."

"Other than April and Connie, I won't say anything," I assure him. "I hope it works out, if that's what you both want, and you're happy together."

"Thanks, Megan." He drops a tool into his toolbox and stands up. "I have to run to my truck for a few minutes. I'll be back."

Ryan hurries through the store and leaves through the back door.

Seconds later, the jingle above the door heralds Eric's arrival.

"Long time no see." I smile, coming out from behind the counter. "Is this a business call or are you taking me up on my offer to teach you how to knit?" I ask, trying to ease the tension in his face.

Eric doesn't appreciate my attempt at humour. His jaw stays firmly clenched and the muscles around his eyes are taut. This is definitely a business call, and whatever brings him here is serious.

"We found Fred Murphy," he says.

I let out a sigh of relief. Why doesn't Eric look relieved?

"Alive?" I ask.

"He was in the back of a rented cube van parked in front of 845 Mountain Road."

Adam's new office! The look on my face must betray my shock because Eric asks if I'm familiar with the address. I sit in a chair in the cozy area.

"Adam rented an office there last week," I explain. "He's not open for business yet, but he showed me around on Thursday."

"Who else knows he rented an office there?" Eric asks, retrieving his trusty notebook and pen from his breast pocket. "And specifically, who knows you were there on Thursday?"

"Hannah," I reply. "We video chatted with her while we were there. Lin, the receptionist. Connie and April. That's it, as far as I know. I'm not sure if Adam has told anyone."

Then I remember!

"Oh! And Ryan Wright. He said Lin told him."

"Is Fred OK?" I need to know. "I mean, he was alive in the back of the cube van, right?"

My short-lived sense of relief disappears with the shake of Eric's head.

In shock, I fidget with my ring while Eric writes in his notebook until the back door thuds, breaking the silence.

"Hey, Detective Sloane," Ryan greets Eric and resumes working on the front door.

"Hello, Mr. Wright," Eric responds. "How are you?"

"I think I'll slip out for a minute and pick up a snack." An excuse to make myself scarce so Eric and Ryan can talk in private. I flip the sign on the door from OPEN to CLOSED. "Would either of you like anything?"

They decline my offer. I leave through the front door and speed walk to Artsy Tartsy.

April is behind the counter serving the only customer in the bakery. I glare at her, wide-eyed. April widens her eyes to match mine and calls for Tamara. Closing the office door behind her, Tamara joins April behind the counter. April finishes cashing out her customer, and we all watch him leave.

Though the bakery is empty, I stand on my tippy toes and lean over the counter. April and Tamara lean toward me until our faces are only inches apart.

"They found Fred," I whisper. "He's dead. He was at Adam's new office. In a rented cube van."

I explain that I can't stay long because I said I was only going to get a snack.

With no time to waste, we brainstorm. Who killed Fred? How did he die? Why did the killer choose the address on Mountain Road? Were they trying to implicate Adam or me? Maybe Fred couldn't live with what he'd done and killed himself. Maybe Fred discovered who the killer was, and they killed him to keep him quiet.

Fred was our number one suspect, and now, defeated, we're back at square one.

"Maybe there are two killers," April suggests. "Maybe Fred killed Paul, and someone murdered Fred to avenge Paul's death."

Her commitment to believing Fred murdered Paul is strong.

"Paul didn't have many friends," Tamara points out. "I can't think of anyone who would kill to avenge his death."

"He has a grieving widow," I remind everyone. "It wasn't Ryan," I affirm, then tell them about Ryan's out-of-town job.

"Ryan's alibis aren't always rock solid," April reminds me.

"He's dating Lin. Why would he leave a dead body outside her office?" I check the time on my phone while April and Tamara process the news about Ryan and Lin's budding relationship. "I have to get back."

"Take these," Tamara says, handing me a warm bag of oatmeal chocolate chip cookies. "They'll make your snack mission look real."

Two stores away from the Knitorious, I pull my phone out of my pocket. With the bag of cookies in one hand, I use my free hand to text Adam.

Me: They found Fred at your new office. He's dead.

Eric looks up when the door jingles. He closes his notebook and clicks his pen closed. Ryan is carrying his toolbox toward the back room; it seems he's almost finished. I turn the sign from CLOSED to OPEN and offer Eric a cookie. He declines. Who says no to fresh-baked oatmeal chocolate chip cookies?

Ryan returns from the backroom and hands me the new keys and an invoice. I offer him a cookie, and he happily reaches into the bag. He says goodbye to Eric and me, and leaves through the back door. I follow him and lock the door behind him, being sure to lock the barrel-lock. Just in case.

Walking toward the front of the store, I sense Eric is waiting to get me alone and ask me more questions.

"Where were you on Friday night, Megan?"

I knew it.

I tell him about my girl's night with Connie and recommend the show we watched.

Does his question mean Fred's died on Friday night? Or was Friday night the last time anyone saw him? Today is Tuesday. We learned about Fred's disappearance on Sunday, so why is Eric asking me about Friday night?

"Where was Adam while you were having a girl's night?"

"I don't know." I shrug. "You'd have to ask Adam. I told you, we don't monitor each other's whereabouts anymore."

Where were you, Adam? I have a mental flashback to his lack of reaction when I told him Fred was missing.

"Why is Friday night important?" I ask.

"The coroner estimates Mr. Murphy's time of death was sometime between Friday night and Saturday morning. With any luck, he'll narrow it down when he conducts the autopsy today."

This is more information than I expect. Or than I'm used to Eric sharing.

"Did you find Fred today?" I ask, hoping Eric still feels talkative.

"Last night, a local resident reported someone abandoned a cube van outside 845 Mountain Road. The caller said they first noticed it early Saturday morning."

That doesn't quite answer my question but is still more information than I expected. I'm surprised news of another crime scene hasn't made its way all over town, and to the WSBA group chat by now. But this happened last night, after business hours. After most people on Mountain Road left their offices for the day.

Eric thanks me for my time. I offer him another cookie, which he declines because his willpower is obviously super-human, and he leaves through the front door.

Adam hasn't responded to my text. I check again, and it says, *Read*, so I know he saw it. *Where are you, Adam? And where were you on Friday night?*

CHAPTER 28

It's almost lunchtime when someone knocks at the back door. Good timing, my tummy is rumbling for lunch.

Connie has her overnight bag in one hand, and Harlow's kitty carrier in the other. Holding the door for her, I notice a box on the ground.

"That must be a delivery." Connie nods toward the box. "I wish they'd use the front door when no one answers back here. Maybe we should put up a sign."

I carry the box into the store and place it on the counter. It's heavier than I expect; whatever is inside this box isn't yarn. Yarn is light, and even large boxes don't weigh this much.

Connie releases Harlow from his carrier and leaves her overnight bag on the apartment stairs.

"Weird delivery," I comment to Connie. "There's no shipping label, no return address, nothing. Are we expecting anything from a local dyer? Maybe they dropped it off."

She shakes her head.

The sender sealed the box with tape and scrawled KNITO-RIOUS across the top in black marker. I grab the letter opener from the cup of pens beside the cash register and slice it open.

A rock. Odd. Who would send us a rock? And why? Upon closer inspection, this rock is familiar. Where have I seen it before? Connie peeks inside the box, but neither of us picks up the grey, heart-shaped rock.

Harlow rubs his head against the open flaps of the box and tries to jump inside. Connie scoops him up and cuddles him. He purrs but pulls away from her, toward the box. Connie takes him to the kitchenette and distracts him with kitty treats.

"Why would someone send us a rock?" Connie asks.

We're both a bit shaken by the strange delivery. I wrack my brain trying to remember where I've seen the rock before. It's on the tip of my brain, but just out of my mental reach. I move the box to the coffee table in the sitting area. Connie and I sit on the sofa and resume staring at it.

Connie asks me if I've heard about Fred's death—and it comes to me!

"This is the rock Kelly uses to keep the back door open at Hairway to Heaven!" I jump up and shout, like it's the winning answer on a TV game show.

Connie and I inspect the rock, being careful not to touch it. It's grey with streaks of darker grey, and on one edge, there are rust-coloured blotches.

"Connie, I think this might be blood," I say. "I don't remember these blotches on the rock the night Paul died."

Calm and focussed, Connie walks to the front door, locks it, turns the OPEN sign to CLOSED, picks up her phone, and calls Eric. Meanwhile, I take some photos of the rock and the box with my phone.

ERIC LOOKS at the rock and nods like this somehow makes sense to him.

"This is another murder weapon, isn't it?" I ask. "Was Fred murdered by chance? Maybe by a hit to the head?"

Instead of answering me, Eric asks questions.

He asks what time we noticed the box. I told him what time I opened the door for Connie.

The last person to use the door before Connie was Ryan.

No, there were no people or vehicles behind the store when Connie arrived.

No, I didn't hear anything. No one knocked at the door.

I give him a list of customers who visited Knitorious today.

No, the store doesn't have surveillance video.

No, we don't think Wilde Flowers has surveillance video either. In fact, we don't think any of the businesses on Water Street have surveillance video. Except maybe Charmed & Dangerous, the jeweler, but they're way up the street.

Eric asks a fellow officer to guard the rock and the box it arrived in.

He tells us they will dust the back door for prints, "just in case," then he goes outside and fetches crime scene tape from the trunk of his car parked in front of the store. He tapes off access to the parking lot so cars can't enter or leave. Then he tapes off the back door to stop anyone from touching it.

Connie and I watch Eric go next door to Wilde Flowers. Knitorious shares a driveway and parking lot with Wilde Flowers, so we presume he's asking Phillip if he noticed the box, or any people, or cars in the parking lot today.

Standing in the store with Connie and the box, I feel a shiver travel down my spine. Why would Fred's killer bring the murder weapon here? Was the killer hoping I'd touch it and leave my fingerprints behind? Are they warning me I'm next? Is Fred's killer and Paul's killer the same person?

If there are two killers, it's unlikely both of them would send me evidence. Vulnerable and scared, I can't shake the feeling someone is watching me. Someone in my cozy, sweet town is murdering people and either trying to frame me for it or warn me that I'll be their next victim.

Connie suggests we close the store for the rest of the day. I agree with her idea, but I don't think we have a choice anyway, since it's a crime scene now.

Another uniformed officer opens the front door and greets the officer guarding the rock. He says he's here to pick up the box and the rock. Out of the corner of my eye, I spy Harlow gracefully and sneakily leap onto the table next to the box. I applaud his persistence. Connie sees him too, and when he launches himself again, she catches him mid-leap, preventing him from getting inside the box.

"I'll take Harlow upstairs, so he won't be in the way," I offer, holding out my hands to take the cat from her.

"Thank you, my dear." Connie smiles.

On my way upstairs, I pick up her overnight bag. I put Harlow and the bag in Connie's apartment and shut the door before he can bolt past me and run back to the store.

Part way down the stairs, I unlock my phone and sit for a moment.

Me: Are you finished questioning me? I'm not feeling well. I'd like to leave.

The low-grade nausea, which arrived at the exact moment I recognized the rock, is getting worse. I need to lie down. Somewhere quiet. Somewhere without a police presence.

Eric: I'll be there in a few minutes to drive you home.

It's a statement, not a question. He's not asking if I'd *like* him to drive me home, he's *informing* me he will drive me home. I suspect he wants to speak to Adam before I do.

Next, I text April and fill her in about the latest murder weapon showing up at Knitorious and send her the photos.

"Maybe I should stay," I suggest, struggling with guilt over leaving. "Or you could come home with me. It would give you a break from this." I gesture to the surrounding chaos.

"No need, my dear." Connie hugs me and rubs my back. "Archie is on his way here. You go home and get some rest." She tucks a stray curl behind my ear. "We'll talk in a couple of hours." She smiles.

Eric and I ride in silence to my house. Adam's car is in the driveway.

I drop my keys on the table by the door and march over to the dining room table, where Adam is doing whatever he does on his laptop.

"Why didn't you reply to my text?" I demand. "I know you saw it!" I'm almost shouting. Not quite, but close.

"Oh, jeez, Meg! I'm sorry," Adam says, smacking his forehead with his palm. "I saw it, but I was on the phone arranging insurance for the law practice. By the time I hung up, I forgot to text you back."

Really?! I tell him someone died, and it slips his mind to text me back?

When I tell Adam everything that happened today, the words explode out of me with such speed and urgency that Eric wouldn't be able to get a word in edgeways if he tried.

Then, after he's sufficiently overwhelmed with facts, I show Adam the photos of the rock I took with my phone.

Adam says nothing and focuses his gaze on the window while he processes the last few minutes.

"You took photos of the evidence?" Eric asks me while we wait for Adam to catch up.

I nod and show him the photos on my phone.

"Other than Connie and April, and now Adam, who else did you show them to?" he asks.

He's right, but I'm a little offended by his assumption.

"No one else," I say.

"Where were you on Friday night, Adam?" I ask.

I need to know, and Eric would've asked him, anyway.

"I was here until about 6 p.m., then I walked over to The Embassy for dinner," he recalls. "Friday's special is Fish and

Chips. Halibut or haddock. I chose halibut. After dinner, I had a couple of pints, chatted with Sheamus about golf, and left after the Leaf's preseason game. I got home around 10 p.m.?" He snaps his fingers and looks at Eric. "Phillip saw me, he pulled into his driveway as I got to the front door. We said hello. He wanted to talk to me about the garden." Adam looks from Eric to me. "Phillip says you're an over-waterer, Meg."

Wracked with guilt for thinking—even for a minute—that Adam could kill Fred, I remind myself the Adam that I know isn't capable of murder. At least I don't think he is. I hope he's not.

Is he really incapable of murder, or do I *want to believe* he's incapable of murder? Now I'm second-guessing myself; I'm exhausted, defeated, and confused.

I flop onto the family room sofa with an exasperated sigh. The house is silent except for the low hum of voices from Eric and Adam talking in the dining room. A few minutes, or an hour later—I have no idea because my eyes are closed and I'm trying to relax by focussing on my breathing—Adam walks Eric to the door, and Eric leaves.

"Meg, I think it's time for us to lawyer-up."

"Of course, you do," I respond. "You're a lawyer, and lawyers always think that."

A lawyer will limit Eric's access to us, which would slow down the investigation. A lot.

"If you want to lawyer-up, go ahead," I tell him. "I'm not doing anything that might slow down the investigation. I have nothing to hide. I didn't do anything."

"Speaking of lawyers," Adam continues, "I have my annual golf retreat tomorrow with the guys from law school, remember? Well, I emailed them and cancelled. I don't feel comfortable being four hours away with all this going on. And I have a lot to do. The practice opens in three weeks."

Wait. What? I forgot about his golf retreat; I stopped putting Adam's events in my calendar weeks ago.

He needs to go. I need him to go. We've been together way too much since this investigation started. We need respite this two-night retreat will provide. I'd have the house to myself for two glorious nights!

"No!" I insist, waving my hands in front of me. "Email them back and tell them you'll be there. You made these plans months ago, and we've already paid for it," I argue, trying to appeal to Adam's sense of practicality.

"I don't know…" he hems and haws.

Think, Megan, think! Give him all the reasons he should go.

"Listen, Adam, the last couple of weeks have been difficult. You left the firm, you were blackmailed twice, attended a funeral, and we've spent an uncomfortable amount of time together, which has been stressful. We're being investigated for murder, we're still adjusting to Hannah being away at school, and you're trying to set up a new practice in less than thirty days…" Gosh, it sounds awful when I say it out loud. "You deserve a couple of days away, to decompress, see your buddies, play some golf, and process everything that's happened." One last push; I put one hand on my chest and the other on his arm. "I think it would be unhealthy if you don't go," I whisper.

"I'll think about it," he says.

CHAPTER 29

WEDNESDAY, September 25th

I sip my coffee and watch through the living room window as Adam loads his golf clubs into his car, relieved he's going to the golf retreat.

Before I leave, I put a bottle of pinot grigio in the fridge to chill. The thought of having the house to myself makes me giddy with excitement. My big plans include movies, wine, popcorn with extra butter, and finishing Hannah's cowl.

AT LUNCHTIME, Connie leaves for another mystery appointment, and it's just Harlow and me in the store for the rest of the afternoon.

I package online orders and chat with the local charity knitting guild who visit the store on Wednesdays to knit, discuss future charity knitting projects, and order yarn for their upcoming projects. This month they're working on *knitted knockers* for the Knitted Knockers organization. Knitted knockers are prosthetic breast inserts that cancer survivors put in their bras after a mastectomy. They're always in demand at local hospitals and cancer support groups. Connie gives the charity guild a discount on the yarn they purchase for charity knitting.

The store closes at 6 p.m., but at 5:30 p.m., Harlow and I are the only ones here, so I close early and gather up the online orders, so I can drop them off before the post office closes.

After I give Harlow his dinner, I hide a few kitty treats in his favourite napping spots.

"Connie will be home soon," I assure the tuxedo cat as he cleans his face with his freshly licked paw.

AT THE POST OFFICE, I join the short line right behind Tamara who's mailing a care package to their daughter, Rachel. Tamara tells me she and April are going out for dinner and a movie tonight.

"You should join us," Tamara offers with a smile.

"Thanks," I respond, "but I've waited months to have the house to myself, and I plan to enjoy every minute."

I also don't want to be the third wheel on their date night.

After Tamara drops off her package, we say goodbye on her way out, then I drop off the on-line orders and leave.

I have to walk back to Knitorious to get my car. Walking past Ho Lee Chow, my tummy rumbles, so I stop and peruse the menu in their window and contemplate adding a combo number seven to my evening plans.

"Hey Megan! It's nice to see you again. Your curly hair gave you away," the unfamiliar man says, walking toward me.

He's next to me now, and even up close I don't recognize him. How does he know my name? I'm sure we've never met.

"Hi!" I smile. "I'm sorry, have we met?"

"You don't remember me?" He clutches his chest and has a mock heart attack. "You're breaking my heart, Megan."

"I was your cab driver the other night," he reminds me, pointing to a taxi parked on the road.

The yellow car has Precious Cargo Cab Company painted on the side and printed on the roof light. I shake my head. He must have the wrong Megan.

"You flagged me down just off Mountain Road?" he says, trying to jog my memory. "Really late Friday night... or I guess it was really early Saturday morning. You're even prettier in the daylight, by the way."

I still don't recognize him, but he piques my interest when he mentions Mountain Road and Friday night.

"You were at a house party and had a few drinks. You said you didn't want to drive home," he recalls. "You were walking home and flagged me down when I drove past. You don't remember any of it? Wow, you must've had more to drink than I thought."

"Where did you drop me off?" I ask.

"At home," he replies. "You live above the knitting store, right? I dropped you off out front."

I confirm he's referring to Knitorious, even though it's the only knitting store in town. He asks again if I live above it, but I don't answer him.

"I was kind of hoping we'd run into each other again," he says, shifting his weight and looking at the ground. "I was wondering if maybe I could get your number? We got along so well in the cab. But I'm not allowed to ask customers for their number. Since you're not in my cab, technically you're not a customer anymore." He shrugs with a smile.

I'm processing his words and twirling my ring.

"Is that a wedding ring?" He asks, pointing his chin toward my ring. "I looked for a ring when I drove you home. You weren't wearing one, so I assumed you're single. I'm sorry if I got it wrong."

"Was I wearing any other jewelry?" I ask.

"I don't think so." He shakes his head. "If you were, I didn't notice. Why? Did you lose something that night? I didn't find any jewelry when I cleaned out the cab after my shift. Sometimes there's an earring, or a broken necklace, or something, but nothing on Friday night." He pauses for a moment. "So, I guess getting your number is out of the question?"

I don't give him my number. Instead, I ask for his name and number, and he's eager to give me both. He's in a hurry to pick up an order from Ho Lee Chow and deliver it to a customer. Opening the door to the restaurant, he says he hopes to hear from me soon, then disappears inside.

He'll hear from someone soon, that's for sure.

I take a couple of photos of his cab with my phone, being sure to capture both the license plate number and the cab number.

I dial Eric's number and hurry toward Knitorious.

Voicemail.

"Hi, Eric. It's Megan Martel. Can you please call me back? It's important. Thanks." I end the call. "Where are you, Eric?" I mumble with a frustrated sigh.

I text him the photos of the cab, and the driver's name and number. Then I send a second text with the highlights of my conversation with the cab driver, and what he said about our alleged interaction on Friday night.

I was neither at a house party, nor intoxicated when the driver said he picked me up on Mountain Road. In fact, I was nowhere near Mountain Road on Friday night, and I was never in a cab.

Unbeknownst to the driver, I wasn't in his cab on Friday night. Fred and Paul's killer was.

The knot in my stomach grows larger with every step I take toward Knitorious. Ignoring the pending sense of doom taking over my body, I pick up the pace as I close the distance between me and the parking lot. When my car is in sight, I sprint across the parking lot, pressing the button on the key chain that unlocks the door, and lock myself inside. I open my phone and plug it into the console, then stare at it.

Now what?

Should I call April? No. This investigation shouldn't upend her and Tamara's life, and I don't want to interrupt their date night. Between raising two kids, running a business, and the hectic pace of life, date nights for them are rare. I'm all too familiar with the consequences of ignoring the required maintenance of your marriage.

Should I call Connie? No. I'm not convinced she's being completely honest about her mystery appointments, and I don't want to cause her to worry or stress if it might impact her health.

Should I call Adam? What good would that do? He's four hours away from Harmony Lake. It's late in the day, so he's finished golfing and probably had at least a few drinks with his buddies by now.

Maybe I should call Kelly. No. Bad idea. If my suspicion is correct, calling Kelly could put one or both of us in danger. I cross this option off my mental list of potential next moves.

Why hasn't Eric called me back?

I take a few deep breaths and devise a plan. Go home, put on my pyjamas, then decide what to do. With any luck, in the meantime, Eric will call me back.

I lock the front door behind me, making sure I have my phone and didn't leave it in the car. Phone in hand, I take a deep breath, and drop my bag on the bench by the door. Looking forward to a chilled glass of pinot, I head toward the kitchen.

I gasp and bring my hand to my mouth.

My stomach sinks and my heart pounds double time.

"What are you doing here?" I demand. "How did you get in?"

CHAPTER 30

STEPHANIE MURPHY STARES at me from my kitchen table. She taps her leather-gloved finger on the handle of the gun laying on the table in front of her. Her curly hair is pulled into a tight bun,—I assume so she doesn't leave any stray hairs behind— and her expression is emotionless, her eyes empty, soulless voids.

I tighten my grip on my phone and move my hand behind my back.

"Hi Megan," Stephanie says, her voice flat. "I let myself in with the spare key. The one under the mat at the back door." She taps the table in front of her. "Put your phone here, please. I know it's in the hand behind your back."

I inch toward the table and Stephanie wraps her hand around the handle of the gun. Her index finger hovers over the trigger while I carefully place my phone on the table, face up. I take a few backward steps, never diverting my gaze from Stephanie and the gun.

"That's far enough," she says.

"How did you know about the spare key?" I ask.

"You're so predictably suburban, Megan," she chortles,

rolling her eyes. "It was literally the second place I looked." she smiles, smug about her resourcefulness.

"What do you want?" I ask.

"To plant some evidence that will prove without a doubt it was you who killed Paul and Fred," she replies, "then kill you. Or more accurately, help you put yourself out of your misery."

"Adam will be back soon," I lie.

"Not according to the GPS tracker I put on his car." She shakes her head. Without breaking eye contact with me, Stephanie reaches into a pocket, retrieves her phone, and places it on the table in front of her. She grips the handle of the gun with one hand and uses her teeth to remove the glove from her other hand. She unlocks her phone. "He's over three hours away at a golf resort. We both know he won't be home tonight." She sneers.

Stephanie moves her hand away from the gun to put her glove back on, but she keeps the gun close to her. I don't have time to do anything, like run away or snatch the gun. I need to distract her while I think of a way out. I have to keep her talking.

"Where's Kelly?" I ask, inquiring about her sister. "Won't she wonder where you are?"

Please don't tell me you've hurt Kelly, or she's your partner in crime.

"Don't worry about Kelly," Stephanie replies. "She's sound asleep until tomorrow morning. I'm getting better at dosing the sleeping medication. Her deep sleep should last long enough that she won't notice my absence, and she won't wake up groggy and suspicious."

"You drug your sister?"

"Only sometimes." She shrugs like it's no big deal. "Like tonight, so I can visit you. And Friday night when I snuck out to... take care of Fred. Other than that, just here and there. It helps her sleep without waking up in the night, crying over her loser husband." Stephanie shakes her head. "What a waste of tears," she scoffs.

It's safe to assume Stephanie hated Paul.

"I also drugged Fred the night I visited Paul," she adds. "And tonight, I'm going to drug you, except you won't wake up." She smiles.

She's a psychopath. I have to get out of here.

"Your phone will give you away," I say. "If the police check it, they'll know you were here. If you leave now, I won't say anything. If anyone asks, I'll say you picked up something for Kelly."

I know she won't fall for it, but I need to prolong this conversation as long as possible while I plan my escape.

"It's a burner," she informs me. "I'll dispose of it as soon as I leave."

Of course, it is and of course, she will. She's thought of everything.

"How? Like down a sewer grate, or something?" I ask, stalling what feels like my inevitable downfall.

Ding!

Before Stephanie can answer me, my phone dings and we both look at the screen. It's a text.

Eric: Call me.

By instinct, I take a step forward. Stephanie points the gun at me, shaking her head.

Brrrrring! Brrrrring! My phone lights up. Eric's name flashes on the call display, and I've never wanted to answer a phone call so much in my life.

Still pointing the gun at me, Stephanie uses her other gloved hand to turn off the phone. "I understand why you killed Paul," I say, trying to sound sympathetic. "He stole the photos you sent to Kelly and used them to blackmail people. He would've exposed your affair with Adam. But why did you kill Fred? He's your husband, and he loved you. He told me at Paul's celebration of life."

"You've got some things right," Stephanie admits. "I didn't want my affair with Adam to become public knowledge, and Paul stealing the photos from Kelly was the final straw. But the biggest reason was to save my sister. Paul was a loser, and he sucked her dry financially again and again. Yet, despite everything he'd done, Kelly insisted she loved him, and refused to leave him. He would've kept dragging her down with him. Paul knew she was too good for him, that's why he spied on her phone and her email. He knew she'd realize she could do better and leave him."

"So, you went to see Paul that night intending to kill him?" I clarify.

Committing murder with yarn and a knitting needle she found at the crime scene, before sunset, with witnesses right downstairs, doesn't seem well planned. And judging by the predicament I find myself in, Stephanie strikes me as a meticulous planner.

"No. I never planned to kill anyone," she explains. "When he discovered my affair with Adam, Fred and I agreed there could be no more secrets. We agreed to be honest with each other to save our marriage. That's when Fred told me he loaned Paul money. He helped Paul pay off his latest gambling debt and stop a money lender from placing a lien on the building. If they lost the building, my sister would have lost her home and business." The tone of Stephanie's voice grows angrier as she speaks, and her jaw clenches tighter until she's speaking through her clenched teeth. "I was furious. To make it worse, Fred told me Paul planned to pay us back by robbing my sister's business and selling her equipment. Fred said Paul already had a buyer lined up. He said Kelly wouldn't lose any money because she had insurance." She shakes her head and tears well up in her eyes.

At least, I think tears are welling up in her eyes. It's hard to tell for sure. The sun is setting, and inside the house is getting darker by the minute.

"Fred seemed OK with this robbery scheme, which made me more furious," she continues. "So, after an early dinner, I helped Fred fall asleep. Then, I left my phone at home and drove to Harmony Lake. My plan was to tell my sister about Paul's latest gambling debt, Fred's loan to stop the foreclosure of the building, and her husband's plan to steal from her."

Tears stream down Stephanie's cheeks. While she pauses for a few breaths and composes herself, I wonder why she left her phone at home if she wasn't planning to kill Paul.

"Would you like a glass of water?" I ask, in part to buy time, and in part to keep her calm since she has a gun.

Maybe I can throw the glass at her head and run away. She shakes her head.

"The back door was open. Kelly used a rock to prop it open and let in some fresh air," Stephanie recalls. "I went inside, but Kelly was busy with a customer and didn't notice me. I didn't want to interrupt, so I went upstairs to the apartment. It never occurred to me Paul would be there. He's part of so many committees, and organizations that Kelly says he's out almost every evening. But when I opened the door, there he was, standing in the kitchen in his undershirt, pouring milk into a giant bowl of cereal. I felt sick just looking at him. I confronted him. I told him I knew about the gambling, the money lender, and the robbery plan. He was so smug and arrogant."

Our eyes are locked, but in my peripheral vision, through the window behind her, the bushes rustle. Like a large animal is there. The largest animal I've ever seen in the backyard is an obese squirrel who eats scraps the neighbours leave him. I blink, attempting to reset my vision in case my eyes are playing tricks on me.

"He held up his phone and showed me the photos," Stephanie recollects, holding up her empty hand as if she were holding a phone. "He admitted he stole them from Kelly's phone. Paul threatened me. He said if I told Kelly, he'd send them to every lawyer and every law firm in the country. He demanded twenty thousand dollars to keep quiet and gave me until midnight to transfer the money to his account. Then he told me to leave, or he'd upload the photos to social media sites that instant. He turned the TV on and sat at the table to eat his cereal."

Stephanie talks like she's in a trance. Her face is emotion-less, and her tone of voice is eerily calm and even. She's looking into my eyes, but I'm not sure if she sees me, or the events she's reliving. Her steady hand rests on the gun.

"I left," she says, "but part way down the stairs, I realized I could have Paul charged with extortion and harassment. I decided to threaten him and beat him at his own game. So, I went back to the apartment. The TV was blaring, and he didn't hear me come in. He was at the table, sitting with his back to me. He slurped his cereal so loudly I heard it over the TV. This was my opportunity. I could rid myself, and my sister, of him forever. Eliminate him. The yarn and knitting needles were right in front of me. The yarn was already in a big loop. I wrapped it around my hands and put one of the knitting needles in my mouth. Then I crept up behind him, looped the yarn around his neck, and pulled with all my might. I couldn't get it tight enough. I wasn't strong enough. Using the knitting needle as a garrote, I tightened the yarn around his neck. Paul kicked his feet and tried to pry his fingers between the yarn and his neck. Then he just stopped. I let go of the yarn slowly, and his head fell forward into the cereal bowl. He looked dead, but I wasn't sure. I hoped he was dead, but I didn't want to check. I crept backwards out of the apartment. I kept the knitting needle in case Paul woke up. If he attacked me, I could stab him with it or something."

Stephanie blinks a few times and rejoins me in the present moment. She dabs her eyes with a gloved finger.

"When you think about it, I did you and Adam a favour

by killing Paul," she proclaims. "If he made those photos public, it would have ruined all of our lives."

I hope she doesn't expect me to thank her.

Stephanie pulls a pill bottle from the pocket of her jacket and places it on the table next to the gun and my phone.

"I could use a glass of wine," I state, ignoring the pill bottle. "Would you like some?"

I don't want wine; I want the bottle. Maybe if I hurl it at Stephanie's head, I can separate her from the gun long enough to escape.

"No thank you," she replies. "But you go ahead. You'll need something to swallow these with,"—she smiles and shakes the pill bottle—"and wine will get the job done."

Making slow, intentional movements so Stephanie won't panic and shoot me, I open the cupboard and get a wine glass. A shard of glass could be a good back-up weapon if my wine bottle idea doesn't work. I inhale and swallow hard, nervous about turning my back on Stephanie long enough to retrieve the wine bottle from the fridge.

"Why did you kill Fred?" I ask, trying to distract her. "Because he found out you killed Paul?"

"No," she replies. "He believed either you or Adam murdered Paul."

As she speaks, I open the fridge and get the wine, then turn to face her again, closing the fridge door with my hip.

"After he died, we found out Paul had no insurance," Stephanie says. "My sister couldn't afford his final expenses, so Fred and I paid for everything. Fred resented spending the money. He wanted to get some of it back by following through with Paul's plan to burglarize the salon. I begged him not to do it. I told him if he got caught, he'd go to jail. Fred relented and promised me he wouldn't rob the salon. Then, on Friday night, Fred said he was going to work for a few hours because something came up.

I open the bottle and leave it on the counter to breathe while I choose my moment.

"He lied," she continues to unburden herself. "According to the GPS tracker I put on Fred's car, he didn't go to work. He went to a truck rental place. I knew right away what he was doing, and I drove to the salon. The rental truck was parked by the back door. I tried to reason with him. I begged him not to do it. He told me everything was my fault. He said if I hadn't had an affair, then you and Adam wouldn't have killed Paul to keep it a secret, and Paul wouldn't have died before he could pay us back."

It's an excellent theory, but Fred couldn't have been more wrong. I pour some wine into the glass.

"He turned his back to me to open the back of the truck. I picked up the rock by the salon door and hit him in the head," Stephanie confesses. "The top of his body fell into the open truck, I just had to lift his bottom half up there too. I locked him in the back of the truck and thought about what to do next. I needed to point the evidence toward you and Adam. I looked at Adam's GPS and saw that he'd spent time at 845 Mountain Road, so that's where I left Fred and the truck. After I dropped off Fred, I hailed a passing cab and pretended I was you. It was late, and I was too tired to walk back to Water Street. I asked the cab driver to drop me off at Knitorious. From there, I walked to the salon to collect my car and the rock."

"The cab driver fell for it," I confirm, picking up the wine glass and swirling the contents while I work up the nerve to put my plan into action.

"I told the driver my name was Megan," Stephanie admits. "It was dark, we have similar hair, and similar body types, so I figured if the police asked the cab driver who was in his cab, he'd lead them to you." She shrugs a shoulder.

Now or never. I bring the glass to my lips and take a small

sip. When returning the glass to the counter, I miss on purpose, and it shatters on the wood floor.

"Darn it!" I yell, jumping back when the wine glass hits the floor.

Stephanie grabs the gun and stands up to assess the situation. Shards of glass and splattered wine cover the kitchen floor. She isn't reacting as I hoped she would. I hoped the breaking glass would startle Stephanie enough to jump up *without* grabbing the gun. Her eyes dart back and forth from me to the mess on the floor.

"I better pick these up." Eying the biggest, sharpest shard of glass, I bend to pick it up.

"Stop!" Stephanie shouts. "Don't move!" She cocks the gun.

"OK, transcription stopped," says Oscar's humanoid voice as I raise my hands to my shoulders and slowly stand up.

I guess Adam didn't uninstall the glitchy dictation app before he left.

Stephanie looks in the direction Oscar's voice came from, then back at me. Her eyes are wide with panic and confusion.

"Who said that? What does it mean?" She's raises the gun higher, aiming it at my head.

I tell her about Oscar and explain the dictation app that Adam installed.

"You know how much Adam loves technology," I quip, trying to de-escalate her stress level. I stare down the barrel of the gun she's still pointing at my head. "He has to try every new gadget." I shrug. "He just can't help himself."

I explain that this specific app has a glitch and sometimes records when it's not supposed to.

"How do we erase it?" She demands with urgency.

"We don't," I reply. "The device emails the transcript to Adam. It's probably in his inbox already."

Stephanie's eyes are wide with horror, and her hand trembles, making the gun unsteady. I mentally ask the universe to please make her scared enough to make a mistake, but not scared enough to shoot me.

"Go get it and bring it here," Stephanie demands, waving the gun between me and Oscar.

With my hands still raised, I take slow steps to the end table in the family room, sensing the gun as it follows my every step. This positions me close to the front door. I could be outside in three seconds. I squat slowly, turning my head toward Stephanie. I explain to her that I have to lower my hands to move the table and unplug the device.

I have no intention of unplugging anything. I have a new plan.

Stephanie nods and I turn my attention back to Oscar. Out of the corner of my eye, an indistinct blur moves near the front door. I blink, looking into the darkness, but there's nothing. The stress of this situation must be messing with me.

I lower my hands and pretend to reach behind the table, but I pick up the ceramic yarn bowl instead. With my back still to Stephanie, I stand up, holding the yarn bowl against my chest like a Frisbee.

In one fast motion, I spin toward Stephanie and launch the yarn bowl, frisbee-style, toward her head. As the ceramic sheep-inspired bowl hurtles through the air, Stephanie instinctively raises her hands and turns her head to protect her face, pointing the gun toward the ceiling.

I run.

"Oscar! Unlock the door," I shout.

"OK," Oscar replies as the lock clicks.

Reaching for the doorknob, something behind me shuffles, and without looking, I imagine Stephanie coming after me. As I turn the doorknob, the door swings open, forcing me behind it, into a corner. Police rush through the open door. I try to weave through the onslaught of blue uniforms and escape. One of them grabs my waist and shoves me into the corner. He stands, gun drawn, with his back to me like a human shield.

Bang! A single gunshot.

A thud.

Stephanie lets out a breathy grunt.

I crouch down to make myself the smallest target possible and try to peek around and through the officer's legs.

I can't see anything except a gun on the family room floor. My human shield adjusts his stance, and Stephanie's top half comes into view. She's facedown with a knee wedged in her back. Someone cuffs her hands behind her back. The cop on her back leans forward. It's Eric.

"He's hit!" a woman's voice yells.

He who? Who's hit? Did Stephanie shoot Eric?

"Who's hit?" I ask my human shield.

No answer. Either he can't hear me or he's ignoring me. I ask louder. No answer.

The house is crawling with police officers, inside and out. The lights from the patrol cars bounce off the walls, creating a strobe effect. One by one, the police turn on every light in the house.

"All clear!" the woman's voice yells.

The human shield turns to me and takes my arm.

"Are you OK?" he asks, pulling me up from my crouched position.

I nod as he looks me over, checking for signs of injury.

Physically, I'm OK. Aside from that, I'm not sure yet, stay tuned.

Still kneeling next to Stephanie, Eric stands up and walks toward me, smiling.

"Were you shot?" I scan him for evidence of a gunshot wound.

"No," he says, shaking his head and smiling.

How can he smile? He smiles in the face of murder, turns

down fresh oatmeal chocolate chip cookies, Eric Sloane is a freak. A freak who just saved my life.

"I heard a gunshot," I insist. "Someone said, *he's hit*."

"She was talking about Oscar," Eric explains. "Stephanie shot Oscar. He was the only casualty tonight. Well, Oscar and your yarn bowl."

"Poor Oscar," I say.

I'll miss him.

ERIC GOT the photos of the cab and the information about the driver I texted to him earlier. When I didn't answer his text or phone call, he knew there was a problem. He came to the house, peeked in a few windows, and assessed the situation. Then he contacted Adam, who used the app on his phone to unlock the house. Back-up arrived without lights and sirens, and officers surrounded the house, positioning themselves so Stephanie wouldn't see them if she looked outside. This explains why the bushes in the backyard were moving; it wasn't my eyes after all.

Eric sneaked into the house and hid. He aimed his gun at Stephanie and waited. Biding his time until she pointed her gun away from me and he could intervene. He was the blur I saw near the front door before I attempted to escape. He heard her entire confession.

When I flung the yarn bowl at Stephanie's head, it gave Eric the opportunity to sneak up behind her while I was out of the line of fire. That was the shuffling, gunshot, thud, and grunt I heard. Eric says he lunged at her and grabbed her wrists, commandeering her arms to keep her from aiming the gun at anyone. Stephanie put up a struggle, and the gun discharged, shooting Oscar. Stephanie hit the floor face first with Eric on her back. Oscar was in the wrong place at the wrong time.

CHAPTER 31

WEDNESDAY, October 2nd

April and I took a road trip to Toronto for a few days to visit Hannah and Rachel. We took the girls shopping and saw a musical. On our way home, we stopped for two days of pampering and spa treatments at Ste. Anne's Spa. The break and change of scenery gave me the time and space I needed to process everything that happened.

When I got home last night, I found boxes scattered throughout the house. Moving boxes. Adam is moving! He's moving into one of the new condos at the Harbourview Condominium complex. He gets possession this weekend and says he'll move on Saturday, if I'm ready to be alone in the house. I am. More than ready.

Besides, while I was away, he had a state-of-the-art security system installed, complete with cameras. I live in the safest house in Harmony Lake.

Today is my morning off, but I work this afternoon. I take my time walking to work and stop at Latte Da. I've missed their coffee.

Standing in the long line, I'm deciding what to order, when someone taps my shoulder.

"I saw you walk past the salon and took a chance that you would stop for coffee," Kelly says hesitantly.

I throw my arms around her. She hugs me tightly and we cry. Ugly crying. Sobbing. The loud, wet, messy crying that isn't discreet. We help ourselves to napkins and find a quiet corner. We start speaking at the same time, apologizing to each other.

She's sorry for not realizing her sister was a psychopath. I'm sorry she lost her husband and brother-in-law. She's sorry she didn't tell me her sister was having an affair with Adam as soon as she found out. I'm sorry I suspected her of murder. She's sorry she hasn't called since Stephanie almost killed me. I'm sorry I didn't call her to warn her when I figured out Stephanie was the killer. When we run out of tears and apologies, we get back in line to order our coffees.

"Eric let me see Stephanie," Kelly whispers while we wait for our coffees. "I asked her not to cause any more suffering with a trial. She agreed."

"It's over?" I ask, dubious. "Like, completely over?"

"It's over," she assures me, nodding.

We get our coffees and go outside. After another long hug, we agree to meet at Ho Lee Chow for dinner after work. Kelly returns to the salon, and I continue to Knitorious.

The jingle of the bell above the door, and the warm, comforting smell of the store hit me and I realize how much I missed the store. I close the door behind me and stand still, taking deep breaths and allowing the comfort to wash over me and through me.

"Welcome back, my dear." Connie gives me a long, swaying hug. "The store isn't the same without you," she says when we finally pull apart.

"Welcome back, Megan," Archie says, hugging me. "Thank goodness you're OK," he whispers in my ear.

We sit in the cozy sitting area, and Harlow wakes up from his nap in the front window. He gives me the side-eye, indulges in a yawn accompanied by a long stretch, then slinks over. Purring, he graces my lap with his presence.

Connie and Archie ask after Hannah and Rachel, so I pull out my phone and show them photos of our visit while Connie fusses over me and strokes my hair.

I tell them about Adam moving out, but they already know. Apparently, I'm the last one to find out.

"We look forward to having him as a neighbour," Connie says, then exchanges a sneaky glance with Archie.

"I don't follow," I say.

"Well, my dear, Archie and I also purchased one of the new condos," Connie explains. "It's time we take our relationship to the next level. I was going to move to Archie's house" —she gestures to Archie—"but Ryan lives there, too, and he wouldn't want to live with two senior citizens."

"And I'd love to move here," Archie adds, "but the stairs to the apartment are too much for my hip." He gyrates his hips to illustrate his point.

"So, we decided a new condo would be perfect," Connie concludes. "It's not his, it's not mine, it's ours." She has that content, optimistic glow that people get when they're in love.

"And it's perfect for the 'retirement lifestyle' we're trying out," Archie says, using air quotes around "retirement lifestyle."

Wow. A lot can happen in a week.

"I'm happy for you," I say. "It's wonderful news. So, does this explain your mystery appointments? You were house hunting?"

"Yes!" Connie taps my knee. "And I'm so glad it's over. If I never shop for another home again, it'll be too soon."

"I assume Harlow will move to the condo too? Or will he make the daily commute?" I ask.

Connie and Archie laugh.

"He's coming with us," she confirms. "But we're planning to do some travelling, and we'd like him to stay at

Knitorious while we're away. If that's OK with you, my dear."

Of course, it's OK with me! Harlow belongs here. He's as much a part of Knitorious as Connie and the yarn.

"Who will run Knitorious while you two globe trot and try out your 'retirement lifestyle?'" I ask, using air quotes for the first time in my life.

"You will, of course," Connie replies, like it's the most obvious thing in the world. "Knitorious needs you, and you need Knitorious. I'm not the only one entering a new phase of life. You aren't a wife and full-time mother anymore, my dear. You're a soon-to-be-single woman who has a grown child and a business to run."

"You want me to work full-time?" I ask, confused.

"I want you to *own* it, my dear," Connie clarifies. "We'll work out the details later, but trust me, you need this store, and this store needs you. I knew when I met you almost seventeen years ago that you would take over Knitorious one day."

For the second time today, tears fill my eyes, and a lump forms in my throat. I blink back tears and try to swallow the lump while Connie takes my hand, and Archie gets the box of tissues from the counter.

"I'll still be here part time, when we aren't travelling," Connie explains, waggling her index finger. "You'll never get rid of me, no matter how hard you try." She winks. "But it's time for me to step aside and watch you blossom. It's time for you to make this store your own."

I don't know what to say, and I'm too choked up to talk, anyway. With tears streaming down my face, I nod and reach out to hug her, squishing Harlow.

When the bell above the door jingles, Connie gets up and greets Eric while I dry my eyes and compose myself. She and Archie tell him about their new condo.

Why does it seem like every time I see Eric, I've either just finished crying, or I'm on the verge of crying? He must think I'm an emotionally unstable mess. I stand up and turn around to face them.

"Hi Eric," I say smiling.

He didn't get any less hot while I was away. In fact, he's hotter than I remember.

"Hi Megan." He smiles. "Welcome home. Don't worry, I'm not here to question you." He chuckles.

I laugh with him, thinking this is the first time he's shared his sense of humour. Solving this case agrees with him; this is the most relaxed I've ever seen him.

"I'm returning the items we took into evidence. The huge purse and its contents." He hands me a gift bag and a large evidence bag filled with smaller evidence bags. "Except the knitting needle," he adds. "We have to keep that."

He can keep the knitting needle forever, for all I care. I never want to see it again. I put the evidence bag behind the counter and open the gift bag, and pull out a heavy wad of tissue paper.

"A small token of my appreciation for your help with this case," Eric explains. "I know it's not the same as the one you made," he says, switching his weight from one foot to the other, "but I wanted to replace the one you lost. Connie gave me the number of a local potter who makes them."

I open the tissue paper and find a new sheep-shaped yarn bowl. Similar to the one that broke when I hurled it at Stephanie's head.

"Thank you," I say. "I love it. It's one of the most thoughtful gifts I've ever received. Actually, I have something for you too."

I reach into my caramel-coloured tote, pull out a gift bag, and hand it to him.

"I was going to drop it off at the station later. To say thank you for saving my life, and my reputation, and believing I was innocent."

He opens the bag and pulls out the hat and scarf I knitted for him. I found the yarn at Romni Wools when April and I were in Toronto. I knit them in the car, when it was April's turn to drive, and at the spa. It's a worsted-weight, merino blend in the same shade of forest green as the polo shirt he wore the night we had dinner at the store and he questioned me. The yarn has honey-coloured flecks of tweed that match the honey-coloured flecks in his eyes.

He saved my life; it's the least I could do. No gift will ever be adequate to thank him.

Either Eric Sloane is a talented actor, has good manners, or he's touched by the gift.

"Thank you. I love them." He clears his throat. "No one has ever knit for me."

"Really? Well, I knit a small gift of appreciation for everyone who saves my life," I tease. "So, there could be more hand-knit gifts in your future if you save my life again."

He laughs. "I'll keep that in mind."

"So, what's next for you?" I ask. "I'm sure you're ready to wave goodbye to our quirky little town and watch us fade in your rear-view mirror as you move on to bigger and better cases."

"Funny you should ask," Eric responds. "Harmony Lake PD is starting their own major crimes unit, and they offered me a position."

"And?" I ask. "What did you say?"

"I hope they offered to make you the head of the department," Connie adds.

"I accepted," he answers me, then looks at Connie. "And yes, I will be in charge of the unit. The unit of one. Me. I will be the major crimes division of the HLPD."

We congratulate him, and Archie shakes his hand.

"This town is perfect for me," Eric says. "I can fish in the summer and ski in the winter. And with the low crime rate, I'll have enough time off to enjoy both."

I guess I'll be seeing him around town since he'll be a local.

He asks if we can recommend a real estate agent since he'll need somewhere to live in town. Connie asks him what he's looking for in a home, and he lists his criteria: something small, no yard to maintain, and centrally located. He says he doesn't have very much stuff but needs enough room to store his fishing gear, ski equipment, and a jet ski.

Connie looks at me. I look back at her and smile. She widens her eyes and upgrades her look to a glare, and I sense I'm missing something. She opens her eyes even wider and nods her head. She's trying to tell me something, I just know it. But I'm not getting it. I'm better at this game when April and I play it.

Giving up, Connie lets out an exasperated sigh, and throws her hands in the air.

"It just so happens, Detective Sergeant, that I'll be moving out of the upstairs apartment in the next few weeks, and it will be vacant," Connie says.

"Would you consider renting it to me?" Eric asks. "It would be perfect!"

"That would be up to the owner," Connie replies, glaring at me.

I smile, sure I'm missing something again.

"Megan, will you be looking for a tenant for the upstairs apartment?" she asks.

It's me! I'm the owner, I realize, catching up to everyone else in this conversation. The idea of owning Knitorious is so new, I haven't grasped it yet.

"Yes! I'd love to have you upstairs," I declare.

An immediate rush of heat floods my face as the last word leaves my mouth, and I realize how it sounds. I'm sure Eric knows what I mean. Talking to him as a cop is easier than talking to him as a... friend? Potential tenant? Neighbour?

Harlow winds himself around Eric's ankles. *Thank you, Harlow, for the distraction.*

"Harlow obviously wants you to move in, and I can't say no to him," I say.

"You've never seen the upstairs apartment, have you Eric?" Connie asks. "Megan, why don't you take Eric upstairs so he can see what he's agreeing to before he commits."

"Sure!" I look at Eric. "Do you have a few minutes?"

"Lead the way," he says.

As we climb the stairs, Eric says, "I didn't realize you own Knitorious. I thought Connie was the owner."

"Ditto," I say, opening the apartment door and stepping inside. "I only found today that I'll be the owner," I explain. "I'm still getting used to the idea. There's been a lot of change lately, you know? Hannah moved away, my marriage ended, I was a murder suspect, then almost a murder victim, and now I'm about to become a business owner. It's a lot to keep up with."

"You'll be an amazing business owner," he says, looking into my eyes. "And landlady." He walks around, giving himself a tour of the apartment. "This place is perfect! I love it!"

"Then it's yours!" I tell him. "You can move in as soon as Connie moves out. Listen Eric, thank you again for saving my life. I'm not sure it would've ended well if you hadn't shown up when you did."

"Yes, it would," he assures me, nodding. "You're smarter and tougher than you give yourself credit for." He walks into a bedroom and raises his voice so I can hear him, "I think you have it backwards. I might have saved Stephanie from you." He comes back into the kitchen. "You were practically out of there when I intervened. You would've fought your way out, and you would've won, whether any cops showed up. Trust me, I have good instincts about these things." He smiles. "And please stop thanking me now."

"Just one more." I hold up my index finger. "Thank you for putting up with me nosing around in your investigation. I'm sure I didn't make your job any easier."

"You were a huge help," he insists. "You'd make a great partner."

"That was it," I say, "The last thank you. Well for this. If you do something else nice for me, I reserve the right to thank you for it."

"Deal," he agrees, extending his hand, and we shake on it.

"Harmony Lake isn't usually this exciting, you know," I warn him. "If you're expecting a steady flow of murder investigations, it might disappoint you when you realize the major crimes unit solves cases like littering, jaywalking, and double parking. Maybe you should sign a short-term lease in case you miss the excitement of the big city."

"I have a feeling Harmony Lake is more exciting than it looks." He smirks. "And if it isn't, that's fine with me. I'm ready for a bit of boredom. It'll be a nice change.

We laugh and head back downstairs.

TURN the page for a sneak peek of Killer Cables: A Knitorious Murder Mystery Book 2

CLICK HERE to download the knitting patterns for the hat and scarf Megan knit for Eric.

CLICK HERE to read an exclusive bonus scene from Knit One Murder Two.

A Knitorious Murder Mystery Book 2

Killer
Cables

REAGAN DAVIS

COPYRIGHT

ISBN: 978-1-9990435-5-1 (ebook)

ISBN: 978-1-9990435-4-4 (print)

CHAPTER 1

"Who's a smart girl? It's you! That's right, you're a smart girl!" I say with a high-pitched and excited voice.

I squeeze the plush duckie to make it quack and toss it across the room.

"Go get it, Sophie!"

Sophie scurries across the wood floor and down the hall. She doesn't apply her corgi-brakes fast enough and slides past the duckie and into the carpet by the front door. She shakes it off, picks up the duckie and prances back to me proudly with her head held high.

Sophie has been staying with me since last week when her human, Laura Pingle, slipped on a patch of ice while taking her trash to the curb and broke her leg in two places. Laura was rushed to the hospital, had to have emergency surgery, and I jumped at the opportunity to look after Sophie until she gets home.

"Which sweater do you want to wear today, Sophie?"

Laura is a knitter, so Sophie has an impressive wardrobe of hand-knit dog sweaters. I grabbed about eight of them when I picked up Sophie's supplies at Laura's house, and I left behind at least eight more. Most of them have some shade of purple as either the main colour or an accent colour.

"How about this one?" I ask, holding up her purple and black hounds tooth sweater with a folded turtleneck.

She doesn't disagree since she's an easy-going roommate, so I slip the sweater over her head. By instinct, she lifts one paw, then the other so I can feed them through the impossibly short sleeves of the sweater. She's done this before and knows the drill.

I attach her purple leash to her purple collar, slip on my winter boots, crush my curly, chestnut-brown hair under a hand-knit hat, wrap the matching scarf around my neck, and put on my coat.

I check my pockets to make sure my gloves are there, check Sophie's leash to make sure we have enough poop bags for the day and grab my cranberry-coloured tote bag.

I take a last look in the mirror by the door, and I remove a stray eyelash from under one of my hazel eyes. Then I pull my lip balm from my purse and smear a layer on my lips to act as a barrier against the cold, dry, winter air.

"Oscar, I'm leaving," I say into the void.

"OK. I'm arming the house," Oscar replies in a humanoid voice.

Oscar is a digital voice assistant. This is my second Oscar. My ex-husband, Adam, and our eighteen-year-old daughter, Hannah, gave him to me for Christmas.

I call him Oscar 2.0. because Oscar 1.0 died suddenly last September when he was shot by someone who broke into my house to kill me. Thankfully, Oscar 1.0 was the only fatality that night. The killer's previous two victims weren't as lucky. They lost their lives, while I only lost a WI-FI enabled device.

Sophie and I leave the house and I hear the door lock behind me. Good job, Oscar.

I started the car ten minutes ago using the remote starter

on my keychain. It's too cold to walk to Water Street, so Sophie and I get in the warm car for the short drive to work.

I PARK in the small parking lot behind the store, and instead of going in through the back door like I would normally, Sophie and I walk around to the front of the store and across the street to the park so Sophie can have a walk and do her business.

This time of year, this early in the day, and this close to the lake, it's too cold to stay outside for very long. As soon as Sophie finishes her business, we high-tail it back across the street to Knitorious.

I unlock the front door and kick the snow off my boots against the brick wall next to it. Then I turn the knob and open the door, listening for the jingle of the bell. It's one of my favourite sounds.

Knitorious is warm, cozy, and feels like home. Other than my house, it's the only place where walking through the door makes me feel both relaxed and reinvigorated at the same time.

I undo Sophie's leash and take her sweater off. She gives herself a shake and follows me to the back room where I put our outerwear and her leash away. I freshen Sophie's water bowl, turn on the lights in the store, and flip the sign from CLOSED to OPEN.

"It's showtime," I say to Sophie, just like Connie always says to me when she unlocks the door and turns the sign.

Tuesdays aren't our busiest day of the week, but we're in the midst of the winter tourist season, so I expect a steady flow of customers.

Despite Harmony Lake's small size, we squeeze in a large population of tourists during the winter and summer tourist seasons.

In the winter, tourists flock to the two ski resorts in the Harmony Hills Mountains, staying at various rental houses or the new condominium development at the end of Water Street. In the summer, they flock to the same places to exchange their city lives for life by the lake and the small-town-living experience.

Besides being small, Harmony Lake is secluded which gives it the feeling of being farther away from the hustle and bustle of the city than it is.

I can see the lake from the front window of the store. It's across the street just beyond the park where I walked Sophie. Behind me, to the north, are the Harmony Hills Mountains. Tiny, as mountain ranges go, it's still a popular destination for weekend skiers and snowboarders. Geographically, Harmony Lake can't be a bigger town without moving either a lake or a small mountain range.

Knitorious is closed on Sundays and Mondays, so I spend Tuesdays returning phone calls, answering emails, and processing online orders placed on the store website over the weekend. I turn on the laptop and power it up while I check the store voicemail.

The bell over the door jingles, and a well-wrapped Connie comes in from the cold.

"Good morning, Megan, my dear."

She always says it in a sing-song voice.

Sophie jumps up from her dog bed to greet Connie. She wags her Corgi butt while following Connie to the back room.

"Good morning to you, too, Sophie," Connie sings from the back room.

Connie is my mother-friend, and I'm her daughter-friend.

We met sixteen years ago when Adam, Hannah, and I first moved to Harmony Lake. We became instant friends and soon after we became family.

I lost my mum just after Hannah's first birthday, and Hannah was born when I was barely twenty-one, so when Connie and I met, I was young, newly married, a new mum, and grieving. She welcomed us, nurtured us and filled the mother and grandmother-shaped holes we had in our hearts. At almost seventy years young, she's the most beautiful, smart, and sophisticated woman I know.

I started working here part-time about five years ago and became the store owner a few months ago when Connie decided it was time for her to retire and move out of the upstairs apartment. She moved into a new condo with her boyfriend, Archie, and I took over as owner of Knitorious. So, now I own Knitorious and Connie works here part time. We've come full circle.

"Today feels bittersweet," Connie says as she crouches down to pet Sophie.

"I know. It'll be hard to let her go," I say. "It's been nice having a pet in the store again, and we fit together so well, you know? We're like kindred spirits. At home, we both like to eat, nap, and cuddle. At the store, we both like to greet the customers and visit with everyone. I'll miss her."

"Well, Archie and I are going south in a couple of weeks, so you'll have Harlow to help you run the store and keep you company while we're away. I know Laura has missed Sophie dearly and can't wait to see her."

Harlow is Connie's cat. When Connie owned the store and lived upstairs, Harlow had unrestricted access to both the store and the apartment. He was a fixture here. Even non-knitters would come in just to visit him. The store feels incomplete without him here, but I get custody of him when Connie and Archie travel, so he stays at Knitorious while they're away.

"Phillip said he's picking Laura up from the hospital and taking her home this morning. Once she's settled, I'll take Sophie home to her," I explain. "According to Phillip, Laura's looking at six weeks in a cast, so he and I will work out a schedule to take turns walking her—Sophie, I mean, not Laura."

Phillip Wilde is my neighbour. He owns Wilde Flowers, the florist next door to Knitorious, and he lives next door to me. We're work neighbours and home neighbours.

Ding! I have a text.

April: Coffee?

Me: Yes! Please!

April and I have been best friends since we met at a Mommy-and-Me group sixteen years ago. Her daughter, Rachel, and my Hannah are the same age and best friends. They're just starting their second semester of university in Toronto. April and her wife, Tamara, also have a son, Zach, who's fifteen, plays hockey, and eats them out of house and home, according to his mothers.

April and Tamara are the owners of Artsy Tartsy, the bakery up the street from Knitorious. Tamara is a talented pastry chef.

About ten minutes after we text, April arrives. She is a tall, blue-eyed, blonde angel bearing the gift of caffeine. She sets a tray of three to-go cups from the Latte Da café on the counter, then pulls off her mitts, puts them in her coat pockets, and pulls a paper bag from her coat pocket.

"Courtesy of T," she says, dropping the paper bag on the counter. "Dog treats from the latest test batch. We hope Sophie likes them."

I open the bag and remove a small, round treat that looks like a tennis ball. Sophie is sitting at attention, staring intently at my hand with the treat in it.

She takes her role as taste tester seriously.

"Here you go, Soph!"

I toss the small treat onto her dog bed, and she devours it.

"She likes it," I say to April.

Tamara is creating a line of organic, artisanal dog and cat

treats to donate to the upcoming silent auction that will benefit our local animal shelter.

Connie and her friends are celebrating their fiftieth high school reunion soon and have decided to host a fundraising event that will be open to the entire town. It will benefit The Vanity Fur Centre for Animal Health & Wellness. (We locals call it the Animal Centre or the AC, for short).

Most local businesses are donating items for the silent auction portion of the fundraiser, and April and Tamara are donating pet treats. At least, they are if Tamara perfects a recipe she's happy with.

Sophie is part of their focus group and enjoys free samples in exchange for her opinion. Her opinion is always the same: more treats please!

"Have you decided what you're donating to the silent auction yet?" April asks me as she hands a coffee to Connie who's sitting on the sofa in the cozy sitting area of the store.

I nod while swallowing my first satisfying sip of coffee and feel its warmth spread through my body. "Yes. The winning bidder will get a bespoke pair of socks, hand knit by me, in a yarn of their choice."

Coffee in hand, I walk over to join them on the comfy, overstuffed furniture.

"I've also been knitting baby blankets using leftover yarn for the charity knitting guild's donation to the AC," I say. "We have about ten so far. The AC uses them to line the kennels for the shelter animals and wrap up preemie and sick animals to keep them warm."

"Who will be your date, my dear?" Connie asks.

Here we go.

"I'm a confident, independent woman who enjoys her own company and can attend a function alone," I reply.

To be honest, I haven't decided for sure if I'm going yet, but if I do, I thought I might take Sophie as my plus one. I could knit her a little corgi-sized dress to wear. After all, it is a fundraiser to benefit animals and Laura is the founder and executive director of the AC. But it might also earn me a crazy-dog-lady label that I don't need.

"You should be dating!" Connie declares, throwing her hands into the air with dramatic flair.

Connie is a hand-talker who visually punctuates her words when she speaks.

"Thirty-nine is too young to be alone. You should be having fun and meeting people," she says.

"And by people, I mean men," she clarifies, in case I don't know what she means.

April nods in agreement to everything Connie says. It's two against one.

"What do you think, Detective Sergeant?" Connie asks, looking behind me. "Don't you agree that Megan is too young for a life of solitude?"

I turn around to see Eric standing near the counter. He's blushing. I look back at Connie who has a look of smug enjoyment on her face for making him blush. She teases him about being shy when he is supposed to be a case-hardened cop.

Eric is my tenant. He lives in the apartment above the store, and he's new to Harmony Lake.

Last fall, when Harmony Lake had its first murder ever (technically, our first two murders), the Harmony Lake Police Department borrowed Eric Sloane from a larger department because they didn't have a major crimes unit.

After he solved both murders (with a little help) and prevented a third murder (mine), Harmony Lake implemented its own unit and offered him a job. He is now the major crimes unit. Just him.

He's forty-ish, divorced, no kids, and hot. Seriously hot. He's distractingly attractive. I've had to train myself to not stare.

"Hi, Eric." I smile.

I walk over to the counter, silently thanking him for his good timing and interrupting an uncomfortable conversation.

"Hi, Megan," he says. "Do you have a package for me?"

I tilt my head and raise my eyebrows. A package? Am I meant to have a package? Did I forget about a package for Eric? I shake my head.

"Phillip was supposed to drop off a package of hand-knit dog sweaters for me to pick up. Laura Pingle is donating them to the silent auction."

I shake my head. "No, Phillip hasn't dropped anything off."

"Amy is expecting me to bring it to the station today."

Officer Amy Andrews is organizing the silent auction portion of the fundraiser. The AC provides free veterinary care for PSD Tundra, Harmony Lake's police dog. Amy is his handler and supporting the AC is important to her. I've heard from some other business owners that she takes her role as organizer seriously. One person likened her to a bride on one of those Bridezilla reality shows.

"I'll text Phillip," I offer.

I text Phillip and ask if he has a package for Eric. While I'm waiting for a response, Connie asks April if there's been any more news about Mega Mart and the AC.

Mega Mart is a huge multi-national big box store that wants to put down roots in Harmony Lake. Residents and town council are divided. Half of them welcome the jobs and one-stop convenience the store would bring. Half of them don't want a large, faceless corporation invading our cozy, sweet town and competing with locally owned, small businesses.

"When I was at the town council meeting in December, the council was divided right down the middle," April says, using her hand like a knife and slicing it through the air. "Laura was there, and she told the pro-Mega-Mart council members that a Mega Mart would go on that land 'over my dead body.' Those were her exact words. Then she said, 'not even over my dead body, because I intend to donate the land before I die to ensure it will always be The Vanity Fur Centre for Animal Health & Wellness.' Then she stomped out of the meeting."

April attends town council meetings on behalf of the Water Street Business Association (WSBA). Each year a different member takes a turn attending the meetings, reporting any relevant details to the rest of the WSBA, and advocating on our behalf.

Ding! I check my phone.

"Laura didn't give him anything for you," I tell Eric. "He says he dropped Laura off at home a couple of hours ago and is going back at lunch to check on her and take her some soup. He says he'll ask her about the sweaters then."

Eric rubs the back of his neck with his hand.

"I'm planning to walk over to Laura's house in a little while to drop off Sophie. I can ask her for the package and bring it back to the store, if that helps," I offer.

"Why don't I walk over there with you," he suggests. "It'll give me a chance to introduce myself and thank her personally. I'm still the new guy in town, and an introduction from an already-trusted community member like you is always helpful."

He crosses his arms in front of his chest. Don't stare at his chest, Megan. Or his biceps. Look away.

"Also, I really don't want to show up at the station and tell Amy I don't have that package," he adds.

"You two should go now while I'm here to watch the store." Connie makes a sweeping motion with her hands to dismiss us.

"I guess I'll get Sophie and me bundled up," I say, shrugging.

"Great," Eric says, "I'll go get my coat."

CHAPTER 2

APRIL SAYS goodbye and heads back to the bakery, and I help Sophie put on her sweater and attach her leash.

Connie asks me how I'll walk with Sophie while carrying all her accessories to Laura's house at the same time.

I tell her about my plan to drop off Sophie's stuff when I go back to Laura's house after dinner to walk Sophie. This trip is just to fill the immediate need to reunite Laura and Sophie.

Sophie has at least three complete sets of everything she needs. She has a bed, toys, dishes, food, and sweaters at my house, Laura's house, and Knitorious. Those are just the Sophie accessories I know about. She's adored and doted on, and there's no doubt Laura makes sure Sophie has everything she needs to keep her comfortable and happy.

"Ready?"

Eric is wearing the hat and scarf I knitted for him after he saved my life. The honey-coloured flecks in the forest-green yarn complement the honey-coloured flecks in his brown eyes. Don't stare at his eyes, Megan.

While Eric holds the back door open, Sophie goes out first, then I step outside, directly onto a patch of ice. I immediately slip and lose my balance as inelegantly and awkwardly as humanly possible.

Eric grabs one of my flailing arms to stop me from falling and helps me recover my balance.

"Thank you," I say.

"Are you OK?" he asks.

"Yes, I'm fine."

Except for my dignity, which is bruised.

"I have to remember to put salt on that patch of ice as soon as I get back from Laura's," I tell him.

"Are you taking Sophie to Aunt Laura's?" Phillip calls out while loading floral arrangements into his delivery van.

"Hi Phillip," I say. "Yes, we'll drop Sophie off, check to see if Laura needs anything, and pick up the dog sweaters she's donating to the silent auction."

We walk closer to Phillip because he's soft spoken, and it's difficult to hear him, even across our small, shared parking lot.

"Thanks again for dog sitting, Megan. I'd have done it, but you know, Kevin," he says, rolling his eyes and jabbing his thumb behind him, toward his store.

He bends down, scratches Sophie between the ears, and stands up again.

"Before I left, I settled Aunt Laura into her chair in front of the TV. She has her knee scooter on one side, but she shouldn't need to get up for anything until I go back with her lunch. I set up a table on her other side with the TV remotes, a glass of water, her knitting, her laptop, and the phone. I also gave her the mail that has accumulated while she's been away, and she already had her daily coffee while she was waiting to be discharged. She shouldn't need anything, but I appreciate you checking in."

Organization is Phillip's superpower; he takes it to a new level. If organization were an Olympic sport, he'd represent Canada and have gold medals to show for it.

"I'm sorry I don't have the sweaters," Phillip says, looking at Eric. "I didn't know I was responsible for delivering them. Her phone rang as I was getting ready to leave. She answered it and probably forgot to tell me to take them."

"No worries," Eric says. "This works out better. I can thank her in person for the donation."

"OK, well I'm picking up her soup after I make these deliveries, so I might see you there," Phillip says, then raises his index finger. "Oh! And her sister, Glenda, should arrive any time. She's coming to stay with Aunt Laura and help her until the cast comes off."

"Got it," I say. "Drive safe."

I give him a wave as we walk away from him.

It's warmer than it was earlier, and the sun is out now, so it's almost a pleasant day for a walk. Sophie is in front of me, crisscrossing back and forth, contentedly trotting from one side of the sidewalk to the other, sniffing as she goes.

"So, Phillip is Laura's nephew?" Eric asks.

Sometimes, I forget he's new and doesn't know how everyone in town is connected to one another.

"Not exactly," I say. "Laura and Phillip's mum were best friends, so she's like an aunt to him. Laura and her late husband didn't have kids, and now that Phillip's mother has passed, Laura dotes on him like his mother did, and Phillip takes care of her like he did his mother. Harmony Lake is a small community with deep connections. Not all families here are biological."

"Like you and Connie," he says.

"Right." I nod.

"If they're so close, and he seems fond of Sophie, why didn't he look after Sophie while Laura was in the hospital?" he asks.

"Kevin doesn't like dogs," I explain.

"Who's Kevin? His son, dad, partner?"

"His chihuahua," I explain. "Kevin is a small dog with a

big personality. He has definite likes and dislikes, and he definitely doesn't like other dogs."

"Can I ask something else?"

"Of course," I say.

"What's going on with Laura Pingle and the Animal Centre? What was April talking about at the store?"

"When Laura, Connie, and the rest of their clique were growing up, Laura's dad was the town veterinarian. He founded the Harmony Lake Animal Hospital. As the hospital grew, he took on a younger vet named Dr. Pingle. Laura and Dr. Pingle fell in love and got married. When they took over the animal hospital, they expanded it to include a shelter and an adoption centre for homeless pets. Then they expanded it again to include a sanctuary for rehabilitating injured and sick local wildlife. Because of its reputation as a haven for animals, the Pingles were often asked to take in exotic pets confiscated in nearby towns or abandoned by people who found their care too difficult. But since the exotic animals and local wildlife they rehabilitated couldn't be released back into the wild, they acquired quite a few permanent residents along with the expenses of caring for them. The AC sits on a huge plot of land so the Pingles built barns, buildings, and fenced-in areas to meet the needs of the various animals who live there. But as the organization expanded, the income from the animal hospital wasn't enough to cover the expenses of the hospital, the shelter, and the sanctuary. So, they created the Education Centre which, in exchange for a fee, provides tours and educational and volunteer opportunities for schools, community groups and anyone else interested in learning about the animals there. The Harmony Lake Animal Hospital evolved into a non-profit organization now called The Vanity Fur Centre for Animal Health & Wellness."

I stop to take my mitts from my pockets and put them on.

"Are you with me so far?" I ask.

"So far, so good," he replies.

"Fast forward to today. Dr. Pingle passed away and Laura is now the executive director of the AC. Mega Mart decides the land the AC sits on would be a great location for a Mega Mart Store and makes Laura and her sister, who own the land together, a generous offer to purchase it. To make the store a reality, they also need to purchase a piece of land from the Willows farm which is next to the AC. Now, this is where it gets controversial. Are you still with me?"

Eric nods, "I think so."

"Mr. Willows wants to sell, but Laura doesn't. Unfortunately for Mr. Willows, the Mega Mart offer is all or nothing. They either purchase Laura's land and the Willows' land, or they don't purchase any land at all, and find a different location for the store. The town council is involved because if the land sales happen, Mega Mart would need permission and permits from the town to build the store. Half the town council wants a Mega Mart in Harmony Lake, and half the town council is against it. It's the most controversial political event we've had since the DuPont's cat was accidentally elected as a town councillor."

I take a deep breath of crisp winter air.

"Did that actually happen?" Eric asks. "The cat thing, I mean."

"Sure did," I reply. "It's still a sensitive subject for some people, so don't mention it to anyone unless you know which side they were on. It's a long story, I'll tell you when we have time."

When we turn onto Laura's street, Sophie increases her tail-wagging speed, and I can feel her pulling the leash. She knows where she is, and she's excited to go home.

"Can I ask you about one more thing?"

"Uh-huh," I say.

"Did someone ask you on a date? It sounded like Connie and April were trying to convince you to go on a date earlier."

I roll my eyes behind my sunglasses and fight the urge to sigh dramatically and shake my head. I sense this going from two against one to three against one.

"No, but Connie and April are of the opinion that I should be dating. They worry I'm lonely."

"Are you? Lonely, I mean."

"No. I'm alone, but I'm not lonely. Alone and lonely aren't the same thing."

We turn up Laura's snowless driveway. I assume from the attention to detail of the snow removal and carefully cultivated curb appeal, that Phillip takes care of the exterior of Laura's home.

"For the first time in twenty years I don't have to answer to anyone, or live with someone else's habits, or ask someone's opinion before I make a decision. Right now, I'm happy with that. I don't want to make accommodations for someone else, you know? You probably think it sounds selfish."

"I get it, and I don't think it's selfish," Eric says, "but there's a middle ground. You don't have to choose between single or fully committed. You can meet people and date on your own terms, with boundaries, and keep your independence. I think that might be what Connie was trying to say, though it might have come across like she's trying to marry you off before you pass your expiration date." He grins.

"Ha ha! You're a funny guy. I think I like you better when you're in cop-mode and don't have a sense of humour."

We climb the two steps to Laura's porch.

"Here we are," I declare.

"Her driveway is spotless," Eric observes. "The other driveways all have some snow on them, but hers is snowless. Phillip must shovel her snow. Did he make these urns too? They're amazing," he says, gesturing toward the large metal urns on either side of the porch that contain beautifully arranged, seasonal foliage.

There is real garland decking the roof above the garage

and porch, and window boxes with sprigs of evergreen and clusters of holly. It's like being at a photoshoot for Better Homes & Gardens.

"Yes," I say. "I'm guessing Phillip takes care of the outside of the house."

"He does a beautiful job. His own house must be awesome," Eric speculates.

"It is," I confirm.

I look at Phillip's perfectly landscaped yard and garden every day since we're next-door neighbours.

"No matter how hard I try to maintain my yard and garden to his standard, I feel like my house is the before and his house is the after on a landscaping reality show."

Sophie is whimpering and bouncing, her little paws tippy tapping in anticipation. I notice there's mail in the mailbox, so I take it out to bring it into the house.

"In case two weeks' worth of mail isn't enough for her to read?" Eric asks jokingly when I take the envelopes from the mailbox.

I turn the doorknob then stop and let go when I feel my body tense up. I take a deep breath.

"Heavy shoulders, long arms," I mutter.

A trick I learned years ago from a yoga instructor to release tension in the neck and shoulders.

Eric puts a hand on my arm.

"Are you OK, Megan?"

"The last time I let myself into a neighbour's home, I found a dead body, remember?"

"The odds of that happening again are next to impossible," he says in a gentle, reassuring tone. "Most people never discover a dead body. It's a rare occurrence. The odds of it happening twice to the same person would be miniscule. How about this? I'll go in first, make sure everything is OK, then you follow."

He's right, the chances of Laura being dead are slim to

none, and slim just left town, as my dad would say.

Statistically, I'm probably more likely to get struck by lightning, or bitten by a shark, than I am to find another dead body.

"Thank you, but I'll go in first. You're right. It'll be fine. And she's never met you. It might scare her to see your giant six-foot frame suddenly appear in her house."

I kick the snow off my boots against the brick wall next to the door, then bend down and detach Sophie's leash. I open the door and Sophie tears into the house and down the hall.

CHAPTER 3

As I WALK into the house, Sophie lets out a high-pitched, excited yelp and disappears around the corner, into the kitchen.

"Hi, Laura!" I shout from the foyer, "I have more mail for you. I'll bring it in and add it to your pile."

I bend down to take off my boots.

"Sophie missed you so much. You should've seen how excited she was when she realized where we were going."

On the table by the door, I see the bag of dog sweaters with Amy's name on it. I point it out to Eric, put Sophie's leash on the table next to it, and walk down the hall toward the kitchen.

"Laura, I brought Eric with me. He's picking up the dog sweaters for the auction."

As I'm about to walk from the kitchen to the family room, I hear Sophie whining and making whimpering sounds.

In the family room, Sophie is crying and pacing back and forth in front of Laura's chair.

"Oh, you're asleep," I whisper.

Sophie whines and puts her front paws on Laura's chair.

"Shhhh." I raise my index finger to my mouth to shush her. "Let her sleep, Sophie."

Laura is asleep in the chair with her casted leg elevated and resting on a cushion on the ottoman in front of her.

I approach Laura, and add the mail I brought to the pile of mail beside the empty coffee mug on the table beside her, and look carefully at her sleeping face.

You are sleeping, right, Laura?

Hello, knot! I get a knot in my stomach when something isn't right. It's one of the things my intuition does to get my attention. The last time the knot formed in my stomach was when I found a dead body.

I touch Laura's wrist. It's not as warm as it should be, and I can't detect a pulse.

No. Please, no. Not again. Please not again. Not Laura. Not today.

"Laura?"

Gently, I squeeze her hand.

"Laura, can you hear me?" I ask softly.

I shake her hand.

"Laura! wake up!" I shout.

Her chest isn't rising and falling.

She's dead.

"Eric!" I scream, "I think she's dead!"

He runs around the corner from the kitchen and checks for a pulse in her neck. His phone is already to his ear, and he's calling for help.

I'm having flashbacks to the last time this happened, and I struggle to inhale deeply enough.

How can this be happening again?

I step backwards into the kitchen and turn, so I'm not looking at Laura, while I try to regulate my breathing. I notice a coffee mug on the drying rack beside the sink, so I focus my gaze on it while I breathe in 1...2...3...4... and breathe out 1...2...3...4...

Feeling a bit more composed, I turn back to Laura and Eric.

He's still on the phone. I put my hand on the kitchen table to steady myself and notice a light purple, slightly faded, card-sized envelope with a yellow sticky note stuck to it. The sticky note says, **I believe this belongs to you**! and the words are underlined twice.

Laura's knee scooter is next to the kitchen table, and her cordless phone is on the table next to the purple envelope.

I pull my phone out of my pocket and snap photos of the envelope with the sticky note, the knee scooter, the cordless phone, and the mug on the drying rack. They seem important, though right now, I'm not sure why.

I also snap a photo of the mug and the mail on the table next to Laura, being careful not to get any of Laura in the photo.

I look back at the knee scooter. Phillip said something about the knee scooter. What was it he said?

Sophie distracts me. She's pacing frantically in front of Laura's chair and lets out a shrill yelp. I walk over, scoop her up, and walk to the front door where I attach her leash. She's still wearing her sweater and must be warm. And confused. I know I am.

I carry her back to the kitchen and ask Eric what he needs me to do. He tells me to wait outside and flag down the first responders when they arrive.

It feels like Sophie and I have only been outside for a few seconds when the first emergency responders show up. Next thing I know, there are emergency responders coming and going from the house. Lots of them. What happened between the first ones showing up and the house suddenly becoming a flurry of uniforms and a hub of activity is a blur.

A van covered in painted flowers pulls up in front of a neighbour's house.

Phillip!

I forgot Phillip was coming here after his deliveries. Should I have phoned him and sent him back to the store? Too late now. I'll have to tell him what's happening.

Sophie and I walk toward Phillip's van as he gets out of the driver's side with a takeout bag in his hand. Laura's soup.

"Phillip, I'm so sorry," I say.

I tell him Laura looked peaceful and comfortable in her chair, like she was asleep. And I thought she was, until I realized she wasn't.

I hug him tightly and he begins to shiver, either from the cold or shock, or both.

We can't go in the house, so I text Eric and tell him that Phillip is here and ask if I can take him to my house. Moments after I hit Send, a uniformed officer comes over and offers us a ride.

CHAPTER 4

I THANK the police officer for driving us to my house in his warm patrol car. Neither Phillip nor I are in a fit state to drive.

I settle Phillip on the sofa in the living room. While he relieves Sophie of her leash and sweater, I get us a box of tissue and send a text to Connie letting her know what happened with Laura and asking her if she can stay at the store until it closes.

Connie: Oh my! That's awful! Has anyone told Phillip?

Me: Yes. He's with me. He came to Laura's house to bring her lunch and now we're at my house with Sophie.

Connie: Please tell him we're here if he needs anything. Take care of him and you <3

Phillip is crying silently and cuddling with Sophie.

I offer him a drink, and we decide we could both use a caramel coffee with a shot of Irish Cream Liqueur. I leave him and Sophie while I go into the kitchen to make our coffees.

I place his coffee on the coffee table and join him on the sofa.

"Phillip, is there anyone I can call for you? Anyone who needs to know?"

I'm rubbing his back, and he's rubbing Sophie's back.

"Glenda, her sister needs to know, but she's on her way here. I can't tell her while she's driving, it'll have to wait until she arrives."

"Is she going straight to Laura's house?" I ask.

"Yes. I don't think I can call her and redirect her without letting on that something is wrong," he explains, choking up and taking a moment to compose himself. "I can't text her while she's driving, so it'll have to wait."

I nod.

"Phillip, do you remember telling Eric and me that Laura answered the phone when you were getting ready to leave her house this morning?"

He nods.

Her phone was in the kitchen. How did it get from where she was sitting to the kitchen?

"Do you know who she was talking to?" I ask.

Whoever it was might be the last person to speak to Laura before she died. Maybe they heard something that could shed some light on what happened between Phillip dropping her off and Eric and me arriving at her house.

"No." Phillip shakes his head. "I have no idea. It sounded like they were planning to come over, though. I heard Aunt Laura say something like, 'yes, I'm ready for company. What time do you want to come over?' You know Aunt Laura, a social butterfly." He chokes up again and we sit in silence for a few moments.

"Did you and Laura have a coffee or anything when you dropped her off? I mean, maybe she ate or drank something that made her sick?"

I'm thinking about the empty mug next to her and the clean mug in the dish rack.

"No," he says, shaking his head. "She had breakfast at the hospital before they discharged her, and I brought her a coffee from Latte Da when I picked her up. She drank it while we were waiting for the nurse to bring us a wheelchair and tell us she could leave. I threw the empty cup in the recycle bin in her hospital room. Aunt Laura only has one coffee per day, and she rarely eats between meals. She is quite disciplined with her eating habits."

"She left the hospital in a wheelchair?" I ask. "She didn't use her knee scooter?"

"It's hospital policy," Phillip says. "I had the scooter in the van just in case, but she left in a wheelchair. When I dropped her off, she used the knee scooter to get to the porch, then I helped her into the house, and she used the knee scooter to get to her chair. She got skilled at using it quickly. There's no way she'd be able to stay still for six weeks, so the knee scooter was a necessity. I was careful to leave it right next to her when I set her up in her chair."

I'm pretty sure this is exactly what he told me earlier. It may look like she died peacefully in her sleep, but my instincts tell me Laura's death wasn't as peaceful as it seems.

CHAPTER 5

THE SOUND of a car door closing gets my attention and I look through the living room window.

There's a patrol car in the driveway, and Eric is walking from the driver's side to the passenger side. He opens the door, and a woman about twenty years older than me, and about ten years younger than Laura, gets out of the car. She has short auburn hair and her gait reminds me of Laura, so I assume she must be Laura's sister, Glenda. Eric closes the car door behind her, and they walk toward the front door.

"I think this might be Glenda," I say.

Phillip turns his head and cranes his neck to see the porch.

"That's Glenda," he confirms.

I open the front door before they ring the doorbell. Eric and Glenda both come in and I take their coats. I introduce myself to Glenda and tell her I'm sorry for her loss.

Glenda and I have never met. Like Laura, she grew up in Harmony Lake, but she moved to Ottawa in her twenties and has only been back since to visit. Our paths haven't crossed on any of her visits. I lead her to the living room where she and Phillip both cry when they see each other.

"Glenda, you've had a long drive, can I get you anything?

We're having coffee, but there's tea, water, pop, and I can get us some snacks."

I want to do whatever I can to make them both comfortable.

"Thank you, Megan. It was a long drive. I've been on the road since before sunup. I don't drink coffee, I could never get used to the taste, but I'd love a glass of water."

Eric follows me into the kitchen, and I make him a coffee with regular cream. No Irish Cream Liqueur for him while he's working.

I purposely take my time getting Glenda's water so she and Phillip can have a few minutes alone.

"Other than Glenda, did anyone else show up at Laura's house?" I ask Eric.

"Uh-uh." He shakes his head. "A few curious neighbours came near the house to ask if everything was OK and ask what's happening, but no one came to the house specifically looking for Laura, except her sister."

He takes a sip of coffee.

"Why do you ask? Was she expecting someone else to show up?"

"Maybe," I say.

I tell Eric what Phillip told me about Laura's half of the phone conversation. Then I mention how the phone mysteriously found its way to the kitchen after Phillip left.

"If we need to find out who called, we can check her phone records, or her call display," he says.

He said, 'if we need to find out,' like finding out who called might not be necessary, which makes me believe he doesn't think her death is suspicious.

I get Glenda's glass of water and we join her, Phillip and Sophie in the living room.

Glenda has taken my spot on the sofa next to Phillip and Sophie. With Sophie nestled in between them, they're both petting her, and she's loving the attention.

Eric puts his coffee on the table next to his chair, unbuttons his suit jacket, and sits down.

"I'm sorry for your loss," he says to Phillip and Glenda.

They both give him a weak smile.

"We're still waiting for the coroner to arrive and give their opinion, but it appears that Laura passed away peacefully, likely of natural causes. But until the coroner confirms the cause and details of Laura's death, we have to treat the house like a crime scene. The house won't be accessible to anyone until we release it.

"How long will that take?" Glenda asks.

"Probably a few days," Eric responds.

Phillip and Glenda nod.

"Did Laura have any chronic health issues that you're aware of?" Eric asks.

He retrieves his trusty notebook and pen from the breast pocket of his suit jacket and uses his thumb to press on the top of the pen. It clicks open.

"No," Glenda says. "She's always been the picture of health. Even as she's gotten older, she hasn't developed any of the health conditions many elderly people seem to get. The broken leg and the surgery for it are the only health issues I'm aware of."

She turns to Phillip.

"She had a cold in December, but that's the only health problem I know about," Phillip says.

"You know, an uncle on our father's side died from a blood clot less than a day after he had surgery. He was otherwise healthy," Glenda says. "It was about thirty years ago now. I think he was in his mid-sixties and had surgery to fix a knee he'd injured falling off a bike."

"Are blood clots hereditary?" Phillip asks.

Glenda and I both shrug and look at Eric.

"I have no idea, but I'll mention it to the coroner," Eric says, then he jots down another note in his notebook.

"I don't know either," Glenda says, "but it's the only other family death I can think of that was sudden. And the circumstances are similar."

"Glenda, were you planning to stay with Laura while you're in town?" I ask.

"Yes." She nods. "I came here to help her until she had the cast removed."

"Well, now you'll stay with Kevin and me," Phillip says, putting his hand on top of Glenda's.

"I don't want you to go to any trouble, Phillip." She puts her hand on top of his hand which is already on top of her other hand.

He insists. She doesn't want to impose. He insists again. She'll only stay because he insists. He insists that he is insisting she stay, and after a rapid exchange of courteous banter and social etiquette, it's settled. Glenda will stay next door with Phillip and Kevin.

I offer to keep Sophie as long as necessary. I assume Glenda wants to take her, but Sophie can't stay at Phillip's house with Kevin there. Staying next door with me is the next best thing, and I'm more than happy to keep Sophie as a roommate for as long as possible.

Phillip and Glenda are ready to go back to Phillip's house. He needs to call the store to give Noah instructions for closing up, and they both have friends and family they need to contact about Laura's passing.

The four of us decide that Eric and I will go to Laura's house to get Phillip's van and Glenda's car and drive both vehicles back to Phillip's house.

I walk Phillip and Glenda next door to Phillip's house and collect their keys. Then I come back to my house and get in the patrol car with Eric.

"You know," I say after we pull out of my driveway, "until I met you, I'd never ridden in a police car in my life. I didn't even know what the inside of a police car looked like. Since meeting you, I've ridden in a police car so many times that I've lost count."

"It's OK, Megan. You don't have to thank me for making your life more interesting."

I laugh for the first time today.

When we get to Laura's house, Eric gets out of the car and one of the first responders ambushes him and starts flirting with him before he even has a chance to close the car door. I don't know why this shocks me, but it does.

Of course, women flirt with him. He's hot. The fact that he's also smart, funny, and kind, helps too. Heck, if I knew how to flirt, I'd probably flirt with him too.

He's trying to walk to the passenger side to open my door, but she's slowing him down, so I get out of the car, close the door and meet him halfway.

I drop Phillip's keys into his hand and watch the paramedic as she giggles, twirls her hair, and talks about some cool, new club in the city.

I admire her flirting skills. I have no flirting skills. If I had to flirt to survive, I wouldn't make it. I'd die while trying to seduce someone with my awkwardness.

I drive Glenda's four-door, silver sedan and park it in Phillip's driveway. Eric sidesteps the coquettish paramedic and follows me in Phillip's van.

I knock on the door and give both sets of keys to Phillip. I tell him to call me if he needs anything. We hug and I walk across the snowy yard to my house where Eric is waiting on the porch. He tells me a patrol car is coming to pick him up.

"Come inside and wait for your ride," I say. "I don't want to stay out here in case I'm struck by lightning or attacked by a shark."

He laughs.

I gasp and put my hand over my mouth. It was an awful thing to say, an inappropriate reference to earlier when I thought both events would be more likely than finding another dead neighbour

"I'm sorry," I say, shaking my head. "I shouldn't have said that. It was insensitive under the circumstances." I unlock the door and we escape from the cold into the warm house.

"No, it's not, Megan. It's important to keep a sense of humour in this job. It makes it easier to cope with the hard stuff."

"But this isn't my job," I remind him. "And I don't want discovering dead bodies to become such a normal occurrence in my life that I'm able to laugh it off."

"I know. I get it. I forget sometimes that you're a civilian. Are you OK? I can cancel the patrol car and stay a while. Or, I can call Connie or April to come over?"

"No, I'm fine, thank you."

We take a seat in the living room.

"It's easier this time," I explain. "Probably because she wasn't murdered and I'm not a suspect. Right? I'm not a suspect?"

"There are no suspects, Megan. It appears she died of natural causes."

"Right," I say. "About that, there were a few things at Laura's house that didn't look right to me."

"I'm listening," he says.

I tell him about the coffee mug on the drying rack by the sink and point out that Phillip is way too particular to leave it there. Phillip cleaned the house before Laura came home and he wouldn't have left the mug on the drying rack, he just wouldn't.

Then I tell him about the empty coffee mug on the table beside Laura, and how Phillip told me twice today that he left her with a glass of water not a mug of coffee. I tell him Phillip is adamant Laura only drinks one cup of coffee per day, and she'd had a coffee when she was waiting for them to discharge her.

"Maybe Laura made herself a second cup of coffee today, decided to treat herself," he suggests.

"How?" I ask. "Her knee scooter was in the kitchen. Phillip insists he left the scooter beside her chair, within her reach. Do you think she walked from the kitchen back to her chair with a cup of coffee in one hand, on a leg with a compound fracture and a plaster cast?"

"I noticed the scooter next to the kitchen table, but not until after the paramedics arrived. I assumed they moved it so they could access Laura more easily," he replies.

His gaze drops to his lower left, something I've noticed he does when he's thinking.

"Or someone else put it there, so Laura would be helpless and unable to move. And they put her phone there while they were at it, to make sure she couldn't contact anyone," I speculate.

I tell him about the light purple envelope on the kitchen table with the sticky note stuck to it. Phillip wouldn't have left it there, and it wasn't with the other mail. The envelope didn't have a stamp, so it wasn't delivered with the other mail.

A patrol car pulls up in front of the house. We get up and walk to the door.

"I think between the time Phillip dropped her off, and you and I showed up with Sophie, someone else was in the house with Laura," I surmise.

Sophie perks up when she hears her name.

"That doesn't mean she was murdered," he points out. "Thanks for telling me all this." He opens the door.

"Lock it behind me," he says and leaves.

I close the door behind him and lock it.

CHAPTER 6

The lights are on inside Knitorious when Sophie and I arrive just before opening time. We go inside and find Connie already there.

"Hello, my dear! Would it be all right with you if I have a small meeting at the store today?" Connie asks. "The alumni association wants to get together to discuss how we can memorialize Laura at the reunion-fundraiser. We don't have much time to plan something."

Connie is part of the alumni association, and so was Laura.

"Of course!" I say.

It will always feel strange to me when Connie asks my permission to do something in the store that she built and owned for almost forty years. It's not like I would ever say no to her.

Shortly after we open, I'm helping a customer substitute the discontinued yarn her pattern recommends with a current yarn that will give her the same result, when I hear the bell over the front door jingle, and I see Mrs. Pearson come in.

Mrs. Pearson is a knitter and a member of the alumni association. She goes straight to Connie at the long, wooden harvest table behind the cash register, so I assume she's here for the alumni meeting, not as a knitter.

My customer finds just the right yarn for her project. While I'm ringing up her purchase, I overhear Mrs. Pearson telling Connie how upset Brian Sweeney is about Laura's death.

Then Connie says, "Of course he is, they were so close."

Who is Brian Sweeney and what was his relationship with Laura?

I finish the transaction, wish my customer a good day, and wander over to the harvest table. I wait for a lull in their conversation, so I can ask who Brian Sweeney is and what his relationship was to Laura.

"Brian is from Harmony Lake," Connie tells me. "He grew up with us. He and Laura were best friends from the time they were small until the spring of our senior year of high school, when they suddenly stopped talking, and started avoiding each other."

"No one knows what happened that made them stop speaking," Mrs. Pearson adds, "but they never spoke again. Laura left right after graduation to take an eight-month secretarial course in Montreal.

"When she came back, she started working at her father's veterinary clinic," Connie says, taking back the story-telling baton from Mrs. Pearson, "and Brian had moved away to attend university."

"Brian and his wife, Anne-Marie, moved back to Harmony Lake about six months ago," Mrs. Pearson explains, "to take care of his dad who died just about two months ago."

"And they decided to stay, now that Brian is retired," Connie adds.

Connie takes my hand and pulls me closer to her.

"Anyway, the rumour fifty years ago, and it was just a rumour mind you, was that Brian and Laura were a couple, and she was 'in trouble'," Connie whispers, using air quotes around *in trouble*. "People said she left town to have the baby. Sadly, it was common back then for girls to be sent away to have their baby in secret. The baby would be adopted, and the girl would be expected to return home and resume her life as though it never happened."

The fact that she's whispering even though the three of us are the only people in the store, tells me that this is still a sensitive topic.

"We really have come a long way since then," she adds, nodding.

"Thank goodness it's not like that anymore," Mrs. Pearson agrees. "Since he's been back in Harmony Lake, Brian and Laura seem to have mended their relationship. He even volunteers at the AC, where Laura spent most of her time."

Interesting indeed.

"I haven't met Mr. or Mrs. Sweeney," I tell them. "It's good he and Laura patched things up before she died."

"Megan!" Mrs. Pearson distracts me from my thoughts, "Have you ever met my son, Craig? He's a doctor at Harmony Hills Hospital, and he's single," she wiggles her eyebrows and nods her head.

Is she trying to set me up with her son? I look at Connie and she's smiling at me and nodding.

I hear the front door jingle. Saved by the bell!

"Excuse me, ladies," I say as I turn to greet the postal carrier.

I've never been so happy to see a postal carrier and have a pile of bills handed to me.

I think my enthusiasm for his arrival and my attempts to prolong our conversation as long as possible are making him a little uncomfortable. He keeps checking his watch and shifting his weight from one foot to the other while inching toward the door. The longer I talk with him, the longer Connie and Mrs. Pearson will have to talk about something else and forget about setting me up with her son, Craig the doctor.

As soon as he gets himself within arm's reach of the door, the postal carrier tells me he still has most of his route to finish, wishes me a good day, and leaves. But while we were talking, the remaining members of the alumni association showed up, so hopefully Mrs. Pearson and Connie will be too busy with alumni business to set me up with anyone.

I put the mail on the counter and pull the letter opener from the cup of pens next to the cash register.

As I open envelopes and separate the need-to-keep papers from the need-to-recycle papers, I have a flashback to standing on Laura's porch yesterday and taking the mail out of her mailbox before Eric and I went inside.

If the mail was delivered before Phillip dropped Laura off, he would have brought it in. For sure, he would have brought it in. That means the mail was delivered after Phillip dropped her off. If my instincts are correct (they haven't misled me yet) and someone was at Laura's house yesterday between Phillip leaving and Eric, Sophie, and me arriving, her postal carrier might have seen who was there.

AFTER LUNCH, Sophie and I go for our midday stroll, and I check the parking lot to see if Phillip's van is there. It is.

I walk to Artsy Tartsy to pick up some treats for Phillip and Glenda, with a plan to drop them off at his store on my way back, as an excuse to check in and see how they're doing.

I choose an assortment of cookies, mini cupcakes, and tarts. As I'm leaving, Tamara slips me a bag of dog treats for Sophie to taste test. I peek inside the bag to see the shape she chose for this batch: bones. Two different sizes of bone-shaped cookies, and they smell good. Pet food rarely smells good to me, but the dog treats Tamara makes smell yummy. Sophie will love them.

"Hi, Glenda," I say, walking into Wilde Flowers and closing the door behind me.

Wilde Flowers smells divine. I inhale deeply and a bouquet of floral aromas infiltrates every breath I inhale without overwhelming my sense of smell.

"Hi, Megan." She comes out from behind the counter. "Phillip is just in the giant fridge. He'll be back in a moment."

Technically, it's a walk-in florist cooler, not a fridge. I know this because when I've called it a fridge in the past, Phillip has corrected me and explained the difference between them. It's something about airflow and humidity. I'm sure if Phillip hears Glenda refer to his walk-in florist cooler as a fridge, he'll correct her too.

I walk up to the counter and say hi to Kevin, who is on the counter perched on top of a royal blue, velvet cushion with gold piping along the edges and gold tassels hanging from each corner. He sits at attention and stretches his neck to present me with his chin for scratching.

"I was at a loose end, so I decided to come to work with Phillip and help out," Glenda tells me.

"Is Phillip keeping you busy?" I ask.

"Not really"—she chuckles—"but I'm able to watch the store while he teaches Noah about florist things in the back room and the walk-in fridge."

"Well, I'm sure having you here is a comfort to him," I say. "Part of me thought he might not come to work today."

"He talked about staying home today, but what can we do?" Glenda asks, shrugging. "The house is off-limits, and Laura hasn't been released to the funeral home, so there's nothing for us to do. At least at the shop we can keep busy."

I nod.

Phillip emerges from the cooler. I give him a gentle hug and ask him how he's doing. He echoes Glenda's sentiments about being at a loose end and needing work to keep busy and distract himself from Laura.

"I brought some treats from the bakery." I gesture to the white confectionery box on the counter. "I wasn't sure what to get, so I picked a bit of everything."

Glenda goes to put the kettle on, and Phillip invites me to sit in his sitting room—a cozy nook within the store where he sits with brides and other clients to discuss their floral orders.

The nook is set up with four plush, overstuffed chairs, a coffee table, and end tables. He carries Kevin's cushion, with Kevin still perched on top of it, and places the cushion on his lap when he sits down.

Glenda brings out a tea tray, and we drink tea and eat bakery treats.

I remember the bag of dog cookies in my tote bag.

"Can Kevin have a dog cookie?" I ask. "They're from the bakery."

"The tennis ball ones?" Phillip asks.

"These look like bones."

I pull the bag from my tote and hand it to him. He peeks inside.

"Ooooh, Kevin hasn't tried these yet," Phillip says.

He holds the open bag so Kevin can see and sniff the cookies.

"Aww...now you have to give him one," Glenda says. "How would you feel if we put the open bakery box under your nose and then didn't give you one?"

"She's right," I add.

Phillip breaks one of the cookies in half and puts it on Kevin's cushion. Kevin sniffs it suspiciously a few times before eating it.

"He loves it!" Phillip declares.

We hear the door open. Phillip stands up, puts Kevin and his cushion on the chair he was sitting in, and disappears around the corner.

"Hello, Detective." I hear Phillip say.

"Please, call me Eric."

Phillip comes back around the corner with Eric behind him. Eric greets Glenda and me, and I ask him if he'd like a treat and gesture toward the confectionary box on the coffee table. He puts his hand up and shakes his head.

"I assume you're here to speak with Phillip and Glenda," I say, "so I'll leave you to it. I should get back to the store, anyway."

I pick up the handles of my tote bag and stand up.

"No, Megan. Please stay. I'm more comfortable with you here," Philip says, gesturing for me to sit back down.

By Harmony Lake standards, Eric is still new, and many locals are unsure around him.

"Please sit down, Detective, I mean Eric," Phillip says, now gesturing for Eric to take the fourth chair.

Eric sits down and Glenda offers him tea. He declines. He extends a hand toward Kevin, who sniffs it, reluctantly at first, then lets Eric pet him.

"I spoke with the coroner a little while ago, and he thinks Laura may have been poisoned."

Phillip, Glenda, and I let out a collective gasp.

"Was Laura ever prescribed a heart medication called Digoxin?" Eric asks.

Phillip and Glenda vigorously shake their heads in unison.

"Laura didn't have any heart problems," Glenda says, looking at Phillip, "Did she?"

"No," Phillip says, "she definitely wasn't taking any heart medication."

"The coroner is still doing tests," Eric explains. "These are preliminary findings. Hopefully, we'll know more over the next few days."

We stop talking and turn our heads toward the shop door when we hear it open.

Henry Willows comes around the corner. He points at Glenda, then at Phillip.

"Which one of you is inheriting Laura's share of the land?" Mr. Willows demands.

He's referring to the land the AC is on. The land Mega Mart has offered to purchase. The land that Laura said she would sell to Mega Mart over her dead body.

Neither Phillip nor Glenda answer him.

"I'm here to make sure you do the right thing and sell that land to Mega Mart," he bellows. He looks at Glenda and jabs his finger in her direction. "Glenda, I know if it's you, you'll do what's right." He looks at Phillip and jabs a finger in his direction. "But I'm not sure where you stand."

Mr. Willows' approach is uncomfortably aggressive.

Eric stands up and positions himself in front of Mr. Willows blocking his access to the sitting area, and to Phillip and Glenda. They're standing nose to nose. Mr. Willows is a big man. He and Eric are the same height, and Mr. Willows has a thicker build. He moves his head to look past Eric at Phillip and Glenda.

"The deadline is soon. The offer has to be signed before the deadline. The right decision has to be made!" He shouts, jabbing his index finger toward Phillip and Glenda.

Eric takes Mr. Willows by the arm and escorts him out of Wilde Flowers. I follow them, lock the door behind them, and turn the sign on the door from OPEN to CLOSED. The two men are speaking on the sidewalk in front of Knitorious.

Phillip and Glenda are both shaken.

"If you two want to call it a day," I suggest, "I'll help Noah look after the store until it's time to close.

Phillip shakes his head.

"Willows' bark is worse than his bite. I'm not leaving my shop because of him."

"I'm staying with Phillip," Glenda adds.

"Glenda, why did Willows say he knows you'll do the

right thing?" Phillip asks. "Have you decided to sell your half of the land to Mega Mart? How would Willows know that?"

"Mr. Willows phoned me about two weeks ago," Glenda explains. "It's public knowledge that I own half the property. Land title documents are a matter of public record."

"What did he say when he called you? Did he threaten you?" Phillip asks.

"No, he was demanding, but he didn't threaten me," Glenda reassures him. "He wanted to know if I intend to sell my half of the land to Mega Mart. I told him we could use the money. I told him I want to sell my share. I didn't say I was *definitely* selling my share."

"Did Aunt Laura know you wanted to sell?"

"Yes," she replies, nodding. "We discussed it. She knew we could use the money, and I knew she wanted to ensure the land is protected for the AC. We didn't agree, but we weren't fighting about it either." Glenda adds, "The last time Laura and I spoke was just after her surgery when she was still in the hospital. I told her I was coming to stay with her and help her until the cast comes off. She said she was looking forward to seeing me and made a joke about how she would have broken her leg sooner if she knew it would get us a nice long visit together."

"That sounds like something Aunt Laura would say," Phillip muses.

"Then she said she was glad I was coming because she needed to talk to me about her will," Glenda says. "She said she changed her will the day she broke her leg, before her surgery."

It sounds like she changed her will in a hurry. Maybe she found a way to make it difficult for Mega Mart to purchase the AC if she died.

Glenda walks behind the counter, pulls out her purse, and plops it on the counter. She reaches into it and pulls out a small notebook.

"Laura said something had come up, that it was family business, and she would only discuss it with me in person."

"I have no idea what it would be," Phillip says.

"Neither do I," Glenda says, opening her notebook and flipping through the pages until she finds what she's looking for.

"Megan," she says, looking up at me, "when Laura phoned to tell me she broke her leg and would be having surgery, she told me if anything happens, I should call her lawyer. He has her will and knows what to do. She made me write down his name." She squints at the page in her small notebook. "Do you know an Adam Martel?" she asks me. "Is he any relation to you?"

Phillip and I look at each other and smile.

"Funnily enough, yes," I reply. "We were married for twenty years."

A concerned look takes over Glenda's face. I reach out and touch her arm.

"Adam is an excellent lawyer," I reassure her. "Laura's estate is in good hands."

CHAPTER 7

Connie agreed to open the store this morning while Sophie and I run an errand.

I have reservations about bringing Sophie with me to Laura's house. The last time we were here, Laura was dead. I don't know how dogs process trauma, or if being outside the house will confuse her because we aren't going inside and she's not staying.

I'm hoping Sophie and the postal carrier will recognize each other and Sophie's familiar presence might make them more inclined to speak to me.

We wait in the warmth of the car outside Laura's house until I see the postal carrier a few houses away. Then we go to the porch. The crime scene tape sealing off the front door isn't obstructing the mailbox, so I assume if Laura has mail, the postal carrier will deliver it today.

A few minutes later, the postal carrier climbs the two steps to Laura's porch, squats down to Sophie's level, and they greet each other like old friends. They've obviously met before since the postal carrier is calling her by name. She stands up and puts Laura's mail in the mailbox. I introduce myself to her as a friend of Laura's and tell her I'm Sophie's temporary guardian. She says she heard about Laura's death from one of the neighbours while on her route yesterday. She gives Sophie her condolences and asks me if I know what happened to Laura.

"I don't know the details," I say. "I heard it was sudden and looked like she died of natural causes. She'd just had surgery, you know."

I hate lying, but I also hate perpetuating gossip. Also, I'm not sure if the coroner's findings are intended to be public knowledge or not, so best to err on the side of caution.

"Do you always do your route at the same time?" I ask. "Is this what time you delivered Laura's mail on Tuesday?

"It would have been very close," she replies. "Sometimes the weather can affect how long I take, and a heavy mail day can slow me down, but I think on Tuesday I was here around this time."

"Did you happen to notice if Laura had company when you were here?" I ask. "We think she had a visitor that morning, but we aren't sure who it was."

"I didn't see anyone," she replies, shaking her head. "There was a car in the driveway that wasn't Laura's. She drives a white SUV, and the car in the driveway was a sedan. I didn't see anyone inside it. It was either grey or silver. A four-door model, I think."

Like the car Glenda drives.

WHEN I ROLL up to Knitorious, I park behind the store. Eric's car isn't here. He's hard at work looking for Laura's killer, and Phillip is loading today's deliveries into his van.

Sophie and I get out of the car and walk over to Phillip to say hi. He crouches down and gives Sophie some love while he and I complain about the frigid wind blowing off the lake today. Then Sophie and I walk across the parking lot to the back door of the store.

Realizing I've left my phone plugged into the console of my car, I open the door and let Sophie inside (there's no point in both of us being cold) while I go back to the car to retrieve my phone before it freezes.

Phone in hand, I lock the car, walk back to the door, reach for the door handle, slip on the same patch of ice that tripped me up on Tuesday, lose my footing, and in a blur of fumbling and flashing limbs, do everything I can to right myself.

The next thing I know, Phillip is kneeling over me telling me to stay awake. The sun is in my eyes and everything is blurry. The back of my head is throbbing, and my ankle hurts. I try to prop myself up on my elbows, but Phillip stops me.

"Nowahhhhhhhh!!" Phillip yells.

I've never heard him yell like that. Phillip is a soft-spoken man with a quiet, gentle voice. He yelled Noah's name so loudly that people named Noah three towns over are probably turning their heads wondering who called them, and looking at the person next to them, asking, "Did you hear that?"

I try again to get up and Phillip stops me, again.

Phillip tells me I can either go to the hospital with him or in an ambulance. I decide to go with him. Noah comes out of Wilde Flowers and Phillip instructs him to go into Knitorious, tell Connie what happened, and to be careful of the ice. Phillip isn't sure if he should move me. I'm stunned, a little out of it, and not contributing much to the conversation.

Connie comes out and Phillip helps her, so she doesn't slip too. They talk amongst themselves and decide Phillip will take me to the hospital. I hear them whispering about my foot being at an unnatural angle, and they're worried it could be broken. This would explain the pain.

Noah goes from Knitorious back to Wilde Flowers and

reappears a moment later rolling an office chair in front of him.

"Smart lad," Phillip says.

Connie holds the chair still, while Phillip helps me into it. Phillip disappears into Wilde Flowers muttering about keys and listing off instructions for Noah and Glenda.

Phillip must have come back outside because his flowered van slowly pulls up next to me and stops. Connie rolls me to the passenger side door of the van. Phillip gets out, comes around to Connie and me, and helps me get inside.

Connie puts my tote bag on my lap. She asks me if I have my knitting, then uses her hand as a verbal eraser to wave away the idea because, apparently, I'm "way too out of it to knit, anyway." She tells Phillip she'll meet us there. I want to ask who will look after the store, but my head is pounding and I'm trying not to throw up.

"Wait!" Connie shouts as Phillip is about to pull away.

She runs into the store, then runs right back out with a plastic grocery bag and puts it on top of my tote bag on my lap. A barf bag. Connie can read my mind. Thank you, Connie!

"Waaatch your steppp!!!" Phillip yells after Connie, as she disappears back into the store.

He yelled in his newly revealed, super-loud voice, and I imagine people all over Harmony Lake looked down simultaneously and watched their step.

I don't remember much about the drive to the hospital aside from being nauseous and sore. I think I dozed off.

The next thing I'm aware of is laying in an exam room, while Connie and Phillip talk to each other across the room. Phillip tells me to feel better, then leaves.

There's a handsome doctor looking at my foot and telling me I'm lucky it's just a bad bruise and a sprain. He says he'd like to have a closer look at the bump on the back of my head.

He keeps talking, and I'm trying to focus on what he's

saying, but it's hard to keep up. Connie is listening and asking a lot of questions, so I give up trying to follow along. She's obviously got this.

The doctor asks me my name. It worries me that he's not resourceful enough to find it on my hospital bracelet, or the chart he's holding.

I hold up my wrist with the hospital bracelet, point to it with my other hand, and tell him, "That's my name."

"Very good," he says, "but can you tell me your name? I want to hear you say it."

Oh, I get it. He's not asking because *he* doesn't know who I am; he's asking to make sure *I* know who I am.

"Megan Martel," I say.

He bends down so we're almost nose to nose and examines my eyes with an ophthalmoscope. I glance at the name tag on his lab coat: Dr. Craig Pearson.

"Are you Marla Pearson's son?" I ask.

He is.

I tell him his mother was just talking about him yesterday. He asks how I know his mother, and I tell him she was at my store and tried to set me up with him.

Hearing the unfiltered words pour out of my mouth, I worry the bump on my head has damaged the part of my brain that stops me from blurting out every thought I have.

He laughs.

"What store?" he asks.

"Knitorious," I say, "on Water Street in Harmony Lake."

"Did it work?" he asks. "Did she convince you to go out with me?"

"I'm here, aren't I?" I reply, opening my arms and gesturing vaguely. "I slipped on the ice, bumped my head, and sprained my ankle just to meet you."

"She doesn't sound like herself!" Connie says urgently, interrupting me and preventing me from embarrassing myself more than I already have. "Is this because she hit her head? Will she go back to normal?"

The doctor explains that the injection I had earlier (I don't remember getting an injection) was pain medication for my head and foot and it's making me loopy and contributing to my weirdness.

Connie tells him that I rarely take any medication, and he observes that it seems to be having quite an effect on me.

I leave the emergency room in a wheelchair with my new crutches laying across my lap.

Connie pushes me into the main lobby of the hospital, and we hear a man's voice calling her name.

Connie stops, spins me around and I see a man walking toward us. I don't recognize him.

He and Connie hug.

"Brian Sweeney, this is Megan Martel." Connie gestures to me.

Mr. Sweeney extends his hand downward toward me, and I extend my hand upward toward him and we shake hands.

"Is she OK?" he asks Connie.

"She will be," Connie says. "Why are you here, Brian? Is everything alright?"

"There's a blood donation clinic here today. I donate as often as possible," he says proudly. "I feel it's my duty as a universal donor."

A universal donor is someone whose blood is Type O-Negative. This means Mr. Sweeney's blood is Type O-Negative. I know this because I'm also a universal donor, and I should donate blood more often than I do.

They're talking about Laura's death. I'm trying to follow along, but mental capacity is limited right now, and I don't catch everything they're saying.

I want to ask them to speak more slowly, but stop myself. This makes me hopeful that the bump on my head hasn't damaged the filter in my brain after all.

"Good luck with the blood donation, Brian." Connie grips the handles of my wheelchair and I sense we're about to leave.

"Thank you, Connie," Mr. Sweeney replies. "You know, I still think of Laura's mother every time I give blood, even after all these years."

Why would he think about Laura's mother?

"It was nice to meet you, Mr. Sweeney." I'm waving at him.

"Mr. Sweeney was my father," he says. "You should call me Brian. I hope you feel better, Megan."

"Thank you," I say, still waving.

He waves back and Connie pushes me through the lobby and out into the cold air. The sun is setting. We've been here all day.

On the ride home, I ask Connie why Brian thinks about Laura's mother when he donates blood.

"Laura's mother, also named Laura, was a Red Cross volunteer. For years, she organized the local blood drives and encouraged people to donate blood," Connie explains. "She was very passionate about it. The same way her daughter, Laura, was passionate about the Animal Centre."

"Laura was named after her mother? I didn't know that," I say.

"Yes, and Glenda was named after their father, Glen."

What a special connection to share with your parents.

We go back to the store so I can get Sophie. Connie pulls up out front, turns off the car, takes the keys from the ignition, and turns to me.

"Stay here," she instructs, pointing at me. "Don't move. I'll be right back."

She gets out of the car and goes into the store.

Determined to figure out these crutches, I follow her into the store about five minutes, fifteen minutes, or an hour later. I'm not sure because I'm having trouble keeping track of time.

I can't wait for this medication to wear off.

Glenda is watching the store, and I thank her. It's close enough to closing time that we lock up. Glenda won't let me pay her for her time. I try to insist, but she won't accept, and I think I might be drooling when I talk, so Connie and I get back in her car.

Sophie jumps up on my lap and Connie drives me home.

Connie pulls into the driveway and April comes out of the house to help me inside. She says she texted Adam, and he used his app to let her into the house. The house has Smart Locks, so the doors can be locked and unlocked with a key, a phone app, or by asking Oscar.

She tells me she's spending the night. I show her my crutches, and tell her I figured out how to use them, but she doesn't seem as excited as I am.

"I see what you mean about the pain meds," April says to Connie.

Connie raises her eyebrows and nods to April.

"Good luck tonight," Connie says as she leaves, closing the door behind her.

Good luck to whom? Me or April?

CHAPTER 8

Friday January 10th

I wake up feeling rough. A feeling I'm not used to. There's a synchronized throbbing in my foot and head, and I have a gross taste in my dry, sticky mouth.

Sophie is laying on the bed next to me. I reach out to pet her and her paws feel damp. Odd.

"Why are your feet wet, Sophie?"

She responds by perking up her ears and wagging her tail.

"Fine, keep your secrets, you mysterious girl," I say.

I look at the time, and it's almost 10 a.m. I can't remember the last time I slept this late. Have I ever slept this late?

I sit up on the edge of the bed and do an internal scan to determine how I feel. There's no nausea, and aside from the incessant pulsating of my injured parts, there's no pain. I use one crutch to stand and find my balance. I hobble over the mirror to see if I look as bad as I feel.

I do. I look horrible. I'm a mess.

I don't remember much after April helped me into the house last night. I must have had trouble finding my pyjamas and the pyjama drawer because I'm wearing an oversized, old, paint-stained U of T t-shirt that, judging by the size,

255

belongs to Adam. I didn't put my curly hair into a bun before I went to bed. It looks like a rat's nest constructed by rats with poor nesting skills.

The house is quiet, except for the sounds of the rubber foot on my crutch thudding on the wood floor, and Sophie scurrying in circles around me.

I wonder if April is still here. I remember her telling me she'd be across the hall in the guest room if I need anything.

Using one crutch, and motivated by a need for caffeine, I make my way toward the kitchen.

"What are you doing here?" I ask, recoiling and clutching my chest with my free hand.

Eric is sitting on the family room sofa, and his presence startles me. The last time he sneaked into my house and surprised me, I was almost murdered.

"Sorry! I didn't mean to scare you." He closes his laptop, places it on the coffee table in front of him and jumps up to help me.

He's gorgeous, and he smells warm and sexy and I've never looked worse in my life. I'm a complete mess. Not a hot mess, as the young people say, but an actual, bona fide mess. My hair is everywhere, I may or may not have brushed my teeth since throwing up in Phillip's van yesterday (I can't remember, but I hope I did), and I'm wearing a giant, old, faded, stretched-out, paint-stained t-shirt and underwear.

Eric eases me onto the sofa and puts a cushion under my swollen, purplish-yellowish foot. He asks me if I want anything, and I motion for the blanket at the end of the sofa. Not because I'm cold, but because it's the only thing nearby that I can hide under.

He covers me with the blanket, goes into the kitchen and opens the cupboard above the coffee maker. Sophie jumps up on the sofa and nestles in beside me.

Eric asks me which coffee I want.

"I think there are two pods of peppermint mocha in the

basket in there," I say. "I'll have one of those please. Be sure to make yourself one. Why are you here, anyway?"

"I ran into Phillip last night in the parking lot and he told me what happened. When I went downstairs this morning to see how you're doing, Connie was instructing Archie to come over, and feed and walk Sophie. I know this cold weather makes his hip act up, so I offered to see to Sophie instead."

This explains Sophie's damp paws.

"Thank you," I say. "Sophie and I appreciate it."

"April let me in. Zach has an orthodontist appointment this morning, so I offered to stay with you while she takes him."

He hands me my coffee and sits on the sofa with me. He puts his coffee on the coffee table and reaches for his phone.

"I'm under strict instructions to text Connie when you wake up," he explains, typing on his phone. "If you didn't wake up by 11 a.m., she was coming over to check on you."

He's finishes typing and puts his phone on the table.

"How are you feeling?" he asks.

"Pretty bad," I say. "But not as bad as yesterday."

His phone dings.

"It's Connie. She says to give you your meds. They're on the kitchen counter."

He texts back a quick reply and goes into the kitchen.

"After Connie dropped you off last night, she went to the pharmacy to get your prescription filled."

He comes back into the room with a bottle of pills and a glass of water.

"I think I'm OK without those," I say. "Whatever they gave me yesterday didn't agree with me, and I didn't like it."

I don't want to be weird and loopy again.

"I heard," he says, "but Connie says to tell you this isn't the same medication, and you're supposed to take it."

He reads the bottle, then opens it and shakes one pill into his hand. I take it with the glass of water he hands to me and hope I don't lose my ability to speak without embarrassing myself.

Eric returns the pills to the kitchen then walks toward the front door. He holds up one of Sophie's dog sweaters, the white one with purple flowers. She gets excited and jumps off the sofa in case this means she's going for a walk. She's always ready for a walk, even on a moment's notice.

He tells me he wasn't sure which sweater she was supposed to wear today, or if there's a system for choosing what she wears each day, and hopes he chose the right one.

I explain to him that Sophie's wardrobe selection is random and thank him for remembering to keep her warm.

"You can leave," I say. "I appreciate you looking after Sophie, and staying to look out for me, but you have a killer to hunt. I'll be fine."

"It's not all field work, you know," he tells me. "I was reading the forensics report on Laura's death, making notes, and filling out paperwork. It's nice and quiet here, I've had a productive morning. Got a lot accomplished."

It takes a village to look after Sophie and me when I'm injured. So far, my mother-friend, best friend, and tenant have had to team-up to keep Sophie walked and fed.

He's back in the kitchen, looking in the fridge and pantry.

"What do you want for breakfast?" Eric asks. "The sticker on the pill bottle says 'take with food.'"

I ask for a bagel with herb butter. He slices a bagel and drops it in the toaster.

"Is there anything interesting in the forensics report?" I ask.

"Not all the forensics work is finished, but so far the empty coffee mug next to Laura's body had undissolved digoxin in it.

I guess this means she was, without a doubt, poisoned.

"This is your second last bagel," he says.

"Oscar, add bagels to the shopping list," I say.

"OK," Oscar replies.

"Apparently, digoxin doesn't dissolve easily. Whoever put it in the mug knew that and crushed it into a powder beforehand," he says, opening the fridge. "You're also running low on milk, bread, and eggs."

Crushing pills into powder isn't something you'd do at the last minute, in a moment of anger. Whoever killed Laura went there intending to kill her and prepared the instrument of her death ahead of time.

"Oscar, add milk, bread, and eggs to the shopping list," I say.

"OK," Oscar replies.

I grocery shop on Mondays, but this past Monday, Hannah went back to school after Christmas break, and I wanted to help her pack and send her off, so I didn't go shopping.

According to Eric, I'm also out of cream. I add cream to the shopping list.

"There's no way you can get to the store on crutches," Eric observes. "Send me the list and I'll pick up your groceries after work. I'll even cook us dinner."

"Won't you be busy working?" I ask.

"Yes, but I have to eat, and so do you."

I thank him and ask him if he's seen my phone.

He retrieves it from the top of the fridge and hands it to me.

Apparently, April put it there last night so I wouldn't text anyone when I was loopy from the meds. This is why she's my best friend. She knows when and how to save me from myself.

I open my phone and text him the shopping list from my Oscar app.

He brings me my bagel and sits down on the sofa. There's a knock at the door. Eric gets up to answer it, but I motion for him to stay where he is. I swallow the bite of bagel in my mouth.

"It's Adam," I tell him. "He'll let himself in."

Adam always knocks. In threes. Everyone else uses the doorbell.

"You're OK with your ex-husband letting himself into your house?"

"He knocks first." I shrug. "And it saves me from getting up to answer the door."

Sure enough, Adam lets himself in.

As Adam takes off his boots and coat, Eric gathers up his laptop and papers and gets ready to leave. He says goodbye to me, and he and Adam say hello and goodbye to each other at the door.

"What are you doing here?" I stretch to put my empty plate on the coffee table and pick up my coffee.

"Connie sent me. She says you're supposed to rest and stay off your foot. I'm here to make sure you comply," he says.

"Don't you have to work today?" I ask.

"I can work before and after my babysitting shift. You look awful, are you OK?"

"Thanks," I say, "I'll feel better after a hot bath."

Adam helps me get up from the sofa and transition to my crutch. While helping me hobble to my bedroom, he recognizes his old t-shirt. I knew it had to be his. I ask him if he wants it back after I launder it. He doesn't.

I brush and floss my teeth then run a hot bath with vanilla Epsom salts and a vanilla bath bomb. After I figure out how to manoeuvre myself into the tub without using my left foot, I have a nice soak.

The logistics of getting out of the tub are a bit of a challenge, but I figure it out.

I dry off, hobble around my bedroom collecting underwear, sweatpants, a sweatshirt, and a pair of cozy, hand-knit socks, then get dressed. The entire process takes me more than twice the time and energy it normally does, but I'm finally clean and dressed.

I sit on the edge of the bed for a moment while I muster the energy for the journey back to the sofa, then hoist myself upright with my crutch, and begin the long hobble to the family room.

Adam hears me thudding down the hallway and comes to check on me. He saves us both a lot of time and effort and carries me to the sofa.

Once I'm situated on the sofa, I pick up the almost-finished baby blanket I'm knitting for the Charity Knitting Guild's donation drive and start stitching.

"Has Glenda called you about Laura's will?" I ask as I knit. "I gave her your number. She told me Laura changed her will in a hurry."

He shakes his head. He doesn't like to talk about his clients or cases in a way that's specific. He takes his clients' privacy and his fiduciary duty seriously, so over the years we've learned to speak in the HYPOTHETICAL.

"Can I ask you a legal question?"

I watch him, waiting for permission to proceed.

He nods.

"Let's say that a HYPOTHETICAL client had a secret child, would it be possible for the HYPOTHETICAL client to amend their will to include that child?"

We always emphasize the word HYPOTHETICAL with a loud voice. I don't know why, that's just how the game is played.

"Well," he replies, "HYPOTHETICALLY a will could be amended to include any secret or recently discovered relative."

Ever since Glenda told me that Laura had her will changed in a hurry, I've been wondering if it could have anything to do with the old rumour Connie and Mrs.

Pearson told me about Laura and Brian Sweeney having a love child.

If there is a secret love child, perhaps Brian moving back to Harmony Lake aroused Laura's curiosity and her desire to find the baby she had fifty years ago.

Or, maybe Brian killed Laura to keep their child a secret. Or maybe the secret love child knows Laura changed her will to include them and decided they'd prefer to inherit sooner rather than later.

We decide to watch a movie. I tell him to pick, and I cover myself up with the blanket. I'm feeling drowsy. I'm not sure if it's the energy I exerted having a bath and getting dressed, or a side effect from the pain medication, but I'm tired, and my eyelids are heavy.

CHAPTER 9

I SLEEP off and on for most of the afternoon.

I'm only half awake when Adam leaves to take Sophie for her midday walk, and I'm semi-conscious when he offers to make me lunch.

The doorbell, followed by Sophie's barking, wakes me up. It's dark outside and there's a Matt Damon movie on TV.

Adam opens the door for Eric.

True to his word, he brought the groceries that were on my list.

He says he's making mushroom risotto with spinach salad for dinner. I love risotto! It's my favourite meal. Adam packs up to leave. Despite both Eric and I trying to convince him to stay for dinner, he insists he has work to do and leaves.

"Thank you for making dinner," I say. "How did you know Risotto is my favourite?"

"I used my detective skills," he replies, winking at me. "I asked April."

He's putting the groceries away in the fridge and pantry.

"Risotto is a lot of work, why don't we have something easier," I suggest. "You don't even have to cook. We can order something."

"It's the least I can do," he says. "The observations you made at Laura's house on Tuesday are helpful. Except for the scooter, I wouldn't have recognized the other inconsistencies you noticed because I'm not as familiar as you are with the people involved."

I was hoping he maybe just enjoys spending time with me, but oh well.

He gets the ingredients out for the risotto and I direct him to the pots and pans he needs.

I suggest we open the bottle of pinot grigio in the fridge, and he says no because I'm on pain killers (I forgot I took them) and offers me a glass of water instead.

"Were you able to find out who Laura was talking to on the phone after Phillip dropped her off?" I ask.

"Someone from The Vanity Fur Centre for Animal Health & Wellness. The call was from their main number. Could've been anyone who was there. We're looking into it," he says.

I remind him that the locals call it the Animal Centre, or the AC for short. If he wants the locals to trust him and open up to him, sounding more like a local would help his cause.

I make a mental note to ask around and find out who was there that morning, and who might have left for a while around the time Laura died.

After we eat, April shows up unexpectedly with dessert. She hands Eric a box of red velvet cupcakes with chocolate buttercream icing, and a bag of dog treats for Sophie to sample. These are shaped like shoes.

"Megan..." April is still standing in the hallway by the door. "Remember that top I asked to borrow?"

I don't remember. Is this something we talked about last night when I was out of it from the meds the hospital gave me?

"You knooooow," she says, "the blue one? With the sleeves?"

She's lying, and she's not good at it. April is an entire head taller than me, her torso and arms are way longer than mine, and she's less busty. There's no way we can share a wardrobe or borrow each other's clothes. She must be trying to get me alone.

"Sure!" I say, "I'm not sure where I put it. Let me help you find it."

I grab my crutch and shuffle off toward my bedroom.

When we're alone, she closes the door and hands me a cell phone.

"Glenda left this at Artsy Tartsy this afternoon," she says. "After she left it rang, so I answered it."

"And?" I ask.

"It was her pharmacist, in Ottawa," she explains. "She had a message for Glenda from the Hav-A-Nap motel. They want her to know that she left her medication there when she checked out on Tuesday morning. The hotel manager called the pharmacist using the phone number on the bottle and asked them to let Glenda know that they would keep the medication at the front desk so she can pick it up."

The Hav-a-nap motel is a motel on the outskirts of Harmony Lake, near the highway.

If Glenda checked out on Tuesday morning, that means she stayed there on Monday night, and was already in town when Laura was killed. Not on the road from Ottawa since before dawn, like she said.

"She doesn't like coffee though," I say flatly.

"Is this the bump on your head talking? Are you having another weird reaction to your meds?" April asks.

"No, it's me talking," I reassure her. "Glenda doesn't like coffee, but I guess you can drink anything from a coffee mug, not just coffee."

April still looks confused.

I have no way of knowing what was in the mug on the drying rack beside the sink at Laura's house.

Eric and I ask April to stay for cupcakes, but she declines, explaining that she already has too much cake in her life.

She leaves and Eric and I enjoy the cupcakes. Unlike April, I'm quite happy with the amount of cake in my life.

While I decide not to tell him yet about Glenda's phone, or the revelation that she was in Harmony Lake the morning her sister died, I do tell him about the almost fifty-year-old rumour that Laura and Brian have a love child, and about Glenda mentioning that Laura amended her will because of "family business" that she would only discuss in person.

"One more thing," I say. "Sophie and I went to Laura's house yesterday morning before I slipped on the ice and met the postal carrier. She's the same postal carrier who delivered Laura's mail on Tuesday after Phillip left and before we got there. She said there was a silver or grey four-door, sedan in Laura's driveway.

"You're brilliant," he says.

I blush.

We note the similarities between the car the postal carrier described, and the car Glenda drives, and we wonder if it's a coincidence that Laura was killed just before Mega Mart's offer to buy the AC is set to expire.

Eric takes Sophie for a walk, returns her to the house and leaves.

"Oscar, arm the house," I say after Eric closes the door behind him.

"OK," Oscar replies.

I hear the click as the front door locks, and the beeping of the alarm system being activated.

CHAPTER 10

Saturday is our busiest day of the week at Knitorious. With winter tourist season in full swing, I can't let Connie work alone, so I hobble off to work.

My head feels almost 100% better and my foot, which yesterday was mostly purple with a little yellow, is now mostly yellow with a little purple.

The swelling is way down, but I still can't comfortably wear a shoe or boot on that foot, so I wear a warm hand-knit sock instead and use my crutch to keep it off the ground.

Sophie and I hitch a ride to the store with Phillip, who tells me Kevin and Glenda are staying home today.

The police have released Laura's house and Glenda says she might go over there later, if she is up to it.

Phillip tells me how Glenda becomes emotional when she talks about being in Laura's house without her sister. He says he might go over there tomorrow and clean. He asks if I know whether the police and coroner took their shoes off when they came and went from Laura's house. I tell him I didn't notice when I was there.

Phillip parks his van, comes around to the passenger side, and helps me out of the passenger seat and onto the ground.

He walks me to the back door of the store, where I notice the ice patch I slipped on has been broken up. The spot where it used to be is covered in both rock salt and sand. Excessive, but effective.

"Phillip, thank you for destroying that patch of ice," I say, looking at where the ice used to be. "It was on my to-do list for Tuesday, but I completely forgot about it after…"

"Don't thank me," Phillip replies, "thank your tenant. I ran into him back here on Thursday night. I was leaving for the day and he was coming home. I told him about your fall, and our trip to the hospital, and he took a shovel from his trunk and destroyed the thing. Then he smothered its remains with rock salt, sand, and I think even cat litter."

Regardless of who did it, I'm grateful it's been taken care of and glad no one else will slip on that patch of ice. I make a mental note to thank Eric for taking care of it.

I thank Phillip for driving Sophie and me to work and go inside.

"It's showtime," Connie says.

She walks over to the door, unlocks it, and turns the sign from CLOSED to OPEN.

"Oh! Before I forget"—Connie raises her index finger—"that sweater quantity of yarn that Mrs. Willows ordered arrived yesterday when you were home recovering. I haven't had a chance to call her and let her know."

"No worries," I say. "I'll drop it off to her personally. I've been looking for an excuse to visit the Willows' farm. I haven't seen Mr. Willows since he burst into Wilde Flowers the day after Laura died."

"You be careful, my dear!" Connie shakes her index finger at me and raises her eyebrows.

"Always," I say.

I sit as much as possible, so I'm not tempted to put any weight on my foot.

After lunch, I'm sitting in one of the plush chairs in our cozy seating area and I hear a familiar voice behind me. A man's voice. I can't place it. Connie is introducing him to Sophie, and he's talking to them both.

"How's my patient doing today?" Dr. Pearson asks as he sits on the sofa across from me.

Dr. Pearson is the familiar voice.

"Do you make house calls to check on all your patients?" I ask.

"Only my favourites." He laughs. "I'm in Harmony Lake visiting my parents and thought I'd stop in to check on you."

So thoughtful.

He asks me questions about my head. He doesn't seem worried, and neither am I.

He asks if he can look at my foot, so I gesture for him to follow me to the back room where I sit on the stairs that lead to the apartment and take my off my sock. He pokes at my yellow foot it and examines it.

"It looks great. Definitely stay off it for the rest of today, but you can try putting some weight on it tomorrow," he says. "You're a fast healer."

"Am I healed enough to have wine?"

In hindsight, I realize that might have come across as sounding a bit eager. Hopefully, he doesn't think I have a drinking problem. I explain to him that I endured mushroom risotto without wine.

"In moderation," he cautions, "wine should be fine. In fact, why don't we have a glass together when you're finished here? Then if there's a problem, I'm right there to help you out."

"Such dedication," I say. "But I've already arranged for my neighbour to drive me home right after we close tonight. Thank you, though."

"I'll make sure you get home. In fact, I'll even come back early and walk Sophie before we leave."

An offer I can't refuse. I haven't made arrangements to walk Sophie this evening. Phillip took her this morning, and Connie took her midday, but I have nothing lined up for her evening stroll.

"Sure," I say, "that would be nice. Thank you, Doctor."

"You have to call me Craig, though," he insists. "Being called Dr. Pearson by my date is weird."

A date? A date!

I immediately worry about what I'm wearing. I was expecting to go straight home after work. I chose comfort over style today because I'm still recovering from my fall. I'm wearing an olive green, cabled, fisherman's style sweater (I knit it myself), over black leggings, a black knee-high boot on my right foot, and an olive-green hand knit sock on the other. My curly hair is in a half-updo with the front and sides pinned up, and the rest falling down my back.

Not what I'd choose to wear on a date, but here we are.

Craig leaves, and I limp out of the back room and into the store where I spend the rest of the afternoon chasing customers around the store on my crutch, and despite my limited mobility, trying to help Connie as much as I can.

Shortly before the store closes, Craig comes back to take Sophie for a walk. I help her with her sweater, attach her leash, make sure they have enough poop bags, and wave them off.

"Do you need a lift home, my dear?" Connie asks.

"No thank you," I reply. "Craig and I are going for a drink, and he's driving me home after."

"You have a date?!"

Connie lunges behind the counter for her phone.

I know she's texting April, and it's just a matter of seconds before…

Ding!

April texts me.

There are no customers in the store, and we close in five minutes, so I call April and put her on speaker.

"It's not a date," I say. "It's one glass of wine, and it'll be quick because I have to come back to the store for Sophie."

"I'll pick up Sophie and drive her home," April offers. "I'm just getting my coat on. I'll feed her and settle her in, so you don't have to rush home."

"Good idea, April!" Connie yells in the background.

My plan was to give Sophie dinner in the kitchenette at Knitorious, then leave her here while Craig and I are out. April's offer is better for Sophie, so I accept. I promise to text her when I get home and hang up.

The bell above the door jingles, and I'm expecting to see Craig and Sophie walk in the door, but instead Eric comes in and offers to drive Sophie and me home and take her for a walk.

I tell him thank you, but we have a lift, and she's being walked as we speak. We wish each other a good evening and he leaves again through the front door, stopping to hold it open for April who's on her way in.

When Craig and Sophie get back, Connie grabs her purse, says goodbye to all of us and leaves.

April extends her hand and introduces herself to Craig. I know she totally rushed over here to meet him; Sophie was just her excuse. I take the leash from Craig's hand and put it in April's, I show her the spare house key I've attached to the handle of Sophie's leash with a carabiner clip, then we all leave.

April and Sophie disappear around the corner, and Craig and I decide to go to The Irish Embassy, the Irish pub on the south side of Water Street.

I start my awkward hobble up Water Street, but he decides we should drive and not risk me falling or otherwise doing myself any further damage. Even with a sprained ankle, it doesn't occur to me to drive somewhere as close as the Irish Embassy. I get into his car, parked right in front of the store.

We get a table behind the bar, it's quieter back there.

Craig explains that he's second on the on-call list at the hospital tonight. Apparently, this means there's a small chance he could be called into work, so he orders a sparkling water, and I order a glass of wine. We also order a plate of nachos. Craig suggests we order dinner, but I'm fine with the nachos, and dinner feels like more of a date than a drink and an appetizer, and I'm not ready for that much of a date, yet.

"Have you been here before?" I ask him.

"A few times, yeah," he replies.

The Irish Embassy is a good-sized pub. It's the equivalent of two of the stores on the north side of Water Street. The main floor has a long double-sided bar in the centre of the space with stools lining both sides of the bar.

The bar is surrounded by various types of seating: booths along the walls, tables and chairs in the centre, and two cozy seating areas with sofas and club chairs around a fireplace.

The tables and chairs can be cleared away, to make space for a dance floor and DJ booth when needed.

There's a centre hall staircase immediately behind the bar that leads upstairs where there are two large function rooms, Sheamus' office, extra washrooms, and a large open foyer overlooking the main floor with an intricate wood railing to lean on.

Beyond the staircase there are more tables and chairs. It's quieter behind the stairs than the rest of the pub, so that's a good place to hang out when you want to hear the people you're speaking with. Past those is the patio door.

The Irish Embassy is one of the few businesses on the south side of Water Street, so the patio overlooks the park and the water. It's a beautiful place to spend a summer night. The patio has tables, chairs, umbrellas, and if there's a live band, they pipe the music out to the patio with speakers.

I'm facing the bar and can see Eric tucking into a big bowl of Dublin Coddle, the dinner special tonight.

He sees me too and lifts his fork to wave. I lift my glass. Craig turns to see who I'm waving to, and Eric nods at him. He nods back.

"My tenant," I explain. "He lives in the apartment over the store."

We talk. He spent his twenties becoming a doctor and his thirties working with Doctors Without Borders; I spent both those decades being a mom and wife. He loves kids; I like them in manageable doses. He wants kids soon; I've been there, done that, and have the university bills to prove it. He's never been married and can't wait to find the right person; I was married for twenty years and not sure I want to do it again.

He's funny and charming. He's handsome, and he's a great conversationalist. Hopefully, my conversation skills are better than they were on Thursday, and I've redeemed myself since my medication-fuelled attempt at interacting with him at the hospital.

"Can I ask you a medical question?" I ask.

"Sure."

"If a seventyish-year-old woman, who's otherwise healthy except for a broken leg, took an overdose of digoxin, how long would it take for her to die?"

"That's an oddly specific question, Megan," he says, chuckling. "Would this have anything to do with Laura Pingle?"

"You know her?" I ask.

Duh. Of course, he knows her. He grew up in Harmony Lake. Why do I keep forgetting that?

"Yeah, she's a friend of my mum's. I knew her, and her

husband, Dr. Pingle. In fact, I saw her the morning she died. I visited her in her room just before they discharged her," he says, shaking his head. "It's hard to believe she's gone. And so tragically. She was such a nice person. Who would want to hurt her?"

That's what I'm trying to figure out.

"Were you her doctor?" I ask.

"No, I was on the surgical recovery floor doing rounds and stopped by to see her and say hi." He leans forward and rests his arms on the table. "She likely died quickly," he explains in a soothing voice.

I imagine this is the voice he uses when he delivers bad news to patients and their families.

"She probably wasn't in much pain or discomfort. Her heart rate would have become erratic. In Laura's case it became too fast, a condition called tachycardia, until her heart couldn't keep up anymore and stopped working. Also, she would have been weaker than normal because she had just had surgery, which may have sped up the process."

"I see," I say.

I hadn't thought about her final moments. She looked so peaceful in her chair, that I just assumed her passing was peaceful and I'm glad to hear that was likely the case.

"I also think," Craig adds, "that whoever killed her knows about digoxin. They either researched it, have some medical education, or are familiar with it because of their own medical history."

"Why do you think that?" I ask.

"Because they knew how much to give her." He raises his index finger. "They timed it so she would be dead when someone found her, which means they knew approximately how long it would take to kill her." He puts up his middle finger next to his index finger. "*And* they crushed it ahead of time because they knew it doesn't dissolve easily." He raises his ring finger.

I didn't realize the information about the pills being crushed was public knowledge. Eric told me and I'm a member of the public, and now that I think about it, he didn't ask me to keep it to myself, so I guess it is common knowledge.

We finish our drinks and nachos and his cell phone starts chiming. The first on call doctor isn't reachable, so he has to go. I totally understand. I try to pay the bill, but he won't let me and suggests that I can get it next time.

He drops me off at home and asks permission to call me. I grant permission, but wonder why, because we are at different places in our lives and we clearly want different things.

April and Connie text me. Whoever their spy is at the pub must have told them we left. They want details and want to know if I want to see him again. I tell them about my evening, put Sophie out in the backyard, and get ready for bed.

CHAPTER 11

I wake up, sit on the edge of the bed, put both feet on the floor, and delicately put some weight on my foot.

So far, so good.

I stand up carefully, keeping most of my weight on my good foot.

No pain.

Cautiously optimistic, I gently shift some weight back and forth between my good foot and my injured foot, adding a bit more pressure on the injured foot each time I shift.

It feels good to have both feet functioning and on the floor again.

The swelling is way down compared to yesterday and almost all the purple bits have been replaced with various shades of yellow. I put some more weight on it and tentatively take a few steps.

Surprisingly, it feels fine.

It only hurts if I poke it, and oddly I get the urge to poke it often. Why is my first reaction to a bruise always to poke it? After thirty-nine years, you'd think I'd know better. Bruises are tender and poking them hurts.

My foot feels good, but I don't want to push it by standing in the shower, so I run a bath instead.

Adam texts and asks if he can let himself in when he gets here. I reply that yes, he can. He says when he gets here, he'll take Sophie for a walk and feed her.

It's Sunday, and Adam and I FaceTime Hannah together every Sunday. He makes breakfast for him and me while we have a virtual visit with our daughter and hear about her week. We've been alternating between his place and mine. This should be his week, but because of my foot he offered to come here.

ADAM IS in the kitchen whisking batter for French toast when I walk in proudly, using both feet.

"Look at you—you're walking!" he says. "Don't do too much too soon, right?"

I nod, then I pick up my tablet and FaceTime Hannah. The three of us get caught up, and I show Hannah my yellow foot.

We finish eating, say our goodbyes and I love yous to our daughter, and I end the FaceTime call.

"How was your date last night?" Adam asks.

"How do you know about that?" I answer his question with a question.

"Everybody knows," he shrugs. "If you don't want people to know, you should go on dates away from Harmony Lake."

"It's not a secret. It wasn't even a real date. It was just a drink with Mrs. Pearson's son who also happens to be the doctor who treated me after my fall." I give him a one-shoulder shrug.

"I'm only teasing, Meg. I'm glad you're putting yourself out there."

"Are you seeing anyone?" I ask gently, treading carefully into what I know is a sensitive subject for Adam.

"No." He shakes his head.

I sense he has more to say but is hesitant, so I sit silently, and wait patiently.

"I've set up a profile on a dating website, but I haven't done anything with it," he adds.

"You should meet people. You deserve to be happy," I say. I mean it.

"We both do," he points out.

"The chances of what happened last time…happening again…are near zero. Zero chances." I bring the tip of my thumb and the tips of my fingers together to make a zero.

"Isn't that what you said about the odds of finding another dead body?" he asks. "And then it happened."

Touché.

"Would it help if I left you a review on the dating site?" I ask, joking.

He throws his head back and laughs.

"I'll give you at least three stars," I add. "OK, maybe four stars. And if I email them a copy of our marriage certificate, maybe I can get one of those *Verified* badges next to my name. You know, like on shopping websites where the reviewer has *Verified Purchaser* next to their name."

"I don't think that's how dating sites work," he says, laughing. "But maybe you can give me a written reference and I'll take it with me on first dates."

We're both laughing hysterically now, and he stops talking to catch his breath. Then, laughing so hard that it's difficult to understand him, he says, "and I'll update my profile so it says, reference available upon request."

Now, it's my turn to throw my head back and laugh. I pick up my napkin from the table and dab tears of laughter from my eyes.

When we do decide to date, whoever dates us will be lucky. We're hilarious!

ADAM LEAVES, and I put on my boots. Both of them. And brag to Sophie when I'm able to get the left boot to fit comfortably on my left foot. It's nice to wear boots on both feet again. I bundle myself in my coat, hat, cowl, and mitts to face the bitterly cold day.

I drive to the store to pick up Mrs. Willow's yarn order, then drive out to the Willows farm, where I pull into the long driveway and park behind Mr. Willows' red pickup truck, which is parked behind Mrs. Willows' silver four-door sedan.

I'd forgotten that Mrs. Willows drives a silver four-door sedan.

I need to find out where this car was on Tuesday morning, and who was driving it.

I get out of my car and walk to the house. The Willows have a large farm with lots of land and multiple buildings. I glance at the barn closest to their house and see the white van from the Animal Centre with its logo sprawled across the side and back of the van, plain as day.

Who would be here from the AC on a Sunday?

I knock on the door to the house, and no one answers. I knock again and listen for the sound of anyone inside. Nothing. Maybe they're in the barn.

I walk to the barn and peek my head through the open door. Mr. and Mrs. Willows are standing in front of one of the horse stalls talking to Dr. Val White, the head veterinarian from the Animal Centre. Mrs. Willows sees me. She smiles and waves, then comes over.

"Let's go to the house," she says, "and get out of this drafty barn."

She leads the way and I follow. She invites me in, and I step into their kitchen.

"Is the horse in the stall OK?" I hand her the bag of yarn.

"Thank you, Megan." She takes the yarn from me. "Yes, it

looks like she's fine. She's pregnant and has been off her food for a few days, so Henry called the vet to come and check on her."

"I'm glad mum and foal are both OK," I say.

"Yes, Henry loves those animals, every single one of them. He worries about them and sometimes he overreacts," she explains.

"I completely understand," I say. "They can't tell us what's wrong, so it's difficult to know how serious it might be, or if they're hurting."

"Listen, Megan, I'd like to apologize for Henry's outburst at the florist shop on Wednesday. I heard you were there and saw what happened."

It's not her job to apologize on behalf of someone else, but I appreciate the sentiment, nonetheless.

"The situation with Mega Mart must be stressful enough. Laura's death probably makes it even more stressful," I say, "especially with her death being so sudden and so close to the deadline for Mega Mart's offer."

She nods, then opens the bag of yarn to check that it's what she ordered.

"I hope Mr. Willows is feeling...calmer...now," I say.

Mrs. Willows closes the bag of yarn and places it on the kitchen table. She uses her hands to cover her face and her shoulders start heaving up and down. She's crying.

We stand in silence for a moment while Mrs. Willows composes herself. She tears a sheet of paper towel from the roll on the counter and dabs her eyes.

"It's not just Mega Mart," she says, pulling a chair away from the kitchen table and sitting down. "Henry's been having..." She pats her chest while she searches for the right word. "...episodes. They thought it might be his heart, so they referred him to a cardiologist in the city. That's where we were on Tuesday."

She looks at me like she's waiting for me to make a connection or draw a conclusion.

"You're saying when Laura died, you and Mr. Willows were in the city at a cardiology appointment?" I ask. "That's funny, I could have sworn I saw you and Mr. Willows in your car driving down Water Street on Tuesday morning."

It's a lie. I didn't see either of the Willows' on Tuesday. I'm trying to determine if they were driving her car on Tuesday, who was in it, and what time they left Harmony Lake for their appointment.

"That would be Henry," she admits. "I was at home until we left for the city just past noon. Henry ran errands in the morning before we left. He likes to use my car because it's better on gas."

"So, you were in town until noon," I confirm.

Laura died before noon.

Her eyes well up with tears and her chin starts to quiver. She dabs her eyes with the paper towel, and nods.

"We lied," she sobs. "We knew Henry would be a suspect, and aside from a couple of errands, and driving around, he didn't have an alibi, so we lied."

Her quiet sobs become loud sobs.

I walk over to the counter, tear another sheet of paper towel from the roll and hand it to her. She dries her eyes and blows her nose.

"He didn't do it, Megan."

She places a hand on my wrist and looks at me pleadingly.

"I know he's loud and short-tempered, but my Henry could never kill someone."

I believe her. I believe that she's convinced he's not capable of murder.

"Who do you think might have done it?" I ask. "Do you have any theories?"

"I think they should ask Dr. White where she was when Laura died," Mrs. Willows says emphatically. "Everyone at the AC knows Dr. White and Laura didn't get along. They argued about everything, especially after Laura found out Dr. White's uncle is the CEO of Mega Mart."

Her uncle is the what? Did I hear her right? The veterinarian at the AC is the niece of the man who's trying to purchase the AC and tear it down?

CHAPTER 12

"ARE YOU OK, MEGAN?" Mrs. Willows asks.

I nod and close my mouth, realizing it's open because my jaw literally dropped when she told me about Dr. White.

"Yes, I'm fine," I say, trying to act like I'm not completely flabbergasted.

I shake myself out of it and refocus.

"How was Mr. Willows' cardiology appointment?" I ask. "Is his heart alright?"

"Yes, thank goodness," she replies, sounding relieved. "The cardiologist thinks Henry has been having panic attacks. We've been so worried, Megan! I can't tell you how many hours we've spent on the internet researching his symptoms and reading about all the different heart conditions we thought he might have. The internet is full of worst-case scenarios. I'm not sure if being able to access all that knowledge so easily is a blessing or a curse, to be honest."

I wonder if they happened to come across information about digoxin on their internet travels?

Mrs. Willows gets up from the kitchen table and throws her used paper towels in the garbage. "Panic attacks brought on by all the Mega Mart stress, no doubt," she mumbles under her breath.

She clenches her jaw and gives me a tight-lipped smile.

I'M ABOUT to back out of the Willows' long, narrow driveway when an SUV pulls up behind me and parks, leaving no room for me to back up around it. I get out to speak to the driver and am shocked to find myself looking at Jay Singh. He rolls down his window.

"Are you trying to leave?" Jay asks.

"Yes, if you pull over a bit, I think I can back up around you," I reply.

He looks at me, smirks, and points at me. A look of realization flashes briefly across his face. He recognizes me, and he's trying to remember where and how we met.

"My friend, April, and I visited you and your adorable twins last September? Right after a mutual friend of ours died?" I say, trying to jog his memory.

I might be forgettable, but a murder isn't easy to forget.

"Right! Of course. How's it going?" he asks. "Hey, solved any murders lately?"

We both laugh.

Not yet, Jay, not yet. But I'm working on it.

I ask after his twins, and when I chide him for working on a Sunday, he doesn't deny he's here for work. Considering Jay's business is providing discreet, high interest, short-term loans, I assume the Willows are having some financial difficulty and might need the Mega Mart deal more than most of us realize.

I PULL INTO MY DRIVEWAY, turn off the car, and root through my bag until I find my phone. I heard it ding while I was driving.

Craig: I'm sorry I had to bail in such a hurry. Hope we can do it again soon? I promise not to run away next time ;)

Me: No worries! I hope everyone made a full recovery. I'll check my calendar and be in touch.

By *check my calendar*, I mean figure out how to shut down this pseudo-dating situation. Craig is looking for someone who wants to get married and have babies, and I'm not comfortable committing to anything more than an appetizer. I need to tell him we're destined for friendship and nothing more. As Hannah would say, I need to Friendzone him. I haven't had to have this conversation with a guy since I was eighteen.

Glenda comes out of Phillip's house carrying Kevin and puts him down on the snowy lawn. Phillip isn't with her. Perfect. I was hoping to get her alone, and her timing couldn't be better, because speaking to her is the next item on my to-do list for today. I almost didn't see her, but Kevin is wearing a tiny fluorescent yellow parka with tiny fluorescent yellow booties, so he's hard to miss.

I get out of my car and we wave.

"Nice to see you back on your feet!" she calls across the lawn.

I curtsey.

We laugh and she gives me a thumbs-up.

I walk across the lawn and join her on Phillip's driveway.

"Don't let Phillip see you do that," she says, smiling and pointing to the footprints I made walking from my driveway to theirs.

"I know, I know, he hates footprints. He prefers the snow to be smooth and pristine," I say.

He always forgives me, and we have a fresh snowfall to

look forward to every few days, so they won't be there long, anyway.

"How are you, Glenda? Phillip mentioned that you were planning to go to Laura's house yesterday."

"I couldn't do it. It's too hard," she replies. "I have to get over it and go tomorrow, no matter how difficult it is. I told Mort I'll drop off Laura's outfit on Tuesday."

Mort Ackerman is our local funeral director. He owns Mourning Glory Funeral Home in Harmony Hills.

My heart goes out to Glenda, I can't imagine having to choose the outfit to bury my sister in.

"I can go with you, if it would help," I offer. "Knitorious is closed on Mondays so I don't have to be at the store."

Glenda unzips her coat halfway, picks up Kevin, puts him in her coat, and zips it until just his head is peeking out.

"I'd really appreciate that, Megan, thank you! Phillip was there for a short while earlier today, but I can tell he's not ready to go back either." She rubs Kevin's head. "Also, he's not comfortable being in her bedroom and going through her personal things."

"I'm happy to help anyway I can," I say.

Glenda cups one of Kevin's ears in her hand, then the other. I think she's checking to make sure they aren't too cold.

"You and Kevin seem to have really bonded," I say, reaching out and scratching Kevin between the ears. "If you want to spend some time with Sophie so you can get to know each other before you take her back to Ottawa, we can figure something out."

"That would be a good idea," she replies, lowering her gaze to the ground, "if I were taking her back to Ottawa with me."

Glenda looks up at me. "We live in a tenth-floor condominium. We don't have a yard for Sophie to run around in. And if I'm honest, I love animals, but I'm not much of a pet person. Never have been. I think growing up as a veterinarian's daughter, I've had more than my share of pets."

I nod.

At least she knows her limits and isn't taking Sophie out of a sense of obligation, that wouldn't make either of them happy.

"I understand," I say, nodding and trying to sound reassuring.

I'm about to ask if she's made other arrangements for Sophie and suggest that I could keep her if no other arrangements have been made, but before I can open my mouth, she starts speaking.

"Is there a chance you might want Sophie? You two are obviously close, and she seems happy living with you."

You think?! Yes, I want to keep Sophie!

I nod enthusiastically.

"I'd love to have Sophie as a permanent roommate! Thank you!"

I clap my hands in front of my chin.

"Glenda?"

I take a deep breath. Tread carefully, Megan.

"Did you misplace your cell phone by chance?" I ask.

"Yes! I did! Did you find it?"

"Not exactly, but I have it," I explain. "You left it at Artsy Tartsy, and April picked it up."

"I must remember to thank her," Glenda says.

"After you left it at the bakery, it rang."

"Oh?" she asks, her interest piqued.

I tell her what April said about her pharmacist in Ottawa relaying a message from the Hav-A-Nap hotel.

"It's true, I'm afraid," she admits. "I arrived in Harmony Lake the night before they discharged Laura from the hospital, not the following morning like I led you all to believe."

"Why didn't you tell the truth?" I ask. "This is the type of thing that Eric can confirm using credit card statements, cell phone pings, and such. Wouldn't it have been better to tell the truth?"

"I left Ottawa early Monday afternoon," she explains. "My plan was to stop at Harmony Hills Hospital on my way into Harmony Lake and pick up Laura's house keys. Then I could pick up some groceries while I was in Harmony Hills and fill the fridge before she got home the next morning."

These are things Phillip would have already taken care of, and I think Glenda would know that.

"Traffic was a mess, there were patches of black ice between here and Ottawa, which means there were lane closures because of the ice and accidents blocking the lanes that were open, and instead of getting to Harmony Hills at dinner time, like I'd planned, it was almost 9 p.m.—far too late to visit Laura, get her keys, and go grocery shopping. I was exhausted, so I got a room at the Hav-A-Nap and went to bed."

"I'm sure if you contacted Phillip, he would've let you into her house or told you where the spare key is," I counter.

"I'm sure you're right," Glenda agrees. "But I didn't want to inconvenience anyone or cause any trouble. I just wanted to put my head down. When I arrived at Laura's house the next day, and Eric told me what happened, I panicked. I knew I didn't have an alibi for the last sixteen hours. Saying I was alone in a motel room isn't exactly a strong alibi, especially when half the town knows that Laura and I weren't seeing eye to eye about the Mega Mart offer."

"Glenda, you have to tell this to Eric."

"I know, and I will," she says, checking the temperature of Kevin's exposed ears again. "I didn't do it. I love Laura. She's my big sister, and I looked up to her. I would never hurt her."

Her eyes well up, and I'm not sure if it's because of tears, the cold temperature, or both.

Glenda asks me if she can have her phone back. I tell her I have to check with Eric first. She says she understands.

We agree we're both chillier than we'd like to be, so we decide on a time to meet at Laura's house tomorrow, and she takes Kevin inside to warm up. I run across the lawn, leaving a second set of footprints in my wake, excited to tell Sophie that she's staying in Harmony Lake.

CHAPTER 13

Knitorious is closed on Mondays, so today's my day for running errands.

After Sophie and I finish breakfast and go for our morning walk, I drive to Water Street and park behind The Pharmer's Market, our local pharmacy.

First stop: acquire caffeine at Latte Da.

Until recently, a daily coffee from Latte Da was part of my morning routine, but it's been demoted from daily necessity, to an occasional treat because Sophie isn't allowed inside Latte Da.

Dropping off Sophie at the store first then going to Latte Da might sound like a good idea, but by the time I drop her off, take off her sweater and her leash, and freshen up her water bowl, going out feels like a hassle and I end up making coffee instead. My wallet is happier with the new arrangement, but my taste buds aren't.

I join the rest of the caffeine addicts in line, right behind Eric. I take a deep breath. He smells so good. Just one more deep breath.

"Hey stranger," I say.

"Hey there! Nice boots," he says, looking at my feet. "It's nice to see you wearing two of them again."

"I know, right?" I agree.

The line moves forward, and we move with it, getting one step closer to the caffeine we both crave.

"How was your date on Saturday night?" he asks.

"It wasn't a date," I say. "Craig is Mrs. Pearson's son, and the doctor who helped me at the hospital after I slipped on the ice. By the way, thank you for breaking up the ice and preventing another accident."

"It looked like a date," he states tersely. "Most doctors I know don't take their patients to an intimate pub for drinks and nachos."

The Embassy isn't exactly what I'd call intimate, but whatever.

"You paid attention to what we ordered?" I ask.

This is both impressive and slightly unnerving, until I remember that I noticed him sitting at the bar, eating a bowl of Dublin Coddle, and drinking a beer.

"I'm a cop. It's my job to be observant. It's hard to turn off when I'm not at work, but I'm trying, trust me."

He sounds irritated. Why is he giving me attitude?

"So, do all his patients call him Craig, or just you?"

Excuse me? He's obviously annoyed about something, and I sympathize, but I don't appreciate him taking it out on me.

"I don't know," I reply curtly. "I'm not acquainted with all of his patients, but if you're really curious, I'll give you his number and you can ask him."

Bad moods are contagious, and now I'm starting to feel grumpy. I move closer so I know he'll hear me when I speak quietly.

"Eric, are you angry with me?" I ask. "Have I offended you?"

His chin falls slightly toward his chest, and his shoulders

droop ever so subtly, causing his normally perfect posture to be not quite perfect with a hint of a slouch. He looks defeated. I've never seen him like this.

Before he can answer, it's his turn to order. He takes a break from giving me attitude and orders a medium roast, double-double.

He moves along to the end of the counter to wait for his coffee, and I approach the cash register to place my order. While I'm waiting for the cashier to come back, I hear Connie's voice.

"Honestly, Eric, why don't you just pull her pigtails!" she says just loudly enough for me to hear and squeezes his arm.

I bite my lips trying not to laugh out loud. The cashier comes back, and I order a cafe mocha with extra whipped cream.

"I didn't see you guys when I came in," I say to Connie and Archie as they both stop and give me a quick hug on their way out of the coffee shop.

"Take care, my dear. I'll see you tomorrow."

I move to the end of the counter and wait for my coffee. The barista hands Eric his order, and he breezes past me, through the door, and onto Water Street.

Good day to you, too, sir!

Acquire caffeine: check!

Next stop: The Pharmer's Market, to replenish my ibuprofen supply.

I think this is the first bottle of ibuprofen I've ever finished before it expired. While there's probably no hurry to replace it, it might be best to keep some on hand in case I find another patch of ice to slip on.

I walk out of Latte Da, and Eric is standing on the sidewalk sipping his coffee. I pretend I don't see him, turn, and start walking toward The Pharmer's Market. I'm wearing sunglasses, and it's easy to ignore someone from behind tinted lenses.

I turn and make my best surprised face.

"I didn't see you there," I fib.

"I'm sorry for being a jerk."

I'd have chosen a different, more swear-y noun, but jerk will do.

"I'm in a bad mood, and I took it out on you. It has nothing to do with you and I'm sorry."

"What does it have to do with?" I ask.

He moves closer to me. If he's trying to speak privately, it's not possible on Water Street.

"I feel like I'm spinning my wheels on this case," he says. "I've solved two murders in Harmony Lake, moved here, joined the local police department, done as much community outreach work as I possibly can, gone out of my way to be approachable, and people still don't trust me. They won't talk to me. Half of them won't even call me Eric, they insist on calling me Detective or Mr. Sloane."

"That sounds frustrating," I sympathize as we stroll toward The Pharmer's Market.

"The only information I get from the community are bits of gossip I happen to overhear, and the information you pass along me, because they trust you. I just want to do my job."

"It takes time," I assure him. "This is a tight-knit community, and the people are protective of their privacy and cautious of outsiders. I know it's not fair and not what you want to hear, but that's how it is."

"How much time?" he asks

"Well," I say, "I once heard a fourth-generation town resident refer to a third-generation town resident as 'that new guy who's only been in town for five minutes.'"

Eric laughs and I decide not to ruin it for him by telling him it's a true story.

"Thank you," he says, "for making me feel better. Please don't think I'm not grateful for all the help and information you pass on to me, because I am. I just wish they'd skip the middleman, er, middlewoman...middlePERSON and come to me directly."

"Speaking of passing along information, can we talk later? Away from potential eavesdroppers?" I ask. "I have a few things to pass along to you."

We try to figure out a time to get together, but I'm meeting Glenda later at Laura's house, and I don't know how long we'll be there. I don't want her to feel rushed. We agree that I'll text him when I get home from Laura's house, and he'll come over.

IN THE PAIN relief aisle at The Pharmer's Market, I'm comparing the brand name ibuprofen to the store brand ibuprofen and enjoying my cafe mocha, when a man sidles up next to me.

"It's nice to see you standing up, Megan," he says. "I almost didn't recognize you."

"Hi Mr. Sweeney, it's nice to be standing up. I'm glad you recognized me, it's good to see you again."

I recognize him as the universal blood donor Connie introduced me to at the hospital. His voice is jollier, and his smile more exuberant than I remember.

"Remember what I said?" He's waggling an index finger at me.

What did he say? Think, Megan.

"Mr. Sweeney was my father, you should call me Brian," he says, reminding me.

"How are you doing, Brian?"

"Pretty good, under the circumstances. Laura and I were friends, you know."

"Connie mentioned that," I say. "I'm sorry for your loss."

His exuberant smile disappears, and a weaker smile, with sad eyes, take its place.

"Yes, growing up Laura and I were very close, but we had a falling out—well our families did—and I'm just glad we mended our friendship before she died."

"I'm sure she was glad to make amends with you too," I say.

"Anne-Marie and I are here to drop off my father's old medication. Finally. He passed away two months ago," he says, changing the subject. "Anne-Marie is my wife. She's over at the pharmacy counter." He uses his thumb to point over his shoulder.

"I'd heard your dad passed away. I'm sorry for that loss too."

"Thank you, Megan," he says. "He had a long and happy life. Ninety-five is a good age, and nothing to be sad about. He was healthy, too, until he turned ninety, that's when all his problems began…"

I suspect I'm about to hear the not-so-short version of Mr. Sweeney's health over the last five years of his life, when we're interrupted by a lovely, friendly lady, who I assume is Anne-Marie.

"Brian, don't bore the poor woman!" Anne-Marie says teasingly while she playfully nudges him.

She smiles at me and extends her hand. I shake it.

"Megan, this is my wife Anne-Marie. Anne-Marie, this is Megan Martel. She just took over Connie's knitting store."

"It's nice to meet you, Anne-Marie."

"Likewise, Megan."

"We're heading to Harmony Hills to look at furniture and paint colours," Brian says. "We're redecorating Dad's bedroom, making it cheerful, and setting it up so the grand-kids can sleep there when they come to visit."

Their faces light up when Brian mentions the grandkids. I

know proud grandparents when I see them and give them the opportunity to brag.

"Oh, you have grandchildren?" I ask.

They have two married sons, wonderful daughters-in-law, three grandsons, and one granddaughter. Their granddaughter adores all things horse-related, and Brian can't wait for her to visit in the summer so he can take her to the Animal Centre to visit the horses.

"She might be able to learn about grooming and caring for them too," he says. "Those are the kinds of educational programs we offer there, you see."

"Yes, I'd heard you were volunteering at the AC. How do you like it?" I ask.

"I enjoy it very much. I originally did it to spend time with Laura, after we became friends again, but it really is a great organization that does wonderful work with animals and the community. I'm happy I decided to do it, and with Laura gone, they'll need more volunteers than ever, so I'll stay on if they'll have me," he replies.

"What do you do there? What's your role at the AC?" I ask.

"Referee, mostly." He laughs, and Anne-Marie joins him. "I spent most of my time distracting Laura and Dr. White when they would argue."

"They argued a lot?" I ask.

"Oh yes," he replies. "Always butting heads, those two. If one says it's raining, I swear the other one would say it's sunny just for the sake of not agreeing."

"Sounds like you had your hands full," I say.

"You can say that again, Megan!" he agrees. "They're so much alike, those two. Dr. White reminds me of Laura with her red hair and fiery temper."

"Do you volunteer there, too, Anne-Marie?" I ask.

"No!" she says, flicking her wrist and letting her hand go limp.

"I'm trying to convince her," Brian interjects, taking her hand.

"The AC is Brian's thing," Anne-Marie explains. "I prefer the company of people over animals. I used to be a nurse, and I like caring for people. I've been volunteering with Meals on Wheels since Brian's dad died. Two days a week I deliver warm meals to infirmed local residents, stop in for a visit, keep them company, and make sure they have everything they need."

"What a lovely way to give back," I say.

I look at Brian.

"Someone from the AC called Laura at home the morning she died," I tell him.

I watch him for a reaction, but he doesn't have one.

"Only Laura's side of the conversation was overheard," I elaborate, "but it sounded like she was planning a visit with the caller. You wouldn't happen to know who might have phoned her, would you?"

"Let me think." He looks up at the ceiling. "I was there. Archie Wright's boy, Ryan was there installing the new safe. Dr. White was there. The rest of the veterinary staff were there and some other volunteers." He looks from the ceiling to me and shakes his head. "It could've been anyone."

"Ryan was there? Why was the AC getting a new safe?"

Ryan Wright is Archie's son. He and Archie are The Wright Men For The Job, Harmony Lake's father-son handyman team. Archie is mostly retired now. Ryan handles most of the jobs, with Archie helping out on occasion.

"Didn't you hear?" he asks.

I shake my head, and he and Anne-Marie move in closer.

"Just before Christmas there was a break-in at the AC, and they stole all the medication," he whispers. "All of it. So, Laura ordered a bigger, better safe. It arrived while she was in the hospital, and Ryan came to install it the morning she died."

Do animals use digoxin? Maybe this is where the killer got their weapon?

"It was lovely to meet you, Megan," Anne-Marie says. "We need to get on the road to Harmony Hills. Furniture and paint colours won't pick themselves."

We all laugh.

"It was lovely to meet you, too," I say. "And it was nice to see you again, Brian."

They say goodbye and turn to leave.

As Brian and Anne-Marie reach the end of the aisle and turn toward the door, she reaches into her coat pocket to pull out her gloves, and a piece of paper falls out.

I place the brand name ibuprofen back on the shelf, pick up a bottle of the store brand pills, then walk over and pick up the fallen paper.

It's their shopping list. The left side of the page is a list of stores they're planning to visit, and the right side is a grocery list.

I hurry to the door to catch up with them, but when I get there, they're pulling away in a grey, four-door sedan, with Brian in the driver's seat.

Who knew grey and silver four-door sedans are so popular in Harmony Lake?

I hate shopping without a list, I always forget some things and purchase extra things I don't need because I can't remember what was on the list.

While I'm waiting in line to pay for the ibuprofen, I take a photo of the list and text it to Connie, asking her to text it to one of the Sweeneys.

This might be far-fetched, but could Dr. White be Laura and Brian's secret love child? She's around the right age, and Brian says she reminds him of Laura.

If she is, maybe she found out and was so angry she killed Laura. Or maybe she endeared herself until Laura included her in her will, then killed her so she could sell the AC land to her uncle, the CEO of Mega Mart.

No, that wouldn't make sense. Laura was a smart lady. She was vehemently opposed to Mega Mart opening a store in Harmony Lake; there's no way she would have bequeathed the land to the CEO's niece.

I pay for my purchase and shove the receipt and the Willows shopping list in my wallet.

CHAPTER 14

I STOP at home to drop off my purchase and take Sophie for her midday walk before I head over to Laura's house.

On my way to the car, I check Phillip's driveway to see if Glenda is still there. We could drive over together. There's no point in taking two cars, but her car isn't there, so I drive over on my own.

I pull into Laura's driveway, next to Glenda's car. We get out of our cars at the same time. She says she waited outside for me because she'd rather not go inside by herself.

"Do you have a key?" I ask.

"No," she replies. "Phillip says he uses the spare."

I walk over to the large foliage-filled urn on the right of the door and rummage through the snowy sprays of evergreen, dogwood branches, and juniper sprouts until I find the pinecone. I twist and pull the pinecone until the semi-frozen soil underneath it cracks and gives way, allowing me to pull the pinecone out of the urn. The pinecone is glued to the cap of an old prescription pill bottle, and inside the pill bottle is Laura's spare key. I turn to Glenda and shake the bottle to show her I found it.

I open the pill bottle, remove the key, and unlock the front door, trying not to focus on the flashbacks I'm having to the last time I opened this door and found Laura's dead body.

We step into the small foyer, and I put the pill bottle and key on the table by the door. Glenda is taking off her boots and coat. I take a deep breath and repeat the mantra, *heavy shoulders, long arms* in my head, in an effort to release the tension I'm feeling. I take off my boots and coat.

"Phillip said to tell you to put the package of dog sweaters in your bag as soon as you get here so you won't forget them when you leave," Glenda tells me.

I put the bag of dog sweaters in my cranberry-coloured tote bag and tell Glenda she can tell Philip it's been taken care of.

Glenda leads the way upstairs, and I follow.

Laura's house is tasteful. Her decorating style is neutral, practical, and tidy; a conventional blend of beiges, greys, and creams.

Until you get to the master bedroom and step into the purple palace.

Remember the movie, The Wizard of Oz? The moment right after Dorothy and her house land in Munchkin land, when Dorothy opens the front door and crosses the threshold from her black and white world into the world of vibrant technicolour? That's what it's like to cross the threshold from Laura's neutral, conservative décor to her polychromatic purple paradise.

"Purple was her favourite colour," Glenda says.

You don't say. Glenda and I are both smiling. It would be impossible to walk into this room and not smile.

Three walls are painted lilac, and the wall behind the bed is a vibrant violet. The bed linens are a geometric pattern of various shades of purple, and the windows have orchid-purple curtains. The dressers and nightstands are black with purple knobs on the drawers.

I peek into the master en suite where the toilet lid has a

plush lavender cover with matching floor mats in front of the sink and bathtub. The walls are the opposite of the bedroom. Three walls are vibrant violet, and the accent wall is lilac. Three purple towels, light, medium, and dark, hang from the towel rack. The countertop is purple faux-marble.

In a million years I would never have guessed that Laura Pingle's bedroom was a shrine to purple. His purple highness himself, Prince, would have been proud.

Glenda pops out of the walk-in closet holding up a lilac sun dress with spaghetti straps.

"This is her favourite dress," she says, smiling wistfully and looking at the dress with a hint of nostalgia in her eyes. "Now I just have to find her purple cardigan to go over it."

We go through Laura's drawers, marvelling at her enviable collection of hand-knit sweaters, until we find the short, fitted, purple cardigan with mother-of-pearl buttons. Glenda lays the dress and cardigan on Laura's bed and stands back to admire the outfit.

There are some creases in the dress, and I offer to iron it. I ask Glenda where I can find the iron and ironing board, and she directs me the linen closet inside the en suite washroom.

They're exactly where she said they'd be. I scan the purple walls of Laura's bedroom for an electrical outlet and set up the ironing board. The iron's water reservoir is empty, so I take it to the sink in the en suite washroom to fill it.

While the reservoir fills with water, I look around, taking in all the purple, and something sitting on top of the amethyst-coloured garbage pail next to the sink catches my eye. A box with the Let Me Take A Cellfie logo on it.

Let Me Take A Cellfie is the online DNA company that provides the who's-your-daddy DNA results on those horrible daytime talk shows. Why would Laura have a box from a DNA test? I pick up the box and inspect it to make sure it is what I think it is, snap a pic of it with my phone, and place it back on top of the garbage pail where I found it.

While I iron the dress, Glenda collects underwear and shoes for Laura to wear and looks through Laura's jewellery box for their mother's pearl earrings and matching pearl necklace.

"Glenda, what happened between Laura and Brian Sweeney? I heard they had a falling out during their senior year of high school," I ask casually while I iron.

"I don't think it was so much them falling out as it was our families falling out," she explains. "Specifically, I think it was between our mothers, but I don't know for sure. We were never allowed to talk about it."

She finds the pearl earrings and necklace and lays them on the bed next to the cardigan. They complement the mother-of-pearl buttons on the sweater beautifully. She disappears into the walk-in closet.

"Our families were best friends before I was even born," Glenda says loudly from the closet. "We celebrated holidays and birthdays together and even took vacations together. Then one day, we weren't talking to them, and they weren't talking to us. That included Brian and Laura."

"Do you remember anything from around that time that might explain what happened?" I press.

I take the dress from the ironing board, place it on its hanger, and lay it on the bed with the cardigan, shoes, and jewellery. Glenda puts a garment bag on the bed next to the outfit.

"I do remember one thing," she says. "You have to remember, I was much younger than Laura, there are ten years between us, so I was only eight when it happened."

Glenda begins carefully covering the dress and sweater with the garment bag she found in Laura's closet.

"I remember being sick that winter with one sore throat after another. I missed a lot of school and took a lot of antibiotics," she recalls, laughing.

"After my third or fourth sore throat and fever, the doctor

diagnosed me with tonsillitis and told my mother that my tonsils had to be removed. A few weeks later, they were and my throat infections stopped. I felt better, but I had to go back to the doctor for a post-surgery follow-up appointment."

I return the ironing board and iron to where I found them while she speaks.

"It must have been early April by the time I went for the follow-up appointment. My mother and I were sitting in the doctor's waiting room when Brian and his mother came in. Brian had been sick with a sore throat and fever, like me. Our mothers were best friends, so they were talking, gossiping, and giggling until the nurse called Mum and me into the exam room."

Glenda sits down on the edge of the bed, and I sit in the royal-purple, velvet chair in the corner.

"I sat on the exam table, and Mum sat in the chair beside the doctor's desk. He came swooping in with his billowy white lab coat and my file tucked under his arm. He sat at his desk, opened the file, perused it, then said, 'wrong file,' and spun his chair around. He looked at me, said, 'you don't look like Brian Sweeney,' patted the top of my head and said, 'Excuse me ladies while I find the correct file.' Then he and his billowy lab coat swooped back out of the office.

"He left the wrong file, what I assume was Brian's file, open on his desk, and Mum craned her neck to look at it. She flipped the pages, and while she was looking at it, she went pale as a ghost. She went quiet and became sullen. It was like her spark went out.

"The doctor came back in with the correct file, examined my throat, took my temperature, said the surgery was a success, and declared me healed. Then we left, and as far as I know, that was the last time we ever spoke to them."

"Wow, I wonder what she saw in his file," I say.

"I don't know, but when my father came home from work that night, I was allowed to eat my dinner in front of the TV—

a big deal in our house—and there was a lot of hushed yelling coming from their bedroom, mostly by my mother. It was still going on when we fell asleep that night. Laura and I could feel the tension between them for a long time after that."

Could there have been a note in the file about Laura being pregnant? Would something like that even be noted in the father's medical file?

"Glenda, are you aware that there were rumours about Laura and Brian?"

I'm hesitant to ask her my next question when she's already dealing with so much, but this could be the key to finding out who killed Laura.

"Back in the day," I say slowly and deliberately, "some people suspected Laura and Brian were more than friends and that she may have been pregnant at the end of their senior year. There was a rumour that her quick departure for secretarial school right after graduation was an excuse for her to go away and have the baby."

"Really?" she asks, her eyes wide. "I had no idea. I was only eight, those types of rumours would have gone over my head. But I can assure you, my sister wasn't pregnant. My parents and I went to Montreal that summer to visit her, and she was her normal, slim self. She wore form-fitting dresses and showed us around the secretarial school she was attending."

She stares off into the distance for a moment. "We went back at Christmas so we would all be together for the holidays, and she was still thin and not-pregnant. There's no way she had a baby." Then she adds, "She and Brian were best friends, there was never any hanky panky between them."

Hanky panky, there's a phrase I haven't heard in years.

Laura's outfit is packed and hanging on the hook on the bedroom door, ready to be delivered to the funeral home.

Glenda sits on the floor beside the bed, crosses her legs, and pulls a long, shallow plastic storage bin out from under the bed. She takes the lid off the box, and it's full to the brim with photos. They aren't organized or filed, just scattered all over the bin. Glenda begins picking through them.

"I'm making a collage for the funeral and for the reunion-fundraiser," she explains.

She pats the purple carpet next to where she's sitting.

"Help me choose some photos, Megan."

I join her on the floor, and we go through photos of Laura, Glenda, their parents, and a bunch of other people I don't recognize. Rooting through the photos, Glenda pulls out a small stack of pretty, light purple envelopes that are tied together with a snippet of thin, ivory lace.

"An envelope exactly like these was on the kitchen table the morning Laura died," I tell her.

"Really?" she replies. "I've never seen these before."

She unties the ribbon and opens the top envelope from the pile. The envelope and the folded sheet of paper inside it look old; the faded and curled edges give them a vintage look. Glenda opens the folded sheet of pale purple paper to reveal a handwritten note.

My Dearest L,

I love you. I miss you. I think of you constantly. Everything reminds me of you. My dreams of a life where we are together have become my haven, and dreaming of you is the only thing getting me through the long days and nights without you.

What I wouldn't give for us to runaway together, somewhere where we can be alone together forever. Happy and at peace.

My heart aches for you, and my arms long to hold you.

Your Darling,

B xoxoxo

"So romantic," I say. "The handwriting is beautiful. It looks like calligraphy."

"In our day, handwriting was important, it said a lot about a person. We wrote everything by hand: homework, letters, phone messages. We didn't have computers, and typewriters were only in offices for secretaries."

"May I take a photo of the handwriting?" I ask.

"Of course," she says as she lays the letter flat on the floor beside us.

I pull out my phone and take a photo. She folds the letter, slides it back inside the envelope, gently places the envelope on the floor next to the bin of photos, and carefully opens the next envelope in the pile, revealing another light purple, aged, handwritten love letter.

We open every envelope and read every letter. Each letter is a flowery, romantic declaration of undying love. All of them are written in the same beautiful calligraphic handwriting, none of them have a date or even a reference to the time period when they were written, and none of them refer to either L or B by name. None of them mention a pregnancy or a baby.

Glenda carefully returns the last letter to its envelope and adds the envelope to the pile beside the bin, being sure to stack them in the same order we found them. She delicately ties the snippet of lace around them and returns them to the bin of photos.

"I guess there was something between Laura and Brian, after all," Glenda acknowledges quietly. "I had no idea. But I'm still certain she was never pregnant."

Glenda collects the photos she's chosen for her collage, and I put the lid on the storage bin and slide it back underneath the bed.

As we're putting on our coats and boots, I offer to take the outfit to the funeral home for her, but Glenda says she wants to do it herself.

"Will your husband be driving up from Ottawa for the funeral?" I ask.

"I wish he could," she replies, "but our daughter is pregnant, and he's on baby watch."

"Congratulations!" I say.

"Thank you," she says, smiling proudly. "This is our second grand baby. Our grandson is almost two. Our daughter is due in two weeks, and my husband is on call to stay with our grandson when she and her husband go to the hospital to have the baby. Then he'll stay close and help look after him while they get the new baby settled."

I ask if she has any photos, but they're on her phone. Since I have her phone, I don't get to see any photos.

"I'm supposed to be the one on baby watch," she says sadly, "but I had to come to Harmony Lake, so Grandpa has to hold down the fort."

"They're lucky to have you and that you're able to help," I assure her.

"I wish we could do more to help," she says. "Raising a family is so expensive these days, but we can't afford to help them financially. That's why I wanted to sell the land to Mega Mart, it would provide a legacy for our daughter and grand-children."

"Did your difference of opinion about the Mega Mart offer cause bad feelings between you and Laura? Did she die before you and she could resolve it?"

"No, thank goodness," she replies. "When Laura called to tell me about her broken leg, and the family business she needed to discuss with me, she also offered to purchase my share of the land. She thought it was the perfect solution. I'd benefit from the sale, and she'd own the land outright. We'd have no reason to disagree about it, and she could refuse Mega Mart's offer."

We leave, locking the door behind us. I return the key to the pill bottle, tighten the cap, and bury it in the urn where it came from.

CHAPTER 15

AT HOME, Sophie sniffs my legs while I prepare her dinner.

Watching her eat, I wonder if she knows from smelling me that I was at her house this afternoon. Could she smell the scent of the killer the day we found Laura? Was it someone she knows? If Sophie could talk, this case might be solved by now.

Last night, I finished the baby blanket I was knitting for the charity knitting guild, and I still need to block it. It's been soaking in the laundry room sink since this morning.

I spread some blocking mats on the kitchen table, squeeze the excess water from the blanket, spread it out on the blocking mats, and pin it down. When it dries, I'll unpin it and give it to the guild to add it to the collection of blankets they're donating to the AC.

I dry my hands and text Eric.

Me: I'm home. We still on for tonight?

Eric: Yes. Have you had dinner?

Me: Not yet. I'll make us something. Shrimp linguine? With salad?

Eric: No need to cook. I'll pick up something.

About twenty minutes later, I open the door, and Eric

comes in carrying two bags from Ho Lee Chow. I take the bags from him and carry them to the dining room while he takes off his winter gear.

"You don't have to feed me every time we see each other," I tell him. "I'm not giving you information in exchange for food. This isn't a quid pro quo."

"It's the least I can do," he replies from the front door. "I was such a jerk this morning."

"Please don't apologize again," I tease.

"I'll try to stop myself," he says jokingly. "But seriously, I like our meals together, it's a nice change from eating alone."

I can't disagree with that.

I put the bags on the dining room table and go into the kitchen for plates and cutlery.

When I come back into the dining room, Eric is standing at the table unpacking the food. He's wearing jeans. I've never seen him in jeans.

They definitely suit him.

He paired them with a cream-coloured, cable-knit sweater. I'm pretty sure the sweater is store bought, not hand knit, but it doesn't matter. The fit is flattering, and the sleeves stretch across his biceps just enough to remind me he has biceps. He looks warm, cozy, and temptingly snuggly. I allow myself to look, but just for a moment. Then I tell myself firmly to stop staring.

I put the plates and cutlery on the table.

"These are all my favourite things from their menu," I say, looking at the spread. "Is that a coincidence or did you ask them what I usually get?"

"I got the same things we ordered in September." He shrugs. "Remember? We ate Ho Lee Chow at the store while I questioned you."

"I remember." I nod. "You can remember a random restaurant order from four months ago?"

"I'm observant, it's my job." He smiles and sits down in front of his plate.

I go back to the kitchen and return with napkins and two beers.

"Before you leave," I tell him, "remind me to give you the dog sweaters that Laura knit for the silent auction. They're in my bag."

He nods.

I open both beers and put one in front of him with one of the napkins.

Sophie joins us. She jumps on the sofa a few feet away in the living room, lies down, and lets out a sigh.

"How was your visit to Laura's house?" Eric asks.

I tell him about the purple palace, the stack of letters under the bed that match the one on Laura's kitchen table the morning she died, Glenda's disclosure that Laura offered to buy her share of the AC, and about me keeping Sophie.

"That's awesome news about Sophie," he says. "I'm not gonna lie, I wasn't looking forward to her leaving. I think she and I have bonded. I enjoyed our walks together when you were off your feet."

Next, I tell him about Glenda lying about her alibi and April finding her phone.

"Glenda would like her phone back. With her daughter so close to her due date, I can see why she needs to be reachable at all times. Can I give it back to her, or do you need it?"

"I'd like to return it to her personally," he replies.

I get up from the table, retrieve Glenda's phone from the drawer in the kitchen, hand it to him, then tell him about my trip to the Willows farm yesterday.

I tell him about running into Jay Singh, Mrs. Willows' confession that they lied about their cardiology appointment because they don't have a strong alibi, and Mr. Willows not wanting people to know about his cardiology appointment.

"Were you as shocked as I was to learn that Dr. Val White's uncle is the CEO of Mega Mart?" I ask.

His eyes open wide, and he tilts his head. "Really?"

"That's what Mrs. Willows told me," I reply. "I haven't confirmed it though."

"I'll look into it," he says.

"Did you notice that Mrs. Willows car is a four-door, grey sedan?" I ask.

His mouth is full of Cantonese Chow Mein, so he nods.

"That's three people who know Laura and have a car matching the description of the car the postal carrier saw in her driveway the morning she died," I observe.

"Who's the third?" he asks.

"The Sweeneys," I say. "I saw them driving it this morning."

He nods, swallows a mouthful of food and takes a swig of beer.

"She was driving that car on Tuesday," he tells me, "when she was volunteering with Meals on Wheels."

I guess that's the Sweeney's whereabouts accounted for when Laura died.

"Speaking of the Sweeneys," I say, "Brian mentioned that the AC was robbed just before Christmas, and they stole all the medication."

"That's right," he confirms. "We arrested two guys from Harmony Hills for it about a week ago."

"Was digoxin among the stolen drugs?" I ask.

"It was," he says, "among many others."

"When you arrested them, did you recover any of the drugs?" I ask.

He shakes his head. "The drugs were long gone. They probably sold them within hours of getting them. And before you ask, they either don't know, or won't say, who they sold the digoxin to."

My phone dings.

Craig: Have you had a chance to look at your schedule? How does tomorrow night look? After that I'm working nights until Saturday.

"Is everything OK?" Eric asks. "Your face tensed up when you read that text."

"Yup," I reply, "it's just Craig."

"Megan, if seeing Craig makes you happy, you should see him. I was a jerk about it this morning, but I promise I won't be a jerk about it again."

"If I want to see Craig," I say smiling, "I wouldn't let you being a jerk stop me."

"I'm sure of that," he says.

We finish eating and turn on the TV to check the score of the hockey game. We settle on the sofa, with Sophie between us, and watch the game until intermission when Eric gets up to leave.

"I don't mind walking Sophie before I go," he offers.

"Thank you," I say, "but now that I'm back on two feet, I won't have to impose on everyone to walk Sophie."

"It's not an imposition." He shrugs. "I enjoy it."

We say goodnight and he leaves. As soon as he drives away, I remember I was supposed to give him the dog sweaters from Laura.

I fire off a quick text to Craig telling him tomorrow night doesn't look good to get together, then I help Sophie put on her sweater, and attach her leash. I bundle myself up, and we go for a walk.

When we get back, I change into my green flannel pyjamas with sheep on them. After I brush my teeth, wash my face, and put my hair up, I cuddle on the sofa with Sophie. I open my laptop and visit the Let Me Take A Cellfie website.

According to their Frequently Asked Questions (FAQ) page, customers receive their DNA results via email, two to three weeks after the samples are received by the Let Me Take A Cellfie lab.

I need access to Laura's email to see if she's received the results.

She must have sent the DNA samples to the lab before she broke her leg, because when she broke her leg, she went straight to the hospital and stayed there for a week. She was only home for a few hours before Eric and I found her. She died six days ago, so it's probably been at least two weeks since she sent the samples to the lab. The results could be sitting in her inbox, waiting to be read.

What the FAQ page doesn't answer is whether the results are sent to both people who provide samples, or just the person who paid for the test and mailed the samples to the lab. If both parties receive the results, Laura's potential love child could already have them.

I'm about to close my laptop when I remember the other thing I want to look up.

I go the Mega Mart website, find and read the About page for the CEO, then search the internet for articles and posts that include information about his family.

CHAPTER 16

It's snowing. Big fat snowflakes that grab hold of each other on their way to the ground and cling to your hair and eyelashes. The air isn't as frigid today. Don't get me wrong, it's still below the freezing mark, but we're enjoying a much-needed respite from the frigid wind chill.

I park behind the store, and Sophie and I walk around to the front, then across the street for a walk in the park.

I shake the snowflakes out of my hair, and Sophie shakes the snowflakes from her sweater and exposed fur.

I'm kicking the snow from my boots against the brick wall beside the front door before we go inside, when Glenda comes out of Wilde Flowers with a broom and begins sweeping the light dusting of snow from the sidewalk in front of the shop onto the street.

"Good morning, Megan," she says. "Thank you again for your help yesterday. I'm grateful I didn't have to do it alone."

"Anytime," I say. "It was nice to see a glimpse of Laura that I never got to know."

I want to tell her about the DNA test packaging I found

315

and talk to her about accessing Laura's email, but Phillip comes outside.

He congratulates me for getting to keep Sophie and congratulates Sophie for getting to keep me.

While we're making small talk, I start to get chilly and want to go inside.

"Glenda, would you mind meeting me at Laura's later?" I ask. "I want to pick up the rest of Sophie's things, and I think I saw a bag of her food in the kitchen."

"You go ahead, Megan," she replies. "You know where the key is, and we trust you."

They laugh.

"I'd feel more comfortable if you were with me," I implore.

She agrees to meet me after we close up tonight.

I go inside, take off Sophie's sweater and my coat, hang them up in the back room, and switch on the lights in the store. Then I turn the sign from CLOSED to OPEN and get to work checking the store email and voicemail.

I hang up the phone, and the familiar jingle of the bell prompts me to look toward the door where I see PC Amy Andrews and PSD Tundra entering the store. Amy closes the door behind her.

Sophie runs over with her tail wagging, excited about having another dog in the store. She's bouncing around him playfully and sniffing him.

"Hi Megan," Amy says. "Is Eric around? He's supposed to have a package for me."

I think she's referring to the package of dog sweaters for the silent auction.

"Do you mean the dog sweaters?" I ask. "I happen to have them right here."

I reach under the counter, pull the package out of my tote bag, and put it between on the counter between us.

"I do," she replies, "but I kind of need to speak to him

about something else too. I sent him a text, but he hasn't replied."

"His car was out back when I got here," I say. "I'll text him and let him know you're here."

Me: A colleague is here to see you.

He replies almost instantly: ***Be right there.***

"He says he'll be here in a minute," I say, smiling.

I nudge the package of dog sweaters toward her. She doesn't pick them up.

I expect Eric to come from the back room because that's where the stairs to the apartment are, but instead he comes through the front door carrying a to-go tray from Latte Da with two take out cups in it.

"Morning, Amy." He smiles at her.

He hands me one of the cups and shakes the snow out of his brown hair.

While Eric and Amy are talking, I sip my surprise mystery coffee and discover it's a cafe mocha with extra whipped cream. I savour the caffeinated treat while watching Sophie try desperately to convince Tundra to play with her.

She sniffs him, lowers the upper half of her body to the floor in a downward dog pose and yelps playfully while wagging her tail. She even tries nipping at his huge Malinois paws.

He notices her, wags his tail, and sniffs her, but then he seems to remember he's a professional dog who's on duty and goes back to ignoring her.

Mixed signals much?

I sense Sophie's confusion, and I feel for her. Sometimes I wish a certain officer of the law would notice me, and just when I think maybe he does, he goes back into cop-mode and talks to me like I'm a witness.

I shift my gaze from Sophie and Tundra, to Amy and Eric. Like Sophie, Amy is flirting with Eric. She's giggling, touching his arm with one hand and twirling a strand of her hair with the other. She's young and pretty. She's thirty-ish, short (about my height), blonde hair, brown eyes, and has deep dimples when she smiles, which I notice she does often when she flirts.

"Amy," I interrupt, "is Tundra allowed to have a dog treat?"

"Sure," she says, "he'd love one, thanks."

I call Sophie, and we go to the kitchenette to get treats for her and her friend.

"You're such a flirt, Sophie," I say, putting one of the shoe-shaped treats from Tamara on the floor in front of her. "I might need you to teach me how to do that, someday."

I come back into the store and put two bone-shaped cookies on the floor in front of Tundra, then I give a second cookie to Sophie.

I hear Amy suggest to Eric that they go to the reunion-fundraiser together. Eric tells her he already has a date.

He has a date? Who's his date?

Then he reminds her that she'll probably be busy with the silent auction anyway, so they wouldn't see each other. She agrees with him, but she sounds disappointed.

They're still talking. I don't know what they're saying, because I'm busying myself in another part of the store, but I hear muttering, punctuated at regular intervals with her giggling.

"Thanks for the dog treats, Megan," Amy calls out.

"Anytime," I say. "Have a good day."

She picks up Tundra's leash and turns to leave.

"Amy!" I call out.

She turns around and I hold up the package of dog sweaters.

"Don't forget these," I say. "They're the reason you came in."

We laugh and she leaves.

I have another sip of my coffee.

"Thank you for this," I say, holding up my cup. "It's such a nice treat. How did you know what to order?"

"I ordered the same thing you ordered for yourself yesterday," he replies.

"Your powers of observation are amazing, Detective Sergeant."

We wish each other a good day, and he stoops down to give Sophie some rubs, then stands back up and leaves for work.

I text April.

Me: I need a huge favour.

April: Of course!

Me: Thank you!

April: Just admit you have a crush on your upstairs tenant, first.

Me: Seriously?

April: Seriously.

Me: Fine.

April: Fine what?

Me: He's hot, not sure it's a crush tho.

April: That wasn't so hard, was it? What do you need?

I tell her what I need, and then I delete these texts so no one will ever see them.

"WE'RE JUST PRETENDING," I remind April. "We aren't really here to adopt a pet. The goal is to talk to Dr. White and ask her some questions."

"I know," April replies. "We can look, but we can't take any home. Except maybe just one."

"No," I tell her firmly. "T will kill me if you leave here with a pet."

"That's an exaggeration," she laments.

"Maybe, but no pets, unless T says it's OK."

It's just after lunch when we pull into the parking lot of the Animal Centre.

The AC is located on the edge of town, near the highway.

"No pets," April murmurs.

I'm pretty sure she's convincing herself and not talking to me.

We enter through the animal shelter entrance and ask the volunteer at the desk to let us into the cat room.

There are about a dozen cats in kennels, and it's heart wrenching to see them locked up. For a brief moment, I forget why we're here and am overcome with the urge to take them all home.

I remind myself to stay focused as April stops in front of a chocolate brown cat. The card taped to his kennel says his name is, Fudge.

Congratulations, Fudge, you're about to be adopted.

April opens her mouth to speak, and before she says a word, I know Fudge will be joining us for the car ride home. I'll probably be on the receiving end of at least one text from a frustrated Tamara in a few hours.

It'll be worth it, but I can't say that to April because she'll interpret it as me agreeing she should take Fudge home. She should, but I can never admit it out loud.

A shelter volunteer shows us to a visiting room where we wait for someone to bring Fudge in, so he and April can have a meet-and-greet and decide if they like each other.

The small room has two chairs, a bowl of water, a litter box, and a scratching post. There are random cat toys scattered on the floor. The entire wall with the door in it is glass, including the door itself.

Fudge enters the room and April lights up. She's in love. She puts out her hand, and Fudge comes to check it out. She strokes his back and gives him scratches between his ears. When he flops onto the floor and shows her his furry, chocolate-brown belly, I know this is a done deal.

The volunteer comes in to ask how we're doing.

"Would Dr. White be available?" I ask. "We'd like to ask her a few questions."

A few minutes later, Dr. White comes in and introduces herself. April asks how Fudge gets along with other cats.

April and Tamara have an orange cat, Butterscotch. It's amazes me that Tamara has maintained their status as a one-cat family for as long as she has, because April would have a house full of cats, given the opportunity.

"He's great with other cats," Dr. White says. "Fudge came to us from a home where he was with another cat."

"Why was he surrendered?" April asks.

"His owner had dementia and could no longer care for them so the family surrendered them to the AC," Dr. White explains. "We tried to have them adopted as a pair, but that isn't always possible. The other cat found a new home last month."

They talk about vaccinations, whether Fudge has been neutered—he has, the AC only adopts spayed and neutered pets—and his health history, while I wait patiently for an opportunity to ask Dr. White my questions.

"Shall I get you an adoption application and a pen?" Dr. White asks.

April nods enthusiastically. "Yes! Please!"

While Dr. White goes to get the form, I take a few photos of Fudge and April together. Dr. White comes back, hands a clipboard and pen to April, and instructs us to give the completed form to one of the volunteers.

She turns to leave. It's now or never.

"Dr. White," I say, "may I ask you a question that isn't about Fudge?"

"Sure," she replies, smiling and putting her hands in the pockets of her white lab coat.

"I'm a friend of Laura's," I explain. "I don't know if you've heard, but she was killed by an overdose of digoxin."

Dr. White nods. She doesn't look surprised. I don't think the digoxin is new information for her.

"What's the question?" she asks, shrugging.

"Don't you think it's an odd coincidence that a couple of weeks after someone steals digoxin from the vet clinic, it's also used to murder Laura?" I ask.

"It is an unlikely coincidence," she acknowledges, "but many drugs were stolen that night. As far as I know, none of the stolen medications have been recovered, and no link has been made between our robbery and Laura's death."

"Two people have mentioned that you and Laura didn't always get along and argued a lot," I say, trying to sound as casual and non-accusatory as possible. But there isn't really a way to say it without it sounding incriminating.

"Are you insinuating that I stole all the medication from the clinic just so I could keep the digoxin and use it to kill Laura?"

She crosses her arms in front of her chest and tilts her head.

"No," I insist, shaking my head. "I'm not, but I know that's how it sounds. Honestly, I'm just trying to help Laura's family, my friends, and Sophie, find answers and get some closure, you know?" I explain.

She sighs, uncrosses her arms, and pushes several strands of red hair behind her ear.

"It's true that we'd argue and get frustrated with one another," she explains. "But not because we didn't like each other. We both love the AC and want what's best for every animal here. Laura was older and did things a certain way, even when that way was outdated, and there was a more efficient way to do it."

She leans against the glass door and puts her hands back in her pockets.

"For example, Laura didn't want the Animal Hospital to use online booking—where owners can book their pet's veterinary appointment online, without having to call the clinic. I explained to her that online booking is common now and would free up volunteers from answering the phone as frequently, allowing them to spend more time working with the animals. However, Laura felt it would make the AC appear unapproachable. We had a similar argument about branding. We have some popular animals in the sanctuary, some of them are local celebrities. Selling souvenirs like t-shirts, mugs, or stuffed animals featuring them could be a good stream of income, but Laura worried that it would be perceived as exploiting the animals."

I feel Dr. White's struggle. It wasn't easy to get Connie to see the benefits of computers when I started working at Knitorious.

"Has your uncle been pressuring you to convince Laura to sell the AC to Mega Mart?" I ask.

"If you know he's my uncle, you should also know that he's estranged from our entire family," she says brusquely.

I didn't know that. Despite spending hours last night combing the internet for information about his personal life and family, I found nothing aside from a couple of articles that mention his wife. There was no information about his family anywhere.

"I haven't spoken to, or seen, my uncle since I was a little girl," she explains. "I'm sure he has no idea I work here, or even that I'm a vet. He lives on the other side of the country, and from what I've heard, he likes to stay there. I doubt he's ever heard of Harmony Lake or has any personal involvement in this land deal."

"Why is he estranged from the family?" I ask.

"He and my dad are brothers," she explains with a sigh, "and they had a disagreement over money. My dad gave... lent... depending who you ask, money to my uncle to help open the first Mega Mart store. When Mega Mart became a huge international success, he paid my dad back, without interest. But my dad thought the agreement was that he would be part owner of that first store and was expecting a share certificate. It got ugly and they haven't spoken since. Most of the family sided with my dad, and they fell out with my uncle too. It's been so long since I've seen my uncle, that I wouldn't recognize him if he showed up here tomorrow."

"It's sad," I say, "that money tore apart two brothers and divided an entire family."

"It is," she agrees, nodding. "And they're both getting on in years. It would be good for them to forgive each other and let go of this grudge before it's too late."

We talk a while longer while April fills out the adoption application and continues to bond with Fudge. I learn Dr. White was at the AC the morning Laura died, and there are lots of witnesses who can corroborate her alibi.

April hands her form to one of the volunteers. They load Fudge into a cardboard kitty carrier, a volunteer hands me a small bag of his food and the blanket from his kennel. The three of us leave the shelter and make our way to the car.

Fudge sings loudly to April and me on the drive back to town. April sings back to him, saying it will calm him, but I think it's having the opposite effect. Her high-pitched mewing is making both Fudge and me more anxious.

"You should ask Eric to the reunion-fundraiser," she stops mewing and says out of nowhere.

I tell her I overheard him decline an invitation from Amy Andrews because he already has a date.

"Ask him anyway." She shrugs.

"I think we're just friends," I tell her. "I'm his landlady, and I act as a kind of community liaison for him, but beyond that, I'm not on his radar."

I drop April and Fudge off at home. Before I back out of the driveway, I send Tamara a text.

Me: Please don't hate me when you see what I did.

T: What did you do?

I send her one of the photos I took of April and Fudge.

T: Just the one? When she told me where you guys were going, I thought this might happen.

Me: Yup. Just one. Name's Fudge

T: Aww... he looks like a piece of fudge!

If she's mad, she's already getting over it.

I go back to Knitorious and offer to close the store so Connie can leave. I lock up, tidy the store, put Sophie's leash and sweater on, and leave through the back door.

At home, I take Sophie for a quick walk so she can do her business. It gets much colder when the sun goes down, so our evening walks are business trips only. As soon as she's finishes, we dash back to the warmth of the house where I take off her sweater, unattach her leash, and feed her dinner.

"I'll be home soon, Sophie," I tell her while I bundle myself in my winter gear. "I'm hoping this meeting will help us figure out who killed Laura. Wish me luck."

I get in my car and head to Laura's house.

PHEW, Glenda came alone. I was worried that Phillip might come with her. It's hard enough talking to Glenda about Laura potentially having a secret love child, I'm not sure I'd be able to have this conversation with both of them.

We both get out of our cars and go in the house. She takes off her boots and asks me where in the kitchen I saw the bag of dog food.

"Beside the fridge," I tell her. "Against the wall."

I follow her into the kitchen.

"Glenda, there's another reason I asked you to meet me here. I need to talk to you about something private, and I needed to get you alone."

"Okaaaaaay" she says hesitantly, looking worried.

"I need to show you something upstairs."

Now she looks terrified and positions herself so the kitchen table is between us.

Of course, she looks terrified. I scheme to get her into the house where her sister was murdered, then talk ominously about getting her here alone. Well done, Megan.

"Actually, you know what," I say, "you wait here, and I'll go get it. I'll leave my phone on the kitchen table, and if you feel even a little bit uncomfortable, you can use it to call someone."

I unlock my phone and place it on the kitchen table, screen side up, between us. Then I run up the stairs, through the purple palace and into the purple en suite washroom, pick up the DNA test packaging, and run back downstairs.

I put the box on the kitchen table where we can both see it.

"I found this in the garbage pail in Laura's washroom yesterday."

She looks at it, curiously but cautiously.

"It's the packaging from a DNA test," I explain. "Glenda, I think between the last time Laura emptied her washroom garbage pail and the day she died, she took a DNA test. Do you have any idea whose DNA she might be comparing hers to?"

She shakes her head.

"What if there was a baby," she utters. Glenda clutches her chest and sits on one of the kitchen chairs. "What if I'm remembering it wrong? Or didn't notice because I was so young?"

Her eyes fill with tears. "Poor Laura," she says quietly.

I offer to get her a glass of water, and she shakes her head.

"Glenda, the website says they email the DNA results to the customer. Would you mind if I check Laura's email? If we can find out who she was comparing her DNA to, that might help us figure out who killed her and why."

"Yes. That's a good idea," she agrees. "I'll get her laptop."

Glenda gets up and goes to the next room to get Laura's

laptop. I sit down at the kitchen table, and she puts the computer in front of me. I open it and move my hand back and forth across the track pad. It's an older computer and kind of clunky.

"Was it plugged in?" I ask her.

She nods.

"I don't think anyone has used it since before she went to the hospital," she says.

When it finally comes to life, it wants a password. Glenda doesn't know what the password is and suggests we try Laura's late husband's name. That's not it.

We try her wedding anniversary. Not it.

We try Laura's birthday and her husband's birthday. No, and no.

I ask Glenda if Laura has any other devices that she used to check her email... a tablet or smartphone, maybe? Glenda doesn't think so. I tell her I need to do a web search on how to hack into a computer.

"I'm afraid if we just keep trying random guesses, it will freeze us out permanently," I explain.

"Take the laptop with you," Glenda suggests, "then you can keep trying. Let me know when you get into her email."

I thank her and put the laptop in my bag.

"Just a second," she says.

She disappears into the other room, returns with the power cord, folds it up, and presses it into my hand. I put it in my tote bag with the laptop.

On our way out, I tell her I spoke to Eric and told him she was in town the night before Laura died. She says she's already heard from him and understands that I had to tell him. She says she's on her way to meet him now to answer some questions and get her phone back.

CHAPTER 17

Wednesday January 15th

I spend the morning sitting at the harvest table with the store laptop, drinking the café mocha with extra whipped cream that Eric dropped off to me on his way to work. Then I search the internet for instructions to access Laura's laptop without erasing any of the information from her computer.

I sigh dramatically every time I come up against a dead end on my search.

It occurred to me last night that even if I figure out the password that unlocks the laptop, her email might be password protected with a different password. I'm hoping that isn't the case.

"What are you doing that's making you so frustrated?" Connie asks after my most recent dramatic sigh.

"I thought I was onto something with Laura's murder," I say, "but apparently, I was wrong."

"Maybe you should tell Eric whatever it is you're trying to do and let him get frustrated trying to figure it out," she suggests. "It is his job."

She has a point. I might have to hand this off to a professional, and I'm sure the police department will know how to access her email.

"At least take a break for a while," she implores, "and go back to it when you feel less frustrated."

Good idea, Connie.

"What are you wearing to the reunion-fundraiser on Saturday night, my dear?" she asks, subtly changing the subject.

"I'm not going," I reply.

"What?! Of course, you're going," she insists. "Don't be silly."

"I don't know," I whine. "It's been a long week and I'm tired."

"It's only Wednesday," she reminds me.

"I don't have anyone to go with, and I don't have anything to wear," I complain.

"Ask Eric," she suggests. "I'm sure he'll say yes."

"Did April tell you to say that?" I ask.

"Don't be silly, my dear," she replies, waving dismissively.

They're totally in cahoots.

I look at Sophie laying on her bed. She looks back at me, perks up her ears and wags her tail.

"Maybe I'll take Sophie," I say. "I could knit a corgi-sized dress for her."

"You know I don't like it when I can't tell whether you're joking," Connie says.

In an effort to change the subject, I ask her if she's seen Fudge. She says she's seen photos on April and Tamara's social media.

Our phones both ding in unison.

It's Phillip, letting us know arrangements have been made for Laura's service. It's scheduled for Monday at the Mourning Glory Funeral Home. He asks Connie to pass on the details to the rest of the alumni association.

The news of Laura's funeral casts a dreary mood over us and the store. Between serving customers, we sombrely distract ourselves with various mundane tasks around the store until the bell above the door jingles, and Mrs. Pearson comes in.

"Marla, you're early." Connie greets her with a hug.

"Yes, my appointment ended early, so here I am."

Mrs. Pearson is a member of the charity knitting guild. They meet at the store most Wednesday afternoons to knit on their latest project, plan future projects, order yarn, and gossip. She situates herself on the sofa and pulls out the baby blanket she's working on for the AC.

Seeing her blanket reminds me to give her the blanket that I knit to help the cause. I reach under the counter and into my tote bag, pulling out the plastic bag containing the blanket.

"Here's my contribution to the blankets for the AC," I say, handing her the bag.

"Thank you," she says, taking the bag. "So, Megan... I hear you went out with my Craig on Saturday night. He hasn't stopped talking about you."

And now we know the real reason she showed up early.

Connie saves me by interrupting Mrs. Pearson to tell her about Laura's arrangements.

"So, Megan... Do you have any plans to see Craig again?" It seems Mrs. Pearson isn't easily distracted. "He says you're both trying to make something work with your schedules."

"Hopefully." I sigh. "We've both just been really busy. When he's free I'm not, when I'm free, he's not. You know how it is."

"Well, you'll see him at the fundraiser on Saturday for sure, he's attending as my plus one," she says.

"Mr. Pearson won't be your plus one?" I ask.

"No. I'm afraid not. He's going to Toronto for the week-end. He's meeting his brother. They have Leafs tickets," she explains and turns to Connie. "They bought them months ago, before we set the date for the reunion-fundraiser."

She asks who I'm going with, and I tell her that Phillip and Glenda offered to take me, or I might take Sophie. Then I tell her my knitted corgi dress idea.

Like Connie, she's not sure if I'm joking, and honestly, at this point, I'm not sure either. Maybe instead of a crazy cat lady, I'll be a crazy corgi lady, and Sophie is the first in what will become my pack of corgis.

Sophie comes over to me when she hears her name, and I bend down to pet her and look into her pretty brown eyes.

While looking in her eyes, it comes to me...

I pull Laura's laptop from my tote bag and take it to the harvest table. I open it and tickle the track pad until it springs to life. When the pop-up window appears asking for the password, I type in: Sophie.

The little circle icon spins. This is further than I've gotten with my other attempts. After a few seconds that feel like minutes, I'm in!

I find the email icon. Crossing my fingers that it's not also password protected, or if it is, that Laura was a one-password-for-all kind of person, I double click on it. The circle spins...and I'm in!

Laura's inbox is full. She's on a lot of mailing lists, mostly animal and knitting related.

I scroll down the first page with my focus on the Sender field. About halfway down, I see an email from Let Me Take A Cellfie with the subject line, *And The Results Are...*

I take a deep breath. Even though I know no one is nearby, I look around to make sure someone isn't looking over my shoulder. I click on the email.

The email contains a link to a pdf, so I click the link.

The pdf is a table of values. The name of the value is in the first column, Donor A's values are in the second column, and Donor B's values are in the third column. There's a fourth column showing the percentage of values the donors have in common.

I'm not science-y enough to interpret this data without doing some research first.

I scroll to the bottom of the long table and find a heading that says, *Interpreting Your Results.* According to this section, Laura's results aren't from a maternity test, they're the results of a siblingship test.

Laura tested her DNA against someone who might be her sibling.

Reading further, the scientists at Let Me Take A Cellfie conclude there is a high probability that Laura and the other donor are half-siblings with a common father.

Whoa.

I email the pdf to myself in case I can't get back into Laura's email. Then, I power off the laptop, close it, and put it back in my bag under the counter.

I text Adam and ask if he has time to see me today. I tell him I can visit him at his office. He says sure and tells me to come by any time this afternoon.

The rest of the charity knitters are starting to show up. I take Connie aside and ask her if she'll be OK for an hour while I run an errand.

"Of course, my dear! You run along."

After Sophie and I go for our mid-day jaunt to the park, I get in my car and head to 845 Mountain Road, Adam's office.

I USUALLY PARK on the road in front of the large, renovated Victorian-era house, but Eric's car is parked there. Interesting.

I park in the driveway, walk up to the wrap-around porch, enter the house, and greet Lin, the receptionist, who works for all the tenants, including Adam.

Four professionals have office space here: Adam, an accountant, an insurance broker, and a family therapist. From behind her large, ornately carved, wooden desk, Lin helps keep all of them organized and makes their clients feel welcome and comfortable.

I tell her Adam is expecting me, and she lets him know I'm here. While I wait, Lin offers me something to eat or drink, which I decline, and she and I talk about the holiday that just passed. I ask her how Ryan is doing since I haven't seen him lately, and we make small talk about what she's wearing to the reunion-fundraiser this weekend. When she has to answer a phone call, I take a seat on the leather sofa in the waiting area and peruse an insurance brochure I find on the coffee table.

Adam comes down the stairs, holding the ornately carved, wooden hand rail, with Eric behind him. At the bottom of the stairs, they shake hands, Eric thanks Adam for his time, and they say goodbye.

Adam gestures for me to follow him upstairs. As I pass Eric I say, "You should come with us, you might want to hear this."

In Adam's office, I can't help but smile at the many photos of Hannah he has on his desk and cabinets. Including the most recent addition, a selfie of the three of us that we took on Christmas morning. We're wearing matching Christmas pyjamas and Santa hats and sitting under the Christmas tree at my house. It's a great photo of the three of us.

"I know, right?!" Adam says, when he notices me admiring the photo. "I had to frame it. It's a great photo of all of us, and Hannah looks so happy."

"If you still have it on your phone can you text it to me?" I ask. "The one I took with my phone isn't very good. Your eyes are closed, and Hannah and I are blurry."

"Yeah, of course, hang on."

He picks up his phone and scrolls through his photos, then my phone dings.

"Thanks," I say. "Listen, do you want me to come to you

on Sunday since you came to me last week after I slipped on the ice?"

"It doesn't matter." He shrugs. "I'm thinking of making frittatas. I've never made them, but I've been looking at recipes online, and it looks like something I can make. What do you think?"

"Ahem." Eric clears his throat. "I'm sorry," I say, smiling at him. "I'm easily distracted by photos of my daughter."

I sit up straight and direct my focus on Adam.

"Adam, do you remember when you were babysitting me last week, and I asked you HYPOTHETICALLY if a HYPO-THETICAL client could amend their will to include a secret child?"

"I do." He nods.

"And you said HYPOTHETICALLY a client could amend a will for *any* secret HYPOTHETICAL relative."

I realize now, that Adam was trying to tell me the secret relative isn't a child.

"That's right." He nods again.

"Why do you keep saying HYPOTHETICAL like that?" Eric asks.

I put up my right index finger to defer his question.

"Well, HYPOTHETICALLY might a HYPOTHETICAL client have amended her will to include a HYPOTHETICAL half-sibling?" I ask, smirking smugly.

"You clever girl," Adam says proudly. "Well done."

"Thank you," I say, pleased with myself as we high-five each other across his desk.

"I'm not feeling very clever," Eric chimes in. "I'm feeling a bit lost."

I tell them about the packaging from the DNA kit in Laura's trash can, and how Glenda gave me Laura's computer. I explain that I figured out the password and found the DNA results in her email. She has a half-sibling on her father's side.

I tell them that I don't know who the other DNA donor is. The email from Let Me Take A Cellfie didn't include any email addresses other than Laura's.

"What?" Eric asks, with a look of shock on his face.

"I need that computer, Megan. You should've given it to me in the first place."

"The police had Laura's house for four days, Eric. They could've taken the computer then. Or found the DNA wrapper in her garbage. It's not like I had access to evidence you couldn't have acquired yourself."

On Monday, he says he's grateful when I find out information; now he's angry at me for finding out information. I can't win.

I look at Adam and take a deep breath.

"OK, so Laura changed her will before she got the DNA results back, so she must have felt pretty confident that this person was her half-sibling. I guess there's no way of knowing whether the half-sibling knows they've been included in the will? Or whether the other beneficiaries know that the will has been changed and their inheritance might have become smaller?"

"HYPOTHETICALLY," Adam says emphatically, "if a client amends their will to include a new beneficiary, the amount the existing beneficiaries would receive would have to be reduced. Everybody's share of the pie gets a little bit smaller if you divide the pie among more people. Also, the HYPOTHETICAL client isn't obligated to inform beneficiaries that they've been included in the will, or to inform their attorney whether the beneficiaries are aware of their status as beneficiaries."

Adam and I have been playing the HYPOTHETICAL game for a long time. I'm pretty sure he is saying the existing beneficiaries will lose some of their inheritance now that the newfound half-sibling has been added to the will. He doesn't know if the newfound half-sibling knows they've been made a beneficiary in Laura's will.

So, Glenda's inheritance was likely reduced when her new half-sibling was added to Laura's will. Could this make her angry enough to kill her sister? She already has a weak alibi and lied about it. Or maybe she killed Laura to stop her from amending the will, on the assumption that Laura's hospital stay delayed her signing the final document.

But, if Glenda knew about the half-sibling, why would she suggest that I take Laura's laptop and try to break into her email for the DNA results? Wouldn't she want the half-sibling to remain a secret to prevent them from claiming any of Laura's estate?

Laura changed her will before she received the results to ensure that if something went wrong during her surgery, both of her siblings would be acknowledged.

Whoever the secret half-sibling is, their new status as beneficiary is a strong motive to murder Laura.

I know Adam can't tell me who the half-sibling is, or even whether Laura and Glenda have a half-sister or a half-brother, and I won't put him in an uncomfortable position by asking him.

"HYPOTHETICALLY, when will the beneficiaries find out the details of the HYPOTHETICAL will?" I ask him.

"HYPOTHETICALLY, I would expect all beneficiaries to receive a registered letter this week," he replies.

ERIC and I are walking to our cars. I press the button on my keychain to unlock my car, then reach for the handle to open the door. I turn to Eric to say goodbye, and as I open my mouth, he starts talking.

"I'm sorry for how I reacted about the laptop and the DNA packaging," he blurts out. "You're right, we should've found it first. This is only Harmony Lake PD's third murder. Ever. The department is still learning and making mistakes. It frustrates me, but that isn't your problem or your fault. I'm grateful you told me what you found out. But I'll still need that laptop."

I nod.

"You and Adam see each other every Sunday?" Eric asks.

"Yup. We have breakfast together and FaceTime with Hannah. We alternate homes, but he always cooks."

"You two are the friendliest exes I know," he says. "You think you might get back together?"

"No," I say, shaking my head. "We get along so well BECAUSE we're not together. But we're still family." I use the same emphasis on BECAUSE as I did for HYPOTHETICAL.

"What's that about, this HYPOTHETICAL thing?" he asks, emphasizing the word HYPOTHETICAL.

I explain how we learned to speak in the hypothetical and use subtext to talk about Adam's cases and clients.

"This new sibling doesn't help eliminate Glenda as a suspect, does it?"

"HYPOTHETICALLY, no," he replies.

CHAPTER 18

Five minutes before it's time to open the store, Sophie jumps down from the front window display, where she was watching the world go by. She trots eagerly toward the back room with her tongue out and her tail wagging. I hear the back door to the parking lot close, then I hear Eric greet her and tell her he's happy to see her.

"Good morning," he says as he puts a Latte Da to go cup on the counter in front of me. "I'm here to pick up Laura's laptop. We've already retrieved the DNA package from her house."

I hand him the laptop and cord.

"Thank you for the coffee," I say. "Again."

This is becoming a habit I could get used to.

"So, what are you up to today?" I ask him.

"Trying to catch a killer." He shrugs. "You know, the usual."

"Well, good luck with that," I say.

"The alumni association gets access to the high school gym today," he says, "to start setting up for the event on Saturday night. I'll probably stop by to say hi, talk to some

338

people, and see if anyone is talking about what happened to Laura."

"Sounds like a good idea," I say.

"Maybe you'd like to come with me?" he asks.

I detect hesitation in his voice.

"As a community liaison?" I ask. "To encourage people to talk to you?"

"It doesn't hurt," he replies. "The people in Harmony Lake trust you. Your insight is helpful, and you notice things I don't. You know what's normal for the people around here and what isn't."

"Why not," I say. "What time?"

We agree to go to the high school together after I drop Sophie off at home and feed her.

I unlock the door and turn the sign from CLOSED to OPEN. Connie should be here any minute, but she's only working until lunchtime, then she's leaving to focus on the reunion-fundraiser and won't be back at work until Tuesday.

A customer comes in with a layette pattern for her niece's soon-to-be-born baby, and I help her find the right yarn for her project.

We're looking at the sport weight yarn and comparing shades of blue, and Eric is still here, loitering awkwardly. I excuse myself from my customer, go over to him and quietly ask him if he's waiting to talk to me.

"Are you going to the reunion-fundraiser on Saturday?" he asks.

"Maybe," I reply, shrugging my left shoulder. "I haven't decided for sure."

"If you go, who are you going with?" he asks.

I shrug again and tell him that Phillip and Glenda have offered to take me with them, Adam offered to drive me, and Sophie is an option. The event benefits Laura's organization, and includes a memorial to her, so it seems appropriate for Sophie, Laura's canine companion, to be there, I explain to him. I joke that she'd have to find something decent to wear.

My customer calls me over, so I leave Eric to help her. She decides on a yarn, and we go to the counter so I can cash her out. We realize she'll need buttons for the sweater, so I show her the wall of buttons, and she chooses cute wooden ones shaped like trains. I cash her out and wish her a good day, then look at Eric who's still here.

"Maybe we could go to the reunion-fundraiser together?" he asks.

"Listen"—I sit down on one of the sofas in the cozy sitting area—"I'm happy to help you any way I can. I want Laura's murder solved, too, but you don't have to feed me dinner, keep me in daily coffee, or escort me to an event to get my help. I always keep my eyes and ears open and pass on whatever I see or hear."

He nods.

"Anyway, don't you already have a date? I heard you tell Amy when she asked you."

"I told her that because I don't want to go with her," he explains. "I want to go with you."

Really?

"Oh," I say.

Before we can continue our conversation, the bell over the door jingles, and Glenda comes in, clutching an envelope in her hand, followed by Phillip, who has a concerned look on his face.

"The other beneficiary is Brian Sweeney," Glenda announces.

Her eyes are wide, and her mouth is open.

Phillip takes her by the arm, guides her to a sofa, and sits her down. I'm about to tell her that the DNA test Laura took was a siblingship test, when she starts speaking.

"I think I've figured out a few things," Glenda says, staring at the empty coffee table while she speaks. "That day in the doctor's office when I was eight, my mother must have seen a note in Brian's file about his true paternity."

She stops talking and I get her a glass of water from the kitchenette. When I return, she's still staring blankly at the coffee table, so I put the glass of water on the table in her line of vision and tell her it's there.

She nods.

I notice she's not blinking often.

"Then Megan and I found those love letters from Brian to Laura," Glenda starts speaking again. "My mother must have found them and realized Laura and Brian were having a relationship—but they're siblings—and she had to make them stop talking and seeing each other. We all stopped talking and seeing each other."

We all sit together in silence for a few moments. Glenda has a sip of water.

"Glenda, I think you're in shock," Phillip says softly. "Noah can handle the store today. I'm taking you home."

I tell Phillip that Connie will be here any minute, so I'll be available to help Noah if he needs anything, and we'll be sure to give him a lunch break before Connie leaves. They leave, walking slowly with Phillip guiding Glenda by the arm.

"Wow," I say to Eric after Phillip and Glenda leave.

"Wow," he agrees, nodding.

Connie comes in through the back door, and Sophie rushes to greet her. Eric tucks Laura's laptop under his arm.

"The password is Sophie," I tell him.

We say goodbye, and he leaves.

BEFORE SOPHIE and I leave the store for the day, I text Phillip to check how he and Glenda are doing and ask if they need anything. He says they're fine, that Glenda is slowly processing the shocking news and says she might reach out to Brian tomorrow to talk to him.

I use the remote starter on my key chain to start the car about ten minutes before we leave so it can warm up. It's been snowing off and on all day, so while I'm getting Sophie and I ready to leave, I explain to her that she can wait in the warm car while I brush the snow off it.

We leave through the back door, and I lock it behind us. Surprise, surprise, someone has cleaned the snow off my car for me. There are no other cars in the parking lot, so I chalk it up to a random act of kindness, get in the warm car, and drive home.

WHEN ERIC and I arrive at the high school, the alumni association is in set-up-and-decoration mode.

We notice Brian Sweeney standing off to the side with Anne-Marie and walk over to them. They're decorating a large bed sheet with the school colours, royal blue and gold.

"This is the photo backdrop for the prom photos," Brian explains.

"After they finish with the photos," Anne-Marie adds, "we turn the sheet over, and the alumni will sign the back of it in permanent marker, then it will hang in the school...somewhere." She gestures vaguely.

"Is it emotional being back in your old high school after all these years?" I ask.

"It hasn't been that many years," Brian jokes, "but yes, the memories have a way of flooding back. You know," he says, pointing a glue gun at me, "I proposed to Anne-Marie at the bleachers in the field out back."

He smiles and puts his arm around his wife's shoulder.

"I didn't know that," I say.

"She's a year younger than me. I proposed to her the

summer after she graduated," he remembers. "We didn't get married until a few years later when we both finished school, but that's where I locked her down."

He looks at Anne-Marie and winks. She smiles back at him, sheepishly.

"We were going to visit the bleachers today, for old time's sake," Anne-Marie says, "but the snow in the field is at least a foot deep, so we'll wait until spring to relive our proposal."

The Sweeneys have an affectionate, loving relationship. They touch each other almost constantly. They hold hands, rub each other's backs, and hug frequently. They make each other smile and laugh, and more than once I've caught them exchanging a sneaky glance, a sheepish grin, or a wink. After fifty years, they're still smitten with each other, and it's inspiring to see.

Eric asks Brian if he received a registered letter today. Brian shakes his head and says he hasn't been home since this morning to receive anything.

Eric tells him that he's named in Laura's will and asks him if he believes he might be Laura and Glenda's half-brother.

Anne-Marie gasps, covers her mouth with her fingertips and looks at Brian with wide eyes. Brian is looking at Eric and nodding.

"We were waiting for the DNA results to come back, so we'd know for sure before we said anything to anyone…"

Before Brian can continue his thought, Mr. Willows barges into the gym, and stomps straight over to where The Sweeneys, Eric, and I are standing.

"I heard a rumour it's you," Mr. Willows bellows, pointing to Mr Sweeney. "You and Glenda inherited her half of the land. Is it true?"

Eric assumes the same position he did the last time this happened, nose to nose with Mr. Willows, blocking his access to Brian.

"Is it true that your car was in Laura's driveway the

morning she died?" I ask. "Witnesses saw a car just like the one Mrs. Willows drives. We already know you were driving around Harmony Lake in her car that morning."

Brian and Anne-Marie gasp, cover their open mouths with their hands, and raise their eyebrows.

"I was there, so what?!" he barks. "I didn't go in her house. I've never been inside her house."

He shakes his head and takes a step back from Eric.

"I'd heard she was coming home from the hospital that morning," he continues, "and thought I'd take a chance she'd be there. I rang the bell and knocked, but no one answered. There was mail in her mailbox, so I assumed she wasn't home yet, and I left."

If Mr. Willows is telling the truth, he was there after the postal carrier delivered the mail, and his car wasn't the one she saw in the driveway. Also, she was specific about seeing the car and not seeing who was driving it. If Mr. Willows was never in Laura's house, like he claims, the postal carrier would have seen him on the porch or in his car.

"Listen, Sweeney," Mr. Willows barks, "I've sacrificed too much to lose everything now. You need to do the right thing and sell that land to Mega Mart!"

Mr. Willows clenches his fists, puts them on his knees and hunches over. His breathing is loud, erratic, and rapid. He starts knocking on his chest with one of his clenched fists and gasping like he's trying to speak.

"Henry!" Mrs. Willows cries.

I didn't realize she was here. Mr. Willows has a knack for attracting all the attention when he enters a room, and Mrs. Willows has a knack for disappearing into the background like she's invisible.

She stands next to her husband, and Eric takes a step toward him, holding his arms to steady him and, I presume, catch him if he collapses.

Brian and I take a couple of steps backward to give Mr.

Willows space to do whatever it is he needs to do. Anne-Marie steps forward, approaches Mr. Willows, places a hand on his back, and begins rubbing reassuringly. She bends down to speak to Mr. Willows and look at his face.

I can't hear what she's saying to him, but he's nodding. The fist that he was using to knock on his chest is now open and reaching for her hand, which she provides.

His breath is still erratic and wheezy, but Anne-Marie looks like she knows what she's doing, so the rest of us are a little less panicked.

Anne-Marie coaxes Mr. Willows into standing upright and turns him toward the wall. The three of them, Mr. Willows in the middle, Anne-Marie supporting him on one side, and Eric supporting him on the other, take small, slow steps toward the bench against the wall of the auditorium.

As they walk away, Anne-Marie turns her head and looks back at us.

"Ambulance," she says voicelessly.

"Got it!" I say, pulling my phone from my pocket and dialing 9-1-1.

Mrs. Willows rushes to the bench by the wall to be with her husband, and Brian and I go to the front doors of the school to wait for the ambulance and point them toward the cafe-gym-itorium.

THE PARAMEDICS SHOW UP and roll Mr. Willows out on a stretcher, with Mrs. Willows holding one of his hands and Anne-Marie holding the other.

He's conscious and alert when the paramedics lift him into the ambulance, and Anne-Marie stays with him until the ambulance door closes.

Mrs. Willows rides in the ambulance with her husband, and Eric follows them in his car.

I stay at the high school and help the Sweeneys finish decorating the photo backdrop. The rest of the alumni association are shocked and concerned about Mr. Willows' episode, as it's being called. The constant flow of people coming over to ask Anne-Marie about it slows us down, but we get it finished eventually. We hang it where the photographer will set up for photos on Saturday night, admire our handiwork, clean up the art supplies we used, and leave. The Sweeneys drop me off on their way home.

Sophie and I have a quick walk, and while filling her in on the evening's events as we get ready for bed, I get a text from Eric:

Eric: Good news! Dr. Pearson doesn't think Mr. Willows had a heart attack. Admitting him for a few tests though.

Me: That's a relief!

Eric: I'm sorry for running out on you at the school tonight!

Me: No worries! I'm a big girl. Mr. W's episode was more important. Next time, we'll take separate cars ;)

Eric: Dr. Pearson says to say hi

FRIDAY JANUARY 17TH

April shows up at the store as soon as we open, she brought coffee for both of us from Latte Da, in exchange for a full rundown of what happened at the high school last night.

It's a quick but thorough conversation. She has to get back to Artsy Tartsy so Tamara can work in the kitchen all day, baking dog and cat treats for the silent auction tomorrow night.

Glenda comes by at lunchtime to watch the store so I can have a quick break.

"How are you doing today?" I ask Glenda.

"Now that the shock has worn off, I'm feeling better." She nods. "Thank you for asking."

"Phillip mentioned that you might reach out to Brian today," I say. "If you need a few more days before you're ready, I'm sure he'd understand. He seems like a lovely, patient, man, and this is a big shock for both of you."

"I'm sure he'd understand too," she replies, "but I think I'm as ready as I'll ever be. I have questions he might be able to answer, and he might have questions I can help answer."

I thank Glenda for helping in the store, grab a quick bite in the kitchenette, then take Sophie across the street to do her business.

The afternoon is busy, which is fine with me because it means business is good, and time passes quickly and effortlessly when the store is busy.

I wish the last customer of the day a good evening about five minutes after closing time, lock the door behind her, and turn the sign from, OPEN to CLOSED.

Even Sophie is tired. She flops onto her dog bed for a nap while I tidy the store, return mislaid skeins of yarn to their assigned shelves, and give the floor a once over with the broom and dustpan.

I'm sweeping around Sophie and her dog bed when I hear my phone ding on the counter.

Eric: I meant to come by today and walk Sophie for you since you're alone, but it's been crazy today and I couldn't get away.

Me: No worries. I won't mention it to Sophie though, she'll be disappointed. ;)

Eric: So, will you go to the reunion-fundraiser with me? If I promise not to abandon you there again like last night?

Me: Sure, let's do it. You can abandon me as long as it's to catch a killer.

He tells me what time he'll pick me up, and I instantly

take a mental inventory of my wardrobe trying to figure out what to wear.

"Eric and I are going to the reunion-fundraiser, Sophie!"

Her tail wags and her ears perk up when she hears her name.

"I have no idea what I'm going to wear, but I have a date —sort of, I think. With my tenant."

Sophie looks up at me, twitching her eyebrows.

I text Kelly at Hairway To Heaven to see if she can fit me in for a wash and blow dry tomorrow. I'm not hopeful, she's probably fully booked tomorrow with everyone wanting their hair done for the event.

Me: Hi Kelly! I know it's short notice, but any chance I can get a wash and blow dry tomorrow afternoon? No worries if you're booked, I totally understand.

Kelly: Hi Megan! There's always a spot for you in my chair. How about 5:30 p.m.? Then you only miss the last half hour at the store.

Me: You're a lifesaver! Thank you, Kelly! I'll see you tomorrow :)

Kelly owns Hairway To Heaven. She's been doing my hair for at least ten years, and she takes care of Hannah's hair too. Kelly and I have always been friends, but everything that happened last September has made us closer and levelled up our friendship. We share a bond that's hard to describe. A bond that you can only have with someone with whom you've shared a horrible, life-altering experience. She's a great hairdresser and an even better person. Thanks to Kelly, my hair will look decent tomorrow night, without me having to fight it with a flat iron for an hour or put it up to hide its unruliness.

CHAPTER 19

Today is the busiest day of the week, and another body in the store would be a big help. I need to hire someone to work at Knitorious part-time. I'm here full-time, and Connie is here part-time. She's trying to ease into retirement, and she and Archie seem to be making new and exciting travel plans every time I talk to them.

Midday, Eric stops by to walk Sophie, which she and I both appreciate. When he brings her back, I'm in the middle of cashing out a customer, so he removes her leash and sweater. Thinking he's in a rush to get back to work, I mouth thank you to him while I bag eight skeins of yarn and a book of knitting patterns.

To my surprise, when I'm finished ringing up her purchase and my customer turns to leave, Eric is still here. He's loitering near the door.

"What are you wearing?" he asks, holding the door for my customer on her way out.

Confused, I glance down at my see-through Converse sneakers (they show off my rainbow-striped, hand-knit

349

socks), dark blue skinny jeans, navy blue tank top, and amethyst hand-knit cardigan.

"I mean tonight," he clarifies.

Oh, that makes more sense.

"Black?" I offer hesitantly. "I think. I haven't decided for sure yet, but probably black."

Most of the not-casual pieces of my wardrobe are black, so it's the most likely option.

"What are you wearing?" I ask. "Tonight, I mean?"

"Black." He smiles.

"Thank you for walking Sophie," I call after him as he disappears through the front door.

Shortly after Eric leaves, Glenda comes over from next door, so I can have a quick lunch. She can only stay for about fifteen minutes because Phillip is busy making corsages and boutonnieres for the reunion-fundraiser.

I completely forgot that the theme is prom, and now I'm wondering if I should get Eric a boutonniere.

"Glenda, I guess I should get Eric a boutonniere?" I ask.

She taps the top of her wrist and winks at me. "Phillip's got you covered," she says.

KELLY DOES an amazing job with my hair, as usual, and I leave Hairway To Heaven with bouncy, smooth, shiny hair that screams: this person has her life together! Instead of my usual curly, unruly, crazy hair, that screams: this person is really nice, but sometimes she loses her knitting needle behind her ear for half a day!

I DIG through my small selection of formal-ish attire and settle on a 1950s-style, black, cocktail dress with a deep sweetheart neckline and belted waist. It's very fitted through the bodice, and has a full, knee-length skirt. A bit more cleavage than I usually show, but I love the dress and it looks great on me, so I decide to embrace the cleavage.

I pair the dress with black, sparkly stilettos and a matching black, sparkly clutch purse. I'm trying to decide whether to go full vintage 1950s and wear a black crinoline under the skirt when the doorbell rings.

Sophie barks at the closed door while I peek through the living room window and see Phillip on the doorstep.

"Hi, Phillip," I greet him, opening the door. "Come in." I jerk my head toward the inside of the house and move aside so he can step in.

He smiles and extends his hand, handing me a small white box. I take it and open it. It's a boutonniere for Eric.

"Phillip, thank you!"

I hug him. Phillip isn't my most outwardly affectionate friend, but he tolerates my show of gratitude.

"Do I need to water it or anything?" I ask.

I don't have a green thumb. Whatever the opposite of a green thumb is, that's my thumb.

"No!" He waves his hands back and forth like he's trying to stop a plane from landing. "Don't water it. Don't do anything to it. Just put it on Eric's lapel."

"Got it," I say.

"Do you know how to attach a boutonniere, Megan?"

He knows I'm not good with plants.

"Yes." I nod. "I've done this before."

Phillip looks at my housecoat and asks me if I need him to walk Sophie while I get ready. I thank him and tell him that's she's been walked, fed, and watered. I thank him again for the boutonniere and tell him I'll see him tonight.

I put on my makeup, get dressed (I decide against the crinoline since the skirt is full enough without it), and dig out my diamond earrings and bracelet to accessorize my outfit.

"You look beautiful," Eric says when I open the door.

Sophie is bouncing and yelping in front of him, trying to get his attention.

"Thank you," I say. "I assume you mean me and not Sophie," I joke.

"Yes, I mean you," he says. "But Sophie's a beautiful girl too." He bends down to give her rubs.

I go into the kitchen to get the boutonniere box, and when I come back, he's standing up again, and Sophie is sitting at his feet.

"You're handsome," I say.

And by handsome, I mean hot. Like, so, so hot.

"And it's not the tux, you always look good."

I stop talking because I'm blushing and probably about to say something that will keep me awake at night, cringing to myself, for the next ten years.

Eric holds the box while I remove the boutonniere and pin it to his lapel. Then I hold the corsage box and smell him while he puts the corsage on my wrist. He smells good. Like a forest on a rainy day. I think I'm doing a pretty good job pretending I don't find him distracting.

WE ENTER the cafe-gym-itorium through an archway of balloons in the school colours. The alumni association did a fabulous job, it feels like walking into a real prom.

We stop at the registration table to check in; we're guided to the photography booth where we have our photo taken in front of the backdrop I helped the Sweeneys decorate.

On the short drive to the school, Eric explained that there are non-uniform police officers mingling in the crowd. He said they're here to watch and listen for anything that might be relevant to Laura's murder. He said that because the Animal Centre is her organization, and there is a memorial to her at the event, it's possible that someone who knows some-thing about her death could be here tonight and say some-thing that could help the investigation. So, when a man I don't recognize walks up to Eric and starts talking to him while gently guiding him to a quiet corner, I assume he's one of the non-uniform officers and entertain myself by walking around, looking at the various fundraising activities, and greeting friends and neighbours.

The first people I encounter are Mrs. Pearson and her son, Craig.

We greet each other and exchange compliments about how dapper we all look. Then Mrs. Pearson sees someone else she knows and rushes off, leaving Craig and I on our own.

"It's nice to see you again," I say. "I'm sorry we haven't gotten together."

"It's OK," Craig replies, "we're both busy people."

"Busy, and not quite ready to hang out with anyone as more than friends," I explain.

He nods. "I understand."

That wasn't as bad as I'd imagined it. Actually, I feel relieved now that it's done.

"See that lady over there with the dog?" he asks, nodding toward PC Amy Andrews and Tundra. "Do you know her? Is she single?"

Well, at least he's not heartbroken and wallowing in self-pity because I just want to be friends.

"Uh-huh." I nod. "Would you like an introduction?"

"That would be awesome, Megan, thanks."

He straightens his suit and tie, pats his hair into place, and we make our way over to Amy and Tundra.

Tundra is wearing a white shirt collar with a black bowtie, and he's the most dignified and handsome dog I've ever seen.

We loiter nearby while Amy finishes speaking with a lady I recognize. She's one of the volunteers from the Animal Centre.

"Hi, Amy," I say as the lady she was speaking with walks away.

"Hi, Megan," she smiles, showing us her dimples.

"Amy Andrews…" I gesture to Craig. "This is Craig Pearson. Craig is a dedicated physician with a great bedside manner. He's also a keen dog walker."

"It's true," Craig interjects. "I love dogs."

"Craig Pearson, this is Amy Andrews." I gesture to Amy. "In addition to being one of Harmony Lake's finest, Amy organized the silent auction portion of tonight's fundraiser and probably knows where the best donations are hidden."

"You're a doctor?" Amy asks him. "The local antique store, Old School, donated a gift certificate, and as part of their display, they brought a vintage 1957 copy of The Physician's Desk Reference."

"Really? I'd love to see it," Craig says.

"Let's go!"

The three of them walk away, and my work here is done. I hear someone golf-clapping behind me and turn around.

"Nicely done," Eric says.

"Thank you," I say. "They make a cute couple. I hope they enjoy each other's company."

We wander the room, moving in the general direction of the bar and stopping to mingle every few feet. When we get to the bar, I order a glass of champagne, and Eric orders a ginger ale.

We notice Anne-Marie Sweeney volunteering at one of the fundraising tables, so we go over to say hi and check out her exhibit.

"Hi Anne-Marie! Have you had many players?" I ask, gesturing to the game wheel she's spinning.

"It's been steady," she says, "but I think the Champagne Toonie Roll is the most popular attraction tonight."

She points to a game a few stations down from hers, and I make a mental note to check it out next.

"I've been meaning to ask you if Connie texted you the shopping list you dropped at Pharmer's Market the other day?" I ask.

"She did!" She touches my arm. "Thank you for noticing that and picking it up. It saved us from making a second trip to Harmony Hills to pick up the things we'd have forgotten the first time."

We laugh.

Eric excuses himself to speak with someone, and I tell Anne-Marie how amazing she was with Mr. Willows the other night when he had his episode.

"Thank you," she says modestly. "It's all in a day's work for a nurse."

"Well, it's not all in a day's work for a yarn store owner," I say. "Not only did you help Mr. Willows through his episode, you helped the rest of us through it too. We wouldn't have known the best way to help him. Thank goodness you were there and knew exactly what to do."

We agree that it's great news he didn't have a heart attack. She admits she suspected at the time that he was having a panic attack and hopes it's nothing more serious.

The game wheel she's spinning looks like one of those wheels on TV a game show, except instead of the wedges having dollar values or prizes, each wedge features a pet currently available for adoption at the AC. You place a bet on which animal the wheel will land on, and if the wheel stops on the animal you chose, you win a donated prize. If it lands on a different animal, you walk away with the satisfaction of contributing to a worthy cause.

I take ten dollars from my wallet and let it ride on a Rottweiler mix named Purl. Any dog named after a knitting stitch is a sure bet in my opinion. Anne-Marie spins the wheel, but it doesn't land on Purl. Oh well, it was fun to play, and I'm happy to support a great cause.

Anne-Marie has another customer, so I move along to investigate the Champagne Toonie Roll game she mentioned.

Bottles of champagne are set up like bowling pins at the end of a long table. The player rolls a toonie—a two-dollar coin—on its edge, toward the champagne bottles. If the toonie hits one of the bottles before toppling over, you win that bottle of champagne. If not, Animal Centre keeps the toonie.

I hand the volunteer behind the counter ten dollars, and he hands me five toonies.

None of my toonies come close to touching a bottle of champagne, but it was fun trying.

"Nice try, Meg."

I turn to see Adam standing by the table with Dr. White. Are they here together? They make a striking couple.

"Hi Adam."

We hug and exchange a double-cheek kiss.

"It's nice to see you again, Dr. White," I say, extending my hand hoping she'll shake it, but aware that she might not.

I basically accused her of murder a few days ago, after all, and I'm sure she hasn't forgotten. Graciously, she accepts my hand and we shake.

"It's nice to see you again, Megan, please call me Val." She seems sincere.

"Thank you, Val," I say. "Listen, about our conversation the other day at the AC…"

She puts her hand up with her palm facing me to stop me from talking and shakes her head.

"It's forgotten," she says. "Laura's murder has shocked all of us. She's lucky to have friends and family who are so concerned about getting to the bottom of what happened to her."

Before I can respond, an older, distinguished-looking gentleman taps her on the shoulder. She turns around, and he moves in close to her and says something in her ear. She turns back to me and, with her right index finger in the air, looks from me to Adam.

"Will you please excuse me? I need to see to something," she says.

Then she walks away with the older man, leaving Adam and I on our own.

Adam and I exchange compliments about how well be both clean up. After commenting on each other's empty glass, we decide to meander toward the bar for refills.

Eric catches up with us on the way, and we make small talk about which games we've tried and what items we might bid on at the silent auction. I haven't been to the silent auction yet, so I decide that'll be my next stop after the bar.

While Adam and I refill our drinks, Amy Andrews, Tundra, and Craig, approach us and start talking to Eric. He and Amy are talking about work-related stuff, so I gravitate toward Adam, and we wander toward the silent auction tables.

"So," he says, "you're here with Eric."

It was a statement of fact, not a question, but I nod anyway.

"Are you two seeing each other?" he asks.

"Not really," I shrug.

"Are you here with Dr. White, I mean Val?" I ask.

"No." He shakes his head. "Tonight is the first time we've met face to face. We've spoken on the phone in my capacity as Laura's executor. She's seems nice."

"Maybe you should ask her out," I suggest.

"Maybe you should ask Eric out," he counters.

Touché.

We're roaming from one silent auction item to the next when we encounter Phillip roaming in the opposite direction.

While Phillip and Adam are talking and getting caught up, my attention wanders. I scan the room taking in all the people, displays, and decorations. My gaze stops when I see

April and Tamara. They're standing by the samples of pet treats they donated to the silent auction, and they both look stunning. They look like someone shook an issue of Vogue magazine, and they fell out from between the pages. I guess when one of you looks like Heidi Klum, and the other one looks like Halle Berry to start with, and you actually make an effort, you look like you got lost on your way to a runway fashion show in Paris.

I catch Tamara's eye, smile, and wave. She smiles and waves back, but she and April seem to be in a deep discussion with the older gentleman who approached Dr. White earlier. Who is he? He looks vaguely familiar, but I don't know him. I don't want to interrupt, and I stay put with Adam and Phillip.

In between smiling and nodding, but not truly listening to Adam and Phillip's conversation, I keep glancing over at April, Tamara, and the mystery man. He appears keenly interested in their pet treats, and… did he just eat a dog treat? Are my eyes playing tricks on me? I mean, they smell yummy, but I wouldn't eat one. I'm sure he's chewing.

Adam and Phillip's conversation has turned to politics, which is my cue to wander away and leave them to it.

I drift along from one silent auction item to the next, looking at the most recent bid for each item, and who's been bidding on what.

I notice Brian Sweeney has bid on both a year's supply of doughnuts from Glazed and Confused and weekday lift passes for the remainder of the season from the Rise and Glide Ski Resort. Time hasn't done any favours for his penmanship. I notice his handwriting looks more like chicken scratch than the beautiful calligraphic handwriting on the love letters Glenda and I found under Laura's bed.

Maybe he has everyday handwriting, the writing I see on the auction bid sheets, and love letter handwriting on the letters to Laura.

When I get to the year's supply of pet treats, delivered fresh weekly that Tamara and April donated, they're still deep in conversation with the mystery man, and the three of them move aside when I approach their bid sheet. I can't hear what they're saying, but it looks like they're in the midst of an intense discussion, and now the mystery man is sniffing one of the treats. I bid on the dog treats and move along, knowing April will tell me all about it later tonight, or tomorrow.

When I look back, Dr. White has joined them, and the older pet-treat-eating-and-sniffing man is talking to all three of them.

I bid on a gold necklace donated by Charmed & Dangerous, the local jeweller, and return the pen to the pen holder next to the bid sheet.

"Hey, stranger!" Eric says.

"You're back," I exclaim. "Any exciting developments?"

"Not really," he says. "I'm sorry I keep getting intercepted and leaving you alone."

I make a sweeping motion with my hand to wave away his comment.

"This is a work event for you, I know that," I say.

"It's also the first time I've seen most of my colleagues outside of work," he says. "Whenever I'm trying to make my way back to you, I get stopped two or three times by a cop who wants to introduce me to their spouse, or partner, or date."

"That pretty much sums up living in this town," I say. "Whatever you're doing, wherever you're going someone will stop you to talk, gossip or catch up. It's a locational hazard."

I just made that up, locational hazard.

"Well, I'm happy I'm meeting people and that the locals are socializing with me. But it would be nice to do something together. Just you and me. Maybe somewhere everyone doesn't want to stop and talk, and there isn't a murder investigation that keeps pulling me away," he suggests, smiling.

"Maybe," I say.

At the end of the silent auction items, there's a table with a memorial for Laura. It's a tasteful display and a popular one. There are quite a few visitors milling around it.

Eric and I look at the huge photo collage Glenda made. There is a second collage next to it made by the staff and volunteers at the AC, featuring photos of Laura in her element with the animals, the staff, and volunteers.

I sign Laura's condolence book, then scan the signatures before mine to see who else has signed. I notice Anne-Marie's signature near the top of the page, and something about her handwriting is oddly familiar and makes me feel...unsettled. A knot forms in my stomach. I stare at her entry, purse my lips and tilt my head, trying to figure out what it is about her entry in the condolence book that's unsettling.

CHAPTER 20

"You OK?" Eric asks.

"Uh-huh," I reply. "I'm fine."

I pull the Sweeney's shopping list from my wallet, then scroll through the photos on my phone until I get to the ones I took at Laura's house the morning she died.

First, I compare the photo of the envelope on Laura's kitchen table with the sticky note saying, **I believe this belongs to you**! to the shopping list. Then I study her condolence book entry, which reads, *Taken too soon, you still belong here with us.*

The word *belong* in the condolence entry, and the word **belongs** on the sticky note both have a unique letter *g*. That same unique letter *g* is repeated on her shopping list. Hmmm.

I move aside and hand Eric the pen, so he can sign the condolence book.

"Ooofff," I utter when I'm bumped from behind.

"Megan, I'm sorry! I didn't see you there," Brian Sweeney says, grabbing my arm to steady me.

I assure him I'm fine, and he turns back to Glenda, Connie, and Archie. He's pointing and blurting out random letters. I stuff my phone and Anne-Marie's shopping list back into my purse and turn to face them and listen in.

"A!" Brian exclaims, jabbing his index finger into the air. "B! O! AB!" He jabs his finger in a different direction each time he shouts out a different letter. Connie, Glenda, and Archie are laughing in near hysterics as he does this.

Connie catches her breath and wipes tears of laughter from her eyes.

"Hello, my dear, you look beautiful," she says as she hugs me, still laughing intermittently at whatever it was Brian was doing.

"Thank you," I say, "so do you."

She's still smiling, and her face is red from laughing so hard.

It's nice to see Glenda and Brian laughing together and getting along. Out of the corner of my eye, I see Archie lift his leg and rotate it, then put it back on the floor and gyrate his hips as he speaks to Eric. I'm guessing Eric asked Archie how his hip is doing and is now listening to the long version of the answer.

"What's so funny?" I ask Connie.

"Laura and Glenda's mother, Laura, took great pride in knowing the blood type of everyone in town thanks to her work with the Red Cross as a blood drive organizer," Connie explains loud enough for me to hear over Brian and Glenda's laughter. "Sometimes people would test her to see if she could really remember everybody's blood type, and she often referred to her friends by their blood type instead of their name."

"She always called my mum and dad, A and AB, even though their names were Lily and Ernest, for example," Brian interjects.

"Oh," I say, "I get it."

I don't think it's as hilarious as they do, but I guess you had to be there.

The four of them laugh loudly again, and I laugh too, even though I don't think it's as funny as they do, because it's impossible not to laugh when surrounded by so much genuine laughter. It's contagious. Eric joins me, and he laughs too.

"Why are we laughing?" he asks.

"Because they are?" I shrug, giggling.

We move along to look at the yearbooks on display next to Laura's memorial. The yearbook from the year Connie graduated is on top. Carefully turning the pages, I stop to look at Connie's graduation photo and marvel at how young she was.

Harmony Lake is a small town, and it was even smaller back then, before they built the highway through the mountains, linking us to Harmony Hills and the city. Their graduating class was small. Instead of small thumbnail photos of each graduate, like you see in most yearbooks, their yearbook features only eight graduates per two-page spread, four on the left side and four on the right. In this copy of the yearbook, each graduate handwrote a message underneath their grad photo.

The handwritten message under Connie's photo says, *If you follow your dreams, you are capable of anything.* Her handwriting was the same fifty years ago, as it is today.

I notice most of the graduates have beautiful, cursive handwriting. What Glenda said about people back in the day having lovely penmanship must be true.

I turn the page, and Brian Sweeney stares back at me from his grad photo. The handwritten message under his photo is scrawled in writing that resembles his handwriting on the bid sheets more than it resembles the beautiful handwriting on the love letters under Laura's bed.

I randomly pick up another yearbook from the pile. This one is from twenty-seven years before Connie and Brian graduated.

I gently leaf through the pages of the old book, stopping when I see a familiar face smiling back at me. I recognize this face from the photos under Laura's bed; it's Glen, Laura and Glenda's dad. I look at the handwritten message under his yearbook photo and recognize his beautiful, calligraphic handwriting immediately.

My heart rate and my breath accelerate in unison as I reach into my beaded clutch and pull out my phone.

I put my purse under my arm and start scrolling through the photos on my phone, my hands shaking with excitement because I'm pretty sure I'm onto something.

"Is everything OK, Megan?" Eric asks softly.

I nod.

"Found it!" I announce.

I lay my phone on the yearbook next to Glen's photo and handwritten message. I compare his handwriting in the yearbook to the handwriting I photographed from the love letter under Laura's bed. I look at Eric.

"Laura and Glenda are named after their parents," I say excitedly.

"Right," Eric agrees.

"Laura is named after her mother," I elaborate. "Brian's mother is named, Lily. Laura and Lily both start with, L."

"Yes, they do." He nods, looking at me intently.

He looks worried, like I'm not making sense or something.

"The love letters under Laura's bed aren't from Brian to Laura," I explain, shaking my head. "They were to Brian's mother, Lily."

"Possibly," he says. "But if they are, then who's B?"

I tell him what Connie just told me about Laura senior calling people by their blood type instead of their names. He's nodding and I can see him making the same connections I am.

"Laura's father, Glen, could be B, if his blood type is B," I justify. "It makes sense."

Eric nods.

He's processing. He looks downwards and to his left, as I've noticed he often does when he's working something out.

"So," Eric says, "maybe Laura kept one of the letters out to show Brian as evidence that they might be siblings, and that's why one letter from the stack was on the kitchen table the day Laura died. But why would Laura have the love letters that her dad wrote to a woman who isn't her mother?"

"Who knows," I reply, "maybe they were written but never sent? Maybe at some point, Laura senior confronted the other woman and got them from her? Maybe she broke into their house and stole them. I have no idea." I shrug.

Who knows what kinds of crazy things happen between husbands and wives and best friends in these situations? I do know that this all happened in the days before DNA. Blood type evidence, along with those letters, may have been the only proof Laura senior had that her husband fathered a child with another woman.

Not just any other woman, her best friend. They would've been pregnant at the same time. I can't imagine how Laura senior had felt when she figured all of this out. It must have turned her world upside down.

"Think about it," I say. "If Glenda and I assumed the letters were from Brian to Laura, then anyone else who saw them would probably think the same thing. If Brian took that letter home, and Anne-Marie found it, she might have assumed it was from Brian to Laura too. She could easily have reached the wrong conclusion, like we did."

I pick up my phone from the yearbook and do a quick web search. Eric waits patiently while I check three sites to confirm what I found at the first site is true.

"An AB and an A can't make an O," I say to Eric, shaking my head.

"Come again?"

I hand him my phone, open to a web page with a chart

that illustrates how parents with blood Type AB and Type A cannot produce a child with Type O blood.

I tell him about the day I met Brian in the hospital after my fall. He told Connie and I he's a universal donor which means he has Type O Negative blood. Brian confirmed a few minutes ago that his mom had Type A blood, and his dad had Type AB blood, so they couldn't have produced a baby with Type O Negative blood.

Eric hands my phone back to me. We stand still, listening intently as Brian tells Connie, Archie, and Glenda that, according to Laura, her mother told her fifty years ago that Brian is her half-brother. She saw how close Brian and Laura were and worried their relationship might become romantic.

Brian assures them that he and Laura were best friends. He says they were more like brother and sister, which it turns out they actually were. He insists their relationship would never have become romantic.

He says when he and Laura reconciled their relationship, Laura told him she was never sure if her mother was telling the truth back then, or trying to keep Laura and Brian apart because she'd had a falling out with Brian's mum.

"When Laura was cleaning out her mother's belongings after her mother died, she found a stack of love letters to L from B and realized it might be true," he tells Connie, Glenda, and Archie. "She thought L, who the letters were written to, was short for Lily, my mother, and B was Glen because her mum always called him B, in honour of his blood type."

"See," I whisper to Eric.

"So how did you and Laura start talking again?" Archie asks.

"She contacted me after my father died, to offer her condolences, and asked me to meet her. She told me when we met and brought the letters to show me. I asked her if I could keep one, and she said yes."

He says they did a DNA test, to be sure before they told anyone else, but Laura died before she received the results.

He and Glenda are hoping to get to know each other and maybe meet each other's families.

I move closer to Eric, and he lowers his head so I can speak into his ear.

"That day in the doctor's office when Glenda was eight, Laura senior must have seen Brian's blood type in his file and realized he can't be Type O Negative with parents who are type AB and Type A. She knew about blood types, and she knew their blood types."

"You're right," Eric says barely above a whisper, "but it wouldn't have proven that her husband was Brian's biological father. How did she make the leap from realizing Ernest couldn't be Brian's father, to assuming it must be her husband?"

"Intuition," I speculate. "If she already had suspicions about her husband having an affair—sometimes women have intuition about these things—it might have been enough for her to confront him. Maybe when she confronted him, he admitted it, either to ease his conscience, or because his wife was worried about Brian and Laura having a romantic relationship. He wouldn't have wanted his two children to be that close, so he would have had to admit it, even if it were only a possibility."

I bite the inside of my mouth while I consider the possibilities. "Or, maybe she confronted Brian's mum, Lily, and she admitted it. We may never know for sure."

I tell him what Glenda told me about her parents' relationship being tense for a long time after that day at the doctor's office.

I hook my hand through the crook of Eric's arm and lead him over to the condolence book at Laura's memorial table.

I turn back to the previous page where Anne-Marie and I both signed. I reach into my purse, pull out the shopping list she dropped at the pharmacy, and open my phone to the photo of the sticky note in Laura's kitchen. I lay all three handwriting samples on the table in a row.

"Look at the g's," I say.

Eric looks at the handwriting samples, then at me. He picks up my phone and presses it into my hand, then folds the shopping list and puts it in his breast pocket.

"I need to keep this," he says, patting the pocket where he just put the shopping list.

We both turn and look toward the table with the Animal Shelter Roulette game where Anne-Marie was volunteering earlier in the evening. She's not there. Mrs. Pearson is working the Animal Shelter Roulette game now.

We scan the room looking for Anne-Marie.

I don't see her anywhere.

Eric and I look at each other.

"She's gone," we both say at the same time.

CHAPTER 21

ERIC PULLS out his phone and sends a quick text.

"Everyone is looking for her," he says. "We'll search every inch of the school."

I watch his eyes scan the room again, and his gaze stops on PC Amy Andrews. He grabs my hand and leads me across the room to where she's standing with Tundra and Craig.

"Andrews," Eric says with an air of authority. "I know you're not on duty tonight, but we need to locate a person of interest."

Tundra must recognize the urgent tone in Eric's voice because he sits up at attention.

"Yes, Detective Sergeant," Amy says as she picks up Tundra's leash.

"Who are we looking for?" she asks as she, Tundra, and Eric hustle across the floor, under the balloon archway, and out of the cafe-gym-itorium.

Craig and I look at each other. I shrug, he smiles and raises his eyebrows.

"If you're going to see her again after tonight," I advise him, "you'll need to get used to it. This is the second time I've been left standing here since Thursday."

"Thanks for the heads up." He nods.

Craig offers to get us a drink. I thank him and watch him stride toward the bar.

"What's happening, my dear?"

Connie approaches me at a fast pace with Archie a few steps behind her.

"A police officer in a tuxedo just asked Brian if he has his car keys or if Anne-Marie has them. Then he asked Brian to go with him," she explains worriedly.

"Do you know where Anne-Marie went?" I ask.

She looks toward the Animal Shelter Roulette table, then looks back at me.

"I have no idea. Is there a problem?"

"Maybe," I say.

Without being too specific, I tell her Anne-Marie might have information about Laura's murder, and Eric needs to speak with her but can't find her.

Connie's jaw drops and she inhales sharply.

"Does he think Anne-Marie might be in danger?" she asks.

He thinks Anne-Marie might *be* the danger.

"I'm not sure," I reply. "Where inside the school would she go if she wanted to hide or be alone?" I ask.

"Marla!"

Connie gets Mrs. Pearson's attention and beckons her over to us.

Mrs. Pearson is asking someone to watch the table for her, but Connie doesn't want to wait, so she grabs my hand and pulls me toward Mrs. Pearson until the three of us meet in the middle.

"Marla and Anne-Marie were best friends in school," Connie explains to me, then turns to Mrs. Pearson. "Marla, what was Anne-Marie's locker number?"

Smart thinking, Connie!

Mrs. Pearson's eyes dart from left to right while she tries to recall the information.

"252," she says. "In the bank of lockers just outside the science lab."

I text Eric with Anne-Marie's locker number.

"Marla, where else might Anne-Marie go if she wanted to hide or be alone inside the school?" Connie asks her.

"Why?" Mrs. Pearson asks. "Is something wrong?"

"Not if we can find her, Marla, now where would she go? Connie is good at this!

"Well, the first time Brian kissed her was backstage at a school dance, so backstage, behind the curtain, maybe."

I text this to Eric.

"She always wanted to be a nurse, so she spent a lot of time in the Nurse's office, helping the nurse and asking questions."

I text this to Eric too.

"She was on quite a few school teams, so maybe the girls' change room?"

I text this to Eric.

"Now someone please tell me what's going on!" Mrs. Pearson demands, visibly upset.

Connie and Archie each take an arm and guide her toward Craig who's heading toward us with a drink in each hand. They intercept him; he hands both drinks to Archie and helps Connie to guide his mum to a chair where she can sit down.

Eric and another officer swoop into the cafe-gym-itorium and toward me.

"We haven't found her," he says. "We have to consider that she may have left the building."

"It's freezing out. She's wearing a dress and high heels," I say.

Eric nods. "And Brian has their car keys. Their car is still in the parking lot, and her coat is still at the coat check. She left in a hurry, either by choice or by force."

He asks the officer next to him to contact Amy and find out if she has boots in her car, telling him that she can't search through twelve inches of snow in open-toed shoes.

Hearing him mention twelve inches of snow reminds me of something the Sweeneys said when Eric and I were here on Thursday night.

"The bleachers!" I blurt out. "Remember? Brian told us he proposed to Anne-Marie at the bleachers in the field, after her graduation."

"You're brilliant." He smiles at me, squeezes my shoulder, then turns and runs out of the cafe-gym-itorium and probably the school.

CHAPTER 22

I SCAN the room looking for April and Tamara. They'd want to know what's happening. I don't see them anywhere.

The crowd is thinner than it was earlier. All the police officers have left to find Anne-Marie. The reunion attendees, most of whom are older and tired from setting up for the event, have started to leave.

I see Dr. White, I mean Val, sitting with the mystery man. They're deep in conversation and apparently oblivious to the commotion around them. I see Craig, Connie, Archie, and Mrs. Pearson sitting together off to the side of the action, and I see Adam speaking with Glenda near the bar.

Phillip walks past me.

"Phillip," I call after him.

He turns and smiles.

"Have you seen April or Tamara?" I ask.

"Yes!" He says. "About fifteen minutes ago, they were at the coat check. I assume they were leaving."

"Thank you," I smile.

"Listen, rumour is, no one is allowed to exit the parking lot? Have you heard anything about that?" he asks. "I need to get back to Kevin. He won't go to sleep if I'm not home."

"Sort of," I admit. "No one can find Anne-Marie Sweeney. The police are looking for her, so I guess they've locked down the parking lot."

He says nothing, but his mouth forms a small letter *o*, and his eyes open wide.

I leave the cafe-gym-itorium and go to the makeshift coat check in the library next door.

I don't have my ticket, it's in Eric's pocket, but the coat check volunteer knows me. She's an occasional member of the knitting group that meets at Knitorious and, I've just learned, volunteers at the AC.

"I'm sorry, I don't have my ticket," I plead.

"No worries, Megan, I know who you are." She smiles. "Do you see your coat?"

I nod and point to my coat.

"It's the black, double breasted, camel hair, knee length, beside the emerald green faux fur," I say. "There's a lip balm in the right pocket and a black, merino-silk blend, lace-weight scarf shoved into one sleeve—just in case you need proof that it's mine."

"Here you go," she says, handing me my coat.

I pull the scarf from the sleeve, and she asks if she can see it.

"Sure." I hand her the scarf.

I put my coat on, button it up, and smear some lip balm on my lips while she inspects my scarf.

"I love this pattern," she says as she hands the scarf back to me.

"Thanks," I reply. "It's called Wisp. I think it's from Knitty in 2006."

"Next time I'm at the store, I'll look for a skein of yarn that matches my coat and cast it on."

"Great! Have a good night," I say as I wrap the scarf around my neck and walk toward the west doors that lead to the field and the bleachers.

Stepping out of the school and into the bitter cold, I wish I'd thought to put a pair of mitts in my pockets or purse before I left the house. I tuck my clutch purse under my arm and shove my hands in my coat pockets.

Eric wasn't exaggerating. There's at least twelve inches of snow on the field. The paved path that leads from the school to the bleachers has been shovelled and salted, so that's where I walk. There's no way I'm stepping into snow that's knee deep with nothing except a pair of stiletto heels and silk stockings for protection.

Walking along the shovelled path, I see a group of people surrounding the bleachers, most of them holding a flashlight aimed at the same section of the metal seats.

Getting closer, I see that they're illuminating Anne-Marie, who's standing in the centre of a row of bleachers, about halfway between the top and the bottom.

I get as close as I can, without breaching the human barricade of police officers surrounding her, and join the crowd of bystanders. I stand as close as I can to my fellow onlookers. Close proximity isn't a choice, it's a survival technique. The path is only about eighteen inches wide, and it's at least minus fifteen with the windchill, so we need to huddle together and keep each other warm.

"An ambulance is on the way!" Someone yells from the snowy field.

"Why an ambulance?" I ask my fellow onlookers.

"She says she took something," a man answers.

When he turns around, I realize it's Mort Ackerman, the owner of the Mourning Glory Funeral Home.

"It won't be long now!" Anne-Marie yells from the bleachers, "I took the rest of your father's digoxin, well the rest that was left after I poisoned Laura Pingle."

The crowd lets out a collective gasp. She just confessed!

"Anne-Marie, sweetheart, please come down and let us

help you. Think of our boys! And our grand babies!" Brian pleads with her.

Brian seems to be standing with the police who are surrounding her.

I hear two deep, loud barks and see Amy and Tundra standing in the snow, Amy holding a flashlight.

I pull out my phone and text Craig.

Me: West doors, near the bleachers. Anne-Marie might need a doctor.

Craig: On my way.

"No, Brian! A life for a life," Anne-Marie shouts.

When did she take the digoxin? How much time does she have?

"I've been so stupid!" She yells, then smacks her palm against her forehead. "I found that letter and assumed you wrote it to Laura. You've been spending so much time together at the Animal Centre."

Brian moves to take a few steps closer to his wife. She puts her hand up and shakes her head.

"Stay!" she commands. "If anyone takes one step closer, I'll take this."

I assume she's holding something up, but I can't see anything in her hand.

"It will kill me immediately," she adds. "Now, please stay back and let me give my dying declaration before it's too late."

Craig rushes past me in the snow and has a word with one of the cops forming the barricade. The cop says something back to him and points. Craig moves quickly through the snow in the direction the cop was pointing. Then the cop speaks into his phone, presumably telling someone a doctor is on the way over.

"The letter, and all the time you were spending together, reminded me of the rumours back in high school that you and she had a secret relationship. Even though you always denied it and swore it was just a rumour, I began to think it was true, that there was a relationship, and now that we were back in Harmony Lake, you were resuming an affair with her."

Anne-Marie sobs and wipes her face with the sleeves of her dress. I hear sirens in the distance, and I'm hoping they get here quickly.

"Then I found a package for a DNA test one morning when I was putting the garbage out. The bag broke and the test package fell out of the bottom."

She goes from standing to sitting on the bleacher behind her. I feel my heart beating faster, and a wave of heat escapes from under my scarf. I'm worried that she's about to drop dead.

"I assumed the rumour about Laura being pregnant when she graduated was true. I didn't want the boys to find out they had a fifty-year-old, half-sibling." Her voice is becoming breathier. "And I didn't want you to leave me for Laura and the family you wish you had."

She grabs her stomach and lurches forward as though she's in pain.

I read about Digoxin poisoning after I found out it was how Laura died. Apparently, one of the early symptoms of toxicity can be stomach pain and nausea. I wonder if Laura had stomach pain and nausea before her heart stopped working?

The sirens grow louder as the ambulance gets closer until they're louder than Anne-Marie's breathless voice. Then they stop.

"Brian, it devastated me when I found out I was wrong. I'm so sorry! Why didn't you just tell me everything? From the beginning?" She draws her knees to her chest, with her feet resting on the bench, and hugs her knees. She must be freezing. And terrified.

"I used your Dad's digoxin. He was on so many meds, I knew no one would notice if it was missing. When we dropped his medication off at the pharmacy, I didn't hand the bottle of digoxin in with the rest of them because I didn't want to draw attention to the fact that we had access to it. So, I kept it. I'm glad I did because this was the only fair way for this to end."

She's rocking back and forth now.

"I went to her house while I was doing my Meals On Wheels route. I convinced her to have a coffee with me, even though she said she'd had her limit for the day. I put the pulverized pills in her flavoured coffee. I confronted her about the affair and the love child, and she denied it. She insisted I had it wrong. I showed her the letter I found from you to her, and she told me it wasn't what it looked like."

She stops talking to cry and catch her breath. Her voice is getting weaker, and the human barricade has moved forward a few steps without her noticing. Or maybe she noticed and assumed it was so they could hear her better. Or maybe she noticed and doesn't care anymore.

"She tried to tell me the truth. I didn't believe her, and it was too late, anyway. I could see the poison taking effect. Her heart rate was so fast and her breathing erratic. I cleaned the mug I used and left it by the sink, then I moved her knee scooter and the phone so she couldn't reach them."

I'm watching Anne-Marie while also keeping my eye on a dark figure climbing up the back of the bleachers. I don't mention it to my fellow onlookers, so I don't draw attention to the climber and ruin their cover. Two paramedics with a gurney have joined us on the shovelled path. We all move aside and huddle even closer together, so they can position themselves as close to the bleachers as possible.

"When I left, she was still alive, barely. I knew she wouldn't be for much longer."

Anne-Marie is sobbing and covering her face with her

hands. Eric has scaled the bleachers and is a few rows above her. He climbs slowly and silently until he's one row behind her then grabs both her wrists, preventing her from taking whatever it was that she'd held up earlier. Police rush the bleachers with the paramedics and Craig Pearson right behind them.

CHAPTER 23

Our FaceTime visit with Hannah is longer than usual today because Adam and I have so much to tell her about the reunion-fundraiser.

On one hand, it was a huge success and people will talk about it for years, but on the other hand, it was sad and scary.

According to a text from Eric, Anne-Marie will be OK. Unlike Laura, she received medical attention before it was too late. He says she's devastated by what she's done, is still in the hospital receiving treatment, and she's on suicide watch.

Eric left right behind the ambulance and followed it to the hospital. I'm OK with it, but I might give him a hard time anyway, because I know he feels bad for leaving me there.

Anne-Marie's confession and trip to the hospital killed the party vibe, and the event fizzled out after all the excitement. A handful of people stayed behind to find out if they won the items they'd bid on in the silent auction, but Amy told them to leave saying she'll notify the winners sometime later today.

Since Amy and Tundra were now working instead of attending the reunion-fundraiser, Craig, Mrs. Pearson, and I stayed behind to help with the clean-up.

Phillip and Glenda went to the hospital to be with Brian. I don't think they're home yet. His van wasn't in his driveway when Adam got here this morning, so I texted Phillip to ask if I could do anything to look after Kevin. He texted back, saying he came home during the night, picked up Kevin, and dropped him off with his apprentice, Noah.

Adam made a mushroom spinach frittata for breakfast and, I must say, our separation has been good for his cooking skills.

"Did you take my advice and ask Val on a date?" I ask him.

"After she walked away from us with that man, I didn't speak to her again. Whoever that man was, he monopolized her time."

He didn't say he wouldn't ask her out.

Our separation has also been good for our communication skills. I've learned that a big part of listening to Adam is listening to what he doesn't say as well as what he does say.

"If you do ask her out," I say, "and you cook for her, make these frittatas. She'd be impressed, they're amazing."

He smiles proudly.

My phone dings.

"Everything OK?" Adam asks with food in his mouth.

"Yes, all good," I say. "It's Eric. He's apologizing again for abandoning me. Like I can't find my way home in my own hometown."

I roll my eyes and have another forkful of frittata.

"He likes you, you know," Adam says, then swallows the mouthful of frittata he was chewing.

"We've become good friends," I reply.

"No, Meg, he *likes* you," he clarifies.

"How would you know?"

"I've known since September when he was investigating us for murder. He doesn't hide it very well, Meg." He takes a sip of orange juice. "Also, he told me."

"He *told* you?"

Adam nods. "On Wednesday, when you came to my office full of HYPOTHETICAL questions, he was already there. He asked me a few questions about Laura's will, the timeline of the changes and such. Then he asked me if you and I were trying to work things out. The babysitting shift I did when you hurt your foot, and how well we get along, confused him. He said he doesn't want to interfere if we're trying to work it out."

"He should have asked me, not you," I say, annoyed.

"That's what I said," Adam agrees. "He said he didn't want to put you in an awkward position because if he doesn't have a chance, he'd at least like to be your friend, and stay in the apartment above the store."

"What did you tell him?"

"The truth," he replies. "We're not a couple, but we'll always be family, and whoever dates us has to be OK with that."

"Good answer," I reply.

AFTER ADAM LEAVES, I sit on the living room sofa and call Sophie up to sit with me. I explain to her that Anne-Marie killed Laura, and I tell her the reasons Anne-Marie gave for doing it. I tell her I'm sorry she lost her person. I tell her I love her, I'm happy we'll be living and working together, and I'll do my best to make her as happy as Laura did.

She wags her tail and listens to me the entire time I talk. I have no idea how much she understands, or if dogs have unresolved issues, but I hope this gives her some closure, if closure is something dogs need.

CHAPTER 24

TUESDAY JANUARY 21ST

Yesterday, Harmony Lake shut down early for Laura's funeral. It was a beautiful service. The entire town attended, including some of the animals, past and present, from the AC. Laura would have been thrilled knowing the animals she loved so much and devoted her life to helping were there.

It's been decided that Brian will replace Laura as Executive Director of the Vanity Fur Centre for Animal Health & Wellness. But not yet, he'll take over in a few weeks. He has a lot to deal with right now. His newfound sister and old friend has died. He has another newfound sister he's trying to build a relationship with, and he's processing the truth about his dad and his father being two different men. On top of all that, he had to explain everything to his own sons and help them come to terms with it all. He's supporting Anne-Marie while she recovers physically, emotionally, and mentally, and arranging legal support for her.

In the meantime, Adam has offered to step in as acting executive director for a short time. This temporary position should put him and Val in the same orbit on a regular basis, so we'll see if anything comes from that. Sophie and I will stop by the AC to visit and look out for any sparks that might fly between them.

The custom hand-knit socks I donated to the fundraiser were auctioned off for two hundred and fifty dollars to Glenda! She loves wearing hand-knit socks, but unlike her mother and sister, she doesn't knit. She's coming by the store later today to choose yarn for her new socks and for me to measure her feet.

Glenda and Brian have decided to decline Mega Mart's offer to purchase the AC. As per Laura's wishes, they'll be donating the land that the AC sits on to the Vanity Fur Centre for Animal Health & Wellness. This also means the town council and residents won't be divided about a big box store moving into our cozy little haven of a town.

I asked Glenda if she and her husband would be OK financially without the proceeds from the land sale, and she said Laura left her the house, so they will be fine. She said their pensions cover their living expenses, and the proceeds from the sale of the house will pay for a few extras, allow them to help their daughter, spoil their grandchildren, and provide a legacy which was what they wanted from the proceeds of the land sale.

It worried me that Mr. Willows wouldn't take the news about the Mega Mart offer well, and it might have a negative effect on his health. However, it seems he's arranged to subdivide a piece of his land and sell it to Jay Singh. Jay and his wife want to move out of Harmony Hills and into Harmony Lake. To a home with enough land for their boys to grow and play. They'll be building their dream home on the property. Mrs. Willows told Connie this sale will improve their financial situation and, hopefully, ease Mr. Willows' stress-related health issues.

Last week one of the regional news outlets ran a story

about the land dispute between Mega Mart and the supporters of the AC.

The news story portrays the situation as another example of a big corporation trying to bully small town residents and threaten local businesses. The story features Dr. White passionately advocating on behalf of the AC and Harmony Lake. She implores Mega Mart's CEO, her uncle, to do the right thing, find another piece of land, and build his store somewhere that won't disrupt the good work of a non-profit organization.

Unbeknownst to anyone in town, Mega Mart's CEO saw the news story, flew across the country, and attended the reunion-fundraiser on Saturday night. He met his niece, Dr. White, and has since contacted the rest of his family. They've started to mend some fences, and he made a sizeable donation to AC.

He told some attendees at the reunion-fundraiser that someone in town (who he had the nerve to describe as "pushy") forwarded the news story to his corporate email, his assistant's email, sent him the link on Facebook and LinkedIn, and left a voicemail message on his direct line at the office informing him the story. No one knows who it was, (wink, wink, nudge, nudge) but I have it on good authority that finding his assistant's email and tracking down the direct line to his office was not easy.

It turns out he was the distinguished, older gentleman who approached Val while Adam and I were talking to her, had a long discussion with Tamara and April about their dog treats (yes, he ate one, April confirmed it), then monopolized Val for most of the evening.

Speaking of April and Tamara, their dog and cat treats were a huge hit! They sold for five hundred dollars at the auction, and the CEO of Mega Mart was so impressed when he saw them at the fundraiser, that he wants to sell the treats under Mega Mart's pet brand. Mega Mart is expanding their pet food line to include organic, chemical-free options, and he thinks their line of cat and dog treats will fit in perfectly with his vision.

April and Tamara are negotiating with Mega Mart. They will also sell them in Artsy Tartsy and online under the brand name of The Barkery: Gourmet Treats For Well-Heeled Pets.

Connie is off today. She was scheduled to work and offered to come in, but she and Archie are leaving tomorrow to head south for two weeks of fun in the sun. I know she has a lot of packing and planning to do before they leave, so I told her to take the day off.

I can't wait until she drops Harlow off this afternoon. For two whole weeks, he'll be back where he belongs, at Knitorious.

Glenda says she'll stay in town for the next few weeks while her sister's estate is settled. She says it'll give her a chance to get to know Brian and be there for him while he works through everything that's happened.

"We are family, after all, and family supports each other," she said to me.

She'll be staying at Laura's house while she's here, cleaning it out and getting it ready to sell. Brian said he'd like to help her, and she thinks it would be a great way for them to get to know one another.

I asked her to please not paint over the purple palace.

Since she'll be around, and Phillip already has Noah helping him at Wilde Flowers, Glenda will work at Knitorious part-time. The timing couldn't be better with Connie going away. Glenda will work here a few hours each day, except for a couple of days around her daughter's due date. Then she'll drive to Ottawa, visit with her family, and meet her new grandbaby. For a non-knitter, she's great at working here. Her mom and sister were both avid knitters, so I guess some of it rubbed off on her.

I need to find another part-time employee, though. I've added it to my to-do list for next month. I don't want Connie to feel like she can't go anywhere.

The bell above the door jingles and a huge arrangement of flowers with legs remarkably similar to Phillip's walks through the door.

The floral scent reaches my nose, and it's divine.

Phillip puts the vase of flowers on the counter and fusses with the arrangement. I guess in case a flower or two moved between next door and here.

"Phillip they're beautiful!" I exclaim. "You're an artist."

I lean closer to them and take a deep breath, inhaling as much of the bouquet of aromas as I can. The smell of fresh flowers in the middle of winter is such a treat.

"Thank you. I'm quite proud of it," he replies. "Do you want me to deliver them here every month? I can deliver them to the house if you prefer." He flicks his wrist. "It doesn't matter, we can decide month to month."

"You're delivering them here? I thought you were just bringing them by so I can ooh and awww over your immense talent."

My birthday isn't until next month. I'm not sure who would send me flowers.

"Wait, did you say monthly?" I ask.

"Yes, haven't you heard? Your upstairs tenant had the winning bid for the year of monthly floral arrangements I donated to the fundraiser."

"No. I hadn't heard. I don't think he's here."

Phillip must be confused. If Eric bid on the flowers, I'm sure he'll want them upstairs in his apartment where he can enjoy them.

"You can leave them, and I'll let him know they're here. Then you don't have to carry them back to your shop. I'm sure he'll want them in his apartment where he can enjoy them."

"Megan," he says, sounding exasperated.

He takes both my hands and takes a deep breath.

"He wants YOU to have them. He specifically instructed that I should deliver them to YOU each month," he explains, using the same voice one would use to explain something to a young child.

"Ohhh. I think I follow now."

He taps the countertop in victory. We have successful communication.

"Where is the best place to put them? You know, so, they get enough light?" I ask.

Phillip picks them up and moves them to the coffee table in the cozy seating area, then fusses with a few of the individual blooms again.

They're so pretty, I feel giddy looking at them.

"Do I need to do anything? Add water, put one of those flower pills in the water to keep them alive?"

Confession time: Plants die on my watch. I try to keep them alive, I honestly do, but I'm better at keeping people and pets alive. If you can scream for food and water, you have a better chance of survival with me as your caregiver.

He looks horrified and starts waving his hands in front of him and shaking his head.

"No. Do nothing. I'll do everything. I'm just next door, I'll pop over and make sure they're getting what they need."

"Thank you, Phillip." I put my index finger up, showing that he should wait here for a moment.

I go to the back room, reappear with a bag of Barkery dog treats, and hand him the bag.

"For Kevin," I tell him. "April and Tamara asked me to drop them off to you."

He opens the bag and pulls out a small, cookie shaped like a shoe.

"Tell them thank you," he says, then he waves his hand

like a verbal eraser. "Actually, never mind. I'll tell them myself. I'll text them as soon as I get back to the shop."

He walks to the door, and as he's turning the handle, he turns to me.

"Please don't do anything to the flowers, Megan. Seriously, I'll take care of it."

And he leaves, closing the door behind him.

I hope these flowers don't die, or Phillip might bring me fake ones next month.

I talk to Sophie about the flowers, ask her if she can smell them, and tell her how lucky we are to have such fun and interesting friends and neighbours.

The bell over the door jingles, and I peer around my large floral arrangement to see Eric placing one of two to-go cups from Latte Da on the counter.

"Thank you," I say, walking to the counter to get my coffee.

This is the first time we've seen each other since Saturday night, when he hopped in his car and chased Anne-Marie's ambulance to the hospital. He looks more relaxed, the muscles in his face are less tense, and his jaw is lax. He looks like he did before Laura died.

"Are things slowing down for you? Now that you've solved the case?" I sip my latte.

"I think you mean since *we* solved the case," he says. "It wouldn't have been solved as quickly or as easily without you. Thank you."

"I'm happy to help, and the flowers are thanks enough. They're beautiful." I gesture toward the floral arrangement on the coffee table.

"I'm glad you like them."

Is he blushing? I think he is.

"How is Anne-Marie? Is she still in the hospital?" I ask.

He nods. "For now. They've moved her to the psychiatric unit for evaluation. I've been able to speak with her though."

I sit on the sofa in front of my flowers and Eric joins me.

"And what has she said?" I ask.

"Not much more than what she said on Saturday night," he replies. "She's fragile right now, so we have to question her slowly and carefully. But I have been busy confirming her story."

"Oh?"

"Brian's dad was prescribed digoxin. I followed up with the late Mr. Sweeney's doctor, and he'd been taking the medication for the last few years of his life. And the pharmacy confirmed that when Mrs. Sweeney handed in his old meds, she didn't hand in any digoxin."

"So, everything she said was true. I guess she had no reason to lie, she thought she was going to die that night," I say.

"She'll be charged. When she gets approval from the doctors, she'll be moved to a detention centre, and her care will be transferred as well."

"I still can't believe we've had three murders in less than six months. We went from no murders ever to having three so close together." I shake my head.

"I wanted to see you sooner," he tells me. "But the last two days have been crazy with all the paperwork and reports that go along with a case like this."

I nod.

"Listen, I'm sorry I bailed on you on Saturday."

I think this is apology number eight, but the first one in person.

"I get it. Really, I do. Please stop apologizing."

He acts like he abandoned me in the middle of nowhere, not ten minutes from home and where I knew pretty much every person around me.

"Well…" He takes a deep breath. "Maybe I can make it up to you by taking you out for dinner?"

I want to reply, but I don't know how to reply in a way that sounds laid back and chill. Yelling YES at the top of my lungs while I jump up and down would come across more eager than I'd like, but that's the only response I can think of right now.

"I like you, and not just because you're good at solving murders," he says.

He smiles at me and I tell the butterflies in my stomach to settle down.

"I wanted to ask you out the day Laura died, when we were walking to her house," he explains. "But you said you weren't ready to date, then Laura died, and things got crazy."

I nod, still resisting the urge to scream, YES and jump up and down.

"Then I saw how close you and Adam still are, so I backed off in case you two were working things out. But then you went out with Craig, and I thought maybe when you said you weren't ready to date, you meant you weren't ready to date *me*. Now I'm rambling, and I'm tired of trying to figure this out, so I'll just put it out there. *I like you.* I want to spend time with you and see if maybe you could like me too."

"I'd like that," I say calmly without jumping up and down.

I smile and shrug, doing my best impression of casual and chill, while the butterflies in my stomach flutter out of control.

"Good," he says with a sigh, sounding relieved. "How about tonight? We could go somewhere in Harmony Hills, where we won't be gossiped about before we order an appetizer. You can tell me that story about the cat who became the town councillor."

Before we can finish our conversation, the bell above the door jingles.

I stand up to see over the flowers, and Mrs. Pearson is closing the door behind her.

"Hi, Mrs. Pearson. How are you?" I ask.

"I'm fine, thank you, which is more than I can say for my sock."

It's Tuesday, and she's here for Stitch-Fix, a weekly drop-in where knitters can bring their knitting mistakes, and we help fix them. I say we, but this week it's just me. She greets Eric and joins us in the cozy sitting area. She drops herself with a sigh into an overstuffed chair across from Eric and me and pulls a mostly finished sock from her bag.

"I was so involved in the movie I was watching last night that I finished the leg and started the foot of this sock without knitting the heel." She shakes her head, laughing.

"Beautiful flowers," she says as we reach around them to exchange the sock.

"Thank you," I say for both the compliment and the socks.

"I'm not sure what type of heel the pattern calls for, but how do you feel about an afterthought heel? Or we can rip out the foot and you can knit the heel in the pattern."

"Afterthought is fine," she says. "Oh, and Megan, thank you so much for introducing Craig to that lovely Amy Andrews. They hit it off so well at the fundraiser. It's too bad all that unpleasantness happened, and she and her dog had to work."

"I'm glad they like each other. They're both nice people," I say.

"They've been texting constantly since Saturday." She grins. "They're going on a date tonight."

I wonder who's happier about the date, Craig, Amy, or Mrs. Pearson?

"That's great," I say. "I hope it works out for them."

"Me too!" she says. "Let's cross our fingers and hope there's no unpleasantness tonight that might cut their date short."

The three of us cross our fingers.

CONTINUE READING for a sneak peek of Murder & Merino: A Knitorious murder mystery book 3.

DOWNLOAD the pattern Megan used to knit Glenda's socks here.

.

A Knitorious Murder Mystery Book 3

Murder &
Merino

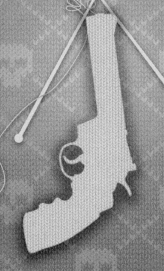

REAGAN DAVIS

COPYRIGHT

ISBN: 978-1-9990435-8-2 (ebook)

ISBN: 978-1-9990435-7-5 (print)

CHAPTER 1

Where can I put five hundred and twenty-eight eggs? That's the question. Eleven boxes with forty-eight eggs in each box. They were just delivered to my yarn store, Knitorious.

Every year, on the Saturday of Easter weekend, Harmony Lake hosts an Easter egg hunt. The Water Street Business Association—we locals call it the WSBA—contributes to the event by stuffing eggs with treats. This year, I volunteered to receive the eggs, divide them up among the businesses on Water Street, and deliver them to each store.

These aren't the plastic Easter eggs of our youth. These are new and improved eggs. They look and feel like the same pastel-coloured, plastic eggs, but these are eco eggs. They're sustainable, made from 100% recycled plastic, non-toxic, and BPA free.

For now, I've stacked the boxes on the long wooden harvest table near the back of the store, but I think I'll move them to the back room until I have time to divvy them up and deliver them. Because I'll forget otherwise, I make a note in my planner, reminding myself to deal with the Easter eggs over the next few days.

Putting the cap back on my fountain pen, the jingle of the bell over the door gets my and Sophie's attention. We look up and Eric is closing the door behind him. He's not alone. He has a large black Labrador retriever with him. The dog is wearing a bright red nylon collar. Instead of a leash, Eric is holding a rope tied to the dog's collar.

"Hey, Handsome!" I say.

Eric grins. "Hello." He blushes and rubs the back of his neck with his free hand.

"I was talking to Cardinal," I say with a wink.

Actually, I was talking to Eric. He's super attractive. Downright hot. I get a flutter in my belly every time I see him. Or smell him. Or hear his voice. Or think about him.

Eric is my tenant. He lives in the apartment above the store. He's a detective sergeant with the Harmony Lake Police Department, and we've been dating for about three months. It's casual. My eighteen-year-old daughter, Hannah, calls it a situationship. Apparently, that's what the young people call an undefined relationship situation.

"You know him!?" Eric exclaims. "I was hoping you would. You know every pet in town."

Sophie is thrilled there's another dog in the store. She runs up to him, wagging her Corgi butt excitedly, yelping, and sniffing the lab's paws.

"Yes, I know him. Cardinal belongs to Father Daniel, over on Mountain Road. Why is he with you? And where's his leash?" I ask.

Father Daniel Lambert is a retired priest. He's in his eighties and lives in his childhood home on Mountain Road.

"I found him running back and forth across Water Street," Eric explains. "He almost became road kill, more than once. I pulled over, opened the car door, and whistled. He came running over and jumped right into the car. I was on my way to the Animal Centre to drop him off, but I got a call about a missing person, so I have to go there instead. Would it be OK if I leave him here with you until a patrol car can pick him up and take him to the Animal Centre?"

"No need for a patrol car," I say, walking from the counter to where Eric and Cardinal are standing. "I'll take him home. April and I are going for lunch soon, and we can drop off Cardinal on our way."

"Are you sure?"

"Of course!" I reassure him. "Anyway, Father Daniel is older and is easily confused, a call from the AC might add to his confusion. Can I keep your rope-leash until I drop him off?"

"Absolutely! Thanks, Megan. You're a lifesaver."

"Hello, Eric. Hello, Cardinal," Marla says as she enters the store from the back room.

Marla Pearson started working here part-time a few months ago. She's lived in Harmony Lake all her life and is part of the town's human landscape. She's an avid knitter, and her son, Craig, and I even went out on a date once. She's a great addition to the Knitorious team, except I keep calling her Mrs. Pearson instead of Marla. Calling her Marla after calling her Mrs. Pearson for so many years is a tough transition.

"Hi, Mrs. Pearson—I mean, hi, Marla," Eric says.

I'm not the only one struggling with the transition. And Eric's only known her for six months.

"Did he escape again?" she asks, walking over to Cardinal and rubbing his head. "Houdini would've been a better name for him than Cardinal. I'll take him into the kitchen and get him some water and a treat."

She holds out her hand, and Eric hands over the rope-leash. She and Cardinal walk through the store and into the kitchenette with Sophie trotting happily behind them.

"How's your day so far?" Eric sidles up to me now that we're alone.

He smells good. Like a forest after it rains and the sun comes out. One more deep breath, Megan.

"Any day I don't find a dead body is a good day," I tell him.

"Wow, your standards for a good day are low," he teases.

"Only since I've met you," I joke back.

We met when I found a dead body. He was the investigating detective. After we solved that case, we found a body together, and solved that case too.

He takes my hand.

I tell the butterflies in my belly to settle down.

"I have to go take this missing person report. Are we still on for dinner tonight?"

"Sure, if you're not busy searching for someone. Who's missing?"

"I'm not sure yet. An adult female. I'll know more when I get there," he winks.

I swoon internally.

"It's my turn to cook," I say. "You cooked last time. Beef Stroganoff?"

"Perfect," he says, reaching for the doorknob. "I'll text you later."

And he's gone.

I take two of the Easter egg boxes into the back room, place them on a shelf, then go into the kitchenette and use my phone to snap a photo of the tag on Cardinal's collar. The tag has Father Daniel's phone number on it.

"Thanks for giving him water and treats, Marla."

"Anytime. He's a good boy. He just has a tendency to wander. Often."

Cardinal is a famous escape artist in Harmony Lake. Father Daniel has a fenced yard, but Cardinal is a tall dog and can scale the fence. He can also dig underneath it and get out that way.

According to Jill Plumb, Father Daniel has become forgetful, and sometimes when he puts Cardinal in the backyard, he gets distracted and forgets to watch him. Jill is one of Father Daniel's caregivers. She's also a local crafter. We carry some of her buttons and stitch markers at Knitorious.

I pick up the landline and dial Father Daniel's number.

"*Âllo?*"

(Hello?)

"Hi, Father Daniel. It's Megan Martel. How are you?"

"*Oui... Madame Martel! Ça va?*"

(Yes... Mrs. Martel. How are you?)

"*En Anglais, s'il vous plaît*, Father Daniel."

(English, please, Father Daniel.)

Father Daniel is bilingual. He grew up in a French-speaking home. Because of our proximity to the Quebec border, there are quite a few francophones in our area. I'm not one of them. Despite twenty years of French in-laws, I'm about as fluent as a French toddler.

"Apologies. How are you, Mrs. Martel?"

"I'm fine, thank you. I'm calling to let you know Cardinal is with me. I'm heading out in a few minutes, and I'll drop him off if that works for you."

"Cardinal! I forgot about Cardinal! I put him outside. Jill didn't show up this morning, and Cardinal can't wait all day, so I let him into the backyard. Thank you for finding him," he says with his thick French accent.

"No problem. I'll bring him home soon."

We hang up, and I check the time. April will be here any minute, and Sophie still needs her midday walk.

Marla assures me she'll be fine if I leave her in the store with Cardinal. I glance over at him, and he's asleep on the floor in front of one of the sofas in the cozy sitting area. His romp through town must have tired him out.

I slip on my rain boots and trench coat, then attach Sophie's leash. We cross Water Street and go to the park for a quick walk. Our timing is good, there's a break in the rain. The air is thick and damp, and I can feel my curly hair expanding as it absorbs the humidity while we walk. The ground is wet and muddy, with lots of puddles for Sophie to hop over; she doesn't like to get her paws wet if she can avoid it.

Water Street is to Harmony Lake what Main Street is to other small towns. It's called Water Street because it runs parallel with the waterfront. Most of the stores and businesses on Water Street are on the north side, and the south side has the park and waterfront. To the north, the town borders the Harmony Hills Mountain Range. The buffer provided by the mountains and the water make Harmony Lake feel farther away from the city and more secluded than it is.

Between the two resorts in the mountains and the rental accommodation around the lake, Harmony Lake is full of tourists in the winter and summer. We're between tourist seasons right now, but in about six weeks, Harmony Lake will be full of escapees from the city.

When Sophie and I get back to the store, April is waiting for us. She's sitting on one of the sofas, stroking Cardinal, who's loving the attention.

April and I met sixteen years ago at a mommy and baby playgroup, and we've been best friends since. Our daughters are the same age and are in Toronto together, attending their first year of university. Watching my daughter pack up and move to Toronto has been hard, but April and I are grateful that the girls have each other, and we have each other to help us through the transition.

We might be soul sisters, but physically, April and I are a study in opposites. She's tall and lithe, I'm short and curvy. Her hair is blonde and stick-straight, and I have chestnut brown, curly hair. She has large, blue eyes, and mine are deep-set and hazel. April has a year-round bronzed glow, while my skin is fair with peachy undertones. There's no risk of confusing one of us for the other.

"I see you have a visitor," April says, stroking Cardinal's shiny, black head.

"He's a lucky boy," I tell her. "Eric found him criss-crossing Water Street. He was almost hit by a car."

"Poor guy!" April says, scratching Cardinal's neck.

"Do you mind if we make a detour on our way to Stop Guac & Roll? To take Cardinal home?" I ask.

Stop Guac & Roll is a new Mexican restaurant in Harmony Lake. One of the perks of living in a tourist town is having a wide variety of restaurants to choose from. We don't have any chain restaurants or drive-thrus, but we have some of the best family-owned restaurants anywhere.

"Absolutely," April replies. "We have to take Cardinal home because he's a good boy."

Her voice is high-pitched and excited. I think she's talking more to Cardinal than she is to me.

WE GET IN THE CAR. Me in the front seat so I can drive and April in the back seat with Cardinal since she thinks he might get lonely.

On the way to Father Daniel's house, we discuss our order at Stop Guac & Roll. We studied the menu online to prepare for our lunch.

"You'll order the chiles rellenos, and I'll order the chimichangas, and we'll share," April reminds me

"And we'll order the nachos to start," I add.

"Of course, we're ordering nachos. We have to order nachos. And maybe a quesadilla," she replies.

I pull into Father Daniel's driveway, and a light drizzle blurs the view through my windshield. It's a messy, early spring day. Lawns and gardens are wet and muddy, and the ground is soft and squishy.

Cardinal recognizes he's home. He whimpers and bounces in the back seat.

I get out of the car and so does April. She's holding Cardinal's rope-leash with both hands. Cardinal jumps out of the car behind her and bounds onto the lawn, almost yanking April right off her feet. His paws are caked in mud, and April has planted herself firmly with both feet on the driveway and her butt sticking out. She looks like she's playing tug-of-war, not wrangling a Labrador retriever.

"I'll ask Father Daniel for a towel so we can wipe his paws," I say, climbing the steps to the front door of the large, Victorian-era, two-storey home.

"Good idea," she grunts, her voice strained from the effort of resisting Cardinal's attempts to wander farther than the length of his rope-leash will allow.

I ring the doorbell and wait. Then I knock. Then I remember Father Daniel telling me Jill isn't here. He's a slow-moving, elderly man in a large house. He's probably on his way to the door, but it's taking him a while.

Sure enough, the door eventually opens with Father Daniel and his walker on the other side.

"*Bonjour*, madame!" He smiles broadly.

"Anglaise, Father Daniel," I remind him.

I stand aside so he can see Cardinal behind me, pulling April.

"Do you have a towel, Father Daniel? Cardinal's paws are too muddy to come into the house."

"Ah, yes!" Father Daniel replies in his thick French accent. "Bring him to the side door. Jill and Vanessa have a paw wiping station set up there." He points to his right. "I'll meet you there."

I nod and turn to leave the porch. Father Daniel closes the door.

Vanessa Grandin is Father Daniel's other caregiver. She and Jill share the job. They help him with his personal hygiene, cook and clean for him, run errands, chauffeur him to and from services at St. Francis of Assisi Church, and organize his appointments. I don't know Vanessa very well. She's in her mid-to-late twenties and moved to Harmony Lake about two years ago when she married a local.

April, Cardinal, and I walk to the side of the house.

"No wonder you escaped, Cardinal, the gate is open," I say when we round the corner.

I approach the ajar gate and pause before pushing it open so April and Cardinal can get into the yard where the side door is located.

A knot forms in my stomach, and I'm overcome with nervous hesitation. The last time I felt this knot, I found a dead body. I convince myself it's just a flashback, and the odds of a dead body lying on the other side of this gate are slim to none, and slim just left town, as my dad used to say. My heart pounds in my chest, and I swallow the lump in my throat.

"Heavy shoulders, long arms," I mutter to myself, too low for April to hear.

Heavy shoulders, long arms is a mantra I learned in a yoga class years ago. It reminds me to release the tension in my neck and shoulders.

I nudge the gate, but something on the other side prevents it from opening. I squeeze into the narrow opening and peek behind the stubborn gate.

Jill Plumb is laying on her back with her head turned to the side. Her eyes and mouth are open; her empty gaze focused toward the overcast sky. Her face is drained of colour. She's so pale, she almost looks fake. Almost. Her head and shoulders are laying in what looks like a puddle of dirty water. Diluted blood.

"What is it?" April asks. "Is everything OK, Megawatt?"

April likes to come up with punny nicknames for me.

I shake my head. This is the opposite of OK. I squeeze back through the narrow opening, being careful not to change the position of the gate or Jill.

"No," I reply. "Jill Plumb is blocking the gate. She's dead."

CHAPTER 2

APRIL TAKES A STEP TOWARD ME. I raise my shaky hand, palm facing her, and shake my head.

"Don't look," I say, still shaking my head. "Trust me, April, you don't want to look. And we don't want to contaminate the scene any more than I already have."

Sadly, I speak from experience.

She nods, and the muscles around her eyes and mouth tighten. Her eyes fill with moisture, fear, and sadness.

I walk toward her and put my arm around her shoulder. I turn her around, and we walk back toward the car.

I take the rope-leash from her and unlock the car door. As soon as I open the back door, Cardinal and his muddy paws jump in. I close the door behind him, walk to the driver's side, open the door, put the key in the ignition, and lower the back windows enough for Cardinal to have fresh air. Then I close the door and press the button on the key chain to lock the car.

I turn my attention back to April. She's standing where I left her with her phone in her hand, her fingers shaking as she dials 9-1-1.

"I'll call 9-1-1," she mutters, raising the phone to her ear.

"OK," I say.

I understand the desperate need to do something. To do anything. To be useful in a helpless situation. It's an awful feeling, and I hope calling helps her feel like she's doing something to help.

I retrieve my phone from my trench coat pocket and send a text to Eric.

Me: Not having a good day anymore.

He texts back right away.

Eric: Are you saying what I think you're saying? Where are you?

Me: 793 Mountain Rd. Cardinal's house.

Eric: On my way.

I slide my phone back in my pocket. April is on the phone with the 9-1-1 dispatcher. Experience tells me they'll keep her on the phone until help arrives.

I take her free hand and lead her up the steps to Father Daniel's front door. I ring the bell and wait.

"What happened?" Father Daniel asks when he opens the door. "You didn't come to the side door. Where's Cardinal?" He cranes his neck to look behind me.

"Cardinal is in my car. Jill had an accident in the side yard. Can we come in?"

Once we're inside and Father Daniel is sitting down, I explain to him that April is on the phone with 9-1-1 because Jill is beside the house, and she's dead.

The retired priest says something in French and makes the sign of the cross with his right hand.

"I must see her," he declares, his accent heavy.

This might not be a good idea. I'm not sure if there's a right or wrong thing to do here, but I find it difficult to say no to old people. Saying no to a priest seems equally difficult, and Father Daniel is both. So, I nod and help him to the side door. I open it and help him step out just far enough to see Jill's upper body.

From this perspective, I can see that if he opened the door to let Cardinal out, but didn't go out himself, he wouldn't have seen Jill's body lying there. She could have been there this morning when Father Daniel put Cardinal outside. How long has she been there?

Father Daniel says what I assume are prayers in French. If I were Catholic, I'd probably understand what he's saying. He makes the sign of the cross again, and we go back inside.

I help him sit in his chair and ask him what he'd like to drink. He says he'd like a cup of tea, so I fill the kettle and plug it in.

April is standing on the porch, I presume waiting for the first responders so she can wave them down.

I hear sirens. Moments later, there are police inside and outside the house, and paramedics are tending to Father Daniel and checking his vital signs.

"Can we get a tent please?" Eric's voice booms from beside the house.

I put Father Daniel's cup of tea on the table beside him and feel a hand on my shoulder.

"How are you?" Eric asks, pulling me aside.

I shrug. "I'm fine. I'm not sure about April, though. This is her first body."

Such an odd thing to say. But it's true. I look around and find her in the dining room. She's sitting at the table, talking with a police officer.

"You can talk to her after you've both been questioned," Eric reminds me.

"I know." I nod. This isn't my first crime scene.

"Tell me everything starting from when I left the store." He retrieves his trusty notebook and pen from the breast pocket of his suit jacket. He flips the notebook open to an empty page and clicks the top of the pen with his thumb.

I tell him everything.

"What can you tell me about Jill Plumb?" he asks.

"I know she's one of Father Daniel's caregivers. She also makes buttons and stitch markers and sells them online. We carry some at Knitorious. She's married to Rob. They have two kids. Their daughter is a year older than my Hannah. She's away at school somewhere in the U.S. I can't remember which school—it'll come to me later—and their son is a few years older. Jill said he's travelling for a year. Last I heard, he was in Asia or Australia. Somewhere far away."

"Is that everything?" Eric asks. "I sense there's more, but you're hesitating."

Gently, I tug his sleeve. He moves closer to me and lowers his head so I can whisper. He's much taller than me, so speaking discreetly can be a challenge.

"Jill can be a bit of a gossip," I say, barely above a whisper. "Not in a malicious way, but if she hears a rumour, she'll pass it along, like most people in Harmony Lake. She was really close with Father Daniel, they're like family. She's one of those people who really had her life together, you know? She and Rob have an amazing marriage. Her kids are happy, she has a successful small business, and she's respected in the community. This is so tragic."

"I understand. Thank you," Eric says, rubbing my upper arms. "Are you sure you're OK?"

"I'm fine," I assure him. "But I'd feel better if I could see April."

I look past him into the dining room, and she's sitting alone now. The officer she was talking with has left.

"Give me a minute," Eric says.

He walks over to April and sits in the chair beside her. After a brief conversation, he gestures for me to come over, and he leaves the dining room.

April and I have a long, tight hug.

"I guess we'll go to Stop, Guac & Roll another day," she says when we pull away from each other.

"I guess so." I agree.

She pulls her phone out of her pocket and calls Tamara.

Tamara is April's wife. Besides Rachel, their daughter who's at university with Hannah, they have a sixteen-year-old son, Zach, who plays hockey and, according to his mothers, eats enough for three people.

April and Tamara own Artsy Tartsy, the bakery on Water Street. Tamara is a gifted pastry chef, and her creations are some of the best baked treats I've ever eaten.

I pull out my phone and text Marla to let her know I won't get back to the store for a while. She insists she's fine and even offers to walk and feed Sophie if I'm not back before closing time.

Speaking of dogs, Cardinal's been in my car for forty-five minutes. He must be anxious, watching all the activity and people coming and going from his house.

Using a mixture of hand gestures and silent speaking, I ask April if she'll be OK while I tend to Cardinal. She nods and waves me away. Then she calls me back.

She moves the phone away from her ear. "T says if we're still here after closing, she can drive Sophie home and feed her."

"Tell her thank you. But hopefully, we'll be out of here by then," I say.

I'm so lucky to have such amazing friends. We're a quirky bunch, but when push comes to shove, we have each other's backs.

She resumes her phone conversation, and I go into the sitting room to check on Father Daniel and figure out what to do with Cardinal.

"Jill, she did not show up for work. I had to put Cardinal outside. He cannot wait all day," Father Daniel explains to

Eric. "I saw nothing when I opened the door. I heard nothing. All day, I heard nothing from the yard."

I swear Father Daniel's accent gets stronger the more I hear him speak.

Eric sees me and excuses himself from Father Daniel to talk to me.

"Cardinal has been in my car for almost an hour," I tell him. "Can I bring him inside?"

"I guess so," Eric replies. "The inside of the house isn't a crime scene."

I look past Eric. "Father Daniel, where can I find a towel to wipe Cardinal's paws?"

"*La porte la-bàs*," he replies.

(The side door.)

Eric follows me to the side door.

"He keeps doing that," Eric observes. "Randomly breaking into French while he answers my questions."

"He's francophone," I explain, "and he has dementia. I think he forgets to speak English. Can you get a bilingual officer to question him?"

"Believe it or not, no one on duty right now speaks French."

"Adam is bilingual," I remind him, "and he's up the street. I'm sure he'd help you out."

Adam is my soon-to-be-ex-husband. He's a lawyer. His office is on the same road as Father Daniel's house.

I grab a towel and go out to my car to wipe Cardinal's paws. A uniformed officer joins me. Cardinal is a strong dog, not to mention a determined one. The officer explains they don't want to risk him getting away from me and contaminating the crime scene.

I open the door, and the officer takes the rope-leash. After a brief moment of silence for my muddy upholstery, I close the door and suggest to the officer that we take Cardinal for a quick walk so he can do his business.

The three of us cross the street and wait while Cardinal relieves himself on the neighbourhood trees. We cross back, I wipe his paws, and the officer takes him into the house to see Father Daniel.

I check the time on my phone and notice my battery is low. I head to the car to retrieve the portable charger from my tote bag.

Charger in hand, I duck out of the car, close the door, and lock it.

"What's going on? Is Father Daniel OK?" a woman's panicked voice asks behind me.

I spin around. "Hi, Vanessa."

She must have the afternoon shift with Father Daniel today.

"Father Daniel is fine," I assure her.

"Then why are all these cops here?"

"Jill isn't fine," I explain. "She had an accident or something. You should come inside."

"What does that mean? She had an accident? Is she OK?" Vanessa asks as we climb the steps to the porch, and I open the front door.

"Vanessa! I'm so glad you are OK. Come here so I can see you!" Father Daniel insists, waving his hands toward himself, beckoning Vanessa over to his chair.

Vanessa bends down, and Father Daniel hugs her. She looks him over, making sure he's not hurt, and he's does the same to her.

Vanessa is a beautiful young woman. Her wavy, shoulder-length, champagne-coloured hair looks like she just stepped out of a shampoo commercial. Her skin is smooth and wrinkle-free with that healthy glow of youth you don't appreciate until the day you notice it's not there anymore. She has large, brown eyes, and I envy her posture. She wears very little make-up, or if she does, she's skilled at applying it and I can't tell it's there.

"Hi, Vanessa, I'm Detective Sergeant Eric Sloane," Eric says, extending his hand for her to shake.

Vanessa stands upright. "Hi," she mutters.

She doesn't shake Eric's hand, so he pulls it back. She makes brief eye contact with him and smiles. Then she averts her eyes to the floor and comes back over to me. She stands at my side, slightly behind me, close enough that our shoulders are touching. Her anxiety is palpable. Some people don't like the police. And let's face it, this situation is overwhelming. There are police everywhere, paramedics are hovering around, and Vanessa doesn't know yet why they're here.

"Vanessa, I need to ask you a few questions. Maybe we can step into the dining room." Eric gestures for Vanessa to walk ahead of him toward the dining room.

Vanessa hooks her hand around my arm and looks at me. "Will you come with me?" she asks.

Her eyes are wide, and her breaths are fast and shallow. She's terrified, and something about her triggers my maternal instincts. I want to reassure and protect her. I put my hand over her hand on my arm, smile at her, then look at Eric.

"Can I?" I ask.

"To start," he says, "but I might need to speak to you alone at some point."

Vanessa nods, looking at her feet. We walk into the dining room and sit down.

April is still here. Still on her phone. When she sees us, she ends her call. "Hi, Vanessa," she says. "Would you like some water?"

Vanessa nods.

"I'll be right back," April says as she leaves the room.

Eric tells Vanessa that Jill is dead.

While Vanessa takes a moment to process the news, April brings a glass of water into the room and places it in front of her. Vanessa wraps her trembling hands tentatively around the glass and mumbles thank you in a shaky, weak voice. April excuses herself to check on Father Daniel.

Eric asks Vanessa to confirm her personal details like her name and birth date. She's twenty-seven. She seems so young. I recently turned forty, and twenty-seven feels a lifetime away when you look back at it from forty.

"I was home with my in-laws," Vanessa says in response to Eric asking her where she was last night and this morning. "Justin spent the night in the city at his brother's place. They went to a concert last night."

Though she's responding to Eric's question, she's looking at me when she speaks.

"I thought Mr. and Mrs. Grandin were in Florida?" I ask. "They're home?"

She nods. "They came home last night. We weren't expecting them until next week. My father-in-law said a storm is heading toward Florida, so they left early." She shrugs.

Mr. and Mrs. Grandin are Vanessa's in-laws. Vanessa and her husband, Justin, live with them. Mr. and Mrs. Grandin are snowbirds, they spend their winters in Florida and the rest of the year in Harmony Lake.

"The last time I spoke to Jill was yesterday when I came to work. We spent about thirty minutes discussing Father Daniel's care. She left, and I haven't seen or spoken to her since," she replies to Eric, while looking at me.

I nod.

"What did Rob say when he found out? Have you talked to Rob?" Vanessa asks, looking at me.

I look at Eric for a response.

"Officers are with him now," Eric replies. "Were you and Jill close, Vanessa? If she were having marital problems, would she confide in you?"

Vanessa looks at her hands, still wrapped around the glass

of water on the table. "They've been struggling lately," she mutters.

"Struggling how?" I ask.

She looks at me. "I think it's been hard for them to adjust to living alone. You know, now that both their kids are gone."

I nod.

"Vanessa," Eric says, "do you know why Jill would have ten thousand dollars in cash in her purse?"

How much? Did I hear him correctly?

CHAPTER 3

WHY WOULD JILL need that much in cash? Ten thousand dollars is a lot of money to carry around. Does this mean Jill's death was a tragic accident and not murder? A murderer would take the money, right? Maybe Jill slipped in the mud and hit her head. Or maybe the heavy gate hit her and she fell over.

"May I be excused?" Vanessa asks, looking at me, her eyes glassy with tears and sadness. "I need to use the washroom."

I look at Eric.

"Of course," he replies.

With her gaze fixed on the floor, Vanessa pushes her chair away from the dining room table, gets up, wraps her arms tightly around herself in a self-soothing manner, and leaves the room.

"Ten grand?" I ask Eric, barely above a whisper.

He nods.

"That means it wasn't a robbery, right? Her death is accidental?"

He shakes his head. "I don't think this was an accident. I'm waiting for the coroner's opinion, but it looks like someone stabbed her in the neck."

"Oh," I reply, feeling a wave of nausea wash through my belly and up into my throat. "How will you manage a murder investigation and a missing person at the same time? Will other officers be assigned to help you?"

Eric shakes his head. "There is no missing person case," he replies. "I've reclassified it as a murder case."

Jill Plumb was the missing person? Vanessa saw her yesterday. When did she go missing? Did her husband, Rob, report her missing? Where did she go when she left Father Daniel's house yesterday? Had she been in his side yard the entire time?

"I doubt I'll make it to dinner tonight," Eric says. "Raincheck?"

"Of course." I smile.

A uniformed officer comes in to speak to Eric, so I leave to check on Father Daniel and April in the living room.

Father Daniel is sitting in his chair. The paramedics have left, and April is standing by the fireplace, looking at the photos on the mantle.

"So, Louise is your older sister, and Lisette is your younger sister?" April asks, pointing to a black-and-white photo of two little girls.

The girls look about five to seven years apart in age. Both girls have curly blonde hair, matching spring dresses, knee-high socks, and Mary Jane shoes. The photo was taken in the front yard. Both girls are squinting into the sun.

"Not quite," Father Daniel explains in broken English. "Louise and I are twins. Lisette is our younger sister. Technically, Louise is older but only by four minutes." He laughs. "Louise inherited the house from our parents. I came to live with her after I retired. When she died, I inherited the house. Lisette didn't agree when our parents left the house to Louise. But Louise devoted her life to caring for them, so it was fair. Lisette didn't think so and hasn't spoken to us since. She didn't even attend Louise's funeral." He shrugs, his eyes downcast and sad.

While Father Daniel explains his family history to April, a glint of metal catches my eye, and I notice a laptop computer on the piano bench, in the corner, tucked under the piano. Father Daniel uses a laptop? And the internet?

It didn't occur to me that his house would be equipped with an internet connection. Everything is so old here, the house itself, the furnishings, the wallpaper, and the rest of the decor. It's like stepping into the Leave It To Beaver house. The laptop is an anachronism, and it sticks out like a sore thumb.

"Is that your computer, Father Daniel?" I ask. "Do you use the internet?"

He flicks his wrist at me. "Pshaw! I've never used a computer in my life. It belongs to the girls. One of them brought it here. They use the computer. Tap, tap, tap. Always tap, tap, tap when one of them uses it." He mimics typing on a keyboard while he explains about the tap, tap, tap.

I nod.

Vanessa comes into the room, her eyes red and swollen. April walks over to her and asks if she can give Vanessa a hug. Vanessa nods, sobbing silently as April hugs her.

When Vanessa pulls away from April's embrace, she wipes her eyes and looks at us.

"I'm sorry," she says self-consciously. "Jill was my best friend in Harmony Lake. My only friend, if I'm honest. I'm shy and I don't make friends easily. Jill was so nice to me. I can't believe someone would do this to her."

April and I each rub one of Vanessa's shoulders.

"Can all ten thousand dollars go in the same evidence bag? Also, do we have to photograph each bill separately?" A police officer calls out.

April looks at me quizzically.

"Jill had ten thousand dollars in her purse," I explain.

"I gave her the money!" Father Daniel exclaims. "I gave it to her to get away from the bad guy. Oh...poor Jill!" He covers his face with his hands, and his frail shoulders heave up and down.

Vanessa attends to him at once. She wraps her arms protectively around his shoulders. They cry together while Cardinal lies at Father Daniel's feet.

"Bad guy?" I ask. "Jill needed ten thousand dollars to get away from someone? Do you know what was going on, Vanessa?"

With her arms still wrapped around Father Daniel's shoulders, Vanessa shakes her head without looking at me.

Was Jill being blackmailed? Or was she using the money to literally get away from someone? If the "bad guy" killed Jill, why didn't he take the ten thousand dollars with him?

The sound of a phone ringing distracts me. Vanessa releases Father Daniel from her embrace and rushes into the kitchen. In a weak voice, she says, "Hello?" when she answers the phone.

"Do you think we'll be able to leave soon?" April asks me quietly, checking the time on her phone.

I shrug and check the time on my phone too. "I hope so," I reply. "I'd like to get back to the store before it closes."

I send a quick text to Marla to make sure everything is OK at Knitorious. She assures me everything is fine. Connie is with her, and they have everything under control. They've even moved the rest of the Easter eggs to the back room.

"That was Father Patrick," Vanessa explains when she walks back into the room. "He heard about what happened. He and someone else from the church are on their way here to see you." She touches Father Daniel's shoulder. "They're setting up a schedule of church volunteers to help look after you now that Jill..."

Her voice trails off before she finishes her sentence.

Father Patrick is the priest who replaced Father Daniel when he retired. "They" would be the church community.

Harmony Lake is a small town, and news travels fast. I'm sure everyone in town has heard about Jill's death by now.

Vanessa and Father Daniel have a disagreement about a sandwich. She wants him to eat one, but he doesn't want to. She's worried he hasn't had enough to eat today, and he insists he's not hungry. As a compromise, Father Daniel agrees to have a nutrition drink so Vanessa won't worry. Before he can change his mind, Vanessa disappears into the kitchen and reappears with a vanilla-flavoured bottle of Ensure. She opens the bottle and hands it to him.

Out of the corner of my eye, I see Eric walk into the living room. April sees him too. She nudges me and whispers, "Let's ask if we can leave."

Eric, noticing us looking at him and whispering, comes over.

"Is it all right if we head out?" I ask.

He shrugs. "You've both given statements, so it should be fine for you to leave."

"Take Vanessa with you," Father Daniel says. "She's upset and needs a break. Someone else can fuss over me today." His accent is thick and not easy to understand.

Vanessa looks hesitant. She shakes her head and says, "It's OK. I'll be fine."

"No," Father Daniel insists, wagging his finger at her. "You've had a shock. You should go home for the rest of today. We'll see each other tomorrow."

I remind her that Father Patrick is on his way, and the church community is organizing volunteers to help look after Father Daniel.

"We won't leave him alone," Eric assures her. "We'll be here for a while yet, and we'll make sure he has everything he needs, and someone is here with him when we leave."

Vanessa nods and picks up her purse from the floor next to Father Daniel's chair.

CHAPTER 4

I DROP OFF APRIL FIRST. I offer to take her home, but she wants to go to Artsy Tartsy because Tamara is there. Speaking from experience, I warn her that people will come into the bakery and ask questions if they know she's there.

Most people don't intend to spread gossip, and their intentions aren't bad. It's human nature to want answers and try to make sense of something so tragic, especially when it happens in a small, cozy town like Harmony Lake. But being peppered with questions is overwhelming when you're in shock.

She assures me she intends to stay out of sight by hiding in the office and kitchen until closing time. I walk her to the door. We have a long, tight hug, and I ask her for the millionth time if she's OK. She assures me she is. We promise to check in with each other later.

"I can tell the three of you are very close," I say to Vanessa when we're alone in the car, on our way to the Grandin residence. "You, Father Daniel, and Jill, I mean."

"We are," she agrees. "Other than Justin and my in-laws, they're really the only people I know in Harmony Lake. We see each other every day."

Her voice cracks at the end of her last sentence, and she uses a shaky hand to wipe the tears welling up in her eyes. Seeing how upset she is, I'm glad she agreed to let me drive her home. The Grandins can pick up her car from Father Daniel's house later.

"Jill never said anything to you about the 'bad guy' Father Daniel mentioned? Or that she needed money to make someone go away?" I ask.

Vanessa doesn't answer me. I turn to look at her, and she's shaking her head. Tears are streaming down her face, and she's wringing her shaky hands on her lap.

"I'm so sorry you've lost your friend," I say.

I reach over to unlatch the glove box, pull a portable tissue holder out, hand it to her, and slam the glove box shut.

In an attempt to distract her, I ask, "So, were you and Jill using that laptop to teach Father Daniel how to use the internet?"

"As if!" Vanessa smiles weakly. "He has no interest in the computer, and I don't think he even knows what the internet is. Jill brought the laptop to his house. We were using it to keep track of his appointments, order his prescription refills online, and to log his symptoms. He also liked us to read him the news from the church website. It's useful."

We pull into the driveway of the Grandin's ranch-style bungalow, and I wave to Mr. and Mrs. Grandin, who are sitting on the covered porch like they're waiting for us. Vanessa must have let them know we were on our way.

When Vanessa opens the car door, Mrs. Grandin rushes from the wicker rocking chair on the porch to her side.

"Vanessa, sweetheart, are you OK?" Mrs. Grandin asks, wrapping her arms around her daughter-in-law's shoulders and steering her toward the house.

Vanessa turns her head toward me, "Thanks for the ride, Megan."

Mrs. Grandin turns to me and smiles, then returns her attention to guiding Vanessa toward the house.

Mr. Grandin reaches for the fancy walking stick leaning against the wall near his wicker rocking chair. He rises, steadies himself with the walking stick, and starts walking toward me. There's a break in the rain, but the driveway is wet and slippery. Mr. Grandin is a tad unsteady on his feet, and I'm worried he might slip on the slick asphalt.

"Hi, Mr. Grandin," I say. "Welcome home. I hear you left Florida earlier than you'd planned."

"Yes, they're calling for a storm later this week." He smiles. "A depression that could turn into a hurricane. We decided not to risk it, so we came home early. It's not even hurricane season yet. Climate change, I guess."

He's almost standing across from me now, and the tip of his walking stick is wet from dipping in and out of the puddles on the driveway. Mr. Grandin doesn't have a limp, but watching his slow amble, it's obvious he has some kind of mobility issue. Each step looks deliberate and planned.

"I don't think I've seen that one before," I say, pointing to his walking stick. "Is it new?"

The handle is a lion's head, ornately fashioned in metal. It looks like it might be antique. Mr. Grandin collects walking sticks. He's proud of his collection and likes to talk about it.

"You mean Leo?" he asks, chuckling and rubbing the top of the lion's head with his thumb. "No, I've had this one for at least two or three years now."

Mr. Grandin adjusts his weight, and Leo's metal head disappears inside the palm of his hand.

"Ghastly business at Father Daniel's house today, eh?" he asks.

"Yes," I agree. "A sad day for Harmony Lake."

Before he can ask me anything else about the murder scene, I turn the key in the ignition, shift the car into reverse, and say, "Well it was nice seeing you, Mr. Grandin. I have to get back to the store before it closes. Tell Vanessa to call me if she needs anything." I smile, wave, and back out of the driveway.

BY THE TIME I get back to Knitorious, it's almost closing time. Instead of pulling into the parking lot, I pull up on Water Street, right in front of the store.

The jingle of the bell above the door and the warm, familiar scent of the store feel like home, and my shoulders drop about an inch, letting go of tension I didn't realize they were holding onto.

"Hey, Soph!" Sophie greets me excitedly at the door, and I squat to pet her. She puts her front paws on my knees and sniffs my face.

"Hello, my dear!" Connie sings as she walks to the front of the store. "Are you all right? You've had quite a shock."

I stand up to greet her, and she envelops me in a tight, maternal embrace, complete with rubbing my back. When she pulls away, she holds my upper arms with her hands while she leans back and scans me from head to toe, checking for herself that I'm in one piece and undamaged.

Connie is my mother-friend and I am her daughter-friend. We met when I first moved to Harmony Lake almost eighteen years ago. I was a recently married, new mum living in a new town. My own mother passed away shortly before we moved here. I walked into Knitorious to replenish my yarn stash because I was knitting my way through my grief, during Hannah's naptimes and after tucking her in at night. Connie took me under her wing, and she's filled the mother-and-grandmother-shaped hole in our lives ever since.

Knitorious was her store. She built it from the ground up. I began working here part-time about five years ago. Last fall, when Connie decided it was time to "ease into retirement"—her words, not mine—she passed the store onto me. Now I run it, and she works here part-time. We've come full circle. Connie used to live in the apartment above the store, but she moved out last fall when she and her boyfriend, Archie, bought a condo together.

"I'm fine," I reassure her.

She tucks a section of her sleek grey bob behind her ear and gives me the side eye.

"Good," she says. "Now, where's April?"

I tell Connie that April is fine, too, and she's with Tamara. Connie mumbles something about checking for herself.

Still holding one of my arms, Connie guides me to the cozy sitting area, and we sit on one of the sofas.

As if they rehearsed it, Marla appears from the back room with a glass of water, a banana, and a container of yogurt.

"We assumed you missed lunch," Marla says, putting the water and banana on the coffee table in front of me and handing me the yogurt and a spoon.

"Yes, we did," I confirm.

Seeing the food makes me suddenly aware of the emptiness in my stomach. "Thank you." I peel the lid off the yogurt and shovel a heaping spoonful into my mouth.

"Poor Rob!" Connie says, shaking her head. "I suppose he'll have to tell the kids. I can't think of a worse phone call to make."

"Do you think he'll have to tell Jill's first husband too?" Marla asks, picking up her knitting and starting a row of her shawl without even glancing at it.

"I hadn't thought of that," Connie replies.

I hadn't thought of it either. They've been together so long, I forgot Rob is Jill's second husband. She moved to Harmony lake around the same time as me. She left an

426

unhappy marriage and moved here for a fresh start with her kids.

When she met Rob, they became a family almost instantly. He was Jill's husband and the kids' dad. They call him "Dad," and they have his last name. Jill never mentioned her first husband to me, and it never occurred to me he might still be involved in the kids' lives. Jill and Rob were the only parents I saw at school plays, sporting events, team fundraisers, and all the other events that require parental attendance.

"I forgot she was married before Rob," I say. "Is her first husband involved in the kids' lives?"

Connie and Marla look at each other and shrug, then they look at me.

"I'm not sure," Connie replies. "When she first moved here, she and the kids became involved in the church community at St. Francis of Assisi. That's how she and Father Daniel met and became close. He helped her settle in and start her fresh life in Harmony Lake. Back then, the rumour was that her first marriage wasn't just unhappy, it was dangerous. People said her first husband was abusive, and she fled to save her and the kids' lives."

Connie raises her eyebrows and nods.

If that's true, could Jill's first husband be the "bad guy" Father Daniel was talking about? Maybe Jill was hiding from him all these years, and he found her. Or maybe he was threatening her or the kids and she was trying to pay him to leave them alone?

"That's awful," I say, shaking my head. "I can't imagine being afraid of my spouse. Thank goodness she got herself and her children out of that situation." I pick up the banana and peel it.

"That's not the only rumour about Jill," Marla adds, rotating the large shawl on her lap so she can begin the next long row.

"Oh, that rumour has no substance, Marla," Connie waves her hand dismissively.

"What rumour has no substance?" I garble, chewing a mouthful of banana.

Connie and I look at Marla.

"Well, I haven't seen it for myself, so I can't tell you who it is or if it's true," Marla begins. "I'm not even sure who claims to have seen it. I heard it from a man I go to church with."

"Spit it out, Marla," Connie encourages.

Marla opens her eyes wide, stops knitting, and puts her needles on her lap. "Apparently, someone saw Jill on a late-night stroll with a much younger man. And they looked close, if you know what I mean." She waggles her eyebrows.

"If it was late at night, how can someone be sure it's a 'much younger man'?" I ask. "Or even that it was definitely Jill. The person who saw them would've had to be pretty close to them to know for sure."

"Exactly," Connie agrees.

Marla raises her hands in a stop motion. "I'm just telling you what I heard," she says as a disclaimer.

"Interesting," I say, putting my banana peel on the coffee table in front of me. "Vanessa mentioned that Jill and Rob were having problems. She thinks they were struggling to adjust to living on their own. You know, empty nest syndrome. But maybe there's more to it."

I find it hard to believe Jill would have an affair. She always seemed so devoted to Rob and their family. Also, Jill was steadfast to her religious beliefs and took pride in living her life as an example of pious devotion.

But do we ever truly know what someone's life is like behind closed doors? Living in a small town has taught me that what you see isn't always what you get. The residents of Harmony Lake are masters at hiding their secrets to avoid the local rumour mill. Did a secret cost Jill her life?

If Jill was having an affair, maybe the man she was seeing

is "the bad guy" Father Daniel mentioned. Could this other man have been blackmailing Jill? Maybe the ten thousand dollars was to pay him off so he wouldn't expose their affair, ruining her marriage and reputation.

Ding! The sound of Connie's phone brings me back to the here and now.

She picks up her phone from the coffee table in front of us and reaches for the reading glasses that hang around her neck. As she raises the glasses to her face, I'm in awe of her knack for making even the most mundane sign of aging–reading glasses–appear sophisticated and elegant. I hope I make reading glasses look refined and graceful when I'm almost seventy years old.

"April's fine!" Connie declares with relief as if we've been waiting confirmation of April's well-being. "Archie just left her and Tamara, and he says they're both well." Smiling, she dips her chin and looks from me to Marla over the top of her glasses.

"Why was Archie visiting April and T?" I ask.

T is Tamara's nickname.

"He was delivering a chicken pot pie," Connie replies, like she's reminding me of something I should know but forgot.

"Oh. That's nice of him." Marla says, "I wish my husband enjoyed cooking. I'd love to go home to a homemade chicken pot pie."

"You will be," Connie assures her. "He made one for you too. He says he'll be here in about ten minutes to drop it off."

Noticing the time, Marla moves her knitting to the sofa cushion next to her, jumps up, locks the door, and turns the sign from OPEN to CLOSED. Sophie steps down from her napping spot in front of the store window, jumps onto the sofa, and snuggles next to my hip.

"Archie is trying all the things he didn't have time to do before he retired," Connie explains. "Right now, he's embracing cooking. He was making a chicken pot pie for dinner tonight, and when I told him about Jill, he decided to make a second one for Rob and the kids. Then he decided to make a third one for Father Daniel since Jill usually makes his dinner for him. When I told him Megan and April were there and found Jill's body, he decided April and Tamara could also use a chicken pot pie for dinner, so he made pie number four. He thought you might like one, Marla, because you're probably tired from staying late to help me in the store until Megan got back, so he made a fifth pie. He's been going back and forth to the store and making pies all day."

I stare blankly at Connie, and she smiles at me.

"What about my chicken pot pie?" I ask.

"Oh, you don't need a pie, my dear," she replies, winking at me. "You're coming over for dinner. You'll share our pie, and we'll send you home with the leftovers."

I open my mouth to protest, but Connie interrupts me before I can speak. "Eric will have to work late, so you won't be having dinner with him, and you've had a stressful day. We're feeding you. You can feed Sophie before we leave the store and walk her when we get to the condominium complex." She taps my knee.

To be honest, I'm too tired to go home and cook anything for myself, and I'm grateful for the company after a stressful day. Also, I'm still hungry, and the thought of homemade chicken pot pie is making my mouth water. The yogurt and banana were a nice snack, but they don't compensate for missing lunch. I'm thankful to Connie and Archie for thinking of me and Sophie.

"Thank you," I say, putting my hand on top of her hand. I look at Sophie. "Are you hungry, Sophie? Do you want dinner?"

Sophie's ears perk up. She jumps off the sofa and wags her corgi tail, looking at me.

"Let's go," I say.

On our way to the kitchenette, we pass the wall of knitting

notions. I tidy a few mislaid stitch markers and button sets. Looking at her logo on the packaging, I realize most of them were made by Jill. The knot in my stomach swells and makes its presence known. I swallow hard and take a deep breath to try to push it down. I can't let this go. Jill deserves justice for what happened to her. "We need to figure this out, Soph," I mumble while moving a mislaid set of stitch markers back where they belong. Who killed you, Jill? And why?

CHAPTER 5

Friday, April 3rd

"It's showtime," I say to Sophie in the same sing-song voice Connie uses when she says it.

Without lifting her head, Sophie looks up at me from where she's laying on her dog bed and twitches her eyebrows.

I inhale deeply, mentally preparing myself for all the friends and neighbours, most of whom don't knit, who will make up excuses to visit the store today so they can ask me about Jill's death.

I unlock the door, turn the sign from CLOSED to OPEN, and return to the harvest table where I'm making a checklist of all the stores on Water Street who are taking part in the Easter egg hunt.

The bell over the door jingles, followed by the clicking sound of Sophie's nails tippy-tapping on the wood floor. I put the cap on my fountain pen, lay it on my planner, and stand up to see who's here.

Sophie is wagging her tail and bouncing excitedly around Eric's feet.

"Good morning," he says when he looks up and sees me walking toward him.

"Good morning." I smile.

He looks tired. Hot but tired. His jaw is doing that clench-ing-and-unclenching thing it does when he's working a murder case.

Eric places a to-go tray with two coffee cups on the counter, then crouches down to rub Sophie before she bursts from trying to get his attention.

"Thank you." I lift one of the coffee cups from the tray, crack the lid, and sniff it. Dark roast, double double. Not mine. I put it down and lift the other cup from the tray. I take a small sip. Coffee crisp. Yum!

Coffee crisp is white hot chocolate with a shot of espresso and extra whipped cream on top. It's my current regular order from Latte Da, our local coffee shop. Current, because every few weeks I fall in love with something else from their menu and change my regular order.

Eric pops up to a standing position and picks up his coffee.

I swallow that first sip and focus, feeling the warmth and caffeine touch my soul.

"I'm sorry about bailing on dinner last night." Eric is an apologizer. He doesn't apologize for a minor inconvenience once, he apologizes several times until I tell him to stop apologizing.

"No worries," I reassure him. "Figuring out what happened to Jill is more important. Did you have dinner last night?"

He shrugs. "If by dinner you mean an energy drink, bag of chips, and cruller from Glazed and Confused, then yes, I had dinner last night."

I shake my head. "No, that's not dinner. You won't solve any murders if you're malnourished. There's a piece of chicken pot pie in the refrigerator for you. Courtesy of Archie." I gesture toward the kitchenette with my head.

"Awesome, thank you," he says, rubbing his flat, muscular stomach. "I'll take it with me when I leave."

"How is the case?" I probe.

He takes a deep breath. Is he deciding how much he can tell me?

"She was definitely stabbed in the neck," he says with a sigh. "Hopefully, when the coroner does the autopsy today, they'll be able to provide more information on the manner of death."

"Manner of death? Didn't you just say she was stabbed in the neck?" I ask, confused.

Eric swallows a mouthful of coffee. "Manner of death and cause of death aren't the same thing," he explains. "Stabbing is the cause of death, the manner of death is how the cause of death is delivered. For example, stabbed with a knife or stabbed with a fountain pen, would be manners of death."

He looks behind me at my fountain pen on the harvest table and raises his eyebrows.

"Was Jill stabbed with a fountain pen?" I ask, shocked.

"I have no idea," he replies. "The coroner should be able to determine the details about the size and shape of the murder weapon when they examine the wound."

"I get it." I nod. "Once you know the size and shape of the weapon, you can narrow the search to items that match those specifications."

"Right." He winks.

I swoon internally, feeling the butterflies in my belly begin to flutter.

"How's Rob? Have you seen him?" I ask.

"I saw him yesterday evening. He's devastated. He tried to answer my questions, but he's in shock. When I was leaving, he said he would phone their kids. I left an officer with him."

Hearing Eric refer to "their kids" reminds me of my conversation with Connie and Marla yesterday.

"About their kids," I say. "Did Rob mention that he's not their biological dad? Rob is Jill's second husband. The kids are from her first marriage."

"I'm aware," he says. "The first husband might be their biological father, but Rob is definitely their dad."

I nod. He's right, and I'm impressed he's making the distinction.

"I don't know how much truth there is to what I'm about to tell you," I caution, "but according to the local rumour mill, Jill's first husband was abusive. She didn't just leave him, she escaped for her and her kids' safety."

Eric nods. "He lives three time zones away, but we're verifying his alibi."

So, he knows about the first husband but neither confirms nor denies whether he knows about the rumour. Answering a question without actually answering the question is Eric's superpower.

"Good," I say. "I'm visiting Rob later today. I'm taking him a tourtiere. Frozen, so he can eat it whenever. I'm sure he's swamped with casseroles and other pre-made food, but I feel like I need to do something."

A tourtiere is a traditional French-Canadian meat pie. I make them a few at a time and freeze them. I pulled one out of my freezer before I left for work this morning and stuck it in the freezer at the store until I visit Rob later today.

"Were you and Jill close?" Eric asks.

I shrug one shoulder. "She wasn't a confidante like April or Connie, but I considered her a friend," I tell him. "I've known her practically the entire time I've lived in Harmony Lake. We'd see each other at school functions and community events. She's been supplying stitch markers and buttons to Knitorious for about ten years, so we had a working relationship too. I think most of her friends were from her church."

Eric smiles.

I lead him to the wall of knitting notions and show him some of the stitch markers and buttons Jill made. She was a talented artist.

The bell above the door jingles, and someone, who I happen to know does not knit, walks into the store. So it begins. This isn't my first murder, and I'm getting good at dodging questions I don't want to answer. A skill I've learned from listening to Eric answer my questions without actually answering them.

Eric says goodbye to Sophie and me, retrieves his chicken pot pie from the fridge in the kitchenette, and leaves through the back door.

WHEN CONNIE ARRIVES for her shift at lunchtime, I'm ready for a break. I'm tired of dodging questions about Jill's death.

I close the door to the kitchenette and eat my sandwich in peace, enjoying the respite from inquisitive friends and neighbours. When I finish my sandwich, Sophie and I go for our midday walk in the park across the street.

It's a perfect spring day. The sun is shining, the breeze off the lake is light, and it's warm enough to not require a heavy coat, yet cool enough to be comfortable. The birds are singing, and buds have sprouted on tree branches with the promise that, in a few weeks, Harmony Lake will be leafy and in full bloom. On such a beautiful day, it's hard to believe there's a grisly murder scene and a devastated family only a few minutes away.

When we return to the store, I put away Sophie's leash and freshen her water. I ask Connie if she'll be all right alone while I visit Rob Plumb.

"Of course, my dear. You go ahead. Give him a hug from me."

"Thank you," I say, "I'll be back as soon as I can."

"Archie and I stopped by this morning to drop off the chicken pot pie," Connie adds. "The poor man is overcome with grief."

I grab two blank notecards from under the counter. I write the reheating instructions for the tourtiere on the first card and tape it to the top of the frozen pie. On the second card, I write a condolence note to Rob and the kids. I seal the envelope and write *The Plumb Family* on the front. I pick up the tourtiere and leave through the back door.

Steering the car onto the street where the Plumbs live, it dawns on me Rob might be overwhelmed with people showing up unannounced, offering him condolences and casseroles.

If he already has company, or doesn't answer the door, I'll leave the tourtiere on his doorstep, then send him a text letting him know it's there. I don't want to add to his burden, but I want him to know I'm thinking of him and invite him to reach out if he needs anything.

I pull into the Plumb's driveway and park next to Rob's truck. The absence of other vehicles makes me think he's between visitors at the moment.

I ring the doorbell and wait. After about thirty seconds, I debate whether I should ring the doorbell once more or put the tourtiere on the doorstep and leave. I extend my arm to ring the bell, when the door opens.

"Hi!"

It's a woman. She's short, about my height with shoulder length wavy, white hair. She has fair skin, blue eyes, and a warm smile. I think I detect a hint of a French accent when she says hi. I'd guess she's in her mid-to-late seventies. There's something vaguely familiar about her, yet I'm certain

I've never seen her before; she must not be local. I assume she's a relative. Jill or Rob's mother or aunt, maybe.

"Hi!" I say. "I'm Megan Martel."

I extend my hand, and she shakes it.

"Hi, Megan. I assume you're here to see Rob?"

She definitely has a French accent. I notice she didn't tell me her name or her relationship to the Plumbs.

"If he's accepting visitors," I say. "I understand if he's not. I don't want to impose. Maybe I could leave this with you, and you could…"

I'm about to hand the tourtiere to the unfamiliar woman when I'm interrupted.

"Megan? Is that you? Come in!" Rob bellows from inside the house.

The unfamiliar woman moves aside and smiles. I step into the foyer. Rob walks out of the living room and greets me at the door with his arms extended. I hand the tourtiere to the unfamiliar woman and hug Rob. During our embrace, I tell him how sorry I am for his loss and for the kids. When we pull apart, we're both crying. He smiles weakly and wipes his swollen, red eyes with his tear-drenched shirt sleeve.

"I didn't realize you have company," I say. "I wouldn't have knocked if I knew someone was here. There were no other cars, so I assumed you were alone."

"I parked on the road," the unfamiliar woman says. "This is cold, should it go in the freezer?"

"Yes, thank you," I say. Then I look at Rob. "It's a tourtiere. You can warm it up whenever. It'll keep in the freezer for months."

"Thank you," he says.

The unfamiliar woman walks into the kitchen, I assume to put the tourtiere in the freezer.

Rob guides me toward the living room and gestures for me to sit down. I sit on the end of the sofa, and he sits in the chair to my left.

"I heard you were there yesterday," he says.

I nod, fearful that he'll ask me what Jill looked like when I found her. I'm not sure what to say or how much to tell him if he asks.

"I'm sorry," he says, tearing up.

Sorry for what? I pick up the box of tissue on the end table and extend it toward him. He takes one and wipes his eyes.

"I'm sorry you found her and had to see her like that," he explains.

"You don't have to be sorry. It's not your fault," I reassure him.

The unfamiliar woman comes into the room and joins me on the sofa.

"I've put the kettle on," she says. "Coffee or tea?"

She looks at me.

"Tea, please," I reply.

Who are you? I want to ask.

She looks at Rob.

"Tea, please," he replies. "Thanks, Lisette."

Lisette? Father Daniel's estranged sister, Lisette?

CHAPTER 6

WHY IS LISETTE HERE? And why is she so comfortable in Jill and Rob's house?

I've been here at least half a dozen times over the years, and I've opened the freezer or answered the door. And I wouldn't know where to find the kettle.

"Lisette…" I draw out the last syllable of her name and pretend to search my memory bank. "Are you Father Daniel's sister, by chance?"

"Yes," she replies, smiling. "Daniel is my older brother."

"Father Daniel recently mentioned you," I tell her. "He said he hasn't seen or spoken to you for many years."

Lisette nods. "That's right. I fell out with my siblings when our parents died. I always felt the twins, Daniel and Louise, were my parents' favourites, and I was the accidental third child. When Louise inherited the house, it triggered my insecurity and, in my mind, confirmed that my parents always preferred the twins over me."

Her accent is much lighter than Father Daniel's, making her easier to understand.

"That must be an awful feeling," I sympathize.

"It was. Growing up, I felt like I didn't belong. Daniel and

440

Louise are older than me, and I didn't have much in common with them. And being twins, they shared a bond I didn't understand. I only knew I felt excluded. Looking back, I see now it wasn't intentional. As soon as I could, I moved away to pursue my education. Then I had a career, got married, and had a family. Daniel devoted his life to the church and helping his parishioners. Louise devoted her life to caring for our parents, at the expense of having a life of her own. I understand now why my parents left the house to her. And why she left it to Daniel."

"Why don't I tend to the kettle," Rob interjects. "You said tea, right, Megan?"

I nod. Rob looks at Lisette.

"I'll have tea too," she says. "Thank you, Rob."

He leaves the room, and Lisette and I are alone.

"Have you been in touch with your brother?" I ask.

She shakes her head. "Not yet. I want to reach out to him. Jill was helping with that. You see, Jill searched for me and contacted me a few months ago."

"Did Father Daniel ask her to find you?" I ask.

"No. He doesn't know she and I are friends. She contacted me because she was worried about him. She said he was in the early stages of dementia and suggested if I wanted to reconcile with him, I should do it soon, while he still remembers who I am."

"Jill was very kind-hearted. She took wonderful care of your brother," I tell her.

"Yes, she and Daniel were very close, and she always looked after him. Sadly, she was more like his family than I am."

"After she contacted you, did you and Jill speak regularly?" I ask.

"Yes, we became close friends. We talked and texted almost every day. At first, it was updates about Daniel, but soon we would talk about our own lives and realized we have a lot in common. We met in Harmony Hills a few times for coffee, and she would invite me here, to her house, for lunch. She was such a lovely person."

Lisette stops speaking and takes a moment to compose herself. I hand her the tissue box from the end table. Their friendship and regular lunches explain Lisette's familiarity with the house.

"Jill was encouraging me to contact my brother," Lisette continues. "She wanted to tell him she had reached out to me and ask him if he'd like to see me. I kept backing out because I was scared he wouldn't want to see me, or if he agreed, I worried that seeing me after all these years would upset him. I said some awful things after our parents died, and I didn't go to Louise's funeral. We've had no contact for over ten years."

"I've always found Father Daniel to be a patient, kind man," I tell her. "I mean, he's a priest and they encourage forgiveness, right?"

"I know," she says, "Jill told me the same thing."

Rob returns carrying a tray with a teapot, mugs, milk, sugar, and a plate of cookies. He puts the tray on the table in front of us, and we each prepare a mug of tea.

"Lately, Jill became more urgent about Daniel and me reconciling," Lisette tells us. "She said Daniel's dementia symptoms were worsening, and he wouldn't be able to live on his own much longer. She thought he needed an assisted living situation. She told me she doesn't think my brother has a power of attorney, and she was worried about who would make decisions for him when he could no longer make them himself. She was planning to tell him about me this week. I'm not sure if she did before she…"

Choking up before she can finish her sentence, Lisette pulls another tissue from the box.

I'm not a lawyer, but I was married to one for a long time, and he told me about powers of attorney. A power of attorney is a document that allows someone else to make decisions on your behalf if you become mentally or physically incapacitated. There are two types of powers of attorney where we live. Power of attorney for property gives permission for someone to make financial decisions on your behalf, like selling your home to pay for an assisted living facility or withdrawing money from your bank account to pay your bills. Power of attorney for personal care allows someone to make healthcare decisions on your behalf, like which treatment to pursue or even whether to continue life support.

We're sipping tea, and commenting on the yummy cookies the Plumb's next-door neighbour made, when a cell phone rings. While Rob and I debate whether we detect a hint of cinnamon or nutmeg in the cookies—I'm convinced it's nutmeg, he's convinced it's cinnamon—Lisette pulls her cell phone from her pocket and looks at the screen.

"Excuse me," she says, "I have to take this."

Lisette leaves the living room and walks toward the foyer where she steps onto the porch, closing the front door behind her.

Now that I have a few moments alone with Rob, I ask him how the kids took the news about Jill.

"Not well," he says, taking a deep breath. "Our son didn't believe me at first. He's in New Zealand 'finding himself'. Between connecting flights and time zones, he won't get home until Monday." He reaches for his tea on the coffee table. "Our daughter thought I was joking when I told her." Rob shakes his head. "I would never joke about something like that. She'll be home from school on Sunday." He takes a sip of tea and swallows it. "I think they're both in shock," he adds.

I don't want to upset him further, but I want to mention Jill's first husband and gauge Rob's reaction. He might know if Jill was having problems with her ex.

"I'm sure you've had to call a lot of people and tell them

about Jill," I say. "It must be a horrible thing to do. If there's anyone who needs to know, but you'd rather not call, I can help you. I know she was married before you met her, maybe her ex needs to know or her former in-laws?"

I look at Rob for a reaction. No hint of agitation or anger on his heavy, swollen, blotchy face.

"He doesn't need to know," Rob replies, shaking his head. "Jill didn't have any contact with him after she left. I don't even think he knows where we live. He hasn't had any contact with the kids either. In fact, he was more than happy for me to adopt them when he found out it meant he'd never have to make child support payments. It's best to leave him be. He and Jill had...an unhealthy relationship. I don't want the kids exposed to him."

I smile and nod.

The hesitation in his voice, when he described the marriage as unhealthy, makes me wonder if the rumour Connie and Marla told me about Jill's first marriage might be true.

"You're a great dad, Rob. I hope you know that."

He blushes and avoids eye contact with me for a moment.

"Really, you are," I tell him. "You attended every school event, sporting event, and field trip. You coached teams and organized fundraisers. You and Jill are two of the most involved parents I've ever known."

"Thank you," he replies. "I wish I was as good a husband as I was a father."

Why would he think he wasn't a good husband?

"I'm sure Jill thought you were a terrific husband," I assure him.

"Not recently." He sighs. "The last time I saw her, we argued. She was so angry, she stomped out of the house. I didn't go after her. I wish I had. You see, I try to give Jill space when she's upset. Her first husband was...controlling, so she's sensitive about personal space. I was always careful to not make her feel threatened or unsafe. If only I'd gone after her that night. Instead, I fell asleep on the sofa, waiting for her to come back. When I woke up at 6 a.m., she wasn't here. Our bed wasn't slept in. She didn't answer her cell phone. I knew something was wrong. That's when I reported her as missing."

"I'm sorry," I reply. "I know how hard it is to adjust to an empty house and the void left when the children, who had all our attention for eighteen years, go out on their own."

"It was more than that," he says, staring into the distance. "Something else was going on with her, but she wouldn't talk to me. She wouldn't let me help her."

"Why do you think that?" I ask.

"For the past few weeks, she was preoccupied. She was anxious and not sleeping well at night. When I'd ask her what was going on, she'd get irritated and snap at me. Sometimes, late at night, I'd wake up to the sound of her whispering in her office. I'd go in there to check that she was OK, and she'd hang up the phone, then accuse me of spying on her." He looks at me, shaking his head. "I wasn't spying. I was worried. Who was she on the phone with in the middle of the night?"

"I don't know," I respond.

Was Jill on the phone with the younger man she'd allegedly been seen walking with at night? I'm not about to ask Rob, though I want to.

"I know about the rumour, you know," he says as if he can read my mind.

I stare at him blankly and shrug. "Rumour?"

"I know there's a rumour that Jill was having an affair," he explains. "She wasn't. She'd never do that."

"I believe you," I assure him.

I believe he's convinced Jill would never do that.

"Is that what you argued about the last time you spoke? Were you asking her why she was anxious and preoccupied?"

"Yes," he admits, nodding, "among other things."

"You don't have to tell me if you don't want to," I say. "But if you want to get it off your chest, I'm here to listen."

Rob inhales and looks up at the ceiling. Then he exhales and looks at me.

"We were arguing because I wanted her to stop working for Father Daniel," he confesses. "I was worried about her safety. Lately, his dementia has progressed, and he can be unpredictable when he's confused. Sometimes, he acts out. A couple of weeks ago, Jill came home with a cut on her hand because he threw a sandwich at her. The sandwich was on a plate. She dodged the throw, but the plate broke when it hit the wall, and she cut her hand cleaning it up. A week before that, Father Daniel woke up confused after a nap. He didn't know where he was. He was scared, and he gripped her arm so tightly that she had bruises shaped like his fingertips. Those are just the incidents she told me about. There might be more she didn't disclose to me."

"I had no idea," I say. "This must be why she told Lisette that Father Daniel shouldn't live alone."

Rob nods. "On top of that, she had a run-in with Saxon Renaud at Father Daniel's house, and it left her shaken up."

"Saxon Renaud? Why do I know that name?" I ask.

"He owns most of the houses on Mountain Road," Rob reminds me.

"Right," I say, "and a lot of the rental cottages along the lake, I think."

"That's him," Rob confirms. "He wants to buy Father Daniel's house. He buys them, renovates them, and rents them out. There aren't many unrenovated houses left, and he's set his sights on Father Daniel's. He showed up one day when Jill was there. Jill said Saxon was trying to convince Father Daniel to sign a sale document. She said Father Daniel was confused, and if she hadn't been there to intervene, he probably would have signed it. She asked Saxon to leave. She says he gave her a hard time and wouldn't leave until she threatened to call the police."

"Wow," I say, shocked.

Imagine trying to take advantage of an elderly person with dementia and bullying his caregiver for your own financial gain!

Her encounter with Saxon Renaud must be the catalyst to Jill looking into Father Daniel's power of attorney situation. If he had designated a power of attorney, Jill could have contacted them, shutting down Saxon's attempt to take advantage of him. Either she couldn't find any documents, or Father Daniel confirmed he didn't have any powers of attorney set up, which made her desire to involve Lisette more urgent.

Rob and I both look toward the foyer when we hear the front door open and close.

"Sorry about that," Lisette says as she enters the living room and takes her seat on the sofa. "What did I miss?"

"Not much," I say. "Rob was just updating me on the kids."

"Yes," Rob agrees, "and commiserating about being empty nesters."

"Well," I say as I stand up, "I should get going. Connie's on her own at the store, and I'm sure she's ready for a break."

Rob and Lisette walk me to the door where I slip on my shoes and pull on my jacket.

"It was nice meeting you, Lisette."

"It was nice meeting you, too, Megan."

Rob extends his arms and we hug.

"If you need anything, or if you need to talk, you can call me anytime," I tell him.

"Thank you, Megan. And thank you for the tourtiere."

I open the door and step onto the porch.

"Megan!" Rob says, following me onto the porch.

I turn to him as I pull my keys from my pocket.

"There is one thing you might be able to help me with. I don't know anything about Jill's business. I know she had some orders to fill, and her website is still active. Would you be able to stop by and help me sort out her final orders and shut down the website?"

"Sure," I reply. "Is Sunday afternoon convenient for you?"

"Perfect. I'll see you then." Rob goes back in the house and closes the door behind him.

On the drive to Knitorious, I mentally unpack the information I just took in it at Rob and Jill's house.

It sounds like Jill's first husband wasn't in touch with Jill and the kids, or if he was, Rob didn't know about it. Also, according to Eric, the ex-husband lives far away, so he seems an unlikely suspect.

I overlooked Father Daniel as a suspect in Jill's death because he's frail and weak, and because I believe he is a kind and gentle person. But if his progressing symptoms make him capable of hurting Jill, maybe he's also capable of killing her.

What's the deal with Saxon Renaud? What kind of person intimidates an elderly, senile priest and his caregiver? Could he want the house enough to kill someone to get it? Jill herself said if she weren't there to stop him, Father Daniel probably would have signed the sale document. By murdering Jill, Saxon Renaud would eliminate the obstacle standing between him and Father Daniel's signature.

Who was Jill talking to in the middle of the night in her office? Is there any truth to the rumour that she was having an affair? I'd love to see the call history on her phone. She could have gone to see him when she stomped out of the house the night before she died.

According to Lisette, she and Jill were close friends. Seeing how familiar and comfortable she is in their house, and with Rob, makes my intuition tingle. It's only been about twenty-four hours since we found Jill's body, and she's already there. Was Lisette one of the first people Rob called? I guess he had to tell her because she'll need to make alternate care arrangements for her brother, but I feel like something else is going on. I don't think they're having an affair. I didn't get that vibe. That palpable energy that hangs in the air when two people are attracted to each other isn't there. Also, there's a significant age difference between them, and her attention toward him felt more maternal than romantic.

Lisette admits she's hesitant to reconcile with her brother, despite Jill's determination to make it happen. Could Lisette want to avoid reconciling with Father Daniel enough that she'd murder Jill to prevent it?

As much as I hate to admit it, Rob doesn't have a strong alibi for the night Jill disappeared. He fell asleep on the sofa. Alone. No one can verify he was there. He admits they weren't getting along, and the last time they saw each other, they argued. Statistically, when a woman is murdered, her partner is the most likely suspect. He appears distraught, but is he?

CHAPTER 7

I ENTER the store through the back door. Connie is helping a customer in the worsted weight section, and there's a young man sitting on one of the sofas in the cozy sitting area, rubbing Sophie. I stash my tote bag under the counter, and the young man turns to look at me.

"Hi, Tyler," I greet him. "I didn't recognize you. I haven't seen you around town for a long time."

Tyler Grandin is Mr. and Mrs. Grandin's younger son. The son who is not married to Vanessa. I glance toward Connie and see the customer she's helping is Mrs. Grandin, Tyler's mother.

"Hi, Mrs. Martel," Tyler replies. "I don't get to town much since I moved to the city. I'm not working today, so I came to Harmony Lake to visit my parents now that they're back."

"And I talked him into driving me around while I run a few errands," Mrs. Grandin adds as she walks to the counter with several skeins of yarn.

"Hi, Mrs. Grandin," I say. "How is Vanessa doing?"

I've been thinking about Vanessa since I dropped her off at home yesterday. I wish I'd thought to exchange phone numbers with her.

"She's doing all right," Mrs. Grandin replies. "Thank goodness we came home early and were there when you brought her home. Justin spent the night in the city with his brother, then worked all day yesterday. If we weren't there, she would've been alone all day."

"It was fortunate timing," I agree, nodding.

"How was the concert?" I ask Tyler.

"It was good," Tyler responds. "Normally we'd go clubbing after, but it was a Wednesday night so we went back to my place and fell asleep watching Netflix."

"That merino yarn you chose is lovely, Mrs. Grandin," I say.

"Thank you! I made a sweater for Tyler while we were in Florida. I'm so pleased with how it turned out, I want to make another one for Justin," she explains.

Connie finishes ringing up Mrs. Grandin's yarn, we wish her and Tyler a good day, and they leave the store.

With a sigh, I drop myself onto the sofa beside Sophie, pick up the sock I've been working on and start knitting. This sock has an easy-to-remember stitch pattern, so I'm able to knit one stitch after another, without looking at the pattern, and let my mind relax.

Connie joins me with the spring sweater she's working on, and we knit together for a few minutes. The store is quiet except for the soothing click of our needles. I hear my phone ding inside my tote bag under the counter and convince myself to get up from the sofa to retrieve it.

There's a photo from April of pastel-coloured meringue cookies piled onto a plate. The caption reads, "Want some?"

Me: Yes, Please!

April: See you in a few minutes.

On my way to the kitchenette for plates, napkins, and drinks, I tell Connie cookies are imminent.

As promised, April arrives a few minutes later, carrying a white confectionery box with the Artsy Tartsy logo on the lid.

"My favourite Easter treats are T's meringue cookies!" I declare, taking the box from her and placing it on the coffee table.

"I think T's favourite part of Easter is making them," April replies, sitting on the sofa and greeting Sophie with a scratch between her ears.

April lifts the lid of the confectionery box and takes out a much smaller box, which she opens to reveal a bunny-shaped gourmet dog treat from their gourmet pet treat brand, The Barkery: Gourmet Treats For Well-Heeled Pets. "We didn't forget about you, Soph."

Sophie jumps from the sofa to the floor and tippy-taps her front paws excitedly until April puts the treat on the floor in front of her.

"She loves it," I say to April. "On behalf of Sophie, thank you."

We eat the soft, chewy meringues, and between mouth-fuls, I tell April and Connie about my visit with Rob and conversation with Lisette.

"It's nice that Jill was trying to reconcile Father Daniel with his sister," April comments.

Connie and I nod.

"Well, Mr. Saxon Renaud sounds like an unsavoury person," Connie surmises.

Connie is a good judge of character.

"I'd love to know who Jill was speaking to on the phone in her office late at night," I say.

"If we were placing bets, my money would be on Justin Grandin," April responds.

"Justin Grandin!?" Connie and I declare in unison.

"Why would she be talking to him?" I ask.

April shrugs. "T heard a rumour that Jill and Justin were having an affair."

"From who?" Connie asks. "Did she hear it from Marla?

Because Marla admits she heard the affair rumour second-hand."

April swallows the meringue she's chewing. "I don't think so." She takes a sip of water. "She said a man and a woman were speaking French in the bakery yesterday. She didn't recognize them, and her French isn't perfect, but she's sure one of them said they'd seen Jill and Justin walking together late at night near the church, looking cozy."

"I wish we knew who started this rumour!" I declare, frustrated. "I'd love to ask this person some questions about what they think they saw."

"I can't imagine Jill having an affair either, my dear," Connie says to me. "But you have to admit, the rumour mill in Harmony Lake has been right more than once."

"OK," I concede. "Even if there is some truth to the rumour, Justin was in the city the night Jill went missing. Tyler confirmed they were at a concert, then at his place all night. The next morning, he went from his brother's place to work. Mrs. Grandin said he was at work all day. It can't be him."

Or can it? Now that I think about it, Tyler told me they went back to his place after the concert and fell asleep watching TV. I suppose it would be possible for Justin to sneak out of his brother's place, drive to Harmony Lake, meet Jill, kill her, then drive back to the city and sneak back into his brother's house. It would be a one-hour drive each way, but it would be possible.

"I have a theory," April offers. "I think Jill was having an affair, Rob found out, they argued about it, and he killed her."

April always thinks it's the spouse.

"He doesn't really have an alibi, does he?" Connie points out.

"No, he doesn't," I agree.

CHAPTER 8

S<small>ATURDAY</small>, April 4th.

Connie and Marla are both working today. Harmony Lake is between tourist seasons, and I don't expect the store to be busy. They'll be fine on their own while I pop over to Father Daniel's house to see how he's doing and offer to walk Cardinal.

I park on Water Street in front of Knitorious and take Sophie across the street for our morning jaunt in the park. It's still early in the day, and the sun is shining but hasn't dried the dew from the grass yet. The breeze blowing off the lake is chilly, and I can see my breath.

After our walk, I drop off Sophie at the store, say good morning to Marla, and walk down the street to Artsy Tartsy.

The bakery isn't open yet, but peering through the window, I see Tamara arranging freshly baked goodies in the glass counter displays. I knock on the door. When she looks up, I smile and wave. She smiles and waves back, walks around from the back of the counter and unlocks the door for me.

"Good morning," she says as we have a quick hug.

"Good morning," I reply. "Thank you for putting some of

those meringues aside for me."

"Of course," she says. "You know we've always got your back. Excellent choice, by the way. Father Daniel loves them. He comes into the shop and buys some every spring."

"I'm glad I can take him something he likes. He's had a rough week. He deserves a treat."

"So do you," Tamara points out, walking behind the counter and retrieving a confectionery box.

"And April," I say.

"Don't worry about April," Tamara reassures me. "She's doing fine. I'm taking good care of her."

I smile. "I know you are. You two are lucky to have each other."

Tamara hands me a white confectionery box with a pastel green ribbon tied around it.

"Thank you," I say as she unlocks the door for me.

PULLING into Father Daniel's driveway, I park next to Vanessa's car, and rummage through the depths of my tote bag for my cell phone. I know it's in there. I heard it ding on the drive over. I finally locate the thing, pull it out of my bag, and unlock the screen.

Eric: Good Morning! I stopped by with coffee, but you aren't at the store. Everything OK?

Me: Yes, all good. I'm about to visit Father Daniel and offer to walk Cardinal. Sorry I missed the coffee.

Eric: Your loss is Marla's gain. Luckily, she likes Coffee Crisp. Dinner tonight? We could go to Pastabilities.

Me: Sure! But how about my place instead? I have some information to pass along to you and the fewer ears the better.

Eric: Sounds good! I'll bring dinner. See you after work.

I pick up the box of meringue cookies from the passenger

seat, throw my bag over my shoulder, and walk up to Father Daniel's front door.

"Hi, Vanessa," I greet her when she opens the door. "How are you?"

"Hi, Megan," she says, moving aside so I can step into the house. "Come on in."

I hand her the box. "Meringues," I tell her. "T says Father Daniel likes them."

"Thank you," she says, taking the box. She looks in Father Daniel's direction. "Look who's here, Father Daniel. And she brought you some treats."

"Bonjour, Madame!"

(Hello, ma'am!)

"It's gotten worse in the past couple of days," Vanessa whispers.

I nod, assuming she means Father Daniel's tendency to speak only in French has gotten worse. The shock of Jill's death, and the change to his routine, must be causing him stress and worsening his symptoms.

"Bonjour, Father Daniel. *Anglais, s'il vous plaît."* I reply.

(Hello, Father Daniel. English, please.)

"Apologies," he says. "Come and sit down."

He pats the arm of the old velour wing chair next to him.

I sit in the chair, and Vanessa disappears into the kitchen with the meringues.

The living room is arranged around Father Daniel's easy chair. His chair is in the centre of the room, directly across from the TV. It's one of those reclining chairs with buttons on the armrest. He can push a button to raise his feet, put them down, or to raise the seat of the chair so he can get in and out with minimal help. There is a wing chair on either side of him, each positioned at a slight angle toward him, allowing visitors to sit close enough for him to hear them.

"How are you doing, Father Daniel?" I ask, lowering myself into one of the wing chairs.

"I'm fine," he replies. "Did you hear what happened to Jill? Tsk, tsk...so sad." He shakes his head.

I nod. "I heard what happened to Jill. I'm sorry for your loss."

I guess he doesn't remember that I was here when we found her. That I was the person who found Jill and told him she was hurt.

He reaches over and puts his frail, shaky hand on top of mine and gently squeezes my hand. His skin is thin and wrinkly, like crepe paper. His touch is light and slightly cool. He's such a gentle soul, it's hard to imagine him hurling a plate at Jill or squeezing her arm tightly enough to leave bruises.

Vanessa returns with a few meringues on a plate. In one swift motion and with her one free hand, she grabs the collapsed TV tray resting against the side of Father Daniel's chair, flicks it open, and positions it in front of him. She puts the plate of cookies on top of the TV tray.

"What a nice treat for you, Father Daniel," Vanessa says. "I'll be right back with your tea."

Father Daniel turns up the TV as if to drown out her voice. He's watching The Price Is Right. Drew Carey is making small talk with contestants about to bid on a showcase of prizes. Engrossed by the program, Father Daniel is oblivious to Vanessa and me.

"I didn't know The Price Is Right airs on Saturdays," I say, following Vanessa into the kitchen.

"I don't think it does," she replies. "It's his favourite show. He also likes Wheel of Fortune and Judge Judy. We have hours of them on the PVR for whenever he wants to watch them."

By "we," I assume she means her and Jill.

"Cardinal didn't greet me at the door," I observe. "Is he in the backyard? I can take him for a walk while I'm here."

"Thank you," Vanessa replies, pouring steamy water from

the kettle into a Brown Betty teapot. "But there's no need, Justin is walking him as we speak."

"That's nice of him," I say. "How are you doing, Vanessa? Are you OK? I know Jill's death was a shock and giving a statement to the police was stressful."

She stops pouring, puts the lid on the teapot, inhales deeply, and looks at me. "I'm all right. I'm keeping busy and that helps. I used to come here for a few hours each afternoon. Jill was his main caregiver. She was here in the morning for his morning routine, then again in the evening for dinner and his evening routine. But now I'm doing his morning and evening routines, and church volunteers are here in the afternoon to give me a break."

"Is there anything I can do to help while I'm here?" I ask.

She shakes her head. "I don't think so. Starting tomorrow, church volunteers will take turns walking Cardinal, and I'll start training a few of them on Father Daniel's routines, so we can try to keep his schedule as normal as possible. Even small disruptions stress him out and make his symptoms worse. Thank you, though."

"Can I ask you something, Vanessa?"

"Sure," she replies, placing mugs, milk, sugar, and teaspoons on a tray.

"Has Father Daniel ever been hostile toward you? Or harmed you physically? Like when he's confused, maybe?"

She shakes her head. "Not me, but I was here once when he threw a plate at Jill."

"Rob mentioned it," I tell her. "Are you ever worried when you're here alone with him that he could hurt you?"

Before she can answer, the front door opens and closes, and the distinct sounds of Labrador retriever ears flapping and dog tags jangling get louder as Cardinal galumphs down the hall and into the kitchen.

"Hi, Cardinal," I say, rubbing his head with both hands.

His tongue is hanging out, and he's panting. When I stop

rubbing him, he heads straight to the water bowl on the floor in the corner and starts slurping water.

"Someone had a good walk," I say. "He looks happy and tired."

"Are you talking about me or Cardinal?" Justin joins us in the kitchen.

"Both of you," Vanessa teases.

Justin is tall and thin. Taller than both his parents by at least six inches. He has dark curly hair and green eyes. He and Vanessa are a stunning couple. They're so young.

I barely remember being that young. When I was twenty-seven, I had a seven-year-old daughter, a workaholic husband, and I was a full-time student. I had to leave university when Hannah was born. When she started school, I went back and finished the last three semesters of my economics degree. At the time, I had no appreciation for how much energy it took to get everything done. That's the paradox of youth; only in hindsight do you appreciate the privileges it provides.

"How are you, Mrs. Martel?" Justin asks, interrupting my self-indulgent introspection and bringing me back to the here and now.

"I'm good, Justin. How are you?" I ask. "And please, call me Megan. Mrs. Martel is my mother-in-law."

And with those last seven words, I realize I sound just like her.

We make small talk. He asks about Hannah. I ask how he enjoyed the concert the other night. He asks how I like being a business owner. I ask about his brother's apartment in the city. His story is the same as Tyler's. They went to the concert, and since Wednesdays suck for clubbing, they went back to Tyler's place and fell asleep watching Netflix. I ask him about his job. He's a technician with a local cable/internet/telephone provider.

"It's a good job. I get a lot of hours, and the overtime is

nice." Justin checks his watch. "Megan, are you hanging around here for a while?"

"I can stay a little while longer, but I have to make an appearance at the store, eventually. Connie and Marla will be ready for a break," I reply. "Why?"

"I need to take Vanessa's car to the shop and get a new tire," he explains. "She's been driving around on a doughnut for a week. But I don't like leaving her here alone after what happened. I'd feel more comfortable if someone else was here with her."

A doughnut is what we call the spare tire in the trunk of the car. The spare tire that's slightly smaller than the rest of the tires on the car.

"I can stay until about noon," I offer.

"Father Patrick and someone else from the church will be here at noon," Vanessa says, "so that will be perfect."

"What happened to your tire?" I ask Vanessa.

"Last Saturday, I took the car to the shop to have the snow tires removed and the regular tires put on," she replies. "Would you believe the very next day I got a flat tire? I have no idea how to change a tire, so I called Justin, and he drove out to Harmony Hills to change it for me. Apparently, the tire isn't fixable, and we need a new one."

"And Vanessa is enrolling in the WOW course at the community centre," Justin adds, starting to walk toward the door.

"The WOW course?" I ask.

"Women on Wheels," he explains. "It's a course taught by a female mechanic. She shows women how to change a tire, check the oil, fill the washer fluid, stuff like that." He shrugs.

"I should take it." I'm not joking.

I have no idea how to do any of those things. I don't think Hannah does either. Maybe I should sign up both of us. And April. And her daughter, Rachel. And Connie. And Tamara too.

While I'm making a mental list of everyone I want to enroll in the WOW course, Vanessa pulls out her phone.

"What's your number?" she asks. "I'll text you the link."

I give her my number and mentally cross off another item on my to-do list: getting Vanessa's phone number. The phone inside my tote bag dings, confirming that I've received her text message.

"Goodbye, Father Daniel." Justin waves toward the elderly man.

Father Daniel's gaze is fixated on the TV. His brow furrows, and he turns his mouth into a deep frown. He looks agitated. He picks up the remote, aims it at the TV, and stabs one of the buttons with his index finger.

"*Homme horrible! Batteur de femmes!*" he mumbles, jabbing the button on the remote.

My French isn't great, but I'm pretty sure that translates to horrible man and woman beater—or possibly woman drummer.

"Uh-oh," Vanessa says as she walks toward him.

I place my hand on her arm. "I'll take care of it. I may as well be useful if I'm going to be here for a while. You say goodbye to your husband."

"Are you OK, Father Daniel?" I ask, gently taking the remote from his hand.

He grumbles something I can't understand. I look at the TV and a news anchor reading one of those thirty-second news updates that sometimes airs during commercials. The anchor is talking about a politician who was arrested last week and charged with assaulting his female partner.

For a moment, I was worried Father Daniel's sudden agitation was in response to Justin speaking to him, not to something he saw on TV. I fast forward through the rest of the news update and remaining commercials until The Price Is Right appears on the screen.

"There you go," I say.

461

I place the remote on Father Daniel's TV tray. He's once again absorbed by the game show, and the tension in his face disappears. I look at Justin and Vanessa and shrug.

Justin kisses Vanessa goodbye, waves at me, and leaves through the front door. Vanessa locks the door behind him.

"The doctor says irritability is part of the dementia," Vanessa explains. "Jill took him to his medical appointments, but she would explain everything to me."

I carry the tray of tea Vanessa prepared into the living room and give a cup to Father Daniel. I place the tea tray on top of the piano—out of Father Daniel's reach—in case he becomes distressed and reaches for something to hurtle across the room.

Glancing at the piano bench, I notice the laptop that was there the day Jill died is gone. I wonder if Eric took it as evidence? I make a mental note to ask him about it.

Vanessa changes the sheets on Father Daniel's bed, starts a load of laundry, refills his pill organizer for the next week, freshens Cardinal's water bowl, and jots down a few notes for the church volunteers while I drink tea with Father Daniel, eat meringues, and watch Judge Judy. Cardinal is snoozing contentedly on the floor next to Father Daniel's chair.

Judge Judy is hearing arguments from a former couple who are arguing over the custody of their award-winning dog. She's about to render her verdict when the doorbell rings.

Cardinal perks up. He moves from laying down to sitting up, his ears are at attention, and he's staring at the door. Sophie would run toward the door, barking. She'd bark relentlessly until I answered it. I'm not used to a dog who remains calm in the midst of door-knocking.

Vanessa opens the door and a thin, middle-aged man pokes the tip of his umbrella at her feet, forcing her to hop out of his way as he pushes past her and walks into the house.

He literally used his umbrella like a cattle prod. He didn't say excuse me or even look at Vanessa. If I hadn't seen it with my own eyes, I wouldn't believe it.

Umbrella man speaks enthusiastically in French, which distracts Father Daniel from Judge Judy.

I reach for the remote and pause the TV because I don't want to miss the verdict.

Umbrella man is wearing neatly pressed khakis with an ironed crease down the centre of each leg to the cuffed ankle, a white, collared shirt with a yellow v-neck sweater layered over the top, and brown penny loafers complete with pennies. In one of his hands he has a legal size, manila envelope, and in his other hand, he holds the umbrella he poked at Vanessa.

The umbrella is a sleek, black, stick umbrella with a fancy whangee handle and long metal tip.

I've never understood why an umbrella would have a long metal tip. The last thing I want to carry around with me in the rain is a lightning rod. But to each his own, I guess.

Father Daniel is delighted to see his guest. Smiling, he reaches for his walker, positions it in front of him, presses the button that helps him eject from his chair, and stands up to greet his guest.

Umbrella man walks over to Father Daniel and tells him, in French, not to get up on his account. They shake hands enthusiastically, and then I hear it. Father Daniel calls the man Monsieur Renaud. Mr. Renaud.

This must be Saxon Renaud. If what I've heard about him is true, the envelope he's gripping probably contains a sale document for Father Daniel's house.

I get up from the wing chair I'm sitting in, and Saxon Renaud sits in it immediately, leaning his umbrella against the side of the chair.

Father Daniel once again positions himself into his easy chair and presses the button to lower himself to a seated position.

Standing next to Vanessa, I ask her quietly if she recognizes the man as Saxon Renaud.

"I don't know," she whispers. "I've never met him. He's pushy, though. He didn't say hello or even look at me. He just poked that umbrella at me to get me to move. Then he walked right in."

"I saw that," I say.

Mr. Renaud hasn't acknowledged either Vanessa or me, so I take the initiative. I muster my friendliest smile, extend my right hand, and walk over to the men.

"Hi there," I say, smiling. "I'm Megan Martel. You must be Saxon Renaud."

He looks at my face, then at my extended hand, then back at my face.

"That's right," he replies. "It's nice to meet you, Ms. Martel. I'll have a cup of tea, please." He points to the teacup on Father Daniels TV tray. "And a couple of those meringues if there are any left." He turns back to Father Daniel and resumes his conversation.

Did he just place an order? I don't recall asking him if he'd like anything. He must think I work here. Even if I work here, his behaviour is downright rude.

I stride into the kitchen, and Vanessa follows me.

"He's very confident," she says.

"He's very arrogant," I correct her.

"I'll make him a cup of tea." She plugs in the kettle.

Saxon Renaud speaks both French and English without an accent. This bothers me, and I don't know why. Adam also speaks both languages without an accent, but it doesn't bother me when he does it. When Saxon Renaud does it, it sounds shifty.

"Am I the only one who thinks it's weird that he brought his umbrella from his car into the house? On a sunny day?" I ask, looking out the kitchen window at the shiny, four-door sedan parked behind me in the driveway. "I don't like him." I shake my head.

Vanessa is placing meringues on a plate. "I can tell." She looks at me. "I don't like him either. Would you mind taking him his tea and cookies? He makes me uncomfortable."

He did poke at her with a pointy umbrella. She seems distressed, though. She's biting her bottom lip, and there are small beads of perspiration on her forehead.

"Are you OK?" I ask her.

She nods quickly, her anxiety palpable. "He just makes me really uncomfortable." She looks at the floor.

"You can stay in here, out of sight. I'll tend to Father Daniel and Saxon," I tell her.

Vanessa hands me the tray loaded with tea, tea accessories, and meringues.

I summon a fake smile, plaster it to my face, and leave the kitchen.

"Here you go," I place the tray on the end table next to Saxon's wing chair.

Not even a thank you.

I stand off to the side, in the doorway between the kitchen and the living room, watching them. Well, watching one of them. My instincts tell me not to take my eyes off Saxon Renaud.

He hasn't touched the tea or meringues he asked for. And he hasn't put down that envelope. Not even for a second.

While watching Saxon and Father Daniel interact, my mind wanders. It's almost lunchtime and I'm hungry, so my mind fixates on food. Pastabilities has the best pizza. Their pasta is amazing, too, but I'm craving one of their pizzas. I'm about to pull out my phone and text Eric to ask him if he's craving pizza, too, and suggest we have that for dinner tonight, when I realize Saxon has removed the documents from his envelope and laid them on Father Daniel's TV tray. He's handing Father Daniel a pen.

CHAPTER 9

I INTERCEPT the pen just as Father Daniel is taking it from Saxon's hand.

"Excuse me!" Saxon declares.

"Father Daniel isn't signing anything today," I state, matter-of-factly.

I gather the papers from the TV tray and hold them out for Saxon to take. He doesn't take them.

"How is this any of your business?" he asks.

It's not, but I'm not about to admit that to him.

"Would you like to take these with you when you leave?" I ask, extending my arm so the papers are closer to him. "Or shall I hang on to them and forward them to Father Daniel's lawyer for review?"

"Your intervention in this matter is neither necessary nor appreciated," he says, snatching the papers from me.

He shoves the papers back inside the envelope, stands up, retrieves his umbrella from beside the chair, and pokes it toward my ankles, forcing me to do a hop-skip to avoid it.

"Did you poke Jill with your umbrella when she asked you to leave too?" I demand.

Father Daniel is calling for Vanessa, but she doesn't leave

the kitchen. He seems distressed. I feel for him. I'm distressed too.

I take a deep breath and conjure up another fake smile. Then, doing my best impression of a calm person, I say, "I'll show you out, Mr. Renaud."

"Why can't you women just mind your own business?"

Misogynist says what?

"*Us women*?" I ask through clenched teeth.

My breathing is shallow now. I can feel my face flushing with anger, and I'm clenching and releasing my fists at my sides. Despite this, I'm careful to maintain a calm, quiet voice to prevent Father Daniel from becoming further distressed.

"You and Jill. Neither one of you knows when to mind your own business," he says.

I walk toward the front door.

"Is that a threat? Did you kill Jill because she didn't mind her business?" I ask.

It feels like a threat. I know I should stop engaging with him and open the door so he can leave, but I'm not good at standing down.

"It's not a threat," he chuckles. "It's a friendly reminder that aggression isn't a very ladylike trait."

He has the nerve to stand there with his pointy umbrella and tell me I'm the one who's aggressive?

"If advocating for my vulnerable friend is an act of aggression, then so be it," I acquiesce.

I open the front door and dramatically sweep my hand toward it, gesturing for Mr. Renaud to walk through it.

"And I'm not a murderer, Ms. Martel. If you want to know who killed your friend, ask your other friend, the one hiding in the kitchen. Her car was here the night Jill died. And her husband had a habit of meeting Jill alone at night."

Saxon looks at Father Daniel and tells him in French that he'll come back later. Father Daniel doesn't reply but unpauses the TV and resumes watching Judge Judy.

"I'm not taking advantage of him," Saxon says to me with one foot in the house and one foot on the doorstep. "The price I'm offering him is more than fair. And I'm giving him time to make other arrangements. I'm doing him a favour. He shouldn't be living here alone."

I close the door, forcing the rest of Mr. Renaud to either leave the house or be hit with it. He leaves. I lock the door behind him. Good riddance.

I hate to agree with anything Saxon Renaud says, but he's right when he says Father Daniel shouldn't be living alone.

"Thanks for your help!" I say to Cardinal, who's still sitting by Father Daniel's chair as though nothing happened. He lays down and sighs loudly.

"Are you OK, Megan?" Vanessa emerges from the kitchen and goes straight to Father Daniel.

I nod. "Are you?"

She looks at me and nods. Father Daniel mumbles something to her.

"I'll be right back," she tells me. "He needs to use the washroom."

While Vanessa helps Father Daniel and his walker shuffle off to the washroom, I drop myself into one of the wing chairs and take a few deep breaths. I check the time on my phone, and I'm about to text Connie and check in at the store when Vanessa comes back into the living room alone.

"He's fine," she says. "Everything takes him longer than you expect. I'm just giving him some privacy. He'll holler when he needs me."

"Did you hear my conversation with Saxon?" I ask.

Vanessa nods. "My car couldn't have been here that night. I was at home, and so was my car. I'm never here at night. Jill always did his evening routine."

"Maybe he saw a car similar to yours," I suggest. "Or he's lying. Who knows?"

"I've never met him before. How does he even know what my car looks like?"

I shrug.

"Listen, Vanessa," I say quietly. "There's a rumour floating around town about Jill and Justin. About them taking late night walks alone together. I don't know who started it or when."

She shakes her head. "It's not true. To be honest, Jill didn't like Justin very much."

"Oh?" I ask. "Why not?"

"Well, it's mostly my fault. Jill was my only friend in Harmony Lake. And the only person I talked to whose last name isn't Grandin. So, whenever Justin and I would argue, or I was upset about something one of my in-laws did, I'd vent to her about it. I think over time, she thought Justin and I didn't get along and we argued all the time. She was protective of me. Also, she had a terrible relationship experience when she was younger and, because of that, I think she sometimes saw red flags where there weren't any."

I nod. "Was she right to be concerned? Are there any problems in your relationship with Justin?"

"No," she says. "Marriage has been an adjustment for both of us. Moving to a new town where I don't know anyone was a struggle for me, and it's not always easy to live with family, but Justin and I are solid."

Father Daniel calls for her, and Vanessa excuses herself to tend to him.

Vanessa drives a fairly common type of car. At night, it would be easy to mistake a similar car for hers. Also, Saxon could've made that up. If he's trying to divert suspicion from himself, it would make sense to implicate someone who had access to Jill every day.

I just can't accept that Jill and Justin would sneak around together. But I can believe that Jill didn't like Justin if she had to listen to Vanessa complain about him all the time. I'm sure what Vanessa said about Jill being protective of her is true. Jill was always fiercely maternal, and with her own kids away from home, maybe she transferred that maternal energy to Vanessa. Did she take it upon herself to meet with Justin alone and talk to him about his relationship with Vanessa? That's the only feasible scenario I can imagine them having a clandestine meeting. Other than Jill and Justin both being out alone and running into each other by happenstance.

The doorbell rings, and Vanessa is still helping Father Daniel. I take a deep breath, brace myself for the possibility that Saxon Renaud has returned for another confrontation, and answer the door.

Father Patrick and a volunteer from the church congregation come into the house. I can't believe it's already noon. I need to get to Knitorious. Connie and Marla need lunch breaks, and Sophie will be ready for a walk. I tidy the teacups, plates, and trays from the living room, then slip on my shoes. When Vanessa and Father Daniel return from the washroom, I say goodbye to both of them and leave.

On the short drive to the store, instead of thinking about who killed Jill and why, I'm wondering if anyone else I know watches Judge Judy. I'm curious to know how that episode ends. Who got custody of the dog?

CHAPTER 10

"I'M SO happy you like to answer the door, yes I am!" I say in the special, high-pitched voice I use to talk to Sophie.

I scratch her back for a few more seconds, then stand up, walk out of the kitchenette and into the store. I stow my tote bag under the counter and say hi to Connie.

"Has it been busy?" I ask. "I was at Father Daniel's house much longer than I'd expected. I'm sorry you and Marla had to hold down the fort."

Connie flicks her wrist. "Don't worry about it, my dear. We had a couple of busy spurts, but aside from that, it's been more like a Tuesday than a Saturday. We coped just fine." She smiles.

"Is Marla having lunch?" I ask.

Connie nods. "She left just before you got here."

"When she gets back, I'll take Sophie across the street for a quick walk," I say.

"There's no need. Marla took Sophie for a walk before she left for lunch."

"That was nice of her," I say.

That's twice today my attempt to walk a dog has been thwarted.

"How is Father Daniel doing?" Connie asks.

We have a seat in the cozy sitting area and pick up our knitting. I cast on for the second sock—I finished the first one last night—and Connie works on her sweater while I tell her about Father Daniel's progressing dementia symptoms, Justin's visit, Saxon Renaud's visit, and Vanessa's revelation about Jill not liking Justin.

"Imagine going around poking people to get them out of your way!" Connie declares. "If I ever encounter him, he might find himself poked by the business end of a knitting needle. Then we'll see how *he* likes it."

"He has a point about Father Daniel living alone," I agree reluctantly, hating to agree with anything that man says. "Spending time with him today, I saw how his symptoms have progressed since Thursday, and it was a shock. Jill was smart to look into assisted living for him."

Connie nods. "It's unfortunate. As much as we all imagine living independently well into our golden years, it's not always possible. What does Vanessa think about Father Daniel moving to a retirement home?"

"She didn't say anything about it." I shrug.

"Well, it certainly affects her," Connie observes. "If Father Daniel moves somewhere with built-in help, she'll be out of a job."

I hadn't thought of that.

"Thank you for walking Sophie," I say to Marla after Connie leaves to have lunch with Archie.

"I'm happy to do it," she replies. "My son's girlfriend has a dog. I want to show them I'd be a good dog sitter, so if they get married, they'll let me dog sit while they're on their honeymoon." She raises her eyebrows and grins coyly at me.

There are a lot of expectations squeezed into that statement.

I have to admit, I'm rooting for Craig and Amy too. If they get married, I'll be able to walk around the wedding reception telling people I introduced them. Craig and I went on a date once, and it was obvious we were meant to be just friends. Amy is a cop who works with Eric, and her dog, Tundra is a police dog. Amy was pursuing Eric, but he wasn't interested, thankfully, and I introduced her to Craig. They've been together for about three months now. Might be early to hear wedding bells, but time will tell.

Marla is telling me about her secret Pinterest board where she pins ideas for Craig and Amy's wedding and pictures of mother-of-the-groom dresses she likes. The bell over the door jingles and Mr. and Mrs. Grandin come in.

"Hi, Mr. and Mrs. Grandin! How are you?" I ask.

"Very well, thank you, Megan. I think I'll take one more skein of that yarn I bought yesterday. I'm not sure I'll need it, but I'm afraid of running out when I'm almost finished knitting the sweater, and there won't be any left from the same dye lot." She laughs.

"Better safe than sorry," Marla says. "You know we have a generous return policy here. You can return any skein of unused yarn for a full refund within a year. As long as we don't smell smoke or see animal fur on the skein you're returning."

"Oh! I didn't know that, Marla," Mrs. Grandin says as she and Marla walk toward the worsted weight yarn.

Mr. Grandin and I are alone at the counter. I smile at him. He smiles back.

"Why don't we sit down, Mr. Grandin. We deserve a rest."

"Yes, we do," he chuckles.

I walk the few steps to the cozy sitting area and sit on one of the sofas. Mr. Grandin follows me with his slow, deliberate steps. When he sits on the sofa across from me, he leans his walking stick against the sofa cushion next to him.

We talk about the weather and our plans for Easter for a few minutes, then Connie and Archie come into the store and join us.

Archie and Mr. Grandin speak amongst themselves, while Connie tells me about her lunch at Stop Guac and Roll, the restaurant April and I were going to for lunch the day we found Jill.

"I haven't seen that one before, Grandin," Archie says, pointing to Mr. Grandin's walking stick.

All the men in town who are around the same age as Archie and Mr. Grandin tend to call Mr. Grandin by his last name. I'm sure there's a story there, but I don't know what it is.

"It's from England," Mr. Grandin explains. "It's bamboo. It was made in 1960. And watch this..."

Mr. Grandin grabs the handle of the walking stick with one hand and holds the stick part with his other hand. Deftly, and with surprising agility, he pulls the handle, and an umbrella slides out from inside the walking stick.

"Well! Would you look at that!" Archie nudges Connie. "Did you see that, Connie? There's an umbrella hidden in there."

"Yes," Connie says. "Very clandestine."

"Do all your walking sticks have umbrellas hidden inside them?" I ask.

"Not all of them," Mrs. Grandin interjects. "He has one that hides alcohol. He collects walking sticks like I collect yarn."

We laugh. Mrs. Grandin is standing at the counter now, and Marla is ringing up her skein of yarn.

"Alcohol?" I ask.

Mr. Grandin nods. "It's from the early 1920s. It was made

in America during prohibition. People used them to smuggle alcohol."

I had no idea there are so many types of walking sticks.

Marla reminds Mrs. Grandin when we host knit night at the store, then she and Mr. Grandin leave.

While Marla knits a hat sample for the store, Archie tries to convince Connie that he could use a few walking sticks with cool gadgets hidden in them for the days when his hip is bad.

There are no customers, so I pick up my planner and go to the back room to divvy up the Easter eggs. Easter is next weekend, and I haven't delivered any yet. A couple of business owners have texted me asking when they can expect their eggs.

The store is slow for the rest of the afternoon, and I'm able to finish dividing the eggs. I also manage to bag them and label the bags with the name of each store. I send a group text to the WSBA and let everyone know I'll deliver the eggs on Tuesday.

The store is still slow when I emerge from the back room, so I let Connie and Marla leave early. I tidy the store, then sweep and mop the floor. A few minutes before it's time to close for the day, I hear the back door open and close.

Sophie leaps down from the window, and trots eagerly toward the kitchenette. It must be Eric because I'm sure I locked that door, and other than Connie and Marla, he's the only one who has a key.

Sophie has different barks. Her bark for someone she knows differs from the bark for someone she doesn't know. This is her I'm-so-excited-to-see-you-again bark. It's a high-pitched, yelp-bark combo.

"Hi," I say when Eric walks into the store. "I thought we were meeting at my house."

"We are." He smiles. "I came home for a quick shower and to change out of my work clothes."

"You don't have to dress up on my account," I tease.

"I want to make a good impression." He winks.

My heart rate speeds up and my knees wobble slightly.

"If it's easier, we can have dinner upstairs," I suggest.

"My place is a mess," he says. "I don't want my landlady to evict me."

It's funny because I'm his landlady.

"I think she'd forgive you," I say.

"Let me walk Sophie for you. You can go home and Sophie and I will meet you there."

Is this town conspiring to stop me from walking a dog ever again?

"Are you sure?" I ask.

He nods. "Sophie and I enjoy our walks together. And the fresh air will be good. It'll help me clear my head and take my mind off work for a while."

"OK." I shrug. "Thanks."

I turn the sign from OPEN to CLOSED, lock the front door, and retrieve my tote bag from under the counter.

Eric walks me to the back door.

"Be a good girl, Soph. I'll see you soon" Sophie looks at me and wags her tail.

"We'll be there in about an hour," Eric says.

I open the door. Eric kisses my forehead and my stomach does a somersault.

"Lock it behind me," I say in the same tone of voice he uses when he says it to me.

He laughs and I leave.

The ride home feels empty and lonely without Sophie in the car with me. I don't care who offers to walk her, the next person to take Sophie for a walk will be me.

I HEAR A CAR DOOR, followed quickly by Sophie's distinct bark and the scraping of her nails on the front door.

"Hey, Soph!" I say when I open the front door. "Your dinner's ready. It's in the kitchen."

She runs past me and bee-lines to the kitchen. I'm sure she could smell it before I told her.

"Hi," Eric says, handing me two boxes of pizza from Pastabilities.

"You got pizza?!" I ask, smiling and with more enthusiasm than pizza usually calls for.

"I didn't know you like pizza this much," Eric says in response to my disproportionate excitement over seeing the boxes.

"I don't," I explain. "I mean, I *do* like pizza, but today I *really* like it. When you suggested Pastabilities for dinner, I got a craving for their pizza. I started to text you from Father Daniel's house to suggest we have it for dinner, but I was interrupted and never sent the text. Yet, here you are with pizza, like some kind of mind reader."

"I aim to please," he says.

I walk into the kitchen and put the pizza boxes on the kitchen table while Eric takes off his shoes and coat. I get plates and napkins and put them on the table, then open the fridge and reach for two beers. I pause.

"Are you off duty?" I shout so he can hear me down the hall. "Can you have a beer, or do you want something else?"

"I'm off duty," he says quietly from right beside me, on the other side of the fridge door.

Startled, I flinch. "I didn't hear you come in." I hand him a beer. "I thought you were down the hall." I close the fridge.

Eric is wearing jeans. They're flattering and distracting. I'm not used to seeing him in jeans; he doesn't wear them often. He's also wearing a light blue t-shirt that's slightly too tight on his biceps and across his chest. Not too-tight as in the shirt doesn't fit him, too-tight as in just the right amount of tightness to outline his muscles.

Don't stare, Megan.

OK, stare, but only while his back is turned to put pizza slices on a plate.

He turns to me. "One of each?" He points to the pizza boxes.

Stop staring, Megan.

"What's on them?" I make intentional eye contact.

One pizza has pepperoni, mushrooms, and green pepper —which happen to be my favourite toppings. I have two slices of that one.

We're sitting at the table, eating pizza, drinking beer, and talking about anything other than Jill's murder. I have so much to tell him and questions I want to ask him, but he's been working non-stop since Thursday. He deserves a break from being in cop mode, so I wait until he brings it up.

"What interrupted you from texting me earlier?" he asks.

Not sure what he's talking about, I look at him, confused.

"About your pizza craving," he reminds me.

"Oh right," I say. "I was keeping an eye on Saxon Renaud and had to intervene when he tried to get Father Daniel to sign something."

"I'm listening," he says.

He's back in cop mode. He's less talkative, his gaze is more intent, and he unconsciously clenches and unclenches his jaw muscles.

I tell him about Saxon's visit and our interaction. I also tell him what Rob told me about Jill feeling intimidated after her interaction with Saxon.

Eric's not impressed. His left eyebrow is slightly higher than the right, and his jaw moves as he grinds his teeth. This must be his angry face. I haven't seen it before.

"At any point did either Saxon or his umbrella touch you?"

I shake my head. "No, I moved to avoid it."

"What about Vanessa?"

I shake my head. "She moved too."

"He sounds like a jerk," Eric says. "Lisette has started the process of having Father Daniel evaluated by a qualified capacity assessor. If he's declared incompetent, it will shut down Saxon Renaud's attempts to get him to sign anything."

"You've spoken to Lisette?" I ask.

He nods. "Rob gave me her information, and her number came up frequently in Jill's phone records."

Lisette told me she and Jill spoke almost every day. It's reassuring to know she was telling the truth. And I'm relieved she's taking steps to protect her brother.

"I noticed the laptop on Father Daniel's piano bench is gone. Did you take it as evidence?"

He nods and swallows a mouthful of beer. "Did Vanessa happen to mention who uses the laptop? Has it been mostly her or Jill?"

"She told me Jill brought it to the house. She said they both used it to organize Father Daniel's appointments, keep track of his symptoms, and check the church website."

"Did she say anything else?"

"Not about the laptop," I reply. "Why?"

"Can I tell you something in confidence?" Eric asks. "I'd like your insight, but I don't want what I tell you to become public knowledge."

"Of course," I say. "I never pass on anything you tell me without checking with you first."

I understand why he needs to ask, but I'm slightly offended, nonetheless.

"I know, but I have to ask," he says. "Someone used the laptop to search for local domestic abuse resources. As recently as this week."

"Do you mean shelters, community agencies, and those types of resources?" I ask, shocked.

I tell him about Father Daniel throwing a plate at Jill. I tell him Rob mentioned it first, and Vanessa confirmed it. I also tell him about the bruises Rob said Jill had after Father Daniel squeezed her arm.

"But I didn't see the bruises myself, and Vanessa didn't mention them to me when I asked her about Father Daniel's physical outbursts."

Eric gets up from the table, disappears down the hall, and reappears with his notebook and pen. He must carry them in his coat pocket even when he's not on duty.

He sits down at the table, clicks the top of the pen, finds a blank page in his notebook and makes a note.

"I know I've mentioned this to you before," I say, "but her first marriage might have been violent. Did you confirm her ex-husband's alibi?"

He nods. "We've excluded him. He was three time zones away the night she died. There's video proof and witnesses who can verify his whereabouts."

I guess it's definitely not him, but I can't shake the feeling that her first marriage is a factor in her death. Maybe not directly, but indirectly.

"The *night* she died?" I ask. "April and I found her at lunchtime. I assumed she died that morning. Maybe on her way to Father Daniel's house for work. She was there all night?" My voice cracks and my eyes fill with tears at the thought of Jill laying there alone in the cold and rain for hours.

"The coroner narrowed the estimated time of death to between midnight and 2 a.m." Eric says quietly.

He hands me a napkin. I dry my eyes and take a moment to compose myself.

"What else did the coroner say?" I ask.

"The cause of death was immediate exsanguination."

He pauses, I suspect to give me a chance to process what he's saying. Exsanguination is medical speak for blood loss.

"That means it was fast?" I ask. "She didn't suffer?"

"The coroner says it was immediate. She wouldn't have suffered at all." He takes my hand. "The puncture wound severed her carotid artery. She would have lost consciousness immediately and likely died within two minutes."

"Does the coroner know what the weapon was?" I ask.

"Something narrow and sharp. The weapon is longer than it is wide. And smooth. There was no evidence that the edge is serrated. The murderer is likely taller than Jill, but the surrounding ground was uneven, so we can't be sure how much taller. The perpetrator is right-handed and was in front of her. There's no evidence of a struggle. She might not have had time to fight."

She saw her killer. They didn't sneak up behind her. She might have been talking to the person who killed her right before it happened.

"Do you have any suspects?" I ask.

"We have people we haven't been able to eliminate yet," he replies, "but no one stands out."

"The person who killed her didn't take the ten thousand dollars she had in her purse. The money must have been intended for someone else," I surmise. "Surely if the killer knew it was there, they would have taken it."

"We spoke to the bank. They confirmed that Father Daniel withdrew the money last week. Jill was with him. I've seen the video footage. He didn't tell the bank employees what the money was for."

"I was hoping to ask him about 'the bad guy' today," I explain, "but he didn't even remember seeing me on Thursday. The stress of Jill's murder has aggravated his symptoms."

He nods. "I know. I've tried to question him twice, but both times he couldn't answer my questions and spoke mostly in French."

"Three times I've heard a rumour about Jill and Justin

having an affair," I tell him. "But Vanessa insists it's not true. In fact, according to her, Jill didn't like Justin."

I tell him what Vanessa told me about Jill's issues with Justin.

"Justin was in the city when Jill died," Eric reminds me.

"It might not be probable, but could it be possible that after they fell asleep watching Netflix, Justin woke up, sneaked out, drove to Harmony Lake, murdered Jill, then drove back to the city? I'm not sure if the timing works with the coroner's report…" My voice trails off at the end of my thought.

"I'll look into it." He makes another note in his notebook.

We decide we've talked about Jill's murder enough for tonight. We move to the family room and sit on the sofa with Sophie nestled between us. We find a stand-up comedy special to watch on Netflix.

When the show ends, Eric yawns and stretches, which startles Sophie awake. She jumps to the floor and shakes it off.

"I should go," Eric says. "First mass is 8:30 tomorrow morning and second mass is 10:30."

"You attend mass?" I ask. "I had no idea."

"Not usually," he says. "Actually, never. I'm not Catholic. I'm going tomorrow because Jill was heavily involved in the church community. A few of us will be there, eyes and ears open. What are you up to tomorrow?"

"Weekly brunch with Adam and Hannah in the morning, Jill's house in the afternoon, and a movie in Harmony Hills with April in the evening. Tomorrow is a full day," I tell him.

"You're going to Rob's house? Alone?" He sounds concerned.

I nod. "Uh-huh. I told him I'd help him with Jill's business. She has a few final orders that need to be processed, and her email and website are still active. He doesn't know anything about her business."

"Can April or Connie go with you?"

"I wasn't planning to ask them," I reply. "Why?"

"Rob hasn't been eliminated as a suspect yet," Eric explains. "I'm not comfortable with you being alone with a murder suspect in his home. If he did it, he'll be stressed out. You're practically made of questions, and if you ask him something that rattles him, anything could happen."

"Made of questions?" I ask. "What does that mean?"

Eric opens his eyes wide and raises his hands in front of him.

Panic. This is the second new facial expression tonight. It's a nice change, he's usually difficult to read. I'm convinced it's a cop-thing, like he's trained himself not to let his facial expressions give away what he thinks or how he feels.

"In a good way," he explains. "It's a compliment. You ask good questions. And you ask them well, without making people feel like they're being interrogated. It's one of the things I lo... It's one of my favourite things about you. But sometimes I worry you could ask the wrong question to the wrong person and get hurt."

"His daughter is coming home tomorrow. She might already be there when I show up. If not, she'll be on her way," I reassure him. "I'll proceed with caution if I get the urge to ask him anything."

"Just be careful, please. Or better yet, ask someone to go with you."

"I'll be careful."

CHAPTER 11

"Nice apron." I point my chin toward Adam's apron when he opens the door to his condo.

The apron was a Christmas gift from Hannah. It combines two of his favourite things: golf, which he's been doing forever, and cooking, which he's been doing since he moved out of our family home in October. It says, *Cooking is like golf: slice it, chip it, and get it on some greens.*

"Thanks," he says, smoothing the bib of the apron. "Come in."

He rushes back toward the kitchen, and I let myself in, closing the door behind me.

We have brunch together every Sunday. We alternate between my house and his condo, but he always cooks. We Facetime Hannah and the three of us have a virtual visit.

We pick up Hannah from university next weekend. She'll be home for the summer, and I can't wait to have Sunday brunch with her in person.

I drop my tote bag on the floor beside the contemporary, sleek grey sofa. The condo itself is new. The builder finished the development a few months ago. It's fresh, modern looking, and has all the modern conveniences you'd expect a fancy new condominium complex to have.

Like the sofa, the rest of the decor in the condo is sophisticated, minimalist, and varying shades of grey. It feels very Adam; he's also contemporary and sleek. The yellow throw cushions on the sofa and yellow artwork on the grey walls are a chic accent to all the grey. He even has a grey pot with yellow tulips on the dining table. It looks like a condo you'd find in a magazine spread about interior decorating, but he did it himself. It's a stark contrast to my warm, wood-accented home full of cozy overstuffed furniture.

A whiff of deliciousness gets my attention and I inhale deeply.

"That smells great," I call out. "What are we having?"

Adam pops his head out of the kitchen. "Grilled naan topped with applewood bacon, spinach, gruyere, and a poached egg."

That sounds amazing. My tummy grumbles in anticipation.

"Anything I can do to help?" I ask, now standing at the threshold between the kitchen and dining area.

"You want to set the table?" he asks, tossing spinach leaves into a heated pan.

"Sure." I collect plates and cutlery, then notice a bag of candy on the kitchen counter. I put the plates and cutlery down and nose around in the bag. Peeps, Cadbury creme eggs, and Lindt chocolate carrots. Hannah's favourite Easter treats.

"They're for Hannah," Adam explains when he sees me looking in the bag. "This is the first time she won't be home on Easter morning and wake up to a house full of chocolate. I thought I'd hide some so when she comes home on Sunday evening, she can find them."

"That's really thoughtful," I say. "You're a good dad."

"I'm a dad with a minimalist aesthetic," he points out.

"Hiding more than a few eggs in this condo will be a challenge. Do you want to take half of them with you so you can hide them at your place?"

"Sure," I reply. "She's become one of those children of divorce who gets two of everything on holidays and her birthday."

Adam and I met and married young. We met in university when I was eighteen. By the time I turned twenty, we were married, and I'd become pregnant soon after. I was focused on being a mum and member of the community, while Adam's ambition to make partner at a large law firm meant he worked sixty-hour weeks and brought work home on weekends. One day, we realized that aside from our last name and Hannah, we had nothing left in common.

We tried to reconnect and make it work, but years of apathy and neglect had taken their toll, and ultimately we decided it would be best for all three of us if we separated. The love is still there, but it's changed. It's not the romantic love that a marriage needs to be happy.

We see each other more often now that we're apart than we did when we were married. It hasn't been easy, but we're figuring out how to be friends, and we have a much better relationship now.

"We're doing OK," Adam reassures me. "Hannah knows we're still a family. We all love each other. We still look after each other. We just don't live together and aren't married. Our family has changed, but it's still intact. I see a lot of failed marriages, Meg, and trust me when I say we're navigating this change better than most of them."

Adam has practiced family law for most of his career, and he has seen some horrible, nasty divorces. He's determined to make sure we don't devolve to that level. We're hell-bent on coming out of this as friends and as a functional family unit.

"I know you're right," I tell him. "It's just... I always promised myself Hannah would always come first."

"She does," he says.

My own parents divorced when I was four. I don't remember the specifics of the breakup, but I remember they didn't like each other. They couldn't stand to be in the same room together. Holidays and birthdays were always a stressful tug-of-war between my parents with my sister and I stuck in the middle. I always swore I'd never get divorced, but here we are.

I set the plate and cutlery on the table, then go back for glasses, orange juice, and napkins.

Adam plates the food, and I use his tablet to Facetime Hannah.

She points out that he's wearing the apron she gave him. He looks surprised that he's still wearing it. He takes it off and puts it over the back of his chair.

While we eat, Hannah brings us up to date on her life as a student in the big city. We need to tell her about Jill Plumb's death, but Hannah has an exam in her Introduction To Sociology course tomorrow, and she and Adam get into a discussion about sociology and criminology that lasts almost an hour. Listening to them and seeing the enthusiasm on both their faces as they talk about law, I realize we'll likely have another lawyer in the family in about six years.

Next thing we know, Hannah has to meet her study group. We say our goodbyes and I love yous and end the call.

"We should have told her about Jill," I say after the screen on Adam's tablet turns off.

He nods. "We'll tell her when we pick her up. So, how are you doing anyway? After finding another body, I mean."

"I'm OK." I shrug. "I hope this is the last dead body I ever see."

"It is kind of eerie, Meg. How you're the person who keeps coming across dead bodies," he says. "I mean, four people have been murdered in Harmony Lake, and you've found three of them. Don't you think that's weird?"

I swallow a mouthful of orange juice. "It's not intentional, Adam. I don't go around *looking* for dead people."

"I know," he agrees. "But you have to admit, finding one body is tragic, finding two bodies is hard luck. But finding three bodies? It kind of seems like a new hobby." Unsuccessfully, he tries to suppress a laugh by clearing his throat and covering his mouth with his hand.

I ignore his attempt at dark humour. I don't want to encourage it.

"Who do you like for it?" Adam asks.

"Who do I like for what?"

"For the murder. Who do you think did it? I know you've been sniffing around. Asking questions."

"How would you know?" I ask.

"I know you. You can't help yourself. You're naturally curious," Adam replies.

"Last night Eric said I'm 'made of questions,'" I tell him.

Adam laughs and throws his head back. "That's the most accurate description of you I've ever heard. He nailed it!"

"I'm glad I amuse you," I say stoically.

"Seriously," Adam's tone changes and he's more serious. "Are you thinking it might be Rob?"

I shrug. "Maybe. Why do you ask? Do you think it might be Rob?"

Adam shrugs. "I don't know. Don't you think there was always something a little off in that family? I mean, they were so perfect it seemed almost fictional."

"Why does it have to be fictional? Maybe they really were that perfect," I suggest.

"Seeing them at school events and games and stuff, it always seemed like they were on a mission to look like the ideal family."

"I never got that impression," I say.

"Maybe I'm being judgmental because Rob always had a way of making me feel like an absent father. He was everywhere. He attended everything. He volunteered for every team and every field trip."

"You're a good dad, Adam," I reassure him. "You didn't attend everything, but when you were there, you were completely present. Emotionally available. I don't think Hannah ever felt neglected or compared you to other dads."

"Thanks, Meg." He reaches over and squeezes my hand. "Since leaving the firm and starting my practice in Harmony Lake, I realize how much I missed when I was absorbed by my career and obsessed with making partner at the firm. Sometimes I wish I could go back and make different choices."

"You were always there when it mattered."

Now that he mentions it, Rob and Jill were always the archetypal couple and parents. Their veneer never cracked. Neither of them ever seemed to have a bad day or even act slightly grumpy.

"I spoke with Jill shortly before she died," he mentions casually.

"Really?" My curiosity is piqued. "About what?"

"She called me at the office and asked if Father Daniel is my client," he explains. "She was hoping I might know whether he designated any powers of attorney."

Interesting. This must've been after her interaction with Saxon Renaud. Father Daniel must not be a client of Adam's. If he were, Adam wouldn't tell me any of this as he takes his duty to client privacy seriously. I ask him anyway, just to be sure.

"Is Father Daniel your client?"

He shakes his head. "No. She asked me if there are any other local lawyers he may have dealt with, then she asked me about having him declared incompetent. She mentioned being concerned about his dementia. We spoke for about fifteen minutes."

"Did she mention anything about Saxon Renaud?" I ask.

"Saxon? No, why would she mention him?"

The familiarity with which he says Saxon's name makes me think they know each other. What if Saxon is Adam's client? What if Adam drew up the sale document Saxon wants Father Daniel to sign?

"Do you know him?" I ask.

"He's my landlord. He owns the building on Mountain Road where my office is located," Adam explains. "We're acquainted, but we're not friends and he's not a client."

I tell him about my experience with him and what Rob told me about Jill's experience with Saxon Renaud.

"Classy guy." Adam's voice oozes sarcasm. His expression becomes serious. "What Saxon is trying to do isn't illegal. It's immoral, but it's within the law."

"What happens if he gets Father Daniel alone, and Father Daniel signs the document, selling the house to him?" I ask.

Adam shakes his head. "Unless Father Daniel has been declared incompetent, it would be legally binding." He has a sip of orange juice.

"Did you tell Eric about your conversation with Jill?" I ask.

"We spoke on the phone on Friday. He's stopping by the office tomorrow so I can give him a statement."

I hear my phone ding inside my tote bag and get up to retrieve it. I find the phone, then use my thumbprint to unlock it. Speak of the devil.

Eric: Just finished mass. Thought I'd say hi and ask what time you're going to Rob's house.

I text back quickly.

Me: Still at brunch. Just realized the time. Heading over there in a few minutes. I'll text you when I get home.

Eric: Stay safe. Keep your cell phone handy. Call me if you need anything.

"Everything OK, Meg?"

I lock my phone and drop it back in my bag.

"Everything's fine. It's Eric reminding me to be careful at Rob's house today," I explain with an eye roll.

"He must think Rob's a suspect," Adam replies. "Why are you going to Rob's?"

I tell him I'm helping him with Jill's business email, website, and final orders.

"Well, watch your back. Hannah still needs two parents," he says.

"I will," I say. "I have to get going. I didn't realize the time."

"We haven't talked about next weekend," Adam reminds me. "We need to finalize our plan to move Hannah back home."

I'm already at the door and slipping on my shoes. "You book the truck, I'll book the hotel. We'll touch base though the week. Sound good?"

He nods. "I'll call you."

I grab my tote bag, we exchange a double cheek kiss, I thank him for brunch, and leave.

CHAPTER 12

At Rob's house, I park on the street because there's an unfamiliar car parked behind Rob in the driveway.

I ring the doorbell.

"Megan! It's nice to see you again."

"Hi, Lisette! It's nice to see you too."

I've been here twice since Jill died, and Lisette has been here both times. Why is she here again?

She moves aside to give me space to step into the house. I close the door behind me.

"I came by to tidy the house and restock the fridge before Rob picks up his daughter at the bus station later," Lisette explains.

"That's thoughtful of you," I say.

"Well, Jill was house proud. She always kept the house tidy and the fridge well stocked. I'm sure she'd want it that way when her kids get here."

She's right, that's exactly what Jill would want. Their friendship may have been cut short, but Jill and Lisette obviously grew to know each other well. I follow Lisette into the kitchen where she resumes clearing old, perished food out of the fridge and replacing it with fresh produce and dairy.

"How are you doing, Lisette? Have you made any progress with seeing Father Daniel?"

"Sort of," she replies. "Father Patrick is helping us. He visits Daniel almost every day. He says he mentions me and shows him my photo. I'm hoping to have a short visit with him next week with Father Patrick."

"That's great news!" I say. "I hope it goes well for both of you."

"Thanks," Lisette replies. "I've started the process of having Daniel assessed. Jill was right about him not being able to live on his own anymore. He needs a safer environment with lots of support."

I want to ask how Vanessa feels about Father Daniel potentially moving into an assisted living facility and not needing her help anymore, but Rob comes into the kitchen.

"Hi, Megan." We hug briefly. "I'm sorry to keep you waiting. I was on the phone upstairs." He places the cordless phone he's carrying on the kitchen table.

"No worries," I reply. "It gave Lisette and I a chance to chat."

I follow Rob upstairs. He opens the door to the spare bedroom they transformed into an office and studio for Jill.

At first glance, it's obvious Jill was organized. The workspaces are clear of clutter, papers are stacked neatly in piles and filed in desktop trays, and the walls are lined with shelves that house multiple containers. Everything is clearly labeled.

"Wow," I comment as I pick up a stack of papers from the tray labelled *To Be Filed*.

"Jill was the organized one," Rob observes. "She kept everything moving along, you know? I don't know how we'll manage without her. We'll fall apart."

His voice cracks on the last sentence. I quietly skim through the orders while Rob takes a moment to compose himself.

"I'm sorry, Megan," he says. "I haven't been in here since...it happened. I never come in here, really. This was Jill's space. I didn't expect to become so emotional."

"Please don't apologize, Rob. You're emotional. I understand." I put the papers on Jill's desk, next to her laptop. "Listen, if being in this room is too difficult, I can figure this out myself."

"No," he replies. "I want to help. I want to do as much as I can for her."

Rob opens Jill's laptop and taps the spacebar until the machine wakes up. He types a password into the computer, and her home screen appears. He clicks an icon, types in another password, a few more clicks, then turns the laptop toward me.

I look at the spreadsheet.

"Her login and password information for everything pertaining to her business," he explains.

"For someone who doesn't know anything about Jill's business, you seem to know your way around the tech side of it," I remark.

He shakes his head. "You're giving me too much credit. Those two passwords are literally everything I know. And I only know those because we use the same few passwords for every device we have. I know nothing about the creative part of it. She has dozens of different button designs, stitch markers, key chain thing-a-mabobs, wine glass charms—whatever those are—and I don't even know what else. I can't tell one of them from the other."

I nod. "Hopefully, I can tell one thing from the other."

I sit at Jill's desk, in her chair, and take a moment to let it sink in that she was the last person to sit here before me, and she'll never sit here again. I take a breath, let it out slowly, and look at the list of websites, logins, and passwords in front of me.

The first thing I do is log into her website. I disable the

online shopping cart and set up a pop-up window, notifying anyone who visits the website that the store is closed and not taking orders. And just in case someone closes the pop-up window without reading it, I set up an announcement bar at the top of every page explaining the same thing.

"Are you sure you don't want me to disable the site?" I ask Rob. "I can hide it so it will still exist, and her website address will still work, but none of the pages will be visible. We could set up a simple cover page explaining the store is closed."

He takes a deep breath. "Can we leave it up? It's weird, but I think sometimes I might want to see it."

"OK," I agree. "Let's leave it. If you change your mind, we'll adjust it later."

Next, we log into her email and print the new orders that have come in since Jill last checked. We set up an auto-responder explaining that Jill isn't taking any new orders, and Rob decides to email each custom order explaining why their order won't be filled and their refund will be processed immediately.

While he does that, I take the first order from the stack of online orders and head to the shelves labelled *Pre-made Inventory*. The shelves contain several tackle boxes. The tackle boxes you'd use for fishing. Each tackle box is labelled with its contents, Stitch markers, ¼ inch buttons, ½ inch buttons, Wine charms, Key chains etc., and a few of them seem to contain the components Jill used to make her products. Like toolboxes, when you open the lid, each box opens into three-layered compartments. Jill made excellent use of her label maker, and for that I'm grateful. Her orderliness and system-ization allow me to find the products for each order quickly and efficiently.

While I create an assembly line for picking, packing, and shipping, Rob finishes his email tasks, and I ask him how the kids are doing.

"I'm picking up our daughter at the bus station in Harmony Hills this evening," he replies, looking at his watch. "And our son will be home tomorrow."

"I'm sure you can't wait to see them," I say.

"I need to see them," he tells me. "I can't explain it, but it's like after Jill died, their absence became so much bigger. I need to see them and hug them and know they're OK. I guess I need to be near the people Jill loved most and who loved her —our kids."

"It makes total sense," I affirm.

I'm about to open a tackle box labelled *Buttons, ½ inch, glass* when my phone dings. I pull it from the back pocket of my jeans and unlock the screen.

Eric: How's it going?

He's checking to make sure I'm OK. I text back right away because I'm sure he'll phone if I don't.

Me: All good. I'll text you when I leave. I've hardly asked any questions.

That last sentence will let him know for sure it's me replying to him, not Rob replying with my phone after he killed me for asking too many questions. I put the phone back in my pocket, open the tackle box, and look for the compartment with green buttons. The tray of the second tier is wobbly and feels unstable. Maybe there are a few buttons underneath the tray.

I lift the tray out of the second tier of the tackle box and look to see what's making the tray wobble.

Well, well, well... Buried under the removable tray of the second tier of the tackle box, I find a cell phone. Without thinking it through first, I hold it up for Rob to see.

"So that's where she put it." He looks at me, sighs heavily, and stands up from behind the desk.

CHAPTER 13

ROB OPENS his mouth to speak. Before he can say anything, Lisette pokes her head into the doorway.

"Excuse me," she croons, the rest of her body following her head into the doorway. "I hate to interrupt…"

Rob and I look at her and smile.

I slip the phone behind my back.

"You're not interrupting, Lisette," Rob reassures her.

"Two things." Lisette holds up two fingers and looks at Rob. "First, I have to leave to meet Father Patrick, but I'll be back in about an hour to finish vacuuming and tidying before you get back from the bus station." She puts down one finger. "Second, you left the upstairs phone downstairs. It rang, so I answered it." She puts down her second finger and extends her other hand, with the phone in it, toward Rob. "It's for you."

Rob looks at me. "Excuse me, Megan. I'll be right back." He takes the phone from Lisette, thanks her, and leaves the room.

Lisette turns to go downstairs.

"Lisette," I call after her.

She returns to her spot in the doorway.

"I just want to mention, because I'm not sure if you know, there's a local man who's tried at least twice to get your brother to sign a document selling him the house."

"Do you mean Saxon Renaud?" she asks.

"Yes." I nod. "Did Jill tell you about him?"

"Yes, she did." she leans against the door frame. "Jill had an unpleasant exchange with him one day at my brother's house."

"I heard," I tell her. "I had an unpleasant exchange with him at your brother's house too. He's quite determined to buy the house."

She nods. "I know. I contacted him after Jill told me about him. I offered him first refusal to purchase the house if he stops harassing Daniel to sell it. I told him I need time to find somewhere for Daniel to move and go through having his affairs taken over, either by me or by a trustee. He was impatient. He wanted something in writing. I told him to put something in writing, and I'll have my lawyer look at it. He didn't like that answer and became rather unpleasant."

"That seems to be his way of doing things," I say.

"Do you think he could have killed Jill?" Lisette asks.

I shrug. "Do you?"

"It's crossed my mind more than once," she admits. "If he did, that means Jill died protecting my brother. I should have been the person looking after Daniel and protecting him. I wish I'd reached out to him years ago and put things right."

Her eyes redden and fill with tears.

"Did you tell Eric—Detective Sloane—about your attempt to reason with Saxon?"

"I did," she replies. "You know Detective Sloane?"

Before I can answer her, she says, "Right! You do. You found Jill. He would have questioned you too."

I smile and nod.

Rob comes down the hall toward the office. He's thanking the person on the other end of the phone and tells them he'll be in touch soon. He ends his call.

"Well, I better get a wiggle on or I'll be late," Lisette announces. She waves and rushes down the stairs.

"I'll just hang this up." Rob holds up the cordless phone in his hand. "The battery is low, it needs to charge."

As if on cue, the phone rings again. Rob takes a deep breath, like he's willing himself to have the patience for another conversation. He pushes a button on the phone, and as he disappears into the next room, I hear him say hello.

I try to unlock the screen of the mystery phone I found in the tackle box. Surprisingly, it isn't password protected. I check the text messages. There's only one text conversation. I check the call history. The phone has only made calls to one number, and it has only received calls from the same number. Obviously, this phone served a specific purpose. Is this the phone Jill used to contact whoever she was having an affair with?

I pull my cell phone from my pocket and use it to take photos of the text conversation on the mystery phone. I also snap a pic of the phone number this phone has been calling and texting with. Then I send a text to Eric.

Me: I'm fine. I found something that might be important. I think you should come see it.

I put my phone back in my pocket. Just as I lock the screen on the mystery phone, Rob comes back into the office.

"You wouldn't believe how busy the phones are since...Thursday," he says. "If it's not my cell phone ringing, it's the landline. I must talk to twenty people a day."

"A lot of people love Jill, you, and the kids," I remind him. "Speaking of phones..."

I hold up the mystery phone.

"I've seen that phone before," Rob tells me. "One day last

week it started ringing when Jill wasn't home. Our ensuite washroom is on the other side of this wall." He walks over to a wall and knocks on it as if to prove what he's saying is true. "I heard it ringing when I stepped out of the shower. I followed the sound and found it under a stack of papers on her desk. I didn't answer it. But when she came home, I confronted her and asked why she had a secret phone. She insisted it wasn't her phone. She said she found it in a parking lot and was trying to get it back to the owner. I came in here to look for it after she died, but I couldn't find it. I assumed she found the owner and returned it."

Didn't he tell me earlier that he hasn't been in this room since Jill died? One of those statements is a lie, but which one? Is this the same phone Jill was speaking on when Rob heard her whispering in her office late at night? Did he believe her when she told him she found it in a parking lot? Do I believe he found an unfamiliar phone hidden in his wife's office and didn't look at the text messages or call history?

I'm gearing up to ask him at least one of these questions when the doorbell rings.

"I'll be right back," Rob says.

He turns and leaves the room. As soon as I hear his footsteps on the stairs, I open the mystery phone again and look at the text messages. They're short and vague. The last text conversation was a few hours before Jill died.

Jill: We still on?

Other person: Yes!

Jill: I'll pick up the money and meet you where we planned in an hour.

Other person: K

It sounds like she went to Father Daniel's house to pick up the money and was intercepted when she was leaving.

I hear Eric's voice.

That was fast. He either broke the speed limit driving here, or he was conveniently nearby.

Two sets of heavy footsteps clomp up the stairs.

Rob enters the room, followed by Eric. I hold the phone out to Eric. He takes it with a gloved hand and drops it in a plastic evidence bag.

I look at Rob. "I had to call him."

Rob purses his lips into a tight smile and nods. "I know," he says quietly.

Eric asks Rob where he'd like to talk. Rob suggests they go downstairs to the living room.

"Megan, can I get you tea or coffee?" Rob asks.

"No thanks," I reply. "I'll stay here and finish packing these orders if that's OK."

Rob nods. He and Eric leave the room. Their voices trail off as they descend the stairs, and Rob offers Eric a drink. Eric declines his offer.

I finish collecting the items for the orders. Jill has a separate table for packing and shipping with all the supplies on it. I package each order, label it, and seal it.

I run the last package through the postage machine and print the shipping label, while the thumping of footsteps grows louder as they get closer.

"Are you ready to go?" Eric asks.

I turn toward the door. He's alone. Rob must be downstairs.

I have a feeling he's not leaving without me, so I nod.

"Can I take these orders with me?" I ask, stashing them in my tote bag. "I'd like to drop them off at the post office. One less thing for Rob to do." I pick up my tote bag, now full with Jill's orders, and put it over my shoulder.

"Did you pack them yourself?"

I nod.

He shrugs. "I guess so. They're already in your bag. If I

say no, you'll probably take them anyway or come back for them."

"Probably," I agree.

I smile and Eric gestures for me to go ahead of him down the stairs.

"All the orders are packed and ready to go," I tell Rob.

I take one strap off my shoulder and open my bag to show him the packages. "Is it all right with you if I drop them at the post office tomorrow?"

"That would be great." Rob gets up from the sofa and walks to the front door. We hug and he whispers into my ear, "Thank you for your help. I'll let you know when the final arrangements are made."

"Call me if you need anything else," I remind him as I leave the house.

Eric leaves behind me, and I hear the door close behind him.

"Do you have time for a coffee?" I ask.

"I wish I could," Eric replies, "but I have to get a search warrant."

I turn to look at him and see a uniformed officer and patrol car in Rob's driveway.

"Why is he here?" I ask, jerking my thumb toward the patrol car.

Eric inhales deeply. "To make sure nothing enters or leaves the house until I come back with a warrant."

"Eric! Rob's daughter is coming home today. Because her mother just died. And you're turning their home inside out?"

Frustrated and mindful of the uniformed police officer watching us from his patrol car, I speed up my pace and hasten toward my car, keen to put some distance between Eric and me before I say something I'll regret.

Eric increases his strides and easily catches up to me as I approach my car door. I push the button on my key chain to unlock the car door.

"I'm sorry," Eric shrugs.

"So am I," I retort. "Honestly, I'm not sure I'd have texted you if I knew this would happen."

I place my hand on the handle of my car door. Gently, Eric puts his hand on top of mine.

I avert my gaze to a nearby tree to avoid making eye contact with him.

"I'm sorry, Megan. I can't help the timing. I didn't have cause for a warrant until you found the phone. If I wait, there's a risk other evidence could be compromised. I assured Rob we'll finish the search as quickly as we can and disturb the house as little as possible. He can delay bringing his daughter home by taking her out for dinner or something in Harmony Hills until we're finished." His voice is soft, and he sounds genuinely regretful.

I shake my head in disbelief and look him in the eye. "That girl is traumatized. She's only a year older than Hannah. She just lost her mother. To murder. She doesn't want to go out for dinner. She wants to come home and be with her dad, in their home, where she can cry, and process, and grieve in peace." I yank my hand out from under his and cross my arms in front of my chest. "There has to be another way."

"There isn't," he says.

"Right," I mumble, opening the car door and flinging my tote bag across the driver's seat and onto the passenger seat.

Eric holds the car door open and moves aside so I can get in. I buckle my seatbelt.

"I need to ask you a few questions about the phone and your conversation with Rob," he advises me. He pauses. "Can we see each other later?" There's hesitance in his voice.

I look him in the eye. His expression is one I haven't seen before. I'm not sure if he's sad, worried, remorseful, or all of the above.

"I have to go. I have to see to Sophie before I meet April. And you should go get your search warrant."

That last sentence sounded more spiteful than I intended. Part of me wants to get out of the car and talk this out with him, but I need to calm down first. Also, I don't want to delay his warrant because that would delay the search, so instead, I start the car, and drive away.

CHAPTER 14

"I DON'T KNOW," I sigh loudly. "Maybe I'm not even angry at Eric. Maybe I'm angry at myself and angry about the situation and I'm taking it out on him. What do you think?"

Sophie pants and wags her tail while I unlatch her leash.

"You're a good listener, Sophie, but your advice-giving skills need work."

Sophie trots off toward her water dish, and I put her leash away. My phone dings and I unlock the screen.

April: Ready, Megaroni?

That isn't a typo, it's one of April's punny nicknames for me. This one is obviously a pun on the word, macaroni.

Me: Ready when you are. Who's driving?

April: I'll drive. Leaving in a few minutes. Will text when I get to your house.

Me: Sounds good.

I prepare Sophie's dinner and put it on the floor, explaining to her that she's eating early tonight because I'm going to the movies with April, and I won't be home at her usual dinner time. She doesn't complain and is scarfing down her food enthusiastically when I leave the room to touch up my make-up and fix my hair.

I swap the long-sleeved, black t-shirt I'm wearing for a short-sleeved, white t-shirt and put a celery green, hand-knit cardigan over top. Movie theatres can be chilly, so layers are my best bet. I hem and haw about whether to change out of my jeans and put on comfier leggings, but the jeans have stretch in them and should be comfortable to sit in for two hours, so I don't bother.

I pull my curls into a high ponytail, leaving the few rebellious coils that refuse to cooperate around my face. While I'm touching up my lip gloss, my phone dings in the kitchen, alerting me that April is outside. I slip on my converse sneakers, grab my tote bag, and tell Sophie I'll be back soon.

"Oscar, I'm leaving," I announce to the digital voice assistant that sits on the end table in the family room.

"OK, I'll arm the house," replies the familiar humanoid voice.

After someone broke into the house last year and tried to kill me, Adam installed a state-of-the-art home security system before he moved out. With my voice, an app, or a keypad, I can lock or unlock the house and turn on or turn off the alarms. This house is like the Fort Knox of Harmony Lake.

The door clicks behind me when I leave, confirming it's locked, and the notification sound on my phone alerts me the alarm is on.

There's only one car in the driveway, and it's mine. Where's April? I walk halfway down the driveway and look up and down the street. April's car is nowhere to be seen. Maybe it wasn't her who texted me. I pull my phone from my back pocket and use my thumbprint to unlock the screen.

Eric: I know you're upset. I'll give you some space. I can arrange for someone else to take your statement about your visit to Rob's house today. Call or text me anytime. I'm here whenever you're ready to talk.

Reading his text, I'm struck with a twinge of sadness and

the urge to call him. I want us to talk but not tonight. When we have time to sit down together and talk properly.

Even though I yelled at him and drove off in a huff, he's the one reaching out. This makes me feel worse than I already do. I regret everything about our conversation today. It definitely wasn't one of my finer moments.

I poise my thumbs to type a response, but I'm not sure what to say. He sent me a thoughtful text, and I don't want to leave him on read.

Me: K

No. Not that. Backspace.

Me: Thanks

That's not right either. Five backspaces.

Me: Okay

Also not right.

Wobb, wobb, wobb. As usual, the bass of April's car stereo precedes her arrival. I glance away from my phone and see her car rounding the corner near my house. I look down at my phone again and realize I sent the "Okay" text message. My thumb must have brushed the Send button when I looked away. Shoot! That isn't what I wanted to send. *Arrrgh!* Frustrated, I lock my phone screen and drop the device into my tote bag.

WOBB, WOBB, WOBB. The bass makes my insides vibrate when she pulls into my driveway.

I get in the car, close the door, and turn the music down about eighty percent.

"Hi." I dramatically rub my ear and pretend the loud music caused hearing loss.

"If it's too loud, you're too old," April teases.

"I'm fine with being called old if it means we can keep the Beastie Boys at a low enough volume to hear ourselves think," I reply.

We pull out of the driveway, and April steers us toward the highway. I turn up the music a bit—OK, a lot—when

Intergalactic comes on. We belt out Beastie Boys songs for most of the drive to Harmony Hills.

Harmony Lake is nestled snugly on the south side of the Harmony Hills Mountains, between the mountains and the lake. Harmony Hills is located on the north side of the Harmony Hills Mountains and is a suburb of the city located farther north.

Harmony Hills is larger than Harmony Lake and doesn't have the same geographic restrictions, allowing it to have a larger population and more amenities. Most Harmony Lake residents make regular trips to Harmony Hills to visit the hospital, big-box stores, various professionals, movie theatres, and everything else our tiny town doesn't have.

Tonight, April and I are driving into Harmony Hills to see the new Kate Winslet movie. We're catching the early show because she has to work tomorrow.

We arrive at the theatre and buy our tickets. There's time to kill before the movie starts. Not enough time for a meal, but enough time for a drink and an appetizer.

The strip plaza where the theatre is located has two big-box, corporate restaurants. We choose one and find a table in the bar area. We order drinks and decide on the spinach, crab, & parmesan dip with tortilla chips from the appetizer menu.

"Why are you so quiet?" April asks me while we wait for our drinks.

I shrug. "I was horrible to Eric earlier," I explain, playing with the cutlery the server just delivered. "Then, he sent me a thoughtful and sweet text, and I accidentally sent him a one-word response. I'm sure he thinks I'm cold and bitter."

"Accidentally?"

"Yeah, my thumb slipped. I think. I looked away for a minute, and when I looked back, I'd sent it."

"Did you send a follow-up message?" she asks.

I shake my head. "You showed up. I tossed my phone in my bag and got in your car."

"Oh, Mega-force, I'm sure he doesn't think that. Everyone has a bad day. He's really into you. He'll understand."

"Mega-force? Really?"

"I just came up with that one on the fly," she brags. "I think it's pretty good."

The server brings our drinks and dip. April unfolds her cloth napkin and snaps it open. She leans back to place the napkin on her lap and drops it. It floats to the floor. When she bends down to pick it up, I see a familiar face a few tables behind her. The familiar face sees me too. I smile.

Saxon Renaud doesn't smile back. He looks away from me, leans forward, and speaks furtively to his companion. A petite woman with white hair. Her back is to me, I can't see her face.

April pops back up and smoothes her napkin over her lap.

"Remember that man I told you about? Saxon Renaud?" I ask her.

"Umbrella man?" she asks, making a poking motion with her hand.

"Yes," I confirm. "He's a few tables behind you. We made eye contact when you were retrieving your napkin."

She turns to look at him. He sneers at us. April waves at him. He doesn't wave back. Once again, he leans forward and speaks to his companion.

"I recognize him," she says when she turns back to me. "He comes into the bakery sometimes. I didn't know his name though." She dips a red tortilla chip into the dip and bites it.

"Does he poke at you and T with his umbrella?" I ask.

"We're always on the other side of the counter," she points out. "But now that you mention it, he always has that umbrella with him. Regardless of the weather or the time of year. It's quirky."

I nod. "He's eccentric, that's for sure."

We finish our drinks and dip fifteen minutes before the

movie starts. The server brings our bill, we pay, and get up to leave.

Saxon and his companion are still here. We have to walk past their table to leave the restaurant.

I plaster a cheery smile on my face and prepare to say hi to him as we walk by him.

"Hi, Mr. Renaud," I exclaim.

"Ms. Martel," he says.

He looks at his companion. I look at his companion.

"Hello, Megan," she smiles.

"Hi, Lisette."

I hope my voice and my expression don't portray the shock I feel seeing her here. With him. This afternoon she tells me she thinks Saxon Renaud might be Jill's killer, and tonight she's having a quiet meal with him? What's really going on here?

"Hi, Mr. Renaud," April says, extending her hand. "You've been to our bakery a few times. I'm April Shaw. My wife, Tamara, and I own Artsy Tartsy."

They shake hands.

"April," I gesture to Lisette. "This is Lisette. She's Father Daniel's sister, and she was close friends with Jill Plumb."

April and Lisette shake hands and make small talk.

Saxon Renaud is wearing another pair of khaki pants—these don't have cuffed ankles, but they have the ironed crease, a light blue collared shirt with a pastel pink, v-neck sweater over the top. The sweater has a light blue and white argyle pattern on the front that complements the light blue collar of his shirt. I glance at his feet, and he's wearing his penny loafers, pennies included.

"No umbrella tonight?" I ask Saxon, trying not to sound sarcastic.

"No," he snaps, "thanks to you. Your police friends have it."

I'm taken aback.

"Thanks to me?" It sounds more like a challenge than a question.

"Yes, thanks to you," he clarifies. "You whined to him about our conversation at Father Daniel's house, and as a result, he came to see me with tons of questions and a warrant for my umbrella."

"Why would he want your umbrella?" I wonder out loud.

He shrugs. "He said something about forensics."

"We better go, Megan, or we'll miss the previews." April tugs my arm.

We wish Saxon and Lisette a good evening and leave.

"Tell your cop friend I expect my umbrella returned to me in the same condition he took it," Saxon calls after me.

"WHAT WAS THAT ABOUT?" April asks when we're safely out of earshot.

"Which part?" I answer her question with a question. "The umbrella situation or the Saxon and Lisette situation?"

"Yes," she replies.

I bring her up to speed about what Saxon said about Eric taking his umbrella and about my conversation with Lisette at Rob's house earlier today.

"You have a knack for finding out everybody's business," April observes. "It's kind of like your superpower."

"It's a blessing and a curse." I'm only half joking.

CHAPTER 15

MONDAY, April 6th

Some mornings I wish I was a person who sleeps in. Today is one of those mornings. It would be so nice to roll over and snuggle under the duvet for a couple more hours. But that's not how I'm designed. For reasons unknown, I wake up with the sun. My brain is wide awake and ready to start the day.

"Good morning, Sophie," I say, reaching out from under the covers to rub her head. "Do you want to go outside?"

Her ears perk up, and she leaps off the bed. I put my feet on the floor, wrap my housecoat around myself, and follow Sophie through the kitchen to the back door. She leaps out of the house and into the morning sun, barking at the birds who dare to hunt worms on the back lawn. They heed her warning and fly away.

While Sophie triumphantly prances a victory lap around the perimeter of the yard, I go into the kitchen and drop a pod of Southern Pecan coffee into the coffeemaker, drop two slices of light rye in the toaster, and prepare her breakfast. Sophie and I eat breakfast, and I look at my planner. Nothing. My day is wide open.

Knitorious is closed on Mondays. I usually run errands and clean the house, but the fridge is full, and the house is semi-clean. I make a quick note in my planner to drop off Jill's orders at the post office.

I intended to text Eric when I got home last night, but the movie went longer than we expected. After April dropped me off, I took Sophie for a walk and got ready for bed. Yesterday was a long day, and by the end of it, I was too tired to compose a text message decent enough to help me redeem myself. Also, I know if I texted him, he would've texted me back no matter how late or how tired he was, and I didn't want to make his day any longer than it already was, either.

After breakfast I shower, get dressed, and take Sophie for a walk around the neighbourhood.

As we stroll from tree to tree, I contemplate the relationship between Saxon and Lisette. Are they scheming to profit from Father Daniel's house? Are they romantically involved? I don't know Saxon's relationship status, but I know Lisette is married. Did Jill know about whatever it is they're up to? If she knew and threatened to disclose their secret, it would give them both a motive to kill her.

But why would Jill give them ten thousand dollars? Unless the ten thousand dollars is unrelated to her death... But that can't be right, the money has to have something to do with her murder. None of this makes sense. What am I missing? It feels like there's something right in front of me, but I can't see it.

This situation is like a giant, tangled ball of yarn. Every time I unravel a knot and think I'm making progress, I find another, bigger knot.

I need to talk to Eric. Not only do I owe him a statement about the mystery phone in Jill's office, but this Saxon-Lisette connection might be relevant to his investigation. I want to ask him about the umbrella Saxon says he took, and most important, I need to apologize to him.

At home, I tidy the house, clean my washroom, Facetime with Hannah briefly to wish her good luck on her exam today, and start laundry. While the washing machine works its magic, I cozy up on the sofa and knit on my sock while I work up the nerve to text Eric and ask if he still wants to talk. By the time I finish the foot of the second sock, the laundry is finished.

As I fold and put away clean clothes and linens, I come up with a plan. I'll go to the post office and drop off Jill's orders, then I'll text Eric and see if he wants to come over for dinner. If he says yes, I'll stop at the butcher for a couple of steaks, pick up a bottle of wine, and maybe a nice dessert from Artsy Tartsy.

DESPITE THE PLEASANT DAY, I drive to Water Street because I don't fancy walking home with my arms full of steak, wine, and dessert.

I park behind Knitorious. Eric's car isn't here, and I feel a pang of disappointment even though I know it's Monday morning, and he's at work.

Because I have priorities, my first stop is Latte Da to get a coffee.

Standing in line waiting to order, I reply to a text from April who wants to know why I haven't spoken to Eric yet.

"Hi, Mrs. Mar—Megan."

I turn around. "Hi, Justin. How are you? You're not working today?"

"I'm on a break," he replies. "Vanessa's not feeling well. She asked me to pick up Father Daniel's prescription from Pharmer's Market and drop it off at his house."

He holds up a small paper bag with the Pharmer's Market logo on it.

"Is Vanessa OK?" I ask.

"Yeah, she has a nasty cold. She says she can't expose Father Daniel to it, so she stayed home. He's out of blood pressure medication, though. She worries about him, so I said I'd take it to him."

"That's nice of you." I smile.

"Before I drop it off, I'll swing home and surprise her with an iced coffee and check on her. She's home alone. My parents went to visit my aunt and spent the night. They'll be back later today."

The line moves along, and it's my turn to order. I ask for a medium Coffee Crisp with extra whipped cream, pay for it, and move down the counter to wait. Behind me, Justin orders an Iced Coconut Latte with a shot of espresso.

"It's her favourite," he says to me as he pays.

He moves down the counter, and we wait for our orders together.

"Justin, can I ask you something?" I ask quietly.

"Sure." He shrugs.

"You know there's a rumour about you, right?" I whisper.

"You mean about me and Jill?" he asks quietly, rolling his eyes.

I nod.

The barista hands me my drink. I thank her, and another barista hands Justin his drink.

Outside on the sidewalk, I ask him if he knows how that rumour started or who started it.

"I have no idea," he says, shaking his head. "Jill didn't even like me. It never bothered Vanessa before, because she knows it's not true. Now that Jill's dead and people still talk about it, it upsets her because she doesn't like people talking bad about her friend."

"They were close," I empathize. "I'd be upset if people were gossiping about my friend. Especially if she couldn't defend herself. Why do you say Jill didn't like you?"

"Because she didn't," he replies flatly. "She told me."

"Really?" I ask.

"It's hard living with your parents when you're newly-weds. At first, it caused some tension between Vanessa and me. We argued a lot, and she wasn't very happy. Vanessa would tell Jill about our arguments and stuff, and Jill decided it was my fault, and I was making Vanessa unhappy. I ran into her one night while she was walking Cardinal, and I was leaving the pub. We walked along Water Street and past the church together. She lectured me the whole time about how I take advantage of Vanessa, how Vanessa's not happy, and it's my fault, and if I'm not careful, Vanessa will leave me. She didn't like me."

"I can see why you'd think that," I agree. "Did Vanessa defend you? Did she ask Jill not to interfere?"

He shakes his head. "I told her to let it go. They had to work together, and Jill was one of Vanessa's only friends. Anyway, if Vanessa defended me, Jill probably would've said I made her do it, and she would've hated me more."

"Fair enough," I say.

"It was nice talking to you, Megan, but my break is almost over. I want to get this coffee to Vanessa, and I still have to go to Father Daniel's house."

I hold out my hand. "I'll drop off the prescription, you go surprise your wife with coffee."

"Are you sure?"

I nod and wiggle the fingers of my outstretched hand.

Justin hands me the pharmacy bag, and I drop it in my tote bag. "I'll drop it off after I stop by the post office."

"Thanks! I really appreciate it."

He turns and walks down the street.

The post office is only a few doors down from Artsty Tartsy, so I stop in to pick up something sweet for after dinner.

"Did you text Eric yet?" April asks before the door closes behind me.

I shake my head. "I got distracted talking to Justin Grandin. Vanessa's not feeling well, and I said I'd drop something off at Father Daniel's for her."

She picks up a small white paper bag. "Let me give you a few meringues for him."

"What are those?" I ask, mesmerized and pointing to small dome-shaped cakes covered in a purple-mirrored glaze. "They're beautiful."

"Mini blueberry mousse cakes with blueberry mirror glaze," April replies smugly.

"I need them," I say.

"How many?" she asks.

"How many do you have?" I ask, half joking.

They're mini, so I take six. While April boxes them, we talk about the movie we saw last night and our appetizer before.

"That reminds me," April says, carefully placing the last mini blueberry mousse cake in the confectionery box. "I was telling T about Saxon Renaud, and she said he's the French person who was in here telling people about Jill and Justin having an affair."

"For sure?" I ask.

She nods. "For sure. The umbrella makes him hard to forget. Also, he has a Facebook account, and I showed her his profile picture to be certain." She looks at me and smiles.

Huh. Saxon is the source of the rumour? It makes sense. If Jill knew a secret about him, he'd want to discredit her so people wouldn't believe her if she told. Also, if Saxon killed Jill, an affair would conveniently distract suspicion from him to her rumoured boyfriend.

Justin says he and Jill walked along Water Street and past the church. The rumour is that they were canoodling at night near the church. Saxon could easily have seen them without them seeing him. Especially if Jill and Justin were having a heated discussion about how Justin treats Vanessa.

Before I leave Artsy Tartsy, April and I agree to have lunch on Wednesday and finally go to Stop Guac & Roll. I pop my head in the office and say a quick hello to Tamara, then leave.

Father Daniel's driveway is full of cars, so I park on the street in front of his house. On my way to the door, I take the prescription bag out of my tote bag and carry it with the bag of meringues.

I ring the doorbell and almost immediately, the big wooden front door opens.

"Hey." He smiles.

"Hi," I say, taken aback. "Why are you here? Is Father Daniel OK?"

Eric nods. "He's fine."

He stands aside so I can enter the house. I glance behind me before I go inside to confirm that none of the three cars in the driveway are Eric's. I would have noticed if Eric's car was here.

"It's getting crowded in here," Eric's colleague says, looking at him. "I'll meet you at the car."

Eric nods to her, and I move out of the doorway so she can leave.

I look past Eric toward Father Daniel's recliner. It's empty.

"He's in the other room," Eric explains.

I nod. This is awkward.

"I was planning to text you after I leave here," I tell him. "I know you're busy, but when you have time, can we talk? I understand If you're too busy with the case and everything."

Stop rambling, Megan.

"When and where?" Eric asks.

"Madame Martel! How are you?"

He knows my name, and he's speaking to me in English. He must be having a good day.

Father Daniel shuffles toward me with his walker. An older lady, who I recognize because she comes into Knitorious occasionally, walks next to him. She watches him with the same level of vigilance you would watch a baby who's learning to walk. She must be one of the church volunteers.

"Hi, Father Daniel! I'm fine. You're looking well. How are you feeling?"

"Fit as a fiddle," he says in his thick French accent, positioning himself in front of his reclining chair. "Come sit with me for a while." He gestures to the wing chair next to him and pushes the button on his reclining chair to lower himself to a seated position.

"I have your blood pressure medication," I tell him.

The volunteer takes the bag from me.

"Thank you," she says. "Vanessa phoned to say you'd be dropping it off. She said he should have one pill right away."

The volunteer disappears into the kitchen with the pharmacy bag.

"Is that Mr. Martel?" Father Daniel asks, looking at Eric.

Maybe he's not having such a good day.

"No, Father Daniel, this is Eric. Do you remember Eric? He was here a few days ago."

Father Daniel looks confused for a moment, then smiles.

"Do you need to speak to him?" I ask Eric quietly.

"No, I was hoping to speak to Vanessa, but she's not here," he replies barely above a whisper.

The volunteer reappears from the kitchen with a glass of water and one pill. She puts them on the TV tray in front of Father Daniel. He obediently puts the pill in his mouth and has a sip of water.

"I just came by to drop off your medication and bring you a few meringues," I say, holding up the other white paper bag.

"I'll get you a plate, Father Daniel," the volunteer says as she takes the bag from me, once again on her way the kitchen.

Again, Father Daniel asks me to sit with him. I slip off my shoes.

"I have to get going," Eric says. "My partner is waiting for me. I need to go to the station and get my car."

"I'll text you in a little while." I smile.

"Any time." He winks, then he looks at Father Daniel. "It was nice to see you, Father Daniel. Have a nice day."

"Thank you." Father Daniel waves.

I'm sure he doesn't know who Eric is.

I sit in the wing chair next to Father Daniel and wonder if he still has that Judge Judy episode with the dog custody fight on his PVR.

The TV is on, and he's watching Wheel of Fortune on mute. The volunteer returns from the kitchen with three meringues on a plate. She puts the plate on the tray in front of Father Daniel. He looks at the cookies and smiles. He gestures to me, offering me one. I shake my head and smile.

"I'll only stay for a minute," I say to the volunteer. "He asked me to sit with him, and I hate to say no."

"Well, since you'll be here for a few minutes, would you mind keeping an eye on him while I run down the street?" she asks.

Does she mean literally run down the street?

"Sure." I smile.

"Thank you!" She slips her shoes on by the door and takes Cardinal's leash off the hook on the wall.

Cardinal! I was so flummoxed when Eric answered the door, I didn't notice that Cardinal isn't here.

"Did Cardinal escape?" I ask, nodding at the leash in her hand.

"Yes!" she replies, laughing, "Father Patrick ran after him and tracked him down but doesn't have his leash. He's hanging on to him by the collar. I'll drive the leash over and pick them up."

She leaves and I don't think Father Daniel notices she's gone.

That explains the third car in the driveway. Eric and his

friend were in one car, the volunteer is in another, and the third car must belong to Father Patrick.

This might be my only opportunity to get Father Daniel alone and ask him some questions. And he knows who I am, so I'm hopeful he's having a somewhat lucid day. I'll try it, and if he seems at all distressed, I'll stop.

"Father Daniel?"

He looks at me. "Yes, dear?" He smiles at me. He has kind eyes.

"Do you remember when you told me you gave money to Jill so she could get away from the bad guy?"

Please, don't let hearing Jill's name upset him.

"Her husband," he says assuredly, nodding his head.

"Rob?" I ask, surprised by his confidence.

"The other husband," he says matter-of-factly.

"Her first husband?" I furrow my brow.

"No, the other husband," he clarifies. "Vanessa's husband."

"Justin?" I ask.

"Yes! Justin," he confirms.

"Justin Grandin?" I verify.

In an unexpected role reversal, I'm confused and Father Daniel seems quite confident about what he's recalling.

"He came here a few days before I gave her the money. He was yelling and calling her names. He was mean to her," Father Daniel explains.

"Justin was mean to Vanessa?" I ask, dumbfounded.

"Justin was mean to Jill. He never came to see Vanessa. He only came when Jill was here, and he was mean." Father Daniel looks at me. "Justin's a bad guy."

"Thank you for telling me," I say to Father Daniel.

He squeezes my hand and smiles at me with his kind eyes. Then he pushes a button on the remote to unmute Wheel of Fortune and bites into another meringue.

Whoa. Could the rumour be true? Were Jill and Justin

having an affair? Was Justin blackmailing her? If Justin killed her, why didn't he take the money? I'm still missing something.

I watch Father Daniel drift off to sleep, still holding a half-eaten meringue, and wonder if the few moments of lucidity he invoked to convey to me what happened between Jill and Justin left him exhausted. Was he lucid? He seemed sure of himself, but Justin coming here to yell at Jill doesn't make sense. Surely, he's confused.

My phone dings inside my tote bag. Quietly, I find the phone in my bag and unlock the screen.

April: You didn't text me! Did you and Eric make up?

Me: I ran into him but he had to go—work stuff—I told him I'll text him. I've been watching Father Daniel because Cardinal escaped. Will text him when I leave here.

I hit send and turn the volume down on my phone so it won't wake Father Daniel if it rings again.

There's a commotion on the porch. I look through the window and see Father Patrick looking disheveled, the volunteer, whose name I should know but don't, and Cardinal, who looks both tired and happy at the same time.

I grab my tote bag, open the front door, and step onto the porch, closing the door silently behind me.

I tell Father Patrick and the volunteer that I need to get going. I let them know Father Daniel is asleep in his chair and suggest they might want to take Cardinal through the side door so they don't wake him. Father Patrick is worried that Cardinal will escape again and wants to take him in the front door. The volunteer wants to take him through the side door. I say my goodbyes and leave them to figure it out.

In my car, I plug my phone into the console and the screen unlocks automatically. I have a text I didn't hear because I'd turned the volume down on my phone,

Connie: Are you near the store? I was there earlier picking

up something I forgot and I think I left the door unlocked. Could you check?

Me: The front door or the back door?

Connie: I'm not sure.

She's not sure which door she used?

Me: I'll check.

Connie: Now?

Me: Yes, now.

Connie: Thank you. Now I can stop worrying.

This text conversation is weird. Why did Connie have to pick up whatever she forgot today? How can she not remember which door she used? Where is she that she can't check the door? Why does she want me to check right now? It's not like stores in Harmony Lake are ever robbed.

I turn the volume up on my phone so I don't miss any more texts and head to Knitorious to make sure the doors are locked.

CHAPTER 16

THE PARKING LOT behind Knitorious is empty except for the Wilde Flowers delivery van. Wilde Flowers is our local florist. They're next to Knitorious. We share a wall and a parking lot.

I walk toward the back door, listening for the chirping sound that confirms the car is locked as I press the button on my key chain. I slip my cell phone in my pocket and tug on the back door. Locked.

I unlock it, go inside, walk straight to the front door and try to open it. Locked. Both doors are locked, just like they were when I left on Saturday. Was Connie really here today?

I walk through the store and the kitchenette to the back door. I reach for the handle to open the door and flinch when the handle turns just as I'm about to grip it.

"Hi again," I say, startled.

"Hi again, yourself," Eric says.

"That's twice today you've surprised me on the other side of a door." I say, trying to ease the tension between us.

"I guess it is." He smiles.

"I'll get out of your way," I say, awkwardly sidestepping around him to get to the parking lot. "Why are you here in the middle of the day?"

He lets the door close without going inside, and now we're both in the parking lot.

"Connie asked me to come by and check the doors. She said she was here earlier and thinks she left a door unlocked."

"Really?" I raise my eyebrows. "That's why I'm here. Both doors were locked, by the way. Why would she ask you? She knows you work on Mondays."

"She said you were watching Father Daniel and couldn't leave. She was worried and asked me to check right away."

"It's a trap," I explain. "She finagled to get us to run into each other."

"Connie wouldn't do that... Would she?" he asks. "Why would she want us to run into each other?"

"I didn't tell her I was with Father Daniel. I hadn't spoken to her all day until she texted asking me to check the store," I tell him.

"How did she know you were there?"

"April texted me while I was there. I told her I was watching Father Daniel for a few minutes. She must have told Connie. She also must have told Connie what I said to her about yesterday. Connie's a worrier and a fixer, and this is her way of getting us to talk."

He looks skeptical. His phone dings, and he looks at it.

"Is it work? Do you have to go?" I ask.

He shakes his head. "It's Connie, she wants to know if I checked the store yet."

As his thumbs type a response, he lowers his phone and moves next to me so I can read their conversation.

Connie: Have you checked the doors yet?

Eric: Yes. Everything is locked up tight.

Connie types a response, and we watch the screen, waiting for it to appear.

Connie: Did you run into Megan, by chance?

"Told you," I say, looking up at him.

In the sunlight, the honey-coloured flecks in his eyes are more distracting than usual. Don't stare, Megan.

"What should I say?"

"Do that thing where you answer the question without actually answering the question," I urge. "I'm sure it'll frustrate her as much as it frustrates me."

His thumbs type.

Eric: Was Megan supposed to be at the store?

"How's that?" he asks.

"Perfect," I reply.

A reply from Connie pops up on his phone.

Connie: No. Thank you for checking.

Eric returns his phone to his pocket, and my phone dings.

Connie: Did you check the store?

I tilt the phone so Eric can read it.

"You were right," he concedes, laughing.

Me: Yes. It's all good. Both doors are locked.

We wait a few seconds, watching the screen while Connie types.

Connie: Was Eric home by chance?

Me: Were you expecting him to be home in the middle of a workday?

"Well done," Eric says proudly.

"Thank you," I reply, "I learned from the best."

Connie: Oh, right. Thanks for checking the doors.

I lock the screen and slip my phone into my jacket pocket when it dings again. I pull it out and look at the screen.

"Connie again?" Eric asks.

I shake my head. "No. It's Vanessa. She's thanking me for dropping off Father Daniel's meds."

I type a quick response telling her it wasn't a problem, and I hope she feels better and is back on her feet soon. The typing icon pops up. I wait for her response.

It doesn't make sense.

"What is it?" Eric asks. "You look confused."

"I am confused," I reply. "Did you catch up with Vanessa after I saw you earlier?"

"No, I called her phone, but she didn't answer. She never answers when I call her phone. Then I called the landline at the Grandin house, and she answered. She said she has a cold and isn't well enough to talk to me today," he explains. "I even brought a female officer with me because I can tell she's uncomfortable around me."

"That's what Justin said too. Vanessa has a cold and stayed home so Father Daniel wouldn't catch it. But look at this." I tilt the phone upward so Eric can read the text.

Vanessa: Thanks! My ankle already feels better, and the swelling is going down. Stupid stairs! Hopefully, I'll be back at work tomorrow.

"Huh!" he says. "What are the odds she has a cold and a sprained ankle?"

"I don't know, but something doesn't feel right."

Eric looks at his watch. I slip my phone in my pocket.

"Do you have to be somewhere?" I ask.

"Not if you want to talk," he replies.

"What do you want first, a statement or an apology?"

"Apology?" he asks. "Megan, you have nothing to apologize for."

The breeze is at my back, blowing my hair into my face. He brushes a few stray curls behind my ear, and I resist the urge to lean my head into his hand.

"Yes, I do," I tell him. "I shouldn't have gotten angry at you for doing your job, and I shouldn't have driven off and left it like that. I'm sorry."

He takes my hand, which makes me feel kind of hectic inside. Then I remember the one-word text reply I sent him and try to explain how that happened, but he's stroking the top of my hand with his thumb which flusters me, so I ramble off a convoluted, incomplete sentence. "And then when you texted me, I wanted to text you back because I didn't want to leave you on read, but my thumb slipped, and April's subwoofer was really loud…"

"It's OK, Megan." Eric interrupts my never-ending sentence; his voice is quiet.

I lean in for a hug, and he wraps his arms around me, enveloping me tightly. I slide my hands inside his suit jacket and up his back, careful to avoid his holster. He's warm and comfortable and safe. He smells like a forest after it rains. His chest expands when he takes a deep breath, and when he exhales, his entire body relaxes. He feels soft and solid at the same time.

"I'm sorry my job makes everything more complicated." He kisses the top of my head.

"We're good?" I ask.

"Yeah, we're good." He sounds relieved. "I thought you wanted to talk to tell me you don't want us to see each other anymore."

I pull away and look up at him. "Why would you think that?"

He shrugs. "Because my job complicates everything, and maybe you decided it's not worth it. It wouldn't be the first time. There's a reason the divorce rate among cops is so high."

Oof! I forgot his marriage ended because his job caused stress in their relationship. I hate that I triggered his biggest insecurity, even if it was unintentional.

"Hey, you two!"

I turn, and Phillip Wilde, the owner of Wilde Flowers, is climbing into his delivery van. I wonder how long he's been out here.

"Hey, Phillip." Eric waves.

"Hi, Phillip," I say.

He waves, climbs into his white van that's covered in painted flowers and turns the ignition.

"Why don't we talk upstairs?" Eric gestures toward the

door with his head. "It's warm up there and there aren't any neighbours."

I collect the mini blueberry mousse cakes from my car and follow Eric upstairs to his apartment.

Though almost five months have passed, it still takes me a moment to get over the shock that this isn't Connie's apartment anymore. The place is completely different now, and it almost feels like she never lived here.

Connie's style is sophisticated and elegant. She likes light neutrals with bright accents, lots of plants in coordinating white pots, furniture with rounded edges and comfy seating.

Eric's aesthetic is more stylishly foreboding. The walls are a light, neutral colour, but they're the lightest thing in the apartment. Everything else is dark, muted colours. His sofa and chairs are dark brown leather. His coffee and end tables are dark brown wood. The throw rug under the coffee table is a deep forest green. He has a few family photos on the walls and tables in chunky, black, wooden frames.

Connie used the second bedroom as a guest bedroom, and it had the ambience of a New England bed-and-breakfast. Eric uses the second bedroom to house his weights and treadmill with a spare bed pushed against one wall like an afterthought.

I put the confectionery box on the coffee table and sink into the leather sofa. Eric's phone rings, and he answers it.

"Yes…Uh-huh…Yup…OK…Right…That would be great…Thanks for calling and letting me know… Have a great day." He hangs up and brings me a glass of water from the kitchen.

"All good?" I ask when he hands me the water.

He nods. "Saxon Renaud's umbrella isn't the murder weapon."

He takes off his suit jacket and loosens his tie.

"You hoped it would be?" I ask.

He picks a cake out of the box and disappears into his bedroom.

"It was a shot in the dark," he says loudly from the other room, "but it was worth a try. The tip of his umbrella is in line with the description of the murder weapon the coroner provided. He has a motive and a history of intimidating Jill."

Eric comes back into the living room, wearing a pair of beige Dockers and a dark blue polo shirt. He's carrying his notebook and pen and joins me on the sofa.

"Does this mean he can have his umbrella back? He accused me of getting you to take it from him." I bite into my second mini blueberry cake.

He shrugs one shoulder. "Eventually. I'm not in a hurry to return it. If he wants to poke anyone in the meantime, he can get another umbrella." He finds a blank page in his notebook and clicks the top of his pen to open it. "When did he tell you I had his umbrella? That's where I was yesterday when you texted me from Rob's house, I was interviewing Saxon and collecting his umbrella."

I tell Eric about my conversation with Saxon and Lisette before the movie last night. I also tell him about Lisette offering Saxon first refusal on Father Daniel's house, and her suspicion that he might be Jill's killer. Then I tell him why April and I suspect Saxon is the source of the rumour that Jill and Justin were having an affair.

"I didn't realize Saxon and Lisette know each other that well," he says.

"Me neither, but there's no proof that anything was going on between Jill and Justin. If Saxon made up a rumour about them having an affair, he could just as easily lie about seeing Vanessa's car at Father Daniel's house the night Jill died." I surmise.

"I don't think he was lying about that," Eric explains. "That's why I want to speak to Vanessa. In his statement,

Saxon said the car in Father Daniel's driveway had a doughnut on the rear driver's side."

"Oh," I say, dismayed that Saxon might be telling the truth. "I don't know which tire it was exactly, but I was there on Saturday when Justin took Vanessa's car to have the tire replaced. She said she'd been driving around on a doughnut since the previous Sunday."

He nods. "I know. I tracked down the tire transaction."

"You really have been busy. Collecting umbrellas, taking statements, searching houses, tracking down tires. I hope you're not overdoing it," I worry out loud.

"I'm fine." He shakes his head, dismisses my concern, and changes the subject. "But I'd be better if I could ask Vanessa a few questions and talk to her in-laws again. They must be the most socially active seniors in Harmony Lake. They're away for the night every time I try to reach them."

"They've been in Florida for six months," I remind him. "They have a lot of catching up to do with friends and family."

Eric asks me about my visit to Rob's house. I tell him how I discovered the phone, and the conversation Rob and I had after I found it. Diligently, he asks questions and takes notes.

"I don't know if it slipped Rob's mind that he'd searched Jill's office for the phone after she died, or if he intentionally lied to me when he said he hadn't been in her office since she died," I say, inserting my opinion amongst the facts. "But he sounded so sincere when he told me how difficult it was to be in her space. I don't think it was a lie. I think he's tired, overwhelmed, and got confused."

"I still can't eliminate him as a suspect, but I also don't have any evidence he was at the scene," Eric says.

"I took screenshots of the text conversation on the mystery phone," I confess. "And a screenshot of the phone number it was communicating with. I haven't called or texted the number, but I'm tempted."

"I figured you took photos." He nods. "Don't contact the number, please."

"I won't," I assure him.

"If it's the killer, you could be in danger if they know you have their number. It's a burner. We haven't been able to trace it to anyone."

"A burner? Like the user discarded it?" I ask.

"Possibly," Eric explains. "It's a prepaid phone. Whoever bought it paid cash. It's not registered to a cellular plan. The user pays cash for minutes and loads them onto the device so they can use it. Whoever has—or had—this phone knows how to not be found. They only turn the power on when they use it, they never use it to connect to wi-fi or search the internet, and they have the location services turned off. We tried triangulating the phone number, but they used it at various locations and were careful to not have another cellular device with them—or if they did, the other device wasn't turned on."

"Can you explain the last part again, but like I'm a civilian, please?"

"We have the phone number, so we can look at the call history and see when the phone was used. To see where it was used, we check the local cell phone towers to see which ones it pinged." He pauses.

"I'm with you so far," I say.

"We can also search to see if any other phone numbers pinged off the same towers on the same dates at the same times. If another number pings off the same tower at the same time, on more than one occasion, maybe it isn't a coincidence. Maybe the owner of the burner phone has another phone in their pocket. A phone that's connected to a cellular plan."

"Can you trace the burner phone to the store where it was purchased?" I suggest.

Harmony Lake only has one store that sells cell phones, and Harmony Hills only has a few.

"Burner phones can be purchased anywhere," he explains. "Corner stores, local buy and sell websites... They can be difficult to trace. This one was purchased at a convenience store in the city a couple of months ago."

"Who would be well-informed enough about using burner phones to avoid being tracked?" I wonder out loud.

"Criminals." Eric answers flatly. "People having affairs and people who disappear and don't want to be found."

People who don't want to be found!

This means something, but what? A surge of certainty rises in my belly. I haven't connected the dots yet, but I'm working on it.

CHAPTER 17

Tuesday, April 7th

I reach for the printer beneath the counter and pick up the online orders I printed. Then I remove the Easter egg checklist from my planner and put it on the counter. As soon as Marla gets here, I'll start delivering the eggs, in batches, to the stores.

"You can't come with me today, Sophie," I explain to her. "I have to carry the bags of eggs, and I won't have a free hand for your leash. Also, some stores don't allow dogs."

She perks up her ears and wags her tail.

"I know, I can't imagine a store without a dog in it, either," I tell her.

I walk to the door, unlock it, and turn the sign from CLOSED to OPEN.

Sophie immediately trots to the front door and bounces excitedly while tippy-tapping her paws.

"Is someone here, Soph?"

The bell above the door jingles, and Eric walks in with two coffees.

"Good morning," he says, putting both coffees on the

counter. "Good morning, Sophie." He crouches down to rub her and tell her how pretty she is.

"Good morning," I say. "I'm glad you're here. I've been thinking about our conversation yesterday..."

"Which conversation?" he interrupts, alarmed.

"About the phone I found at Rob's house," I clarify.

"Oh, right," he exhales.

"Remember when you told me the laptop at Father Daniel's house was used to search for information and resources for victims of domestic abuse?" I ask.

"I'm listening," he replies.

"Someone fleeing domestic abuse definitely wouldn't want to be found. They would be diligent about using a burner phone to plan their escape. They would have a lot at stake because being found could kill them."

"You're suggesting the person Jill was talking to doesn't want to be found because they're in danger?" he probes.

"Maybe she was helping victims of domestic abuse to get out of their abusive situations safely," I theorize.

Eric fixes his gaze down and to the left, a thing he does when he's connecting mental dots. I sip my Coffee Crisp while I wait for him to finish contemplating what I said.

"It's possible. Jill's phone was always used either at her house or Father Daniel's house. She also left the power on when she wasn't using it. She wasn't the one who was trying not to be found. She was always reachable." He looks at me. "So, the money was for someone she was helping?"

"Maybe." I shrug. "I'm not sure how the money fits in. Every time I think I'm on to something, the money doesn't make sense. Maybe she helped someone, and their abuser found out and confronted her."

"It's a good theory. I'll look into it. Thank you." Eric smiles.

"There's one more thing, but it doesn't make much sense, and my source might be confused," I say.

"Is your source Father Daniel?" he asks.

I know Father Daniel's forgetfulness makes him an unreliable witness, and what he told me seems far-fetched, so I debated whether to mention this to Eric at all.

I nod. "He seemed lucid yesterday."

"Except for when he thought I was Adam," Eric reminds me.

"Right, except for that," I agree. "I asked him again who the bad man is. He insisted, confidently and more than once, that the bad man is Justin Grandin. He said Justin came to the house when Vanessa wasn't there and yelled at Jill. He said Justin was mean and threatened her. But he must have it wrong."

"Why do you think he must have it wrong?" Eric asks. "Is there a reason other than his dementia?"

"Vanessa and Justin both told me their transition to married life wasn't easy. They both say they argued and didn't get along very well. They also both admit that Vanessa confided in Jill about it. So, the more I think about it, the more I wonder if Father Daniel heard Vanessa confiding in Jill or maybe witnessed Justin and Vanessa arguing and confused the events in his head. And mixed up the people involved."

"You don't sound sure," Eric responds. "It almost sounds like you're looking for reasons Father Daniel might recollect it incorrectly."

"Maybe," I agree. "I told you it might not be very helpful."

"Even if he was certain, I don't think a statement from him would be admissible. Any lawyer would use his dementia diagnosis and accounts of his symptoms to have it thrown out." Eric checks the time on his watch. "Are you free for dinner tonight?"

"I can be," I tease. Then I take his hand and summon my serious, concerned face. "The real question is, are you free for dinner tonight? This case has you working around the clock. You won't solve anything if you burn out. Maybe you should take some time to relax. We can see each other when you're less overworked. I don't want to be another demand on your time. I'm not going anywhere."

"I have to eat and seeing you is my downtime. Even if I can't get away for very long, at least we can say hi and spend a little time together."

"I'd like that. I still owe you dinner," I remind him. "Text me when you know what time you can come over, and I'll time it for your arrival."

"I can't wait. I'll text you later." He and his to-go cup of coffee open the door, leave, and close the door behind them before the bell above it stops jingling.

I check my list and head to the back room to collect the first several bags of Easter eggs on my list. The bell over the door jingles while I'm gathering the bags, signaling that either Marla has arrived for work, or there's a customer in the store.

"Good morning, my dear!" Connie sings from the cozy sitting area where she's greeting Sophie.

I place the bags of Easter eggs on the coffee table beside her.

"Good morning." I bend down to hug her. "Why are you here? You're not on the schedule today. Is Marla sick?"

Connie flicks her wrist in that familiar, dismissive way she does. "No, everybody's fine." She stands up. "Marla and I talked about it, and we decided that she would help you deliver the eggs, and I would stay here and take care of the Tuesday morning tasks. Have you checked the voicemail and the email yet?"

I shake my head.

"Thank you, but are you sure you don't want to enjoy your day off?" I ask.

"Archie is making lasagna today," she replies, walking behind the counter. "I'm happy to be here while he indulges his inner chef. He said to tell you he's dropping off a lasagna for you before the store closes."

"That's thoughtful of him," I say.

"He's also making one for Father Daniel, Rob and the kids, and Ryan."

Ryan is Archie's son.

"Wow, he's really embracing this cooking hobby."

"Yes, he is," Connie agrees, nodding and looking through the online orders I printed. "Each new hobby lasts about two weeks. We have about one week of cooking left."

Her face lights up, and she raises her eyebrows when she sees my coffee on the counter. I walk over and pick it up. I take a sip, then smile at her.

"Did Eric bring you that?" Connie asks.

"He did," I confirm.

"Does that mean you two worked out your differences?" she asks with a hint of triumph in her voice.

I nod. "Yeah, it was weird, though. When I came to check the store yesterday after you texted me, he was here."

"What a happy coincidence," she says coolly.

"It was," I agree. "He said he was here to check the store too."

I glare at her.

She glares back.

It's a standoff. We stare at each other, waiting to see who will give in and speak first. It won't be me. I'm determined to wait her out.

"I didn't interfere," she finally concedes, breaking the silence. "I nudged."

"Right," I say, "you nudged."

"April said you were having trouble stepping over your pride, or fear, or something—she wasn't sure what it was—

but I knew if you and Eric were in the same room alone, you'd figure it out." The hint of triumph in her voice has morphed into smugness.

I nod and take another sip of my coffee.

Connie points to my coffee. "And that coffee proves I was right."

"We would have worked it out anyway," I reassure her. "But I appreciate your concern."

"Well, I'm glad I could expedite it." She puts her hands on my shoulders. "My dear, you two are the slowest-moving couple ever. If this relationship progresses any slower, it will go in reverse. He's obviously smitten with you, and you practically turn to goo when he's around. Why are you both so hesitant?"

Wow, don't sugarcoat it, Connie. Say what you mean.

"I don't know," I admit, throwing up my hands in frustration. "I literally haven't dated in two decades and have no clue what I'm doing. Eric makes a big deal about not rushing me because he doesn't want to scare me off. His marriage ended because his job caused stress in their relationship, and he's worried history will repeat itself. It's not like we can separate his work from our relationship when I practically trip over dead bodies on a regular basis, and I'm always either a suspect or a witness in whatever case he's working."

My jaw and shoulders relax from the relief of saying it out loud.

"Oh, Megan!" Connie opens her arms. "Come here, my dear." We hug and she sways while she rubs my back in that maternal way that moms do. "You two will figure it out, but you have to talk."

"Good morning, Eric!"

My heart leaps into my throat. My eyes open as wide as they can. Connie and I pull away from each other, and I look at her, wide-eyed and panicked.

Connie looks back at me, also wide-eyed, her mouth agape. She shakes her head in disbelief.

I speed walk toward the kitchenette, passing Marla on my way.

"Good morning, Megan!" she says in a chipper voice.

"Morning, Marla," I utter, already past her.

I stop dead in my tracks and cover my mouth with my hand when I enter the kitchenette and see Eric. He's sitting on the stairs that lead to his apartment and rubbing Sophie.

I was so engrossed in my conversation with Connie, I didn't hear Eric come in, and I didn't notice Sophie leave the store and come into the kitchenette.

My heart is beating in my ears. I drop my hand from my mouth. "I didn't hear you come in."

"Apparently," he says.

I'm not sure if there's a hint of a smile on his face, or If I want there to be so I'm convincing myself I see one.

"Is everything OK?" I ask.

He stands up. "I forgot my notebook and pen." He pulls them both from his breast pocket to show me, then puts them back. "I ran upstairs to get them. I parked out back, that's why I came in through the back door."

The back door that doesn't have A BELL above it. Yet.

I take a deep breath and let it out.

"How much did you hear?" I ask, my voice quiet and cautious.

"Connie knew if we were in the same room we'd figure it out," he recites. "I wasn't being sneaky or listening on purpose. I was coming down the stairs when I heard my name, and it got my attention."

I now understand that when people say they wish the earth would open up and swallow them whole, they mean it.

"Eric, I'm sorry. I truly don't make a habit of talking about us to other people." I shake my head and throw my hands up in frustration. "I feel like I keep messing this up. First Sunday, now this."

"I'm not mad," he promises. "I just wish you'd said it to me."

The bell over the door in the store jingles, and I look over my shoulder. There's at least one customer in the store. I close the door to the kitchenette, but it's hardly soundproof, and the people in this town have a sixth sense for detecting private conversations. They'll be browsing the yarn on the back wall and listening to us in under a minute.

I look back at Eric. As if reading my mind, he opens the back door and gestures for me to step into the parking lot ahead of him.

"I was planning to talk to you," I tell him after he lets the door close behind him. "After Jill's case was over. When you were less busy and less stressed."

"This is what I mean when I say it's hard to be with a cop," he explains, taking both my hands. "There will always be a case. I'll always be busy, and I'll always be stressed. You'll always wait to talk to me because you're worried about how busy and stressed I am. I'll stop talking to you about the stressful parts of my job because I won't want you to worry. After a while, there will be too much unsaid, and you'll resent me for being busy and stressed, and resent that we never talk. There will be a huge disconnect between us and…"

He shrugs, his voice trailing off before he finishes his last sentence.

"I get it," I tell him. "How do we make sure that doesn't happen?"

"That's what we need to talk about," he replies. "Do you want to talk now or later?"

"Megan!"

Eric and I both look toward the back door at Wilde Flowers and see Phillip carrying floral arrangements to his van. "When are you going to drop off my eggs? I set aside time today to stuff them."

"Hi, Phillip," I say. Eric and I both wave. "Soon. I was waiting for Marla to show up, and she just got here."

Phillip gives me a thumbs up and closes his van door.

I look back at Eric.

"Later," I reply. "I have to deliver these eggs before the entire WSBA comes looking for me."

CHAPTER 18

MARLA and I are two hours in, and just over halfway done with egg deliveries.

Living and working in a small, tight-knit community means knowing everyone and stopping to say hi, talk about the weather, and ask about their kids, spouse, parents, pets, recent surgery, recent trip, hobby, and whatever else is important to them. Then taking the time to answer when they ask the same about you.

Besides the usual small talk, the shock of Jill's murder is still recent, and everyone is scared, sad, and full of theories. The most popular theory so far is that her younger boyfriend killed her because she wanted to break up with him.

Other, less common theories include Jill interrupting an attempted burglary at Father Daniel's house—obviously perpetrated by someone from either Harmony Hills or the city, because a local would never do such a thing. Also, Rob finding out about the younger man Jill was allegedly seeing, following her to a rendezvous with him, confronting them, the boyfriend running off, Jill and Rob arguing, and Rob killing her. I really hope their kids don't hear this theory. Or, Father Daniel seeing her outside with Cardinal and, unable to recognize her because of his dementia, believed she was dog napping Cardinal, gained a sudden surge of adrenaline and strength, killed her, then immediately forgot because of his illness.

We're about to walk into Charmed and Dangerous, the local jeweler, to drop off eggs when a lady farther down the sidewalk waves at Marla.

"Hi, Trudy!" Marla waves, then looks at me. "It's Trudy. From book club."

"I'll go into Charmed and Dangerous and drop off eggs to Winston. You stay out here and say hi to Trudy," I tell her.

"OK," Marla replies. "If you're not back when I'm finished talking to Trudy, I'll be delivering eggs to Old School." She points next door to the antique store.

"Sounds good," I say.

I LEAVE Charmed and Dangerous twenty minutes later, with my amethyst and diamond ring freshly cleaned, and having learned that Ruby, Winston's red Eclectus parrot, loves pomegranate. I even got to feed her some. Highlight of my day, so far.

I look up and down the street and spot Marla talking to a man about four stores down. Walking toward them, I realize the man she's speaking to is Saxon Renaud. Why does it feel like he's everywhere I go? He's wearing his cuffed khakis with the ironed crease, penny loafers—I'm not close enough to confirm pennies—and a peach-coloured, v-neck sweater over a white-collared shirt. Noticeably absent is his umbrella.

"Hello again, Mr. Renaud." I smile, approaching him and Marla.

"Ms. Martel," he nods. "Are you following me?"

Seriously, Saxon?

Marla laughs, and he laughs with her, so I laugh too.

"I was about to ask you the same question," I tease.

We all laugh again.

"Well, it was nice seeing you, Saxon," Marla says. "I'll see you on Sunday."

"Very good, Marla. Have a nice day." He smiles at Marla, then sneers at me. "You, too, Ms. Martel."

"Bye, Mr. Renaud," I call after him in an extra cheerful voice.

Something about that man rubs me the wrong way.

"I haven't been into Old School yet," Marla tells me. "As soon as Trudy left, boom! There was Saxon."

We turn and walk back toward Old School.

"Why will you see him on Sunday?" I ask.

"We attend the same church," she explains. "In fact, remember when I told you someone from my church told me that rumour about Jill and the younger man she was supposedly seeing?"

I nod.

"It was Saxon," she declares.

I knew he was the source of the rumour!

We walk into Old School, and the bell over the door jingles.

Artie, a boisterous extrovert, comes out from behind the counter to greet us. I hand him a bag of eggs, and we talk about today's weather, the chance that it might rain on Saturday and dampen the egg hunt, and what everyone's plans are for Easter.

When Marla and I turn to leave, I see an ornate, antique walking stick leaning against a roll-top desk.

"That walking stick looks like it belongs in Mr. Grandin's collection," I say, nudging Marla's arm.

"Oh, it does," she agrees.

"It does belong in Mr. Grandin's collection," Artie pipes in from behind us. "He found it at an antique store in Florida. They didn't have room for it in the car on the trip home, so he asked the antique dealer to package and mail it to Harmony Lake. He had it shipped to Old School, in case it arrived before he did. I'm giving it a cleaning before Mr. Grandin picks it up."

"It's lovely," I say. "It'll be a nice addition to his walking stick collection."

"It's not just a walking stick," Artie says, walking over and picking it up.

He grips the stick with one hand and the handle with another, and in one smooth motion draws a sword from inside the walking stick.

"A sword," Marla observes. "How clever."

"Yes," Artie begins. "Swordsticks, as they're called, became popular in the late eighteenth and early nineteenth centuries in England. It was no longer acceptable for a gentleman to carry his sword in public, but a gentleman wanted to be sure to have his sword with him at all times, so he would conceal it inside a walking stick."

"I didn't know that," I say. "Mr. Grandin showed me another walking stick with an umbrella inside it and told me about one that conceals alcohol, but I didn't know they also hid swords."

"Oh yes," Artie confirms. "Umbrellas, pool cues, swords, alcohol... Walking sticks were used to hide all kinds of things. Swords and umbrellas are the most popular, though. Mr. Grandin has quite a few of both in his collection. I'm sure he'd love to show you if you're interested."

"Our book club once read a book set in the Victorian era, and the female lead character hid her sword in an umbrella," Marla says.

"Oh yes," Artie agrees. "Men used walking sticks and ladies used umbrellas to hide things."

"It was nice seeing you Artie, but the rest of Water Street is waiting for their eggs, so we have to get going," I say as Marla and I head for the door.

When Marla and I run out of eggs, we return to Knitorious for a break before we reload and finish our deliveries.

I take Sophie for a quick, midday walk, then settle in to hold down the fort while Connie and Marla go for lunch together.

True to her word, Connie cleared the voicemail, answered all the emails, and processed and packaged the online orders.

With not much for me to do, and no customers in the store, I collapse onto a sofa with a cup of coffee and pull out my phone to see what I missed while Marla and I were delivering eggs.

The first message is from April.

April: Are we still on for lunch tomorrow?

I type a reply:

Me: Yes. Who's driving?

April: I'll meet you there. I have to go straight from lunch to pick up Zach for his orthodontist appointment.

Me: OK, see you there.

The next message is in the family group chat with Hannah, Adam and Me.

Hannah: Psych 101 exam done!

Adam: Well done! Can't wait to see you on Sunday.

I reply.

Me: Yay! Only one more exam to go!

A message from Eric.

Eric: I can be at your place at 7. Can I bring anything?

Me: Sounds good. Just yourself.

And finally, Adam.

Adam: You forgot to take your half of Hannah's Easter candy. Also, we need to firm up our plan for Saturday/Sunday.

Me: I can pick up the candy tomorrow at your office. We can talk then. What time works for you?

Three dots appear and I watch the screen while Adam types a response.

Adam: After 1 p.m. I have a lunch thing.
Me: K. See you then.

I collect the rest of the bags of Easter eggs from the back room and put them on the coffee table, along with the online orders that Connie prepared, so they're ready to go when Connie and Marla get back.

I look around at the tidy, smoothly running store. "It's like I'm not needed here, Soph."

Sophie wags her tail at me and jumps up on the sofa.

"I agree, Soph. We should relax," I say, sinking back into the sofa.

I pick up the socks I'm working on and knit. I finish at least an inch of the leg by the time Connie and Marla come back from lunch.

"Hi, ladies," I greet them. "How was lunch?"

"It was lovely, my dear," Connie replies.

I put away my knitting and get up from the sofa.

"Marla," I say, "thank you for helping me with the egg deliveries this morning, I really appreciate it. I only have a few bags left to deliver, and I can deliver them alone. Why don't you stay here and take it easy?"

"Are you sure, Megan?" she asks. "I don't mind."

I shake my head. "You deserve a rest. You've gone above and beyond the call of duty. Besides, stitch-fix is today, and Connie might need your help."

Stitch-fix is a weekly drop in program where knitters bring in their knitting mistakes and Connie or I help fix them. Marla's a great knitter, but she's not confident enough yet to manage stitch-fix on her own, so I make sure either Connie or I are here.

"I bought some Easter treats for the Knitorious eggs," Connie interjects, "and if it's slow, you and I can stuff them." Connie winks at Marla. "I made sure there are more treats than eggs."

I gather the bags of eggs and the online orders and pound

the pavement, making the rest of the deliveries, chatting with my fellow Water Street business owners and neighbours, then stopping at the post office to drop off the online orders.

I open the post office door and hold it open while a petite, white-haired lady leaves the post office.

"Megan," she says, "I was hoping to see you today."

"Hi, Lisette. How are you?" I let the door close without going inside.

"I'm fine," Lisette replies. "I'm running a few errands for Rob before I meet up with Father Patrick. We're going to look at an assisted living facility, then we're going to my brother's house for dinner."

"How is Rob?" I ask. "I haven't spoken to him since Sunday."

She shrugs and tilts her head. "As well as can be expected, I suppose. Both kids are home now, and I think he's relieved that they're all together. But he's not ready to face...this...yet." She gestures vaguely around her.

"I understand," I say, nodding. "This town might be small, but it can be overwhelming. You're having dinner with Father Daniel? That's progress. How is the reconciliation coming along?"

"Again," she shrugs and tilts her head, "as well as can be expected, I think. Sometimes he knows who I am. Sometimes I have to remind him. He's always happy to see me, and he doesn't seem angry or bitter about our falling out."

"That's good," I say supportively.

"Listen," Lisette whispers, checking over one shoulder than the other, making sure we're alone.

I move closer to her so I can hear her.

"About my meeting with Saxon on Sunday evening," she says. "The one at the restaurant where you and your friend bumped into us."

She says "the one" like it was one of many meetings she's had with him.

549

"What about it?" I ask, switching the bag of online orders to my other hand and shifting my weight.

"I don't want you to get the wrong idea," she explains. "I agreed to meet with him because he's so impatient to buy my brother's house—you'd think it sits on an oil patch or something." She laughs awkwardly.

"Are you even in a position to negotiate with him?" I ask. "I thought Father Daniel doesn't have a power of attorney."

"He doesn't," she confirms. "Not yet. I'm working on it. It's a process, and it takes time. In the meantime, I don't want Saxon to pester Daniel or any of his caregivers, so I meet with him to discuss the house and humour him. As long as I keep him in the loop, he promises he'll stay away from Daniel."

"That sounds like coercion, Lisette," I observe. "He's bullying you into spending time with him, or telling him your family business, or whatever it is he wants."

Lisette nods. "I know. But right now, it's the path of least resistance. I don't need a battle with Saxon Renaud when I'm trying to reconcile with Daniel and have him assessed. And Daniel doesn't need Saxon Renaud pestering him when he's confused. Jill's death, and having different people in and out of his house to care for him, is overwhelming for him. He gets distressed easily and doesn't understand why."

I nod. "Have you told the police about Saxon's behaviour?" I ask. "If you mention it to Eric Sloane, he might be able to encourage Saxon to back off."

Lisette shakes her head. "I know what Saxon is like. I don't want to get on his bad side and risk him resuming his campaign to get my brother to sign sale documents.

"I get it," I tell her. "And I'm sorry you feel like you have to give in to his demands."

Saxon Renaud is a bully. I hate bullies.

CHAPTER 19

EMPTY-HANDED, I arrive back at the store. Connie is helping a knitter fix a hole in an heirloom baby blanket she'd like to pass on to her grandbaby. I hear Connie assure her the blanket is salvageable, suggesting the knitter leave it behind for a few days, so Connie can find matching yarn and figure out how to repair it. The knitter is happy to leave the blanket with Connie and grateful that it might be saved.

When the knitter leaves, Connie holds up the blanket. "What do you think?"

"I think the hardest part will be matching the yarn," I reply. "It's a beautiful blanket, but the fabric has aged and has a vintage look that will be difficult to match."

"I agree," she says. "But I think we have some crochet thread that might work."

Connie moves her glasses from around her neck to her face and, blanket in hand, walks over to the shelves where we keep the crochet thread.

"Where's Marla?" I ask.

"I sent her home," Connie replies. "She was exhausted, and it was dead in here. She might not mind delivering Easter eggs, but it took a lot out of her, and I could tell her feet were bothering her."

"Good call," I say. "You're right, it's dead in here today. Why don't you go home too?"

Connie checks her watch. "Are you sure, my dear?"

I nod. "I'm sure. We close soon anyway, and today was your day off. You're not even supposed to be here."

Connie picks up her cell phone. "I'll text Archie. He's supposed to pick me up when he drops off your lasagna."

When Archie arrives to pick up Connie and drop off my lasagna, we are in the cozy sitting area. Connie is working on her sweater while I inspect the heirloom baby blanket, trying to recreate the lace stitch pattern and write it down.

"Thank you, Archie. It smells wonderful," I say, taking the lasagna tray from him.

"You're welcome, Megan," he replies. "The heating instructions are written on the lid. I saw Eric earlier, and he says he's looking forward to having it for dinner tonight."

"Where did you see Eric?" I ask.

"He was at Father Daniel's house. I think he said he was looking for Vanessa," Archie replies. "I stopped by there earlier to drop off a lasagna."

"How is Father Daniel?" Connie asks him.

"And how's Vanessa?" I interject. "Is she feeling better?"

"Father Daniel and Vanessa weren't there," he responds to both of us at the same time. "There was someone there tidying the house, and she said Vanessa and someone from the church took Father Daniel into the city for a medical appointment. I left the lasagna with the lady who was tidying the house."

We wish each other a good evening, and Connie and Archie leave through the front door.

I check the time—less than an hour until I close the store— then take the lasagna to the kitchenette and put it in the fridge.

I pull out the broom, and I'm sweeping around Sophie and her dog bed when the bell over the door jingles. Sophie jumps to attention and trots toward the door excitedly.

"Hi, Mr. and Mrs. Grandin," I say, leaning the broom handle against a shelf of yarn.

"Hello, Megan," Mrs. Grandin says, closing the door behind her.

"How's your sweater coming along?" I ask.

"Nicely!" she replies. "I brought it with me so I can show it to you." She taps her knitting bag.

Mrs. Grandin puts her knitting bag on the counter and starts going through it.

"The real reason we stopped by, Megan," Mr. Grandin says, approaching the counter and standing next to his wife, "is to see your tenant, the detective."

"Oh," I say. "Is he expecting you?"

Other than me, I've never known Eric to question anyone at his apartment or at the store.

"No," Mr. Grandin shakes his head, "he isn't. But he's been trying to get hold of us. We're leaving for the city. We have tickets to a musical tomorrow. A matinee. We're staying with our son and won't be home until Thursday."

"Well, Eric isn't here. He rarely meets people here for work," I tell them.

"Where does he meet them?" Mrs. Grandin asks, visibly confused.

I shrug. "His office at the station, I think. Or their home. I'm not sure. I'll text him and let him know you're here. Why don't you sit down?"

While Mr. and Mrs. Grandin make their way over to the cozy sitting area, I text Eric.

Me: Mr. and Mrs. Grandin are here. They said you want to speak to them. They're going out of town tonight.

Eric: They're at the store?

Me: Yes.

Eric: OK. Be there in 15 minutes.

I tell the Grandins that Eric will be here soon. Mrs. Grandin shows me the back and most of the front of the sweater she's knitting.

"You're a fast knitter," I remark.

"Well, I get lots of knitting time in the car when we take our road trips," she explains.

Mrs. Grandin picks up her needles and continues knitting the front of the sweater.

"That's a nice walking stick." I gesture to Mr. Grandin's black, wooden walking stick with a silver handle.

"Thank you," he replies, skillfully pulling the handle and revealing the umbrella that's cleverly hidden inside.

His lower limbs may be slow and unsteady, but his upper limbs aren't.

"They made it in 1922 in Switzerland. The stick is ebony," he says proudly, then he slides the umbrella back into the wooden sheath.

"When I was at Old School today, I saw the walking stick you purchased in Florida. How many do you have all together?"

"Many more than I can use," Mr. Grandin laughs proudly. "I have over thirty, but only about a dozen are in regular rotation. Some are too valuable to use and…."

We're interrupted by the jingle of the bell over the door. I stand up.

"Here he is," I say to the Grandins, then I look at Eric. "It's almost closing time, so I'll lock the door and turn the sign. Then Sophie and I will head out, and you three can talk in the store."

Sophie's two front paws are on Eric's knees to get his attention. He bends down and rubs her quickly. I walk past them, lock the door, and turn the sign from OPEN to CLOSED.

"Can I get anyone tea or coffee before I leave?" I ask.

"I'd love a cup of tea, Megan," Mrs. Grandin replies, putting her knitting aside. "Let me help you."

As she moves to get up, I raise my hand in a stop motion. "It's fine, Mrs. Grandin. I've got it."

"I'll have tea, too, please," Mr. Grandin says.

I nod and walk toward the kitchenette, collecting the broom and my tote bag on the way.

I fill the kettle and plug it in, get the teapot from the cabinet above the sink, drop two tea bags in it, and put it on a tray. I collect two mugs, two spoons, sugar from the countertop, and milk from the fridge. While I'm in the fridge, I see the lasagna and put it on the counter so I won't forget to take it with me when I leave. I'm plating some tea biscuits when Eric comes in.

"Sorry about taking over the store," he says from the doorway to the kitchenette.

I smile. "Don't worry about it. It's closing time, anyway. And what's the alternative? Your apartment?"

"I only ever question my favourite witness in my home," he says, smiling.

I smile. He's referring to me.

"Is that our dinner?" he asks, pointing to the lasagna.

"It sure is," I confirm. "It needs about 45 minutes in the oven, so If I put it in about half an hour from now, will that give you enough time to finish up here and get to my place?"

I pour water from the kettle into the teapot.

He nods. "I'll take the tray, you leave."

I don't need to be told twice. I call for Sophie, then realize she's sitting right behind me. I attach her leash and leave through the back door.

TODAY WAS A LONG DAY, and I'm ready for it to be over. I don't know if it was all the walking and socializing, or if the busy-ness of the last few days is catching up to me, but I'm tired.

I feed Sophie, turn on the oven to preheat, then change out of my clothes and into my blue, plaid, flannel pyjama pants, and long-sleeved, blue pyjama t-shirt. I put my hair up in a messy bun, securing it with the hair elastic on my wrist. After I slide the lasagna into the oven and set the timer for forty-five minutes, I fetch a wine glass from the cupboard and take a bottle of pinot grigio out of the fridge, along with a bag of Caesar salad.

The knock at the door excites Sophie, and she races out of the kitchen, barking.

"That was quick," I say, when I open the door.

"I only needed to ask them a few questions," Eric replies, stepping into the house. "They were eager to get on the road to the city, anyway. Most of the time I spent with them was making small talk and waiting for them to finish their tea."

Eric closes the door behind him, bends down to greet Sophie, and unties his running shoes.

"Great minds think alike." I gesture to Eric's outfit, then my own.

"Are you thinking of going for a run after I leave here too?" he teases, smiling.

"Definitely not," I assure him, shaking my head. "If you ever see me running, you should run, too, because something scary must be chasing me."

I'm not a runner.

Eric is wearing a pair of grey sweatpants and matching grey hoodie. He looks cozy and cuddly. This is the first time I've seen him in sweats.

"How did the egg deliveries go?" he asks, following me into the kitchen.

"Good," I reply. "I gather you weren't able to talk to Vanessa?" I yawn and cover my mouth.

I hold up a wine glass and he nods.

"No, she took Father Daniel to a medical appointment. I've left messages for her. I'll only have one glass of wine, in case she gets back to me, and I can talk to her tonight. I doubt I'll hear from her, though. She doesn't like me. Or maybe she doesn't like cops, I don't know."

He sounds tired. I hand him a glass of wine.

"It's not just you," I observe. "She was the same when Saxon Renaud visited Father Daniel's house. She stayed in the kitchen to avoid him. Maybe she has issues with authority figures." I take a sip of wine. "But her in-laws confirmed her alibi, right? I mean, I assume if they didn't, your conversation with them wouldn't have been so quick."

I grab a salad bowl and pour the bag of salad into it, then add the dressing and toss it.

"Their story is the same. They arrived home. Vanessa's car was there. Vanessa herself was in the house. They parked behind her. Their car was full of stuff, but they were too tired to unpack it, so they unpacked it the next day." He sighs, exasperated.

Eric follows me while I put the bowl of salad on the kitchen table, then we go into the family room and drop our weary selves onto the sofa.

"Do you still have Saxon Renaud's umbrella?" I pick up my knitting and start stitching.

He nods. "Why?"

"When Marla and I were dropping off eggs at Old School today, I learned that back in the day, women hid swords inside their umbrellas. I know you said the tip of his umbrella wasn't the murder weapon, but maybe there's a secret compartment or something, where the murder weapon is hidden."

"I hadn't thought of that," he says. "And I don't think the forensics people did either. If they did, they didn't note it in the report." He reaches into his pants pocket and pulls out his cell phone. "Do you mind if I text them quickly?"

"Go ahead," I reply, taking a long sip of wine.

He finishes typing his text message and tosses his phone onto the coffee table.

"No more work," he says, "not tonight."

"Unless Vanessa calls," I clarify.

"That's the only exception," he insists.

I turn on the TV, and we watch the news until the oven timer rings.

We eat on the sofa in front of the TV, channel surfing until we come across a home renovation reality show. We watch it and eat in silence.

After dinner, Eric puts the dishes in the dishwasher, and I cover the remaining lasagna and salad and put them in the fridge. I pour myself another generous glass of wine and him a glass of water.

"Are you too tired to talk?" he asks when I hand him his glass of water.

"Nope," I reply. "Are you?"

He shakes his head. Sophie whimpers from the back door.

"Want to take Sophie for a walk?" he asks.

I nod.

SOPHIE HAS A NICE, long walk, and Eric and I have an honest, overdue conversation. We set a few guidelines for how we'll communicate with each other from now on.

He won't presume to know how fast or how slow I'm ready to take things; he'll let me decide for myself. I won't avoid talking to him because I'm worried he's stressed or overwhelmed. Instead, I'll check in and ask him if he has the mental and emotional bandwidth to talk. He won't dismiss my concerns when I think he's working too hard, and we'll both admit when we feel stressed or overwhelmed.

Basically, we'll both stop being so concerned about scaring off the other person, and talk to each other about it instead.

"If you ever feel like I'm putting my job ahead of you, I need you to tell me," he says, nodding as if he's trying to convince me. "You always come first, before work."

"Got it," I say, unlocking the door when we get back from our walk.

He takes off Sophie's leash, and we go into the house.

We resume our positions on the sofa, this time with Sophie nestled between us. We watch another home renovation show, and I finish my glass of wine, too tired to pick up my knitting.

Next thing I know, Eric is nudging me awake.

"I need to get going," he says quietly. "You should go to bed."

He stretches his arms and blinks like he's trying to force his eyes to stay open. He must have fallen asleep too.

I nod and check the time. Midnight. Two hours past my bedtime. By the time I lift myself off the sofa, Eric is already at the door, tying his shoes.

"You're on your own for coffee in the morning." He winks. "I have an early meeting, but I'll swing by and say hi when I get a chance."

Yawning, I nod. We kiss each other goodnight and he leaves.

"Oscar, I'm going to bed," I announce to the empty house.

"OK, I'll arm the house," Oscar replies as Sophie and I make our way to the bedroom.

CHAPTER 20

WEDNESDAY, April 8th

"Good morning, my dear," Connie sings as she enters the store from the back room.

Late morning but still morning.

We hug, and when we pull apart, Connie grips my shoulders and inspects my face.

"You look less tired today," she observes. "Good night's sleep?"

"Yes," I agree, not realizing I looked tired yesterday. "Archie's lasagna helped. It was nice to have a home-cooked meal without having to cook. Please tell him his lasagna was delicious."

"Aww, thank you, my dear. He'll love that. All this positive feedback might extend his cooking hobby another week." She smirks at me.

I check the time. I have to leave soon to meet April at Stop Guac & Roll, and Sophie needs her midday walk before I leave.

"Will you be OK if I take Sophie for a quick walk?" I ask.

"Of course, my dear." Connie waves me away like a fly.

"You go ahead. I think I'll get a start on this heirloom baby blanket repair." She collects the baby blanket, crochet thread, and my notes on the stitch pattern from underneath the counter.

I attach Sophie's leash, slip on my jacket and sunglasses, and leave through the backdoor.

"Megan!"

I spin around. "Hey stranger," I say as he jogs toward me from his car.

"I was just coming to see you," Eric says, catching up to me.

"Can we walk and talk?" I ask. "I have lunch plans, and I'm in a bit of a hurry."

We turn the corner onto Water Street, cross the street, and walk in the park.

"I heard from forensics about the umbrella," he says.

"And?" I ask, stopping while Sophie sniffs the base of a tree.

He shakes his head. "No hidden weapon in Saxon's umbrella."

"Oh," I reply, disappointed.

"I don't like him either," Eric tells me.

"They took the umbrella apart and put it back together again that quickly? You only texted them last night."

"I think they use x-ray, actually," he clarifies.

I tilt my head to the side and look at him. "That would be easier than my idea."

We talk about our day. I tell him I'm having lunch with April, then visiting Adam at his office. He tells me he's hoping to finally track down Vanessa today and catch up on paperwork.

"I brought some leftover lasagna and salad for you," I tell him as we cross the street to go back to the store. "They're in the fridge in the kitchenette."

"Thanks." He winks. "I'll probably have it for dinner."

We say goodbye, I go in through the front door, and he walks around to the parking lot.

WHEN I ARRIVE at Stop Guac & Roll, April is already there, sitting at a booth, waving to get my attention.

"Hi!" I extend my arms, and she stands up to hug me.

"How are you? I feel like we haven't seen each other for ages." She sits down, and I slide into the booth across from her.

"I know," I say. "I'm sorry." We saw each other yesterday when I stopped in at Artsy Tartsy to deliver eggs, but I was on a mission and didn't stay long.

"Did you see the group text from Adam?" April asks.

April, Tamara, Adam, and I have a group text thread. Adam texted a suggestion that we share a truck. Neither Hannah nor Rachel have enough stuff to fill up an entire truck on their own, but they each have too much stuff to move with just a car.

I nod. "I did. It's a great idea."

Our server delivers tortilla chips and salsa to our booth. She takes our drink order and, impressed and shocked that we studied the menu before our visit, she takes our food order too. While we wait for our food, we talk about our girls and how their first year of university flew by. Parenthood is weird like that, the days are long, but the years are short. We're excited to have them home and can't wait to see them.

I haven't seen Hannah since she went back to school after Reading Week, and it feels like a lifetime. Facetime is great, but it's not the same as seeing your child in the flesh, hugging them, touching them, and even smelling them.

"I even miss the piles of laundry all over her room," April jokes.

The server brings our food, and I immediately cut my

chiles rellenos in half and transfer one half to April's plate, while she moves half of her chimichangas to my plate. We shuffle the dishes around the table so the quesadillas are conveniently between us.

The food is fantastic. We compare notes and enjoy our lunch, while talking in between mouthfuls about everything from the rumours about Jill's murder, my intense dislike of Saxon Renaud, to the Harmony Lake Easter egg hunt on Saturday.

We're almost finished eating. I'm about to tell April how I wish I'd thought ahead and worn leggings, instead of my wide legged, cotton pants with a button and zipper, when a familiar voice gets my attention.

"Ladies," he says in a dulcet tone.

"Hi!" I reply. "What are you doing here? I thought you had a lunch thing?"

Adam bends over, and we kiss cheeks.

"Sit." April pats the vinyl bench beside her after she and Adam exchange cheek kisses.

He slides into the booth next to April.

"My lunch thing was here," he explains. "Friday is Lin's birthday, but it's Good Friday, and we won't be at work, so we took her out for her birthday lunch today."

Lin is the receptionist at the office where Adam works. The "we" refers to the other professionals he shares office space with, an accountant, an insurance broker, a financial planner, and a therapist.

I nudge my plate toward him, and he takes a chimichanga.

"Can you stay for a minute, and we'll confirm the plan for this weekend?" April asks.

"We're just leaving," Adam gestures toward the door. "We came in one car, so if I stay, I'll miss my ride."

"I'll drive you back to the office," I tell him. "I'm going there anyway to pick up Hannah's Easter candy."

Adam leaves the booth briefly to tell his colleagues to

leave without him, then slides back in next to April and helps himself to a wedge of quesadilla.

After more nibbling and friendly conversation, April announces she has to leave in five minutes to pick up Zach for his orthodontist appointment.

"OK," Adam says, "I've booked the truck. I'm picking it up on Sunday morning at 7 a.m. in Toronto."

"I've booked the hotel for you and me," I say, looking at Adam. "Two rooms with a late check in on Saturday night."

"We aren't staying at a hotel," April informs us. "T's cousin lives in Toronto, and we're crashing there for the night."

"We'll leave right after work on Saturday. That should get us to Toronto about 10 p.m.," I say.

"One car or two?" April asks.

We hesitate while we hem and haw.

"Coming home, one car is enough, because two of us can ride in the truck. But getting there, five of us squeezed into one car is a tight fit," Adam suggests.

"Especially when three of you are so tall," I point out, referring to Adam and Zach who are both six feet tall and April at five feet, ten inches.

"You're right," April agrees, nodding. "And at least two of us would have to squeeze into the backseat."

"Two cars it is." I tap the top of the table.

"T, Zach and I in one car, and you and Adam in the other. Done." April picks up her phone from the table. "I have to go."

Adam slips out of the booth so April can get out. They hug and exchange an air kiss. Then I stand up and hug her goodbye. April leaves, and Adam and I slip back into the booth.

"As soon as I get the bill, we can leave," I tell him.

He checks his phone as I wave down the server and ask for the bill.

"We won't need a storage unit," I assure Adam on the drive to his office. "Between my basement, the garage, and your storage unit at the condo, we have more than enough room to store Hannah's stuff for the summer."

"You're right," he agrees. "I just thought a storage unit would be easier than unloading the truck at April and T's house, then your house, then my condo. I have to return it to the rental place in Harmony Hills by 7 a.m. Monday morning."

"We'll be fine," I say, turning the car onto Mountain Road. "We'll be back in Harmony Lake by 5 p.m., and we have six adults plus Zach to help unload. We'll unload, then you can drop the truck off after dinner. I'll follow and drive you back."

"Ryan and Eric are helping too," Adam says. "Lin volunteered Ryan, and Eric offered when he came to the office on Monday to take my statement about my conversation with Jill."

Ryan is Archie's son. He and Lin have been dating for about six months.

I slam my foot on the brake pedal, and we lurch forward.

"Are you OK?" I blurt out after narrowly avoiding hitting Cardinal.

"I'm fine," Adam reassures me. "Are you OK?"

I nod. "Yeah, I'm OK. Is Cardinal OK?" I loosen my grip on the steering wheel.

I'm sure I didn't hit him. He came out of nowhere, lumbering across the street in front of my car. I think I stopped less than a foot away from him. Too close for comfort. My heart is pounding.

"There he is!" Adam throws his hand in front of my face and points to my left.

I look over, and sure enough, there's Cardinal. He's meandering casually from tree to tree, stopping to sniff each one as he comes to it.

I pull the car over on the wrong side of the road, unbuckle my seatbelt, open the door and step out, leaving my door open. I open the back door and whistle. Weakly. A pathetic, feeble whistle. I've never been a strong whistler.

"Cardinal! Here, boy!" I bellow, slapping my knees.

I call his name again and wave my arms over my head, trying to get his attention.

From inside the car, Adam lets out a shrill, loud whistle, causing Cardinal to stop sniffing and look over at us.

"Wanna go in the car? Who wants to go for a ride in the car? C'mon Cardinal." I use the high-pitched, enthusiastic voice that always gets Sophie excited.

It works. He gallops over and leaps into the backseat. I close the door behind him before he can escape again and get back in the car.

"It would be a community service if the town got together and extended the height of Father Daniel's fence," Adam declares as I pull away from the curb.

"He digs under the fence to escape too," I remind him.

"Well, something needs to be done. At least three times a week I hear stories about someone returning him to Father Daniel's house. One of these days he'll cause an accident."

I pull into Father Daniel's empty driveway. "Wait here," I say as I unbuckle my seatbelt and open the door.

"Are you talking to me or Cardinal?"

"Both of you," I clarify, closing the car door behind me.

I ring the doorbell and wait. I wait longer than I normally would because Father Daniel isn't quick. When no one comes to the door, I knock. Then I walk along the porch, and using my hand to minimize the glare, I squint into the living room window. The TV is on, but no one is in the room. I walk in the other direction and cup my hands around my eyes so I can peer through the kitchen window. The kettle is plugged in, but again, there's no one in the room.

Something's wrong. The knot in my stomach makes its presence known, and a sudden, confident urgency swells inside me. I need to get inside the house. Now.

I lift the mat by the door, no key.

I stand on my tippy toes and try to reach the top of the door frame. I'm too short.

"Everything OK, Meg?" Adam calls, getting out of the car.

I turn to him and shake my head. "Something's wrong. Can you feel around for a key?" I point upward.

Adam takes the stairs two at a time and sweeps his hand across the top of the door frame, coming away with a key.

"Maybe Father Daniel isn't home," he suggests.

"No," I say shaking my head again. "He can't go out alone, and whoever is with him would've let Cardinal in before they left."

I take the key from Adam.

"Maybe we should call the police and let them go in." He's using his calm, reasonable voice.

This isn't the time for calm and reasonable.

"Father Daniel could be hurt," I insist, "or worse." I jab the key toward the lock.

Adam swipes the key from my hand.

"I'll go first." He's using his authoritative voice now.

How cute.

"Adam, he has dementia. He hardly ever sees you. He might get scared. I've seen him a lot lately, and I'm not as big and...imposing as you. I think I should go." I swipe the key back from him.

"Fine," he retorts, jabbing at his phone. "I'll wait inside the door. I have 9-1-1 dialed on my phone, and if anything happens, I'll hit Call." He turns his phone and points to the screen with 9-1-1 on it, showing me he's serious.

I open the door and let myself in, holding the door for Adam, who steps inside the house behind me.

"Father Daniel!"

I walk toward the kitchen and look in. No one.

"It's Megan Martel. Adam is with me, and we have Cardinal!"

I walk toward the dining room. Empty.

"Father Daniel! Are you here?"

A sound. What was that?

"Listen!" I hiss, looking at Adam. "Do you hear that?" I whisper.

We stand in silence for a moment.

"I don't think anyone's here, Meg."

I put my index finger to my lips. "Shhhhh."

Quietly, on the balls of my feet, I walk toward the repurposed main floor den that is now Father Daniel's bedroom. I pass the washroom on my way and pause to peek in the open door.

I gasp and grab the door frame for support.

"Adam!"

CHAPTER 21

Hɪs ꜰᴏᴏᴛsᴛᴇᴘs ɢʀᴏᴡ ʟᴏᴜᴅᴇʀ as he gets closer to the bathroom.

"Get a blanket!" I yell.

His footsteps get duller as they move farther away, then grow louder again and faster as he runs toward the bathroom.

"It's OK, Father Daniel! You're OK." I lunge from the doorway to the floor next to him.

Father Daniel lays crumpled and shivering on the cold, tiled floor. He's on his side, partially covered by a towel. The towel rack from the wall is on the floor next to his head, a layer of drywall dust sprinkles his hair and the floor around him. He's moaning feebly and muttering unintelligibly in French.

"Here." Adam hands me the afghan from across the back of Father Daniel's reclining chair.

I lay the afghan over him. He's cold and clammy to the touch. I rub his arm and back through the afghan, hoping the friction will help warm him up.

"He needs an ambulance," Adam says, his cell phone already up to his ear.

He steps away from the door when he speaks to the dispatcher.

"Shhh. You're OK, Father Daniel," I say in hushed tones.

"Adam! I can't understand him, what's he saying?"

Adam, still on the phone, pops his head around the corner.

"He's muttering something in French," I explain.

Adam extends the hand that's holding his phone toward me. I take the phone and stand up. Adam takes my place on the floor next to Father Daniel. Now they're both muttering in French.

I answer the dispatcher's questions as best I can and make sure the front door is open for the first responders when they arrive.

As soon as the dispatcher lets me hang up, I run back to the washroom.

"He's confused," Adam says without looking at me. "But it sounds like no one showed up this morning. He tried to bathe himself and slipped while getting out of the bathtub. The towel rack came off the wall, and he fell. It doesn't look like it hit his head, but I can't tell and he's not sure. He says his hip hurts."

When the EMTs arrive, Adam and I retreat to the living room, giving them space to work.

"It's after lunch," I say. "He could have been laying there for hours."

Adam nods. "He can't spend another night alone in this house, Meg. I'm a mandated reporter. If the hospital doesn't report this, I have to."

A mandated reporter is a person who, because of their profession, is legally required to report any suspicion of abuse or neglect to the relevant authorities. As a lawyer, Adam is a mandated reporter.

"I know," I tell him. Then I remember. "The kettle!"

I rush to the kitchen with Adam following me, remembering that when I peered through the kitchen window, the kettle was plugged in.

I pull the plug out of the wall and pick up the kettle.

"Dry," I say. "He must have tried to make himself a cup of tea and forgot he plugged it in."

"Lucky the house didn't burn down," Adam states.

We both notice the schedule on the fridge at the same time. Vanessa should have been here this morning.

Adam looks at his watch, then points to the schedule. "It's almost 2 p.m. Someone else is scheduled to relieve Vanessa at 2 p.m."

Where are you, Vanessa?!

An EMT comes looking for Adam. Neither EMT speaks French, and they need a translator. They return to Father Daniel, and I'm alone in the kitchen. I pull out my phone and text Vanessa:

Me: It's Megan. Are you OK? I'm at Father Daniel's house and you're not here. Text back so I know you're OK.

I watch the screen, hoping to see the three dots that indicate Vanessa is typing a response. No dots.

I recoil when a hand touches my shoulder, shocked by my own jumpiness.

"What happened? Are you all right? I came when I heard the address over the radio."

"Hi," I say. "Father Daniel fell. I'm fine."

I hold up my phone so Eric can read the screen.

"Where is she?" he asks.

I gesture to the schedule on the fridge. "According to this, she should be here."

"Can you call her cell phone for me?" he asks. "She won't answer if she sees my number on her call display."

I nod and call her. It goes to voicemail immediately. I end the call and try again. Voicemail again. This time I leave a message.

"Hi, Vanessa. It's Megan Martel. I'm at Father Daniel's house, and I thought you were working today. Can you call me when you get this so I know you're OK? Thanks." I end the call.

I don't tell her about Father Daniel's fall because I don't want her to panic. I also don't want to make her so scared that she doesn't call me back.

Eric is talking to the EMTs who are rolling Father Daniel through the living room on a gurney. They cocooned father Daniel in a blanket, with another blanket on top of him. The cocoon wraps around his head like a hood. He looks tiny strapped into the gurney. There's an IV in one of his frail hands and an oxygen mask on his face. They stop at the door, and Father Daniel mumbles something in French. One of the EMTs moves the mask so he can mumble it again.

"His hip," Adam translates. Then he looks at me. "I'm going in the ambulance."

"I'll follow in my car and drive you home."

"Thanks," he replies quietly. "Also, he's asking for Lisette, his sister." He steps onto the porch and holds the screen door open for the EMTs while they wheel Father Daniel out of the house.

My phone dings.

"Vanessa?" Eric asks.

I look at the screen and see a text from Connie. I shake my head.

"Connie," I reply. "She wants to know what's going on. She heard there are emergency vehicles at Father Daniel's house, and that my car is here too."

I text her back.

Me: Father Daniel fell. He's on his way to the hospital. Adam went with him to translate. I said I'd follow and drive Adam home. Will you be OK if I go?

Connie: Yes! Marla is here, anyway. She's the one who told me about the commotion at FD's house.

Me: Thank you! Can you please text me the Grandin's phone number?

Connie texts me the number, and I call it from my cell phone. It rings and rings. The Grandins don't have voicemail. I hang up.

Eric and I are alone in Father Daniel's house, and it's eerily quiet.

"I have to go to the hospital," Eric says. "I'll need statements from you and Adam about what happened."

"Statements?" My heart pounds. "Will we be charged? For breaking into Father Daniel's house?"

"No," he says calmly. He rubs my shoulder and inhales deeply. "Heavy shoulders, long arms." He reminds me. "I need a statement because we were called, and I have to file an incident report. And just in case Vanessa not being here is somehow related to Jill's murder, I'm just covering all the bases."

I nod. "Adam and I were on our way to his office, and I almost hit Cardinal when… CARDINAL!" I grab his leash from the hook by the door. "He's still in my car."

Eric follows me outside, and we retrieve Cardinal from my car. We bring him in the house, and I give him fresh water. Glancing at the side door next to the kitchen makes me think.

"Eric," I say cautiously, still staring at the side door. "What if Vanessa *is* here? The same way Jill was here the day April and I found her."

He follows my gaze to the side door and raises his index finger. "Wait here."

He opens the side door and steps outside. I hear him walking around, then he comes back in the house and closes the door behind him, locking it.

"Nothing," he says.

We exhale loudly, relieved.

"I told Adam I'd go to the hospital and drive him home. If I hear from Vanessa, I'll text you."

"I'll probably see you there," he responds. "I'll call Lisette from the car and tell her what happened. I'll call Justin, too, and ask if he knows where Vanessa is."

We leave the house, locking the door behind us and placing the key on top of the door frame where Adam and I found it.

CHAPTER 22

IN THE EMERGENCY DEPARTMENT, I sit on a chair in the hallway outside Father Daniel's room, knitting on a sock.

I have four sock projects in progress. One in my bag, one at the store, one beside the sofa, and another one in my bag, in case I run out of knitting when I'm not near my house or the store.

I'm watching the doctors and nurses walk purposefully up and down the hall, coming and going from the various rooms.

Eric and Adam are with Father Daniel. I can't hear what they're saying, but I'm aware of the low drone of their voices.

A nurse goes in, then Eric and Adam come out.

"How is he?" I ask.

"Asleep," Adam replies. "He's disoriented and a little dehydrated. We're waiting for test results, but they think his hip is bruised, not broken."

"That's good," I say, realizing immediately that it sounds like I'm happy Father Daniel has a bruised hip. "I mean a bruised hip is better than a broken hip, right?"

"We know what you mean, Meg," Adam says. "I'm getting a coffee. Can I get either of you anything?"

Eric and I shake our heads. Adam disappears down the hall.

"Lisette's on her way," Eric tells me, sitting in the chair next to me. "And I called Justin. He's at work and he thought Vanessa was at work too. He sounded worried."

I nod.

We sit in silence until Adam returns with his coffee.

"I'll stay until Lisette gets here," Adam says, looking at me. "You can leave. Eric can drive me back to Harmony Lake, or I'll find my way home."

"I'll wait. It's the least I can do. If I didn't insist on going in the house, you wouldn't be here."

Adam opens his mouth to speak—probably to argue with me—when we hear Father Daniel's voice. He sounds agitated. The nurse comes out of his room.

"He's all yours," she says, smiling. "I'll be back in a few minutes to draw blood. Will one of you be here to translate for me? I need to ask him about his pain level too."

Eric and I point at Adam, the only French speaker among us.

"I'll be here," Adam confirms. Then he looks at Eric and me. "I'm going back in."

"I'll go with you," Eric says, getting up and following Adam into Father Daniel's room.

I knit for a few more minutes until I'm bored and stiff, then get up to stretch my legs.

Wandering up and down the halls, a familiar voice gets my attention.

"Hi, Craig," I greet Dr. Craig Pearson, Marla's son.

He's standing in the hallway, looking at an iPad screen. The nurse or doctor he was talking to is walking away.

"Hey, Megan! What are you doing here?" We exchange an air kiss.

"An elderly neighbour fell. I'm hanging around until his sister gets here."

We make small talk. I ask him how Amy, his girlfriend, and Tundra, her dog, are doing. He asks me how working with his mom at the store is going.

Craig is called away, and when he leaves, I have a clear view of the room behind where he was standing. Vanessa Grandin is sitting on the bed. She's wearing a blue hospital gown and has an ice pack on her wrist. I blink and do a double take, making sure it's really her. I knock gently on the open door. She looks up, and the muscles in her face tense up. Her expression turns to panic when she recognizes me. I step into the room.

"Hi, Vanessa," I say softly. "What happened? Are you OK?"

Beads of perspiration appear on her forehead and upper lip.

"I'm fine." She speaks quickly and laughs nervously. Her voice is shaky, and she looks uncomfortable in her body.

"Then why are you here?" I ask.

"It's embarrassing," she says with her shaky and too-fast voice. "I was getting ready for work and slipped on the stairs. I sprained my wrist and hit my head."

I look at the ice pack strapped to her wrist. "Again?" I ask gently. "Didn't you just sprain your ankle falling down the stairs on Monday?"

"I'm a klutz," she rationalizes. "Justin says I'm the only person he knows who can trip over things that aren't even there." Her laugh sounds more panicky than amused.

"Who brought you here?" I ask.

"I drove myself," she nods. "Justin had already left for work, and his parents are away until tomorrow."

A knock at the door makes Vanessa flinch. I turn around.

"Hi again," I say to Craig Pearson.

"Is this the neighbour you're here with?" he asks.

"No." I wave my hand. "Vanessa and I running into each other is a coincidence."

He smiles and approaches the bed where Vanessa is sitting.

"Your wrist isn't broken," he says to her, "but it is badly sprained. And I can't rule out a concussion. You can leave, but I can't let you drive yourself home."

"I'll drive her home," I offer.

"Is that all right with you, Vanessa?" he asks her.

She nods. "Yes."

"The nurse will be in momentarily to give you a prescription for the pain and the swelling, and then you can leave." He smiles, looking from Vanessa to me, then back to Vanessa.

Craig leaves, and Vanessa flips over the ice pack on her wrist.

"Why are you here, Megan? Dr. Pearson said you're here with a neighbour."

"Right." I hesitate. "Father Daniel had a fall..."

I put my hand on Vanessa's shoulder when she tries to get off the bed.

"Omigosh! Is he OK? Who was with him?"

"He'll be fine." I speak slowly, trying to work out what to say and how to say it as I go along. "He was alone when it happened, but Adam and I found him, and he's fine. He's here now."

"No one was with him?! I left messages for Father Patrick on his cell phone and his office phone. I even sent him a text. Where is Father Daniel? I need to see him."

Before she can try to get up again, the nurse comes in.

"Here you go, Vanessa," she says, handing Vanessa a piece of paper. When Vanessa reaches out to take the paper, the nurse takes her hand and looks in her eyes. "I hope we don't see you here again. I hope you stop having all these accidents. I wrote a phone number on the back of the prescription. They can help you." The nurse releases Vanessa's hand. Vanessa averts her gaze and looks down at the floor.

I realize that my instincts about domestic abuse being a

factor in Jill's death might be right, but I was focused on the wrong victim.

I look at the nurse's name tag. Jenna Singh. Jay's wife. Jay is an "alternate money lender," as he likes to call himself, in Harmony Hills and Harmony Lake. He helped me out when I was a suspect in a murder investigation.

"Do you need help getting dressed?" the nurse asks.

"No thank you," Vanessa replies. "I can do it."

The nurse turns to leave.

"Vanessa, do you want me to call Justin for you?" I watch closely for her reaction.

She looks terrified. Suspicion confirmed.

Shaking her head vigorously, she replies, "No."

"OK, I won't," I assure her. "But I need to tell you that when you didn't show up for work today, Eric called Justin looking for you."

"What?! Justin knows I'm here? He can't know I'm here."

"He doesn't know you're here," I reassure her. "We didn't know you were here. He only knows you didn't go to work."

"He'll figure it out," she says, grabbing her clothes and starting to get dressed. "I need to get out of here before he shows up."

"Do you want me to help you?"

"No, I can do it, but close the door so Justin can't see in when he shows up."

I step out of the room and close the door behind me. Jenna Singh is at the nurse's station working at a computer. I decide to introduce myself and hope she might answer a few questions for me.

"Hi, Jenna," I say, my voice chipper. "Are you Jay's wife?"

She stops typing and looks up. "Yes. You know Jay?"

"Uh-huh. I've met your gorgeous twin boys too," I tell her. I extend my hand. "My name is Megan Martel. Jay helped me out last year when a mutual acquaintance of ours was murdered."

"Are you the knitting lady?" A look of recognition flashes across her face.

"That's me," I confirm.

She extends her hand, and we shake. I ask her about her boys and how the house is coming along. She and Jay are building a home in Harmony Lake. She says it's coming along nicely, and they should be ready to move in by July.

"Can I ask you something, Jenna?"

She nods.

"I know you have a duty to protect patient privacy, but Vanessa is a friend of mine. Am I right that you suspect she might be a victim of domestic abuse? I understand if you can't tell me, but I have to ask. Vanessa isn't one to advocate for herself."

Jenna looks down at the keyboard and starts tapping on the keys.

"You're right," she says without looking up from the keyboard where she's now typing furiously. "I can't possibly comment."

"I get it," I tell her. "I'm sorry if I put you in an awkward position."

I turn to go back to Vanessa's room and check if she's finished getting dressed.

"Don't worry about it, Megan," Jenna says, causing me to turn back to her. She spins the monitor just enough for me to see it and looks me in the eye. "I have to check on a patient. I'll be back in exactly sixty seconds." And she's gone.

I think she just gave me sixty seconds to look at the computer screen, but it feels sneaky. Is this a trap? I look around. Everyone is focused on doing their own thing. No one is looking at me.

I lean over the desk and look at the screen. It's a history of Vanessa's emergency room visits since she moved to Harmony Lake. Bruises, broken rib, stitches, broken finger, concussion, broken collarbone. I don't know anyone that accident prone.

The magnitude of this situation hits me. Justin knows Vanessa isn't at home or at work. He'll be looking for her. He knows she's injured and will assume she's seeking medical treatment. He'll figure out she's here. If he's not here already, he's probably on his way.

I burst into Vanessa's room and close the door behind me.

"You ready?" I ask, grabbing her bag.

"Let's go," she says.

Walking down the hall, I stay a few steps ahead of Vanessa, checking our surroundings constantly for any sign of Justin. I turn the corner into the main lobby, thinking we're almost free and clear, when I see him. Justin walks through the automatic doors that lead from the parking lot to the main lobby.

I stop dead in my tracks and back up around the corner, intercepting Vanessa as she's about to round the corner after me. I guide her by the shoulders to the ladies' washroom a few feet away. Once inside, I lock the door. It's a single stall, no one else can come in.

"Justin's in the lobby," I tell her.

Tears fill her eyes, and her breathing becomes erratic.

"He'll find me." She sounds defeated.

"No, he won't," I tell her. "I know what he's doing to you, Vanessa, and I won't give him the chance to hurt you again."

The door is locked, but I lean against it, just in case. I pull my phone out of my tote bag.

"A friend of mine is in the hospital," I tell her as my thumbs move back and forth across the screen of the phone. "I'll get them to distract Justin while we leave."

I don't tell her my friend is Eric because she's either scared of him or doesn't trust him, and I don't want her to second guess our plan.

Me: I need a HUGE favour. Vanessa is with me. Justin is

in the hospital. Please distract him while we leave. Keep him away from the main door. He can't know she was here. Please drive Adam back to Harmony Hills, then come to my house. Vanessa will be there. Text me when it's clear.

Three dots. He's typing.

Eric: Looking for him. Hang tight.

"My friend is looking for Justin. They'll text me back when it's safe to leave." I get my car keys from my tote bag so I don't have to search for them when we get to the car.

Ding!

I look at my phone.

Eric: He's with me. Go. Text me when you're in the car.

"Let's go," I say, opening the washroom door.

I glance up and down the hall, just in case. When we get to the end of the hall, I turn the corner first, then gesture to Vanessa when I confirm it's safe. We do an awkward jog-trot to the car and lock ourselves safely inside.

"Deep breath," I tell her. "You're safe."

"Deep breath," she replies.

I plug my phone into the console and text Eric.

Me: We're in the car. Thank you. See you soon.

Eric: Text me as soon as you get home. Park in the garage. Lock and arm the house.

I send him the thumbs-up emoji and start the car.

CHAPTER 23

"How's your head? And your wrist?" I ask Vanessa as we merge onto the highway toward Harmony Lake.

"Sore," she replies, "but I'll survive."

"We'll figure out how to get your prescription filled once we get you somewhere safe," I tell her.

"Where are we going?" she asks.

"My house," I respond.

"I don't think I should go back to Harmony Lake, Megan. He'll find me."

"You'll be safe," I say. "Power your phone off so he can't use the signal to find you."

"It is off," she replies. "That's why he didn't know I was at the hospital. We have that 'find my friends' app on our phones. I know if my phone is on, he can find me."

"That was smart," I tell her. "You'll be safe at my house. I have a state-of-the-art security system, and it won't occur to Justin that you'd be with me, so I doubt he'll come knocking, anyway."

She inhales. "You underestimate him."

"Vanessa, did Jill know about the abuse?"

"She figured it out a long time ago," Vanessa explains.

"Her first husband was abusive. She recognized the signs almost as soon as I started working for Father Daniel." Then she adds quietly, "She was helping me leave him."

"Does Justin know she was helping you?" I ask.

"I don't think so. I don't see how he could. We were so careful. But one night they ran into each other when she was walking Cardinal, and she told him she knew. He didn't like that at all. Then when those rumours started about them having an affair, he was angry. He said if he found out who started those rumours, he'd kill them."

Surely, Justin didn't murder Jill because he thought she started the rumour. Why would Jill start a rumour about herself? A rumour about an affair with someone she didn't like?

We drive in silence for a while. From the corner of my eye, I see Vanessa wincing occasionally, leading me to believe she's in more pain than she admits.

When we get to the house, I drive around the block and Vanessa and I keep an eye out for Justin's car. There's no sign of him.

As we approach the driveway, I push the button on the remote and open the garage door. I pull into the garage and turn off the car, but leave the doors locked. I push the button on the remote again, and we wait in the car while the garage door closes. Then we get out of the car and enter the house through the garage. I tell Oscar to disarm the house. When Vanessa and I are both safely inside, I instruct Oscar to re-arm the house. I tell Vanessa to make herself comfortable in the family room. I walk around the main floor, closing the blinds and drapes, partly to keep out prying eyes and partly because of her possible concussion.

My phone dings.

Eric: You home yet?
Me: Just walked in the door.
Eric: Lock it. Turn on the alarm.

Me: Done and done.

Eric: Lisette just got here. Adam and I are leaving shortly.

Me: K. Drive safe.

Vanessa sees me texting and asks if everything is OK.

"Fine," I tell her. "I have to text Connie about closing the store and arrange for Sophie to get home."

Me: I just got home from the hospital. I can't go into details but something has come up and I can't come back to the store today. Can you and Marla close? And can you bring Sophie home for me?

While I wait for a response, I get Vanessa a glass of water and ask her if she's eaten today. She says she doesn't think so. I tell her I'll heat up some leftover lasagna for her.

Connie: Of course! April is here. She says she'll bring Sophie home. I'll lock up. Let me know if you need anything.

Me: Thank you! You're the best.

Vanessa winces and rubs her wrist. Before I make her something to eat, I fetch an icepack from the freezer, wrap it in a towel, and give it to her.

"Lay down, I'll cover you up." I say, reaching for the blanket on the back of the sofa.

Vanessa does as she's told and slides down the sofa until she's horizontal. I spread the blanket over her, then go into the kitchen to heat up a piece of lasagna.

Vanessa picks at her food but eats hardly anything.

When the doorbell rings, she jumps. I open the app on my phone and show her it's April bringing Sophie home.

"Hey Soph, who's a good girl?" I bend down to greet Sophie after she and April are in the house, and the door is closed and locked behind them.

"What's going on?" April mouths.

I gesture for her to follow me into the family room.

"Oh, hey, Vanessa," April says, shocked to see Vanessa on my sofa. "What happened to your wrist?"

"It's sprained," Vanessa replies.

"She might also have a concussion," I add. "Would you do us a favour and fill her prescription?"

"No problem," April says. "Where is it?"

"I don't want it filled," Vanessa blurts out. "You never know who is in the pharmacy when they call your name to tell you your prescription is ready."

"Who might be at the pharmacy?" April asks.

"Justin," I say quietly.

"I understand," April says, nodding. "I'll take it to a pharmacy in Harmony Hills, and I'll ask them to call my name instead. How's that?"

Vanessa nods and hands the prescription to April.

I walk April to the door and thank her as she leaves. I give Vanessa the TV remotes, then go into the guest bedroom to get it ready for Vanessa to spend the night.

When I come back into the family room, Vanessa is watching an episode of Friends.

"You're welcome to use my phone if you want to phone your family or anyone else," I offer.

"Thanks," she says, "but it's not a good idea. When Justin can't find me, he'll reach out to them. If I contact them, whatever I say to them will get back to him. They don't know what's been going on, and they like Justin. It wouldn't occur to them not to trust him."

"Why haven't you told them?" I ask.

Vanessa shrugs. "I don't really have much opportunity. Justin only lets me talk to them in front of him, and he monitors the call records on my cell phone, and the landline at his parents' house. One reason Jill brought the laptop to Father Daniel's house was so I could use it to email my family. But I didn't. I was afraid Justin would kill them, and me, if I told them."

That's twice Vanessa has mentioned killing someone, and Justin's name, in the same sentence.

Eric texts me to let me know he's in the driveway and asks me to text him when he can come inside.

"Vanessa, do you remember Eric? The detective who was at the house the day Jill died?"

She nods. "What about him?"

"He's in the driveway." I gauge her response. She looks mildly concerned. "He wants to come in. He's been at the hospital all afternoon. He'll be able to tell us how Father Daniel is doing."

"He texted you?" she asks.

I nod. "Just now."

"Is he the friend who distracted Justin at the hospital?"

"Yes," I admit. "He's a good person. I trust him."

"Fine," she says after a moment. "But what if I don't want to talk to him?"

"You can go into the guest room, and I'll tell Eric to leave." I gesture to the rest of the house. "But I hope you will talk to him. He can help."

I text Eric and meet him at the door.

"Hi, Vanessa, It's good to see you again," Eric says in a quieter than usual voice.

He keeps a respectable distance and hangs near the far wall.

"Hi," Vanessa replies. "How's Father Daniel?"

"He'll be fine." Eric nods, shifting his weight and leaning against the wall. "He has a bruised hip and a few other superficial bruises. The hospital is keeping him for a night or two while Lisette makes other arrangements for him."

"Thank goodness he's OK," she says.

"I spoke with Father Patrick," Eric tells her. "I know you tried to contact him to make other arrangements for Father Daniel's care today. He was in meetings all morning and didn't check his messages. He asked me to tell you he's sorry."

"It's not his fault," Vanessa concedes.

"What happened to your wrist?" Eric nods his chin toward her ice pack.

"Megan didn't tell you?" she asks suspiciously.

He shakes his head. "No, she didn't. But is it safe to assume since you wanted to avoid Justin when you left the hospital that he has something to do with it?"

Vanessa looks at me.

"I haven't told him anything other than you were with me, and we wanted to leave the hospital without Justin seeing you. Oh, and I asked him not to tell Justin that you had been to the hospital at all."

She looks at Eric and nods. "Justin did it."

I offer Eric a drink. He would like a glass of water. And I offer to switch Vanessa's ice pack for a new one. She accepts.

I come back with the water and ice pack, and I sit on the sofa beside Vanessa.

"What did you say to Justin to distract him?" Vanessa asks Eric.

"We've met before," Eric reminds her. "I said hi. I asked him what he was doing at the hospital. He told me you phoned him and asked him to come."

"That's not true," Vanessa says.

"I told him I'd been at the hospital most of the day and hadn't seen you. I made small talk until Megan texted, letting me know you were safely out of the building and in the car, then I asked him if he needed to file a missing person report for you. He said he must've misunderstood your message. We talked a little more, then his boss called him. There was a work emergency somewhere, and he had to drive into the city."

"Thank you for doing that. Justin warned me to never go to the hospital again. He was scared they'd catch on." Vanessa squirms and rubs her temple.

Eric raises his left eyebrow, and his jaw muscles tighten.

His angry face. I'm worried Vanessa will see it, too, and misinterpret it.

"April should be back any minute with your meds," I tell her, so she'll look at me instead of Eric.

Instantly, Eric lowers his eyebrow and relaxes his face.

"Vanessa," Eric says. "I need to ask you some questions about Jill. And about Justin. Would you prefer to speak with a female officer? I don't have to be in the room when you talk to her. And you won't have to go to the station if you don't want to."

"You can do it here," I suggest.

The doorbell rings, and Sophie zooms down the hall at full speed, barking. I get up, but Eric motions for me to stay.

"I'll get it." Eric pushes himself off the wall and walks down the hall.

"It's April," I say, showing Vanessa the app on my phone that shows me who is at the front door.

April comes in and places a pharmacy bag on the coffee table in front of Vanessa. "The pharmacist said if you take one now, you can take another one at bedtime."

"Thank you," Vanessa says, looking at April.

Vanessa opens the bag and inspects the pill bottle. She reads the label, then opens the bottle, and puts a pill in her mouth. She chases it down with a sip of water.

"May I lie down?" she asks, looking at me. "And it's OK, you don't have to tell him to leave." She points toward Eric.

"I'll show you where the guest room is," I say, standing up.

"Well, I should get going. If you guys need anything, you know where I am," April says, already at the door.

"Thank you," I say. "I'll text you later."

April leaves, and Eric locks the door behind her.

I settle Vanessa in the guest bedroom and come back to the family room. Eric is sitting on the sofa, with his feet on the coffee table.

"You were going to tell me to leave?"

I nod. "I told Vanessa if she was uncomfortable with you here, I'd tell you to leave." I shrug.

"I'm glad I get to stay," he says, gesturing for me to sit next to him.

I collapse onto the sofa and rest my head in the crook of his arm.

"Crazy day," he says.

I look up at him. "Thank you for trusting me earlier. At the hospital when I asked you to distract Justin. You could have asked a ton of questions, demanded to see Vanessa, or pulled rank as a cop, but you didn't. Thank you."

"You wouldn't have asked me if it wasn't important. You have good judgment. When you texted saying Vanessa was at the hospital, I thought back to Justin's response on the phone when I told him she didn't show up at work. I realized what I interpreted as worry might have been panic. And Vanessa's behaviour around me might be fear."

It sounds like the pieces fell into place for both of us around the same time.

CHAPTER 24

ERIC FEEDS Sophie while I heat up the last two pieces of lasagna for us.

"Did you take Adam home?" I ask.

"Yes, and I thanked him for giving up his afternoon to help." Then he adds eagerly, "Hey! Did you know Adam golfs?"

"Yup."

How could I not know that? We were married for almost twenty years. I place two plates of lasagna on the kitchen table and sit down.

"Right," Eric says, sitting down at the table "Of course you do. Well, he's a member at the Harmony Hills Golf Club, and he and I are going golfing." He smiles. "On a Saturday, when you're working," he adds.

I'm not sure how I feel about Eric and Adam being friends. Eric is new to town and doesn't have a lot of friends here. Adam's friends were mostly other lawyers from his firm, so when he left the firm, he left them too. I guess it'll be nice for them to have each other to golf with. It feels weird though.

"Cool," I say, trying to sound encouraging and not think about how weird it is.

I put a forkful of lasagna in my mouth.

"How did you and Vanessa find each other at the hospital?" Eric asks.

I finish chewing and swallow my food. Then I tell him everything, starting from when I went for a walk to stretch my legs up to Vanessa and I pulling into the garage. I leave out the part where Jenna walks away from her computer screen; she doesn't need her name brought into this.

After dinner, I load the dishwasher and turn it on, and Eric takes Sophie for a walk.

"Hey!" I say when Vanessa appears in the kitchen. "Can I get you anything? Are you thirsty?"

She nods. "Water would be great."

I gesture for her to sit at the table, then I turn to get her a glass of water.

"Are you hungry?" I ask, putting the glass in front of her.

She shakes her head.

"How are you feeling?" I ask.

She shrugs. Vanessa is an enigma. She either doesn't talk at all, or she talks a lot and shares very personal information.

"Where's Eric?" she asks, looking around.

"Walking Sophie," I reply.

She nods and has a sip of water. "If I talk to him, will you stay with me?"

"If I'm allowed," I respond. "I'm not sure what the rules are for these things."

As if on cue, the front door opens, and Sophie charges down the hall toward the kitchen. Eric follows shortly after. I reach down to stroke Sophie, who is panting and happy after her walk.

"Oh, hi, Vanessa, how are you feeling?" Eric asks, keeping some distance between him and the kitchen table where Vanessa and I sit.

"Better," she replies. "I can try to answer some questions if you want. If Megan can stay with me."

Eric's eyes narrow, and he looks to the side, contemplating Vanessa's offer. After a moment, he nods.

We decide the living room will be more comfortable than the kitchen table. When Eric excuses himself to get his notebook and pen, I excuse myself to get a glass of water and intercept him in the hallway.

"I promise I won't interfere," I whisper. "I won't ask anything. I'll even try not to react to anything she says."

"Thank you," he says silently.

I get my water and join Vanessa and Eric in the living room.

Vanessa confirms that Jill was helping her to leave Justin. Jill had a carefully constructed plan. Vanessa says they spent weeks getting all the pieces in place.

According to Vanessa, the ten thousand dollars in Jill's purse when she died was intended for her. She was meant to use that money—cash because there would be no paper trail —to cover her expenses until she arrived down east where her family lives.

"I would have paid him back, I swear," she insists.

They intended to carry it out on Wednesday night, but it didn't go as planned.

"I was supposed to pack my car with only the essentials," Vanessa explains. "Then Jill and I would meet at Father Daniel's house where I would abandon my car, and Jill would drive me to a women's shelter in the city. The shelter was expecting me, it was all arranged."

"Why Wednesday night?" Eric asks.

"Because Justin was spending the night at Tyler's place after the concert," she replies, "and his parents were still in Florida. I'm hardly ever alone. It was the only opportunity."

"But Mr. and Mrs. Grandin came home early," Eric prompts.

Vanessa nods. "I was packing the last of my things in my car when they pulled into the driveway behind me. I couldn't believe they were there. They could see that I was packing to go somewhere. When they asked me where I was going, and where Justin was, I told them he was at a concert with Tyler for the night and that I was leaving him because I wasn't safe, and this might be my only chance."

She composes herself and has some water. She nods at Eric, indicating she's ready to continue.

"What did they say when you told them?" Eric asks.

"They didn't believe me," she shakes her head. "You have to understand, they think their boys are perfect. They're blind to either of their sons having any flaws. We might live with them, but the Grandins are oblivious to what happens in their own house. She's always busy organizing their hectic social schedule, and he's always busy tending to all his collections. And Justin is careful. He's not always mean, but when he is, it's when they aren't around. Most of the time he's a sweet, loving guy."

"Why do you say they didn't believe you?" Eric asks.

"Because they told me I was overreacting. They said if Justin and I had an argument, I should stay and talk to him. They didn't get it," she explains. "They told me if I went through with leaving, they'd go in the house and call him and tell him. He would've come home."

"What did you do?" Eric asks.

Vanessa shrugs. "What could I do? I unpacked the car. Mr. Grandin helped me bring my stuff back into the house. I put everything back where it belongs, so it wouldn't look like I tried to leave. Then I went to bed."

"Did you contact Jill and tell her you weren't able to meet her?" Eric asks.

"No," Vanessa says, shaking her head. "My mother-in-law stayed close to me all night. And the cell phone I used to contact Jill was in my car, so I couldn't get to it without making them suspicious."

"Where in the car was the cell phone?" Eric asks, leaning forward, keenly interested.

"In the trunk," she replies. "Under that flap where the spare tire is hidden."

Forgetting my promise not to ask questions or show a reaction, I smack my forehead with my palm. Eric and Vanessa both look at me.

"Sorry," I mumble.

"What is it?" Eric asks.

I look at Vanessa. "Was the cell phone hidden with the spare tire four days before? On Sunday? When Justin changed your flat tire?"

Vanessa's jaw drops, and she closes her eyes. "Oh, my god. I never even thought of that. Yes, it was there. He would have found it for sure."

"He didn't react when he was changing your tire and found the phone?" I ask.

"I wasn't there," she explains, shaking her head. "I discovered the flat when I parked at the Shop'n'Save in Harmony Hills. I phoned Justin and waited with the car until he showed up. When he got there, I went into the store and did the grocery shopping while he changed the tire. He didn't say anything when I came back."

"When was the last time you used the phone?" Eric asks.

"Several days before the flat tire," Vanessa recalls. "I don't know when exactly. We didn't use cell phones often. Only for emergencies. Jill and I did most of our talking in person, at Father Daniel's house."

"You didn't contact Jill from the cell phone the night she died?"

"No," Vanessa insists.

"You didn't call or text that number?" he specifies.

"No, absolutely not."

Someone did. I remember seeing the text conversation. I have photos of the screenshots on my phone.

"What do you think happened to Jill that night?" Eric asks Vanessa.

She takes a deep breath and sits up straight. "I think one of his parents phoned him. I think Justin came back from the city, confronted Jill, and killed her," Vanessa declares with conviction. "I wasn't sure before, but now that I realize he knew about the cell phone, if he saw the texts between Jill and I, he would've figured out she was helping me."

"Thank you for talking to me, Vanessa. I really appreciate you trusting me." Eric looks down and writes furiously in his notebook.

Vanessa and I get up to go in the kitchen and find her something to eat.

"Vanessa," Eric calls after us.

She turns to look at him.

"Where's your car now?" he asks.

She shrugs one shoulder. "At the hospital, I guess. That's where I left it."

"Thanks." He continues making notes.

While Vanessa eats a sandwich, Eric comes in to tell us he's leaving and to remind me to turn on the alarm after he leaves.

"I'll walk you out," I say, leading the way to the door.

"Well?" I whisper while he puts his shoes on.

"I need to get Vanessa's car towed to Harmony Lake for processing, find Justin, and question him," he replies quietly.

I step outside with him and close the door almost all the way.

"Maybe when Justin is at the station with you, Vanessa can go home and get some of her things," I suggest.

"We'll make sure she's able to go home safely and collect her things," he says. "We have procedures in place for situations like this."

"That's sad," I observe.

"What's sad?"

"That procedures for situations like this are necessary."

He nods. "I know."

We hug. He kisses my forehead, and I tell him to stay safe.

"Lock the door and set the alarm," he reminds me. "I'll be in touch when Justin is in custody. It might help Vanessa relax a little."

"Sounds good," I say. "Be careful."

He waits until I'm in the house, then he leaves.

April was texting me for an update while Eric was interviewing Vanessa. Before I get ready for bed, I send her a quick text letting her know we're fine, Vanessa is spending the night, and thanking her again for bringing Sophie home from work and picking up Vanessa's prescription.

Vanessa has a soak in a warm bath while I launder her clothes. I lend her some pyjamas. The sleeves and legs are a tad too short, but other than that she looks comfortable. After taking another pain reliever, she goes to bed.

Sophie and I turn in shortly after her.

CHAPTER 25

When Sophie and I wake up, it takes a few minutes before I remember Vanessa is asleep in the guest room. I put Sophie in the backyard and drop a chocolate raspberry truffle coffee pod in the coffeemaker.

While I fix Sophie's breakfast, I hear my phone ding in the other room. I put her bowl on the floor, let her in, and retrieve my phone.

Connie: April tells me you have your hands full. No need to worry about the store today, Marla and I will handle it. Stay safe, my dear.

Would it be possible to have better friends?! I text back right away.

Me: Thank you! You're the best. Please tell Marla thank you for me.

I check the time. It's early. Too early to text anyone, but I'm eager to find out if Vanessa's car was towed and if the cell phone was in it. Hopefully, it was there and the killer's fingerprints, or DNA, or some other forensic evidence is on it.

I slip my phone into my housecoat pocket and get my

coffee cup from the coffeemaker. I knit while I enjoy my coffee and settle cross-legged in the corner of the family room sofa.

After a few rounds of peaceful, quiet knitting, my phone dings.

Eric: You up?

Me: Yes.

Eric: You going to the store?

Me: Not this morning.

Eric: Coffee crisp?

Me: No thank you, I already have a coffee, but come over anyway. Don't ring the bell, or knock, V is sleeping, and Sophie can't control herself when she hears the door.

Eric: K. C U soon.

I contemplate putting my knitting away and getting dressed, but I decide against it and knit until Eric texts me, telling me he's at the door.

I call Sophie, and she follows me to the door. I open the door, and she runs outside to greet Eric.

"You look comfortable," Eric says, looking at my jammies-housecoat ensemble as I step onto the porch, closing the door quietly behind me.

"I am," I reply.

"I'm jealous," he says.

He stands up after greeting Sophie. I notice the stubble on his face and realize he's wearing the same clothes he wore yesterday.

"Did you go home last night?" I ask, concerned.

"For about five minutes," he replies, "to get my laptop. Then I arranged for Vanessa's car to be towed. More paper-work than you'd expect because her car is in Harmony Hills, and I'm in Harmony Lake. Then I went to the hospital to take some photos of the car and do a preliminary search of the vehicle. Then I went home and fell asleep for a couple of hours on the couch."

"And?" I ask, referring to his search of her car.

Eric shakes his head. "No phone."

Darn!

Sophie is calm now, so I open the front door and we go inside.

"Where is it?" I wonder out loud.

"That's the million-dollar question," he replies.

"Coffee?" I ask.

"Yes, please," he replies when he's finished yawning.

I pop a pod of dark roast in the coffeemaker and place a mug under the spout.

"Good morning," Vanessa says, walking into the kitchen.

She bends down to rub Sophie, who's super excited to have visitors so early in the morning.

"Good morning," Eric and I say in unison.

"Coffee?" I ask.

"No thank you," Vanessa replies. "I'm not a hot-coffee person. I'd love tea if you have any."

I hand Eric his coffee and open the cupboard where the tea and coffee pods live.

"Let's see," I say, pulling down the basket of tea pods and putting it on the counter.

"I can do it," Vanessa says, taking over and rummaging through the basket.

I leave her to it and join Eric at the kitchen table.

"We towed your car," he tells Vanessa.

She turns toward him. "I don't want it back."

"OK," he replies. "I didn't find the cell phone, but I found a GPS tracking device."

My interest is piqued. If the car has a tracking device, why didn't Justin know Vanessa was at the hospital yesterday?

Vanessa nods. She doesn't look shocked. The tracking device isn't news to her.

"Jill found it a few weeks ago," she explains. "She checked my car regularly for stuff like that. It was part of the plan. She disabled it a few days before she died. She said removing it would be too dangerous because Justin would know I found it, so she disabled it, hoping he'd assume it broke or stopped working or something. She found instructions online. It's one reason I was supposed to abandon my car at Father Daniel's house." She retrieves her mug of tea, opens the fridge, and takes out the milk.

Jill was good at this. I had no idea she was so shrewd and cunning. I wish she were here so I could tell her how amazing she was for helping Vanessa like this.

"On your left," I say, watching her search for a spoon to stir her tea.

She puts the milk away and gets a spoon from the drawer on her left.

"She thinks he flattened my tire too," she says casually while she stirs her tea. "I'm not sure, though."

"Why would he flatten your tire?" I ask.

"You're not supposed to drive very far on a doughnut, right? She thinks it was a way to control how far I could go, you know, so I couldn't leave Harmony Lake."

That level of control would never occur to me. I wonder what day Jill disabled the GPS tracker. If it was before Sunday, maybe she's right, and Justin sabotaged Vanessa's tire to limit her mobility until he could replace the tracking device.

"I'm questioning Justin later this morning," Eric says. "He was at a job site in the city until late last night."

I look at Vanessa for a reaction. She's stoic, as though he commented on the weather or something equally benign.

She sips her tea. "Megan, is that offer to use your phone still open?"

"Of course," I tell her. "It's on the counter behind you. You're welcome to take it to another room if you'd like some privacy."

Please don't call Justin.

"Thanks," she says, removing the phone from its base. "I want to phone my family and tell them what's going on."

"Take your time," I encourage.

Vanessa takes her mug of tea and the phone and sequesters herself in the guest room.

"I'll walk Sophie before I go," Eric says.

We sit in silence while he finishes his coffee, and I check my email and the store email on my phone.

While he walks Sophie, I empty the dishwasher, then retrieve Vanessa's clothes from the laundry room, fold them, and place them on the kitchen table.

Eric and Sophie return from their walk. Eric puts her leash away and turns to leave.

"Be careful," I remind him. "Text me and let me know how you're doing."

"Will do," he says.

I SHOWER, get dressed, and make my bed. When I emerge from my bedroom, the door to the guest room is still closed, and Vanessa's folded clothes are untouched on the kitchen table. Hopefully she's having a long, detailed conversation with her family, and they're giving her the support she needs.

The doorbell rings. I check the app on my phone and see April holding up a white confectionery box in one hand while making faces and waving at the doorbell camera with her other hand. I let her in, and Sophie is way ahead of me, yelping and pawing the back of the door before I get there.

"Good morning." I give her a big hug.

"Good morning," she says to Sophie. "Good morning to you too." She hands me the white box. "Croissants."

They're fresh. I can feel the heat radiating through the box. The combination of the aroma and the warmth make my mouth water.

"Thank you," I say, already halfway to the kitchen. "Do you want one?"

"Yes, please," April replies, following me. "How was your night?"

"It was OK," I tell her. "Vanessa's head and wrist seem to be a bit better. She had a good conversation with Eric last night, and he's going to talk to Justin today."

"Where is she now?" April asks.

"In her room. Talking with her family down east, I think."

"That's good." April nods.

We eat croissants and drink coffee while I tell April about Eric and Adam's budding friendship and how they're bonding over their mutual love of golf.

"Do you think it's weird that Eric is friends with Adam?" she asks.

"I think it's weird that *I'm* friends with Adam," I joke.

We both laugh and Vanessa walks in, carrying the cordless phone and her empty mug. Her eyes are swollen and red, yet there's a distinct air of relief about her. Her body is less tense, and her facial muscles are more relaxed. She places her mug in the dishwasher, and April pats the chair next to her, inviting her to sit with us at the kitchen table.

"Have a croissant," April says, nudging the box toward Vanessa. "They're fresh."

"Thank you." Vanessa smiles and takes a croissant from the box.

She breaks a piece off and pops it in her mouth.

"How did your phone call go?" I ask.

"Good." She nods. "I want to go home. My parents are helping me get a plane ticket."

My shoulders drop about two inches from the relief I feel.

"We're here to help you too," I remind her.

"Whatever support you need, we've got your back." April smiles.

"Thanks," Vanessa replies. "I want to get my things from

the Grandin's house." She looks at me. "Will you come with me?"

I nod. "For sure. Eric said there's a procedure to help you collect your things safely. If you text him, I'm sure he can make whatever arrangements are necessary."

"I don't want to turn my phone on," Vanessa reminds me. "It'll be full of messages from Justin."

"Right!" I exclaim. "I forgot. I'll text for you."

She smiles.

I pull out my phone.

Me: Vanessa says she'd like to collect her things.

Eric: Leave it with me. Tell her I'll arrange it.

While she finishes her croissant, Vanessa tells April and me that she wants to visit Father Daniel before she leaves Harmony Lake.

I tell her I'll contact Lisette and try to make that happen. She asks who's taking care of Cardinal, and I tell her he's staying with Father Patrick for the time being.

"I'd like to stay until after Jill's funeral," Vanessa says quietly. "I'd like to be there."

I nod. "Rob said he'll let me know when the arrangements are finalized. Sometimes, when the police are involved, final arrangements are delayed."

"Well, I should get dressed." Vanessa gets up from the table, scoops up her folded clothes, and walks toward the guest room.

"THIS IS GOOD," Eric says, before he takes another bite of the croissant he's eating right out of the confectionery box.

He's standing in the middle of my kitchen. I gesture for him to follow me into the family room and sit on the comfy furniture.

"I know, right?! April brought them fresh out of the oven," I tell him. "You just missed her."

"Is Justin in jail?" Vanessa asks anxiously, joining us in the family room.

Eric shakes his head while he chews and swallows the last bite of the last croissant. "There isn't enough evidence to charge him with Jill's murder. Everything is circumstantial. He admits he found the cell phone when he was changing your tire. And he says he had a feeling you were planning to leave him. He admits to putting the tracking device on your car, but technically the car is in his name, so he put it on his own car, which isn't illegal. He admits he didn't like Jill but insists he didn't kill her. I can't place him at the scene." He looks at me. "I don't even have a murder weapon." The exacerbation in his voice and demeanour is almost palpable.

"Can you charge him for what he did to Vanessa?" I ask.

"Mandatory charging," Eric replies, nodding.

"What does that mean?" Vanessa asks.

"It means I'm obligated to charge him if I have reason to believe violence has taken place."

That's a relief.

"So, he's in jail?" Vanessa clarifies.

"He's being processed, then he'll be released with a no-contact order," Eric explains. "He won't be allowed to contact you."

That doesn't mean he won't try.

"Like that'll stop him," Vanessa says.

Since Justin will be at the station a while longer, Eric suggests this would be a good time for Vanessa to collect her things from the Grandin's house. He will accompany her, and a uniformed officer and patrol car will be nearby.

VANESSA RIDES WITH ME, and Eric follows in his car. When we pull up in front of the Grandin house, Mr. and Mrs. Grandin are in the driveway, getting out of their car. Their son, Tyler, is with them. I assume they're arriving home from their trip to the city to see a matinee.

I park across the street from their house, and Vanessa and I wait in the car. Eric pulls up in front of the Grandin's driveway and walks over to my car. Vanessa lowers the passenger side window so she can talk to him.

"I can ask them to leave while you collect your things, but I can't make them leave," Eric explains.

"It's fine," Vanessa says. "I don't mind if they're here. I'll talk to them."

She opens the door and gets out of the car, so I do the same.

She and Eric cross the street and approach the three Grandins. I follow, staying several steps behind but close enough to hear them speak.

Vanessa shows her sprained wrist to Mr. and Mrs. Grandin. She also tells them about her possible concussion, then itemizes a list of previous injuries she's suffered because of Justin.

Mrs. Grandin's eyes bulge, and she blinks rapidly. "Justin could never do those things," she says in a shaky voice.

Mr. Grandin stomps his walking stick into the driveway. "You're making this up." His eyes are narrow and intense.

Tyler says nothing, his gaze darting back and forth between Vanessa and his feet.

"I know you don't want to believe me," Vanessa says with more understanding than I'd be able to display in her position, "but it's true. All of it. And I think Justin might have killed Jill too."

"Now, I know you're lying," Mr. Grandin accuses. "Justin was with Tyler that night. Everyone knows that."

"I was asleep, Dad," Tyler comments. "He was there when

I fell asleep, and he was there when I woke up, but I don't know where he was in between." Then he looks at Vanessa and gestures toward her injured wrist. "A girl Justin used to date made similar accusations about him."

Mr. Grandin stabs his walking stick into the driveway again. "That's enough, Tyler!" Mr. Grandin growls through clenched teeth, shooting Tyler a sideways glare.

Watching Mr. Grandin stab his walking stick into the driveway reminds me of the way Saxon Renaud pokes his umbrella at people, and how the tip of Saxon's umbrella was consistent with the shape of the murder weapon used to stab Jill.

Mr. Grandin has about thirty walking sticks, and according to Artie at Old School, several of them have umbrellas, swords, and other stabby things hidden inside them.

There's no way he took all thirty of them to Florida for the winter. Mr. and Mrs. Grandin pack everything they need for their annual Florida trip in their car. Their car was so full that Mr. Grandin couldn't fit one extra walking stick in it and had the newest addition to his collection packaged and shipped to Harmony Lake. Justin would have had access to Mr. Grandin's collection of walking sticks, and he'd know which ones conceal weapons inside.

I think I just found the murder weapon.

CHAPTER 26

"THAT'S A NICE WALKING STICK, Mr. Grandin," I comment out of nowhere, nodding toward the wooden walking stick in his hand.

Everyone turns and looks at me with expressions somewhere between surprise and concern. Surprise because they forgot I was here, and concern because the timing of my comment would indicate I haven't been following along with the discussion.

"Thank you? Megan," Mr. Grandin says, his voice weak and with a hint of either confusion, concern, or both.

"Did you take it to Florida with you this year?" I ask. "Do you take all of your walking sticks to Florida?"

"I can't remember if I took this one with me," he replies, holding his walking stick at arm's length and inspecting it. "I only take a few of them. We can only fit a few in the car."

I look at Eric and raise my eyebrows, hoping he'll take it from here. He smirks and a look of comprehension flashes across his face, then he looks at Mr. Grandin.

"Is your collection locked up, Mr. Grandin? Who has access to it?" Eric asks.

"My walking sticks are on display," Mr. Grandin replies.

"I know what you're getting at—Justin did not use one of my walking sticks to stab Jill Plumb!"

"I never suggested he did," Eric says calmly. "Do you remember which walking stick *you* were using the night you arrived home from Florida?"

Eric thinks Mr. Grandin is Jill's killer?

Mind blown.

"I don't know," Mr. Grandin replies tersely. "It could've been any of them." He shrugs one shoulder and shakes his head with his eyes half closed.

"I need to see the one you used that night. You can help me, or I can come back with a warrant and seize your entire collection," Eric warns him calmly.

Mr. Grandin opens his mouth as if to speak, then closes it again. I get the feeling he's not thrilled about his entire collection being confiscated and handled by the police.

"Douglas." Mrs. Grandin uses Mr. Grandin's first name. "I believe it was the dark wood with the mother-of-pearl handle, wasn't it?"

"Maybe," Mr. Grandin concedes. "Like I said, I can't remember."

Mrs. Grandin looks at Eric. "If you'll follow me, Detective, I'll show you where Douglas keeps his walking sticks."

"Vanessa and I will wait in the car." I touch Vanessa's shoulder, and she turns to follow me across the street.

Once we're in my car, I lock the doors and we both take a deep breath.

Keeping an eye on what's happening across the street in the Grandin's driveway, I watch as Tyler opens the car door, and Mr. Grandin sits on the seat, sideways, with his feet on the driveway.

I look at Vanessa, who's also watching the driveway intently.

"They're coming back," she says without looking away from the window.

We get out of the car and cross the street. Neither Eric nor Mrs. Grandin is carrying a walking stick.

"Where is it?" Eric asks.

Mr. Grandin says nothing.

"C'mon, Dad, tell him. You're only making it worse for Justin by not cooperating," Tyler advises.

"Justin didn't do it!" Mr. Grandin insists. "I did it! It was me, OK?! I killed Jill Plumb!" Then he adds, "But it was her fault! She made me do it."

What?!

"When we came home, Vanessa was packing her car. Like for a trip. We thought she and Justin might be going away for a long weekend. But she told us she was leaving. She told us she and Justin weren't getting along, and she was scared of him."

So far, this is consistent with what Vanessa says happened when the Grandins returned early from Florida.

"We convinced her to stay. She agreed as long as we didn't phone Justin and tell him we caught her trying to leave." He looks at Eric and shakes his head. "We didn't phone him."

"What happened next?" Eric urges.

"I helped Vanessa empty her car. I lifted the cover of the spare tire well to see if she'd packed anything in there. I found a phone. I turned it on, and it buzzed. There was a text from someone she was supposed to meet. I looked at the previous texts and figured out where she planned to meet them. I pretended to be Vanessa and went in her place. Vanessa was in bed. I took her car because ours was full of stuff, and I didn't want whoever I was meeting to get spooked by a strange car and leave."

He stops speaking.

"What happened when you got there?" Eric asks.

"I didn't see anyone, but Jill's car was parked on the street, two houses up. I got out of Vanessa's car and walked around the house. The gate was ajar, and she was standing by the side door. It was dark, I had to open the gate more to get into the yard. The gate creaking got her attention, and when she realized I wasn't Vanessa, she demanded to know where Vanessa was and if she was OK."

"And then?" Eric prods.

"It was an accident," Mr. Grandin explains, shaking his head and looking at his feet. He looks up at Tyler. "I just wanted to warn that busybody to stay out of Justin's business. She freaked out and started yelling. She called me an enabler. She said I was part of the problem. I pulled the sword out of my stick to make her calm down. She accused me of being abusive, too, and started screaming."

He thought brandishing a sword during an argument would calm the situation? Really, Mr. Grandin?

"It did the opposite," he recalls. "She yelled more and screamed. Her ruckus would draw attention. I didn't mean to. I just wanted her to be quiet and listen to me. It was supposed to be a little poke. A warning. She was flailing and flapping her arms. She practically pushed her neck into the blade."

We gasp collectively, and Tyler reaches out to steady his mother.

"Douglas," Mrs. Grandin says breathlessly, "what have you done?"

"She would have told everyone these lies about Justin," Mr. Grandin reasons, looking at his wife. "She was helping Vanessa leave him. I couldn't let her spread lies about our family and ruin our reputation."

Mrs. Grandin looks at Mr. Grandin, horrified. Mr. Grandin looks back at her with desperation in his eyes.

"I planned to talk to Justin," Mr. Grandin continues, "and tell him to be more patient with his wife, maybe not argue as much." He looks at Eric, defeated. His hand disappears below the steering wheel of the car for a second, then the trunk opens automatically. "The walking stick you're looking for is in the trunk."

Mr. Grandin stays seated sideways in the car, and the rest of us gather around the open trunk, staring at the walking stick, lying diagonally across the otherwise empty space. Eric pulls out his phone and takes some photos of the walking stick without touching it, then he reaches into a pocket and pulls out a latex glove.

"Is the phone in here too?" he shouts to Mr. Grandin.

"In the spare tire well," Mr. Grandin shouts in reply.

Eric pulls a second glove from his pocket and puts it on. He moves the walking stick and lifts the cover of the spare tire well. I can't see what's in there, but he takes out his phone again, snaps a photo, then reaches into the spare tire well and pulls out a cell phone identical to the one I found In Jill's office.

CHAPTER 27

Monday, April 13th

Friday was Good Friday, so the store wasn't open. I spent the day tidying the house and cleaning the yard now that spring had sprung. It might be a holiday, but the Harmony Lake rumour mill didn't take the day off. In between chores, I fielded phone calls and texts from friends and neighbours who'd heard about Mr. Grandin's confession and wanted details. Eric spent the day working. He said he had a lot of paperwork and loose ends to take care of from Jill's case.

Saturday was a picture-perfect spring day, and the annual Easter egg hunt was a huge success. It meant fewer customers in the store, but Connie, Marla, and I had a chance to watch the kids hunt for eggs. We chatted with friends and neighbours who'd ventured down to Water Street to either help with the event, watch, or both.

I took an overnight bag to work with me on Saturday, and Adam and I left for Toronto as soon as I closed the store. Sophie stayed with Eric in his apartment on Saturday night, and I'm sure she was happy with the arrangement since he dotes over her, walks her longer and more often than me, and overfills her bowl at meal times.

We made good time picking up Hannah at university and arrived back in Harmony Lake before 4 p.m. yesterday. Thanks to additional help from Eric and Archie's son, Ryan, we unloaded Rachel and Hannah's stuff before 5 p.m. Hannah stayed at the house to unpack while I followed Adam to Harmony Hills and drove him home after he dropped off the rental truck.

On the way back from Harmony Hills, we picked up Hannah and went to Connie and Archie's condo for Easter dinner. It was the first family dinner they've hosted since they moved in together. The twelve of us fit quite comfortably in their cozy condo. Connie's cat, Harlow, was the host with the most and made sure everyone had a chance to rub him and sneak him some turkey.

Archie did most of the cooking. Adam left him and Connie with a key to his condo so they could use his oven in addition to their own. It was a huge spread, turkey and ham, two different kinds of potatoes, and at least half a dozen other side dishes. Dessert was courtesy of April and Tamara, who brought pavlova with them. It was amazing.

The only awkward moment was Eric almost choking on an asparagus tip when Connie asked him if he's a leg man or a breast man. She was trying to offer him a second helping of turkey, but he misunderstood.

Mr. Grandin was charged with Jill's murder. Eric says the forensics unit confirmed that the sword inside the walking stick in Mr. Grandin's trunk was the murder weapon. They also confirmed the cell phone from his trunk was the same phone Jill and Vanessa were using to communicate with each other, and it had Mr. Grandin's fingerprints on it.

Justin was charged with domestic abuse. When he was released after processing, he and his mother went to stay at Tyler's place in the city.

Vanessa is staying at the Grandin's house until after Jill's funeral tomorrow. I offered her my guest room, but she said she wants to stay at the Grandin's house.

Vanessa spent Easter with Rob and the kids. They had Easter dinner with Father Patrick and Cardinal. Vanessa and I texted earlier today. She says Lisette is taking her to visit Father Daniel today, and she's excited to see him. She plans to spend the rest of her day packing. We'll see each other at Jill's funeral tomorrow and say our goodbyes. After the service, Lisette will drive Vanessa to the airport where her family has a ticket for her to fly home.

My phone dings.

Eric: Can I stop by?

Me: Yes! Don't ring or knock, H is asleep, and Sophie doesn't care.

Eric: C U soon

I check the time, put my knitting aside, and get dressed before Eric arrives.

When he texts me to let me know he's here, I open the door so Sophie can greet him in the driveway.

"You've got your hands full," I say when I see him with a to-go cup from Latte Da in one hand and a huge bouquet in the other.

He uses his foot to close his car door. "Hi, Sophie," he says. "Give me a minute."

Sophie is pawing at Eric's knees, eager for him to bend down and rub her.

"Let me help," I say, walking toward him and extending my hands to take something from him.

He reaches toward me with the coffee cup, so I relieve him of it, and he puts the bouquet on the hood of his car so he can greet Sophie properly before she explodes.

"Nice flowers," I say, gesturing toward the bouquet of tulips, daffodils, daisies, and a bunch of other spring flowers with names I don't know. "Very spring-like."

"It's your April bouquet." He smiles, stands up from

greeting Sophie, and picks up the bouquet from the hood of his car. "I ran into Phillip this morning in the parking lot behind the store, and he asked me if I'd like to bring them to you. Since I'm always looking for an excuse to see you, I said yes."

In January, Eric and I went to a fundraiser with a silent auction. He placed a bid on one of the silent auction items, a bouquet every month for a year, courtesy of Wilde Flowers. He won, and now I get a beautiful bouquet of seasonal flowers every month.

"Thank you." I think I'm blushing. "Yours or mine?" I hold up the coffee I took from him.

"Also yours," he clarifies.

I gesture for him to follow me into the house.

I open the door, and Sophie runs in first, followed by Eric, then me. I take the flowers from him while he takes off his shoes.

"Have you spoken to Lisette?" he asks, joining me in the kitchen where I'm arranging the flowers on the kitchen table.

"No," I shake my head.

"She found an assisted living facility for Father Daniel."

"That's good," I say.

"It is," he agrees. "It's near where she lives. She'll keep Cardinal, and the facility will allow her to bring him for regular visits with Father Daniel."

"Best outcome for both Father Daniel and Cardinal," I comment.

"Adam's helping her navigate through the process of becoming her brother's guardian, then she can sell the house to Saxon, and use the proceeds to pay for the assisted living facility. He's doing it pro bono."

"I'm not surprised," I tell him. "Adam's a nice guy. I'm glad Lisette has a plan and a buyer for Father Daniel's house, but I'm not thrilled that at the end of all this, Saxon Renaud gets what he's wanted all along." I finish fussing with the floral arrangement and stand back to admire it.

"Would you feel better if I told you his umbrella is still in the evidence room?" Eric asks.

"Maybe a little," I admit, sipping my coffee. "You still haven't given it back to him?"

Eric shrugs. "He hasn't asked for it."

"Oh, I have something for you!" I snap my fingers, remembering the socks that have been drying in my laundry room for days. "I'll be right back."

I retrieve the blue and grey striped socks from the sock blockers in the laundry room and hand them proudly to Eric.

"Those were for me?" he asks, taking the socks. "I watched you knit them and assumed they were for someone else. Thank you."

"I hope they fit," I say.

"I love them," he says. "I've never worn hand knit socks before." He sits down, takes his socks off, and puts the hand knit socks on.

"So, you've never washed hand-knit socks either, I guess? Just give them to me. Like your hat and scarf. I'll wash them."

"Like a glove!" He wiggles his toes.

Smiling, he looks at his feet admiringly.

"Morning, Mom. Morning, Eric. Morning, Sophie." Hannah pads into the kitchen and grabs a bowl from the cupboard.

Watching her pull a box of cereal out of the pantry and take the milk out of the fridge, I realize how different the house, the town, and my life are when she's not here.

"Good morning, Hannah Banana," I say, thrilled to have my daughter home where she belongs, waking up in her own bed, sauntering into the kitchen, and splashing milk onto the counter.

"How did you sleep?" I ask, wiping the splash of milk off the counter.

"Good," she replies. "It's nice to be home. It's so quiet and calm here compared to school. Don't get me wrong. I love going to school in Toronto, but it's nice to be back in Harmony Lake for a few months where nothing exciting happens, you know?"

Eric and I look at each other. No, we don't know.

KEEP READING for a sneak peek of Twisted Stitches: A Knitorious Murder Mystery Book 4.

Click here to download the sock pattern that Megan used to knit Eric's socks.

TWISTED STITCHES

CHAPTER 1

Monday July 6TH

"Megan!"

The disembodied voice comes from nowhere. Just loud enough to hear, but not loud enough to recognize. There's nobody around. This is the third time in fourteen hours the voice has called my name. Am I hearing things? Is this a neurological symptom?

The voice called out to me when I walked Sophie last night, again this morning during our morning walk, and just now, while I load groceries into my trunk at the Shop'n'save in Harmony Hills.

I make a mental note to search the internet when I get home, in case this is a symptom of a stroke, or a brain tumour, or something.

Returning the empty cart to the cart corral, I see Mr. and Mrs. Willows across the parking lot. They're getting into their older, oversize, white pickup truck that Mrs. Willows affectionately refers to as "The beater." They see me, too. We smile at each other and exchange waves. Could one of them have called out to me?

Like me, Mr. and Mrs. Willows live in Harmony Lake. They have a farm on the outskirts of town.

It's not uncommon to run into other Harmony Lake residents in Harmony Hills. Harmony Lake is a small town with limited amenities. Most of us who live there make regular trips to Harmony Hills to visit the big box stores, medical facilities, and other businesses and services we don't have on the other side of the Harmony Hills mountains.

Standing in an asphalt parking lot with no shade, at noon on a July day, with the heat from the hot pavement radiating up my sundress, makes a hot summer day feel downright scorching. I start the engine, turn the stereo down and the air conditioning up.

A few uncooperative curls insist on hanging rebelliously around my face as I twist my hair into a bun and secure it with the hair elastic I wear on my wrist.

I pull down the sun visor and open the mirror. With my sunglasses resting on top of my head, I check the mirror and wipe a smudge of mascara from below my left eye. I squint into the bright, midday sun as I grab the lip balm from the cup holder, and smear some on my lips. Ready! I return my sunglasses to my face and turn up the stereo so Beyoncé and I can sing Crazy in Love together.

Merging onto the highway that will take me through the mountains and home to Harmony Lake, Beyoncé fades out and Mr. Brightside by The Killers takes its place.

"*Destiny is calling meeee. Open up my eager eyes 'cause Iiiiii'm Mr. Brightsiiiiiide…*" I'm dueting with Brandan Flowers when I check the rearview mirror and notice a small white car following way too close.

I'm in the left lane. I turn on my indicator to let the driver know I'll change lanes and get out of their way. I check the mirrors and shoulder check to make sure it's safe. As I press my foot into the gas pedal and begin to move over to the right lane, the driver of the small white car guns the engine and slams into me from behind.

I grip the wheel tightly to maintain control of the vehicle and stay in my lane.

That was intentional. Why did the car rear end me?

The driver revs the engine again and veers right.

The car is beside me now.

There's an exit coming up. The last exit before Harmony Lake. I need that exit. If I miss it, I'll be stuck on the highway with this crazy driver for twenty minutes until we get to the Harmony Lake exit.

I accelerate again, hoping to pass the car and veer across to the right lane toward the exit. When I press the gas pedal, the other driver accelerates, too, and won't let me pass.

The car swerves toward me. I steer left to avoid it and almost hit the concrete median that divides the north and south lanes.

Why is it trying to side-swipe me?

Easing my foot off the accelerator, I change tactics. If I slow down, maybe it'll pass me. Then I can switch lanes behind it and get to the exit before we pass it.

As I slow down, I look to my right and see the driver of the white car is wearing a disguise. One of those fake-nose-fake-glasses-fake-moustache disguises that makes you look like Groucho Marx, paired with a fuzzy wig-hat combo like the ones you find at a party store.

Why would someone drive around incognito, intentionally hitting another car on the highway?

The driver's side window in the white car lowers about halfway down. The wind from the open window causes the driver to take a hand off the wheel and adjust the hat-wig disguise. I look at the road and accelerate again, hoping to pass the car. I'm running out of time. I turn my head to the right, and the driver is pointing a gun at me!

A gun!

POP!

The impact shakes my car and rattles my nerves. I wrestle with the steering wheel and manage to keep control, narrowly avoiding the concrete median.

What the?! The driver shot at me. Whoever is in that car is trying to kill me!

My grip on the steering wheel is so tight, my knuckles are white.

I look to the right and make eye contact with the shooter and they lower the gun.

Clunk!

The shooter lurches forward immediately following the distinct sound of metal against metal. The disguised head almost hits the steering wheel. Someone rear-ended the car. The shooter recovers, looks right, guns the engine, and glides across the highway, just making the exit.

The car is gone.

It's over.

What just happened?

I barrel instinctively down the highway toward home. My heart is racing. There's a lump in my throat, and a knot in my stomach.

Honnnnnnk!

Mr. Willows is beside me in his big white truck, gesturing at me to pull over.

I indicate, check my mirrors, turn my head to check my blind spot, then pull onto the left shoulder. I should have pulled over to the right, but I choose the path of least resistance.

Mr. Willows pulls up behind me. He appears at my window and cranks his fist.

Thankfully, I'm old enough to remember when cars had crank windows and understand his hand motion. I lower my window.

"Are you OK, Megan? Is it in park? Put it in park."

I nod. My vision blurs as my eyes fill with tears and I unclench my hands from the steering wheel and put the vehicle in park.

Mr. Willows reaches through the window and turns the key, shutting off the engine. Then he pushes the button on the dashboard that turns on the hazard lights.

I inhale deeply and take my foot off the brake.

"Is she OK? Was she hit?" Mrs. Willows is beside him now with her face in the window.

"I'm OK," I mutter. "I need to get out." I open the car door and try to get out, but the seatbelt stops me.

Mrs. Willows reaches across my lap and unbuckles it. Clutching the car door for support, I stand up. My stomach roils. I take the two steps to the concrete median, grab on, heave the top half of my body over it and throw up on the paved shoulder of the north bound lanes. The wind is at my back, and I'm grateful I put my hair up before I left the grocery store.

"Henry! Get her some water!" Mrs. Willows shouts as she rubs my back. "Shhh," she says quietly. "You're OK, Megan, you're safe."

With his cell phone to his ear, Mr. Willows nods in acknowledgement, and jogs toward the back of his truck.

"Why don't you sit down?" Mrs. Willows suggests as she guides me back toward the car.

I sit sideways with my feet hovering above the pavement. Mr. Willows reappears with a bottle of water. He removes the cap and hands it to me.

"I hit him! His car will have rear end damage." I'm not sure if Mr. Willows is speaking to me, or to the person on the phone. "I rear-ended him as soon as I caught up to them. He was chasing her." He uses his hand to cover the microphone on his cell phone. "The police are coming, Megan. It's going to be OK." He speaks to me in a quieter voice than he uses on the phone.

In the moments before the police arrive, Mrs. Willows tells me that she and Mr. Willows saw the whole thing. According to her, the driver of the white car followed me onto the highway. She thinks the driver targeted me. She doesn't believe it was road rage because she says I didn't do anything to the other driver. She says she got the car's license plate number.

Good. I want to know who tried to kill me.

CLICK HERE to read the rest of Twisted Stitches in Knitorious Murder Mysteries Books 4-6

OTHER BOOKS IN THE KNITORIOUS MURDER MYSTERY SERIES

Sign up for Reagan Davis' email list to be notified of new releases and special offers: www.ReaganDavis.com Follow Reagan Davis on Amazon

Follow Reagan Davis on Facebook and Instagram

ABOUT THE AUTHOR

Reagan Davis doesn't really exist. She is a pen name for the real author who lives in the suburbs of Toronto with her husband, two kids, and a menagerie of pets. When she's not planning the perfect murder, she enjoys knitting, reading, eating too much chocolate, and drinking too much Diet Coke. The author is an established knitwear designer who regularly publishes individual patterns and is a contributor to many knitting books and magazines. I'd tell you her real name, but then I'd have to kill you. (Just kidding! Sort of.)

http://www.ReaganDavis.com/

ACKNOWLEDGMENTS

First, a big thank you to you, dear reader. Your love and support of books 1 & 2, inspired me to continue the series.

Shout out to Kim of Kim's Covers for another perfect cover.

Thank you to Chris and Sherry at The Editing Hall fixing my mistakes, streamlining my ideas, and rearranging all the misplaced punctuation marks.

Eternal love and gratitude to the Husbeast and Kidlets for everything.

Made in United States
North Haven, CT
20 December 2021

13371785R00349